I0722100

Eckleburg

Founding Editor | Rae Cline

Eckleburg is published annually in print, with new original daily content published online at eckleburg.org, by Moon Milk Press, Inc. Established as Moon Milk Review in 2010, Eckleburg is printed in the U.S.A. All rights reserved. No part of this periodical may be reproduced without consent of Moon Milk Press, Inc. The magazine's name and logo and the various titles and headings herein are trademarks of Moon Milk Press, Inc. The views expressed in the writing herein are solely those of the authors and artists.

Cover Art *Bernadette and Bob* by Bobby Neel Adams

Internal Artwork, *L'urlo* by Monica Marioni

"Frittura" by Judith Goode originally published in *Menacing Hedge* (2021)

Contents

FICTION

ESSAY

GALLERY

Five Fictions

KIM CHINQUEE

What's Your Emergency?

When I woke from surgery, I wondered where my arm went.

It was still attached, I was assured. I saw it there, hanging from my body.

I'd been dreaming about dogs, I told the attending person. It's not my first time going under. I went under just weeks before at a different hospital, and the attending there told me, when I woke, we changed our minds. You're healing after all. You don't actually need surgery.

In pre-op at that hospital, that's what they told the guy in the next bed. He was healing after all. His foot did not need surgery. He did not go under.

I fell two months before, taking out my puppy. It wasn't my puppy's fault. She woke me up too early.

I fell onto the concrete tile in the sunroom. I hit my head. I fell onto my wrist and on my shoulder. I had to use the bathroom.

It was five a.m. I let out the puppy and my two other dogs, then cleaned myself. I changed my clothes. My wrist was deformed. I let the dogs back in and held my wrist—with my other arm—in a cradle.

I called one friend I relied on though she is sometimes unreliable.

I'd only been in my house for a year and didn't want to bother neighbors—I respect people's boundaries, especially when it comes to COVID.

I called 911.

"What's your emergency?" I heard.

I'm kind of addicted to Dateline. Nobody was dead yet.

I just really needed a ride to the hospital.

The men came, with the lights on the truck. They said I might want to put some shoes on.

In the ER, the people gave me morphine. I kept dry heaving. I leaned into the trash.

The ambulance men had taken me to the VA. That seemed the most convenient since I'm a veteran. I served during war. I had injuries, long-lasting, while serving in the air force.

Six weeks after having on the cast, the surgeon was concerned I wasn't healing. Two days later, I woke up from anesthesia there, hearing that same echo: We didn't actually do surgery. You're actually all healed now!

Three days later, a doctor who had been my lover and lived the next city over recommended a trauma surgeon, who took me in right away and after seeing an X-ray, said my bones are healing way out of alignment.

After that my doctor friend took a road trip to my house. It wasn't a short drive. I wasn't dating anyone. We'd had sex before. He was wearing scrubs. He wasn't exactly gentle. I'm not sure what he was. He made me feel things I hadn't felt in a long time. He made me bleed. He took a shower on his way out and said he had to get back to his patients.

I'm at his hospital now, where I actually had surgery. He comes to visit me. He sits on my bed. He feeds me fruit from my tray.

I have a nerve block. I cannot feel my arm. It used to be my dominant. I carry it on me like a deadweight.

Seedlings

The nurse cuts my dressing down the middle. Two weeks before, after finally having surgery, I woke up to a soft cast wrapped over a hard splint that covered my incision. I didn't see what was under it until now.

The underside of my forearm has a zipper, or perhaps a train track. A candy cane if I feel like sounding pretty. It's a longer cut than I'd imagined, though gauging by the pain, it could have been much longer.

Some of the gauze is still stuck to my arm, which still has swirls of purple, green and yellow. A precipitation of dead skin cells make me think of seedlings—it's finally actually spring now—I broke my wrist the day after Christmas.

Two days before, stepping around my yard, it was mushy from the recent snow melt, and I found little things that prove to me things heal, that there is hope after a hard season. I took pictures the best I could using mostly my left hand, which has learned to become dominant, my right one merely an assistant. Purple buds sprouted between stone cracks. And there were white buds in large patches all throughout the yard. I looked the buds up on my app: the purple is a woodland crocus, and the white a snowcap. Hearty green stems also shot up in bunches: the wild daffodils I remember coming up the year before: so bright! Oh, how the collection grows. How these miracles surround me!

The nurse asks if I've had sutures before. I had a C-section once, I tell him

That was over thirty years ago. In three weeks, it'll be almost thirty-two. Those sutures were staples. Not like these, that look like thick eyelashes. When my son was just fifteen, I had stitches on my pointer finger, tiny, on its tip, the left one. Nine, I remember. I'd cut down to the bone while slicing a bagel. I don't recall my age then—just knew my son's, since he couldn't officially drive yet. He accompanied me, a passenger, while I, behind the wheel, had a blood-soaked towel wrapped around my finger. I cried while he said, It'll be okay, Mom. I never had those stitches properly removed—I tried doing it myself and that's probably why that finger is still numb there. I don't tell the nurse that.

I lay back on the bed and extend my arm. It's resting on a pillow. I look up and breathe into my mask. I feel a pinch harder than a pinch. It's more like a sharp knife stab, not the persistent throb and ache when I broke my wrist and the on and off pain.

The nurse asks, Are you OK?

I say, How many sutures are there?

He counts. One two three four and five and six...twelve and thirteen, fourteen....

Right-Handed

The pollen count is high.

I kind of like the act of sneezing. An uncontrollable act. My body telling me it's working.

The deep veins of my backyard aren't even in full bloom yet. Though some buds flirt with me: the snowdrops and the squills. It's only my second spring in my new home and things this year are behind, compared to the last one.

The coltsfoot has shown up, with its yellow color. My backyard isn't huge, but it's big enough to offer me surprises, and even over one year in, I feel lucky to say this is my property, though I don't feel I own this property so much as it owns me.

Flowers so alive last year lost their blooms and died in fall, and I felt a part of me died with them.

I took a hard fall in the dead of winter, diving in the sunroom.

I spent months in a cast. I spent months with a bad surgeon, then another who did a good job taking months to fix it.

I sit in the sunroom now, doing my wrist homework.

Squills and crocuses and snowdrops appear, offering surprises. They capture me. I exercise myself and, with my healing hand, do my best to capture the new yellows and purples and pinks of it.

I take picture of the flowers, the soil underneath them.

I look up, far off. The sky is an envelope.

Hunt

He was a hunter. He said he was Catholic. He seemed solid, determined about his shooting ability.

I was new to Minnesota, having just left the Air Force. He was in the Reserve unit I had to join as part of my agreement to get out of active duty early. It was one weekend a month, much different than active, here people reporting late, with wrinkled clothes and hair that went over their collars.

He wore a mustache, and his body had muscles. I drew blood and he was one of my patients. That's how I met him. He had nice veins. I stuck him with the needle, and then he asked me to come over.

I didn't usually say yes right away, but I hadn't been with a man in ages. He lived ten minutes from my place, in a suburb of St. Paul, where I had my new apartment. So that night, I got a sitter to take care of my baby, and after the guy picked me up, he took me to this steakhouse.

As he talked, I had a hard time concentrating, thinking about his arms, his voice, his hunt.

I ate sirloin and he ordered a rump.

At his place, he warned me that I might not be ready. I laughed and said I had the good stuff. Stepping in, I studied the things on the wall, the jackalope, the deer heads. There was a bear rug. Horns. The picture of a steeple.

He stayed himself, just looking at one of the jaws. From somewhere I heard music. As, I danced and moved around him, he got on all fours and he showed me his choppers.

Halo

He came home with a halo. I wasn't sure where it came from/how it got there, but when he walked in the door at his usual five p.m., stepping into the den where I was doing graphics, this bright light shone above him.

I asked him where it came from.

What? he said.

That thing, I said. On your head.

He said he didn't know. He said the only thing on his head was a bald spot.

No, I said, that light. Are you fooling me or something?

He went about his thing, going upstairs to iron his shirt for the next day, probably watching his same sitcom. I assumed he didn't notice the azaleas I'd bought him, since there was no mention. They were purple, not quite blossomed, on the table where he'd put the Poinsettias before I'd arrived the month before, where we'd watched them eventually brown. He'd thrown them away over the weekend, and, this morning, since I'd planned on driving out, I thought it would be nice to add some color, leave it there as a reminder of me.

After he came down, he put on his hat and said it was time to blow the snow out. He got out his jacket. He said it was probably good I didn't leave yet. He said the roads were bad, on his way, on the highway.

I looked up from my laptop. I was a designer, and taught at a college states away, and the next week there'd be classes again. He said, I'm glad you didn't leave. I get to have you even longer.

Perks, I said, touching my mouse. Even with a hat, his halo rose above him. It seemed to get brighter.

I asked if he had wings. I sipped my wine. I said, Have you changed your perfume, your aroma?

He said he was named after a saint, laughed, put on his coat, and I remembered the day before, when I got annoyed with him for putting his butt out in a beer can—I'd told him that was gross, like that cheat of my ex-husband, and went up to take a bath, locking the door, soaking all my germs out, then after he'd knocked, and I told him I was soaking, he'd knocked again, said he had a surprise, and I'd gotten out, unlocking, seeing him there naked with something like a sheet knotted around his neck, making a cape. Ta-da! he'd said, flexing his biceps. He wore that same white cap. I didn't remember any halo then, but I'd remembered even the day before that, when, before going to manage the bank where he worked, he'd said he had to make the donuts, salt the mines—go out to save the world, and I'd told him I'd love to see him in a cape, and only in that.

He'd said he could only find a sheet. It was flannel. I'd invited him into the bath and we bathed there, him on one end, me on mine with my head kinked.

Now, today, I told him, I bought you flowers for the table. I reminded him why.

He said he never would forget me. He got close, and as he got closer, I watched the halo. He kissed me. His halo seemed steady.

He stepped back and zipped his jacket. I heard him go. I looked out to see the light.

I Am Not Antigone: Notes on Losing My Brother

JESSICA LANAY

> "But he is mine. And yours. Like it or not, he's our brother. They'll never catch me betraying him."
>
> —Antigone

- My brother Mike died while incarcerated in Jacksonville, Florida on December 23, 2021. He was found in his cell, alone, at 3:24pm.

- I was not raised with Mike or my other brothers from my father's first marriage. I only learned recently that he abandoned them. Shortly after he abandoned them, their mother was murdered. Nevertheless, Mike and I shared my biological mother or "mommy." And she loved us both the same.

- But there were the pictures. Old pictures with the weight of nearly deflated balloons, early polaroids. I met Mike at a gas station in Albany, GA when I was in my early 20s and from that moment he was in my life.

- I miss my brother. I miss Mike. Goddamnit I miss my brother. He was mine. My brother. I have to live without my brother. I have to breathe this air that he no longer exhales into. And I miss my brother. I miss my motherfucking brother. And I hear my mother's wail in the cathedral of my vagus nerve. Do you understand that I miss my brother? He was me. And I was him. Which means we are both dead. A part of me broke away and left with him. I couldn't hold him when he died. We couldn't hold each other when we died. I miss my brother. The sky will never be blue again. Mike was the blue sky and I lost my breath. I miss my brother. He was mine . . . for a time.

- Maybe I am Ismene. I hate the potential because it raises the question, did I abandon my brother? Maybe. Ismene never had her own story; she was there to remind Antigone that if she protected her brother in death, that she too would die. A disaster. No one wrote Ismene's story. No one recorded her grief. By the time Antigone dies and the epic ends, we can only assume that Ismene was left alone, her family dead (Maybe this is why). She refused to break laws of the world. She advised her sister Antigone to not bury their brother Polynices in order to preserve Antigone's and her lives. Maybe this is about survivor's guilt. Ismene and I become mirror images in survival. We each watch our families disappear into untimely deaths that are the product of a social curse, a social death that neither of our families can be blamed for initiating, but blamed, sardonically, for preserving. Like Sam Cooke said, like it is tattooed on my right thigh, like I am sure it was in Ismene's heart: it's been too hard living but I'm afraid to die. (Otis said AND I'm afraid to die, these are two very different matters).

- Mike was found dead in his jail cell from a fentanyl overdose. Guards help conceal it as it passes into the jails and prisons: on books pages, on clothing, in food, inside of people. Mike in a cell : Antigone hung herself after being walled alive into a tomb : being left to rot alone on a hill like Polynices : sitting inside myself, receded from the shore of reality…refusing.

- My father too was a man of war. The most honest story he ever told me—because he lies more than he reveals the truth, so the difference is distinct—was of shooting an Afghani herder while overseas. Oedipus—the father of Antigone, Ismene, Polynices, and Eteocles—forgot his family while away at war. His crimes as a broken personality cursed his children and similarly my father's trespasses curse my brothers and I with violence, with lack, with uncertainty, with being forgotten. Ismene bends like the branch of a willow, whirls with and around the shape of winds, survives through pliability. Antigone is a stone wielding a stone and for love, regardless of the curse, risks herself to preserve her family. Polynices and Eteocles are both inheritors of Thebes; Mike and our brother Robert fought similarly over who would be the metaphorical "man of the house." There are many stories about how Polynices and Eteocles ended up dying on each other's sword, but the apropos word for it all is neglect.

- Mike was not buried justly and I did not interfere in that lack of justice. I couldn't.

- What other crisis of ancestry and inheritance opens a story about honor, love, social death, and accounting for your kin? What other story in our recent human history begins with a curse born in the corners of the most unforgiving illogic?

- Maybe I am both Ismene and Antigone. Ismene is my sense of self-preservation, but Antigone is my willingness to indict myself in the life and death of my brother Mike.

- I did not attend my brother's funeral. I do not remember what I did that day. My mind drew a white sheet over it. I have thought about it one million times. What did I eat? What did the day smell like? Did I hold my mother? In the end I do remember one thing…screaming.

- I dreamed of Mike after his death. The last time I embraced my brother was in the last dream I had of him. His embrace always pushed me back. His wide chest would lean its full weight into me : a wave. Even in moments where he made me feel unsafe, when he hugged me, it was like passing into sanctuary. His shirt was electric blue, the original blue, bright indigo. I can see it now. He said, "Hold me bay'sis, just hold me." I awoke with my arms wrapped around the dark. I cannot help but envision Antigone smiling as her last breath escaped her as she hung in her tomb. Why do I see her in relief at being joined with her brother?

- My mother and I were getting coffee on December 23, 2021. A practicing driver, I was hesitant to answer when I saw Robert calling. I answered and said, "I am driving, let me call you back." He said, "No sis. You can't. You can't call me back." I asked, "Why? What is going on?" And he said, "Mike's dead."

- Godfuckingdamnit. Godfuckingdamnit. Godfuckingdamnit.

- I was screaming over and over again, rage a monsoon blanching my blood. But more than my own lamentations, I heard my mother. Hers was a wail that blotted out the blue. Hers was a wail that cut the blue from my sight and I can no longer see it. Do you know what it is like to lose a blue sky? I haven't seen a blue sky since that day. And no matter how many times people try to explain to me that—yes, Jesse, the sky is still blue—I cannot see it.

- Mike loved the feeling of being loved, even when he fought it. Mike loved to dance and he could yell out a tune when he wanted to. Mike's perspective of the world was one of wildness. Mike's love was a command: delectable, irresistible, and heavy as a mountain. You could climb Mike's love, if you dared. Mike knew people well, although he did not often heed his own cautions. He was a man of many emotions channeled through the one trumpet of anger. After spending ten years in prison, suffering COVID in prison, being banned from the state of Georgia, he was incarcerated again: possession of a firearm by a felon and possession of prescription pills that didn't belong to him. Isn't it obvious that punishment is justice for no one? It is unhuman to not run when you are hunted. They diagnosed him with bipolarism and depression and still hunted him.

- Like all of us who are the children of my father, we have a strange relationship with violence, a love of it that we respect. We learned the effectiveness of violence through the actions and hands of adults. Mike greeted violence with giddiness, he would swallow his prey whole, tilting his head back, like a vicious bird. Me—I will pretend I love you, if that means I get to watch you die; a Hannibal complex, I will eat my prey morsel by morsel while alive. Afterall, our father is a violent man, selfish to our mothers, a victim in his mind; he creates the disaster and then wants everyone to wait for him to be a hero.

- When Mike died, I understood the nature of his death in a way that my family cannot accept or admit and so I will not specify here. A year before, on Thanksgiving, we sat on the couch together and rested against one another. He was tired, tired of his own shit, tired of the accumulation of people in his life fucking him over since birth, tired of the accumulation of time he did not take to address how those failures affected him. He slept and slept and slept. This was the first time that Mike, Robert, our mommy, and I had shared a holiday together. I have never been in a room with our father and Mike; Mike was clear, he intended to kill him. Our mommy has never been in a room with our father and all of us. Despite this disconnection, together we found peace. We found rest. Mike and mommy both melted into a love grounded in lives refracting each other. They were both abandoned by a parent, both grew up with many siblings, they both fought tooth and nail for everything they had even though the world would not let that be much.

- Mike had a long life that even I have trouble making sense of. Our father did not raise his sons. The story father tells: Mama C, Mike's mother, died and when our father sought custody, Mama C's family intervened. Before Mike's death, mommy and I uncovered the truth when Robert called to say that there was another brother, aged 33. Our father lied about Mama C being dead, she was alive until I was two years of age, I am 35. The rest hides in vital documents and no one will speak about the in-betweens, the real reasons for him losing my brothers. Mike was adopted within Mama C's family and my brothers, for most of my life, were a dream to me.

- I had him for 10 years, minus the additional three he served in prison, and the one he was serving when he died.

- I left the day after Christmas. I changed my flight and flew to Robert in Fort Myers. I flew my nephew down as well. I knew how important it was for us to be together, to just sit with family even if we were not discussing Mike's death in depth. The week was spent attempting to figure out when Mike would be shipped to us so we could make funeral arrangements. We were waiting for the coroner to call so we could prompt the funeral home to transport our brother. We were all shocked when Mike's ex-partner, who I will call Tiffany here, took legal custody of the body and proceeded to text both Robert and I that we could "do what we wanted with the body when she was done." She produced a marriage license, they had not been together for years, but they never divorced.

- Our father took this as an opportunity to assert himself as a parent over a brood of children that he did not raise, and when he was present, he maimed. I was conflicted, did he have a right to grieve his first-born son? It seemed easier than showing up and being there for Mike when he was alive. Even though Mike always swore he would "whoop that cracker's ass (our father)" when he saw him. Robert was emphatic, "Mike needed you, Dad."

- Would Mike have even asked for our father at his own funeral? Seeing as how he told anyone who would listen that he would, "Kill that cracker."

- Mike's body never arrived. No one—not the coroner, not the jail in Jacksonville, not the detectives—would tell us anything. All I could do was go back to my life, go home to my partner. While Robert drove me to the airport, DMX sang "Slippin" on the radio. He glanced at me in the rearview mirror as I started to cry. They were DMX's lyrics, but everything, in that moment, was spoken by Mike.

- There is an unspoken well at the core of Black masculinity, it is a position that will always be defined as usurper. There are violations, humiliations, trespasses that can never be spoken out loud. Fitting into the world is compelled through threatening the life of those that do not comply. But compliance with white fantasies of race means we die anyways. How does one escape a calamity that keeps closing in while taking no shape at all?

- The people that believe in this system, this legalized hunting, believe that it makes them safe. Quite the contrary—they are helping manifest a violence in the world that will return to them. I promise.

- Mike was a marrier, maybe in an attempt to reassemble the home he saw degrade in his youth. If I am remembering correctly, he married each woman he had a child with, save for the last. Like the women before Tiffany, he married her and subjected her to the same pattern that he followed with the others: love bombing, sex bombing, contributing to household necessities, quickly moving in, and around the time each of these women became pregnant, he cheated, and continued cheating until the relationship deteriorated.

- Tiffany, as do many of the women in Robert's and Mike's lives, had a preoccupation with being close to me. They wanted to know the who, what, where, when, and why of me which was something I did not give any of them. They each, in their own way, wanted me to know who the "woman" was in the lives of my brothers. I understood the dynamic, gender in the Black American experience is about survival: hardline matters, discussions and expressions at the crossroads of the question of liberation and what others will think.

- Crenshaw was clear on intersectionality, the answer to Black men's misogynoir is not to imbue them with more rights to white-defined masculinity, but to transform Black masculinity so that it does not occur at the expense of their humanity or the humanity of other Black folks, especially Black women and femmes. The gender debate within Black publics (digital and otherwise) oscillates between erasing the concept completely, and best-selling instruction manuals published by Steve Harvey about what Black women need to do if they want to be wives. But how obedient can we be when it means we lose everything in the process? How can we obey this delusion when it kills us so often? My mother was never saved by gender, I was never saved by it. My brothers are maimed permanently by masculinity. Antigone, Ismene, my mommy, and I cannot escape the truth that more than anything our humanity, our human right to care for each other, is continuously violated by these expectations.

- And I am guilty. I am guilty because Tiffany had a place, like the others, and it was in a place with a rotating face. I helped my brothers isolate their partners because I wanted them to love me. And yes, I know they are at best romantically and serially unfaithful, and at worst, yes, they are abusers. I recognized their behavior through my own survival. I am a victim of domestic violence in my childhood home and my adult romantic relationships; I was raised by a narcissist. And yet—for as much as my brother's trigger(ed) me—I want(ed) their love and need(ed) their recognition. The mothers of their children trigger me. Despite all I have learned, despite all of the history and theory I jam into my head—to respect all Black women regardless of our choices, to respect myself as a part of that community— there is a voice inside my head that screams why do you trust them? Why don't you know better? Are you (am I) stupid? I hear these questions having lived the truth that what the world thinks are choices are actually no choice at all. I harangue myself with the questions everyone uses to signal virtue at the expense of survivors.

- Tiffany left Mike at the coroner to rot for a month. He had to be burned and not buried by the time Tiffany made arrangements.

- I didn't help. I didn't send money.

- I could not tolerate her violation against my brother's body even if he did break her heart and maybe her personhood. I didn't care that he broke her heart.

- I still don't. My lack of care for Tiffany protects me from the totality of my grief.

- My partner now—an intensely vulnerable, deliberate, and honest person—told me that in Egypt there is an Arabic saying that translates to "The shadow of a man is better than the shadow of a wall." Ismene chose the shadow of the men, and Antigone, entombed, chose to dangle behind her wall. Wall—have mercy—fall on me.

- I didn't go to the funeral or the cremation. How could I go? Who would protect me? Who would hold space for my grief? My father? My remaining brothers? Tiffany?

- The day of the cremation I hollered 800 miles away. I broke my voice. I lost my breath. I beat the dirt. They burned all of his 6'2, 200-pound body down to four handfuls of ash.

- Some things are unspeakable while you go through them. The weather is already haptically beating against you, but to speak it? I do not know that I will ever be able to speak of this.

- I grieve for the "whole huge disaster of us."

Four Poems

KATHLEEN HELLEN

on the nature of exception

shi in Japanese means death / herself reflected / his singular pos-
    sessive
projected by the he who (doer of the sentence) substitutes affec-
    tion

in other words indefinite/not quite determined / not that or this
    but object of the proposition
we

not interrogating / pleasures of a self-delight that ravish the sin-
    gularity —
transformed / non-binding / made undressed with stroke of luck
    to manifest

the force that topples worlds erecting boundaries / takes eternity
    into itself

Abby, I don't want to play anymore

we poured our tea like Brits
i said i had two kids
she said she had two kids
and let's pretend
this process does not end
with childhood
(*see Piaget*)
see women in the USA
68.45 percent
with two kids
i said i had
Abby as attachment
friend
who knew
next to nothing
about me
though i was caught up
in her tangles. red hair
freckles. acquaintances
in narratives of play
imagination
the connection
when things got tough
when things you know
for sure
won't get better
Abby bit her lip
i bit mine
(*like tea, like kids*)
copping cues
like mimic
replicant
like snapping turtle

alligator
chameleon
scared the predators
might eat us
but who
would eat us?
red hair, freckles

theory of one who parachuted from the tower

It's easier to focus on occurrences that support
than fighting the uphill battle.
It could be work related.
I looked out from portfolios of
steel and its accounting,
the inconsistencies in RFP's,
my braided thoughts plunging
into lunchtime
        when men in their Armanis
strutted blindly, searching for the one who took
her salad in the garden. Said
good morning, ignoring
evidence to the contrary.

It could be Spell Check,
the sad and lonely song
of the Rapunzel.

i've cased this understanding for as long as i can remember

tethered to the clinging
i scuttle crawl

on city busses
to the restroom of the arts collective

on a wall on a wire on a nail
                              a balloon

taking shape. sailing over ice caps over striated rocks
to a beach leaking hardwood

get over it, i tell myself
what i breathe a dirty blue the same as sky

what i eat a basket of red flowers
eating me

This Is Jeopardy!

JULIE MARIE WADE

from
THE ZEITGEIST
category:

"What is the New Normal?" for $200•

First, please silence your cellphones. Not *lower the volume*, not *put them on vibrate*—silence all electronic devices now. Next, check your spam filters. Junk mail is the digital flipbook for our fiercest obsessions, desires, & fears: Christian Mingle. "Let's Go Brandon" bumper stickers, t-shirts, flags, & more! The Squirting School. (*Definitely don't click that!*). Lendafy: get an unsecured personal loan, no credit check. Leaky Gut: 5 warning signs. PayPal account temporarily suspended. Trisha wants to meet you! Click for hot pics. (*Definitely don't click that!*) Jewish Mingle. Trial CBD Oil: just tell us where to send your free bottle. Transvaginal mesh class action lawsuit (have you added your name?). FarmersOnly: Single in the Country? Hi, it's Jim & Chris from 1-800-Flowers. We're just emailing to check up on your mental health. [cell phone rings softly] Now Facebook's asking, "What's on your mind?" but it's so hard to articulate sometimes, especially in a public space at a reasonable length, so you upload a picture of stirfry on a bed of rice instead. Surely that won't offend anyone. You're wondering, does anyone even use Facebook anymore? Does it matter if only five people like your dinner? These are questions you will have to answer for yourself. [cell phone vibrates] Now those chips you're eating for a late-night snack boast they're "Paleo-friendly" on the bag, which may or may not be why you bought them. Consider this: what caveman had tortilla chips to go with his wild boar & berries? Sure, you get nostalgic for the past sometimes but try revisiting *Jagged Little Pill* on Apple Music. It's healthier than modeling your diet on what people whose average life expectancy was 35 ate two & a half million years ago right before they died. I do recommend a few Post-Its (old school) on the mirror: *YOLO & Paleo are not compatible. YOLO & Keto are not compatible. Bet Dr. Atkins has some regrets. P.S. Bread is not the devil. It's called "the bread of life."* [cell phone plays *Jaws* theme music, indicating a "Scam Likely" call] That's clever—but knock it off! I know about the Dirty Dozen Shopper's Guide to Pesticides, but whatever happened to "fruit's a gamble"? These days Netflix streams *Seinfeld*—big win for retro comedy—but why does it seem like when we talk about nothing in real life, it's nowhere near as funny as the sitcom? Scrunchies are back. Leggings are back. Maybe we *are* funny in our present-day potpourri of panic, boredom, & polarized non-sequiturs—it's just that no one can hear us through our masks. [cell phone chimes eight times] Vaxxing is the waxing of the 2020s, except it hurts way less & more people are afraid of it. Also, the hirsuteness of my neighbor will neither kill me nor make me stronger. I cannot say the same for his cough, sneeze, wheeze, or prolonged proximity. There's no app that will vax you, but there is an app for almost everything else. Somehow LinkedIn is still a thing, & people you haven't seen for 12 years & weren't close to even then will inexplicably appear to wish you a happy work anniversary. LinkedIn should change its name to Lazarus for all the ghosts it restores to life. [cell phone plays Taylor Swift's "All Too Well," indicating an ex is calling] *Now* will you put it away? The language is fecund, always generating new ways to name ourselves. Of course short-hands & omissions proliferate, too. She must be more than a Q-A-Mom, & he more than a MAGA man, & "they" aren't reducible to a pronoun any more than "she" is or "he" is. Things get expansive, & things get restrictive, & so often they're the same things in rapid succession. Ever struggle putting on compression socks? Then, you know what I mean—how they stretch & how they snap back. I started wearing them on long flights because a poet I love named C.D. Wright died of a blood clot after flying all day. Death is the first known form of cancel culture, though the odd few flourish postmortem. Last year our niece came out as enby & bi. They have language we didn't have at 13, but we still haven't figured out how to gender-neutralize the word "niece." Daughter is child, sister is sibling, mother is parent, wife is spouse, but what of the niece who is not a niece or a nephew? Meanwhile, Evie says our cats would be instant stars on Instagram. We've only gone as far as #CatsOfTwitter. Nibling! There's the word at last.

also from
THE ZEITGEIST
category:

"Who is Karen?" for $800

If you search Wikipedia, you'll find two entries—one for the name & one for the slang. Full disclosure: I've always liked this name, the way it puts me in mind of an act of kindness. (Ironic now, I realize.) I've always heard a verb in it, a soft verb where the "ing" gives way to apostrophe. Think how *Carolyn* sounds like *carolin'*, like a woman spreading good cheer through song. The slang version is harder to confront: pseudonym, meme, caricature in some cases, but more often, cringingly real. I'm terrified of being mistaken for her, pushing my cart through the supermarket or dropping my ballot in the specially marked box. *Who do people see when they look at me?* Three adjectives qualify the archetype: white √ privileged √ middle-aged √ I've spent years checking my whiteness, haven't I? Checking my privilege, too? But this is the first time I've had to acknowledge my age. What happened? Wasn't I "young" just a minute ago? Now I work the math & face a different music: *If I don't live at least to 85, then I'm already past my fulcrum.* Of course part of privilege is the permit to take a tangent instead of staying the course, instead of staring the hardest truths in the eye. So here's my white, privileged, (*write it!*—& not like disaster) middle-aged self turning to Buzzfeed to absolve her sins: "Good news! You're only about 5% [this kind of woman]! Not only are you nice to everyone, but you mind your own business as well. Keep doin' you, bestie." *Phew*! Now where can I post these results to counteract the unpleasant fact that I am visually indistinguishable from the demographic that elected Trump? Tangent (aka looking for a loophole): "This was the third most popular name given to girls born in the U.S. in 1965." *Phew*! Most of the women for whom this term was coined are 14 years older than I, closer to Boomer than Millennial, closer to "older" than "middle-aged." They have AARP cards! Some may be retired—hence the extra time for poking around in other people's lives! Course: You're all Gen X, & you've all got work to do. Stop obsessing about the noun, & start putting the verb into practice. Tangent (aka unconscious wishing): I saw a t-shirt the other day that proclaimed, "I'm so woke I can't sleep!" & the thought flickered briefly though bright as a cat's eye—*Could this explain my recent, persistent insomnia?* Course: But then you realized you dreamed that t-shirt, right? You took a Tylenol PM so you could turn off your brain for a while, & what does your sleep-brain do but conjure a catchphrase to let you off the hook? Tangent (aka covering bases): Tylenol has been implicated in studies as an "empathy-reducing agent." Course: It's not that you're lacking empathy; it's that you ascribe to the fantasy that empathy is enough. What if empathy, all by its lonesome, only leads to paralysis? Tangent (aka virtue signaling?): In grad school, I had a panic attack when we watched *Night & Fog*. More recently, I had a panic attack when I joined the 8 minute 46 second silent memorial for George Floyd. I left the screening room quietly. It was dark, so no one could see. At home, there were no witnesses when I flushed & choked, so dizzy I had to forego my chair for the floor. Course: You may not have been seeking attention, but that sounds like the epitome of white fragility to me. Tangent (aka tears): Oh, shit! You're right. Course: Seriously, you're gonna cry now? Like *boo-hoo*, everything bad happens to you—watching documentaries & meditating on other people's pain? I don't feel sorry for you. Full disclosure: I don't feel sorry for me either. But my white, privileged, middle-aged self can backpedal faster than any elliptical at the gym. Tangent (aka rationalization): *In most depictions & videos, she has a fancy haircut, expensive, too. That's not me! I barely ever get my hair cut, & everybody knows I'm more Great Clips than salon. I don't own any make-up or designer handbags. I've never had a facial, a pedicure, a massage. I mean, I drive a Prius, for Chrissake, the smallest one—the C! How entitled can I really be? I always tip 20%, even if the service is terrible, & after Covid, I started tipping 25. And let's be honest: don't we all assume this woman is straight? Divorced, widowed, somebody's horrible mom? I'm not trying to be heteronormative, but I'd like to think most lesbians would behave better. We don't call the police because we think someone doesn't belong*. We're used to being the ones who don't belong. Course: I have to call bullshit here. Yes, you strive to avoid conflict, but isn't that mostly because you're terrified of taking after your mom? The moniker may be new, but the phenomenon isn't. Before all the "Permit Pattys" & "BBQ Beckys," there was Mother Linda, a meddling white woman prone to pettiness, paranoia, & unreasonable demands. When she set foot inside Pay 'n' Save, you watched the cashiers call for a manager. No one waited for the inevitable scene. My advice: instead of the 95% of ways you're not like her, focus on the 5% of ways you are. What could you be doing differently, better? And remember: "nice" isn't always a synonym for "kind." Researching the origin of the name, I learned it means "pure." (OK. I'm still obsessing.) And what's more dangerous than the stakes we place on purity: that all-or-nothing, good-or-bad, blueblood, thoroughbred, binary-embracing bilge? "The longing is to be pure; what we get is to be changed," from a poem I love. Time to revise: not terrified of being *mistaken for* her—that was my mistake!—terrified of *being* her, of *becoming* her, of not seeing if/when/that I already am.

from the
ACRONYMS & MNEMONICS
category:

"What is D.E.A.R. (Drop Everything and Read)?"
for $400

Which was easy for you as the child of a teacher—by title, a Reading Specialist for the Tukwila Public Schools. She was a fixer, a closer, a maven of literacy. She could teach anyone how to decode the squiggles & symbols on a printed page. You pictured your mother striding through halls, draped in a red cape with a winged, silver book on the back. *When we read, we take flight!* might have been her credo. At three, you were already "sounding out" words, already in love with all 26 letters. At four, you could read whole books on your own, though your mother also read to you—a quiet time at the end of each day, free from conflict & fear. At five, permed & bespectacled, you confused your classmates, talking to them about phonics, preaching the Gospel of prefix & suffix. "Are you a teacher's aide?" they asked, & you replied proudly, "No, I'm a teacher's *daughter*." Sometimes your mother substitute-taught at your church school, & the whole focus of Pre-K shifted. A book was a skeleton key primed to unlock any door. She made her students locksmiths. "Cooking is reading!" your mother explained. *If you can read a recipe, you can make a quiche!*, which you understood as a cornerstone of female accomplishment. "Housekeeping is reading!" your mother extolled. She was always consulting *Hints from Heloise*, a rival Bible in your home. You had many rival Bibles, first the *Ramona* series followed closely by *Nancy Drew*. You liked the last name Quimby especially & the moxie exuded by both admirable girls. Reading for you became a kind of detective work, shadowing the person or persons you wanted to become. *If you can read a book, you can emulate a character!* you might have said. That's why it surprised you that the school had to "incentivize" reading. (Wasn't reading its own reward?) Inspired by *Ramona Quimby, Age 8*, they joined the national program to pro-

37

mote reading at home—30 minutes a day as a family. It seemed so simple, so paltry to you. (30 minutes was only halfway around the clock-face after all.) But then, eponymous of the mascot Leviticus the Lion, your school added another program—Roaring for Reading—where for every 30 minutes read, the student received a gold star. Laminated lions (pink for girls & blue for boys) soon adorned the central hall. You found the lion bearing your name & every week presented to Mrs. Olson a slip of paper signed by a parent. Guardian of the books, a stone-faced angel of shorn hair and orthopedic shoes, the school's librarian doled out your stars. *30, 60, 90...300, 330, 360...*After 2100 minutes read, she took your picture with her Polaroid camera & taped it to the lion's chest. His mane already rimmed with stars, his tail already a trail of stars, & now your face square in the middle. Was it weeks or months each year that the competition went on? (Wasn't reading its own reward?) Your pictures became a flipbook of sorts, stacked one atop the other—permed, bespectacled, gap-toothed, & grinning. The only thing that changed from week to week was the color of the bauble in your hair. Some kids began to grumble that it wasn't fair, that there was really no point in trying since a certain know-it-all was always a shoo-in for the grand prize. Over time, Mrs. Olson saw a marked decline in the number of stars your classmates earned. Someone drew devil horns on your lion. Someone else drew glasses and shaded one eye with a patch. (Instead of Four Eyes, they called you "Three Eyes," & you knew why.) On the playground, you heard a lot of "Hey Pirate, why don't you go read a book?" which they meant a lot like "go jump in a lake," but you reasoned it was good advice for a girl like you. Your comeback so simple, so paltry, it defined your early life: "OK. I think I will." *If you can read a book, you've already made a friend!* you might have said.

"What is Divorced, Beheaded, Died; Divorced, Beheaded, Survived?" for $800

Three Catherines, two Annes, & one Jane. Even the duplicate names were spelled the same, which shouldn't have surprised us. We were learning, often tacitly, though sometimes explicitly, too, how wifehood—*wifedom?*—*wifery?*—foreboded a certain, inter-changeable quality. "The wives" became a collective of women who answered to "Mrs." and wore (*flaunted?*) large, glittering rings on their left hands. They also comprised the group that served food & congregated in a kitchen, or, depending on sta-tus, oversaw the serving of food while congregating in a balmy atrium or sunlit salon. History was never just a class we took. History wasn't even history, since the modern news was teeming with men—rich, powerful men—*American kings?*—who replaced wives like any object beginning to lack luster for them. (Stocks, sports car, wife…Toupee, pied-à-terre, wife…) Three Catherines, two Annes, & one Jane. Her surname was Seymour, like the ac-tress who played the title role on *Dr. Quinn: Medicine Woman.* We didn't all love that show the way I did. We weren't all carry-ing a high school torch for Michaela Quinn while pretending our torch really blazed for Sully, the shaggy man she would later wed. "How strange that her name is the same as the third wife of Hen-ry VIII," I remember musing aloud as I mooned privately over her eyes—one brown & one green. (*O, heart-throbbing hybridity!*) Now imagine my surprise upon learning that Jane Seymour was christened Joyce Penelope Wilhelmina Frankenberg, then later changed her name in homage to the English queen. (*Joyce, Penelo-pe, Wilhemina—three names, & she kept none!*) Of "Jane Seymour," the former Frankenberg said, it seemed more "saleable" as sobri-quet. So Joyce became Jane, & the lady-in-waiting to Henry's first wives became Queen, only to die at 29 following complications from childbirth. The history books tell us, repeatedly, "She gave Henry his only male heir." What a way to go down in the annals, at least some of us thought—dead before your 30th birthday, then buried beside the king's plot simply because you didn't demean him with a daughter. (Barrenness, of course, would get you the guillotine.) Our teacher wanted us to remember the notorious monarch's sequence of wives, the way we might memorize courses for a fancy meal or the placement of silverware to accompany each dish. History & Home Economics ran parallel sometimes. But—changing the name to "Family & Consumer Science" didn't do much to renovate the content. We were college-track girls in a single-sex school, & still we knew to think of women in relation to their husbands. Now, in order to pass our history test, we'd have to learn to think of each wife—*course?*—*dish?*—in direct relation to her demise. Three Catherines, two Annes, one Jane. Henry divorced two, beheaded two, & one Catherine went on to outlive him. Sometimes—and this was sad to admit—it seemed like a woman's greatest accomplishment was simply staying alive. We didn't all think of Catherine Parr as often as I did, but I related to her as someone who also wished to publish a book. (*Would I have to wait until my own family died to tell the truth about us?*) In 1546, shortly after Henry's death, Catherine Parr crossed the quavering bridge from writer to author. *Lamentation of a Sinner* was a kind of testimony we now recognize as "memoir"—intimate, confessional, self-examining. Women were capable of so many things. This we had also been taught. Our high school led the state in "female success in physics and calculus" after all. But—I didn't take those classes. I didn't raise those bars for the high-achieving girls who surely came after me, just as they came before. Nope. I hid in the library at lunch. I wrote books no one has ever read. And—I aced my history test: *Catherine of Aragon, Anne Boleyn, Jane Seymour, Anne of Cleves, Catherine Howard, Catherine Parr.* (See how I know them to this day!) Then, under my name I noted, in my tidiest script: "Accurate recollections of historical information should not be equated with endorsements of this or any other lesson."

from the
LESSER KNOWN LESBIANS
category:

"Who is Mary Poppins?" for $800

What do we really know about our title character? Not where she comes from, not how she was raised, & nothing at all prior to her stint on Cherry Tree Lane. Almost certainly a Virgo, she packs heavy but travels light. Her singing voice is unrivaled, even by the impish doppelgänger in her mirror. A careful planner, perpetually self-possessed, & yes, it's true, also a bit arrogant, she's the provider of practically perfect outings—& she's rubbish at saying goodbye. Here's my supposition about this wind-borne woman, with her black swing coat & sensible boots. Pop with me, if you will, into a picture: Wickwar, a village in South Gloucestershire, at the Victorian *fin de siècle*. Father's a farmer, & mother tends the home. She's the only daughter, hearty first-born, followed by four, sickly sons. Alongside her mother, she raises them—fixing the stews, stitching the clothes—& sometimes, for secret exercise, pitching hay in the barn. Late nights in the loft with an old, mousing tom, our heroine reads the Bible, only book her family owns, drawn in particular to Ecclesiastes: "For everything there is a season, & a time for every matter under heaven." She memorizes the litany that follows & holds closest in her tight-buttoned heart: "a time to keep, & a time to cast away." In town, there's a woman called Aster who keeps shop while her merchant husband's gone. How lovely, the girl muses, to be called after a flower instead of her own impossible name—that holy paragon no mortal maiden could ever hope to attain. She finds herself lingering, looking for reasons to be sent to the shop, so she can steal glances at Aster. "I love it when you pop in," the shopkeeper smiles, & all the pale hairs on her arms arise, ecstatic. Over the years, Aster confides in her about the life she lived in London—"such glorious grit & appalling noise!" Then, a cloud passes over her shimmering, hazel eyes. "Of course when I married Henry, it all changed. His family

41

is from these parts, so this is where he wanted to make his home."
One day, when the girl is seventeen, Aster beckons for her to come
close. In a whisper, she says, "I have something for you," then
opens the proprietor's cupboard to reveal a carpet bag. "There
are things I don't have words for. There are words I would like to
invent. But suffice it to say, dear one, I see myself in you—self-
taught, stubborn, longing for a life you can't lead here." A furtive
touching of hands, & the girl's knees wobbling beneath her. "Take
this. There are a few shillings inside, enough at least for a railway
ticket. And an umbrella that once was mine, for rain is inevitable
where you're headed." The girl wishes she could kiss her good-bye,
wishes she could ask how Aster has read her mind. But the woman in the crisp blouse & frilled white apron shoos her through
the door as a tiny bell dings. "*Spit-spot*! Be gone with you before
they come looking." Our heroine never wanted a husband, but
what reasonable way might she find to escape that fate? Our heroine never wanted children either, but by golly, she knew how to
mind them! Aster had tucked a letter in the bag, sealed with wax,
though it did not bear a message baldly meant to woo. (Such a
fool she felt for hoping!) Instead, the note simply read, *Here is the
address of a dear friend in the city who helped me through a difficult
time. You can trust Bert—he's one of us.* What did that mean? What
was it Aster had recognized in her that she could not yet name for
herself? Bert played many instruments, also self-taught, & offered
her a cot on which to sleep. Sharply, though trembling within,
our young heroine asked him: "And what is it exactly you'll expect
from me if I permit myself here to repose?" A wooden screen par-
titioned the room, & he lifted it so she could see: "This is David,
my gentleman friend. All I—all either of us— expect from you is
discretion." One bed & two pairs of stockings stretched before the
fire. She nodded as a new light began to dawn. How many ways
there were, in fact, of living—though some might require a certain sleight of hand, a certain, cultivated ease around taking one's
leave. She patted the parrot head on Aster's umbrella. "Help me,
strange bird. There is a time for everything, & this is the time for
a new surname—for a story that starts *in medias res*."

Mother F***

FILIZ TURHAN

I. Alphabet City

When I told my parents that I was pregnant with my first child, my father's face kind of fell. It wasn't that he was unhappy about the baby. It was just that I was still a student, and as an English major my job prospects were sketchy at best. It had always been important to him that I finish my schooling and get a reliable job before having kids. His own mother had been widowed young, and he had seen first-hand her struggle to feed her four sons. My situation, of course, was nothing like hers had been. Sure, it was a hot and humid summer in the city and hauling myself up the stairs to my fourth-floor walk-up on Avenue D wasn't easy, but it was a far cry from her life on a farm in Eastern Turkey in the early decades of the twentieth century.

II. [Inhale] I am [exhale] your Father

As a teenager, I never sought out babysitting because I just didn't care for children. I was never inspired to coax infants away from their mothers at a party or to talk to weird toddlers. I knew this was something other adolescent girls sometimes enjoyed but not me. Maybe it's because, growing up in America, I never got to spend much time with my younger cousins so many miles away in Turkey.

I sort of tried babysitting once. The mom was a friend of my best friend's mother and she had somehow gotten the implausible impression at a backyard barbeque that I was both mature and responsible. On the Friday I was supposed to show up at her house, I took off instead with my brother and his friends to see *Return of the Jedi* which had just opened at the cineplex. I couldn't wait to find out if it was true: was Darth Vader really the father of Luke Skywalker? Impossible!

I did not call to cancel and deluded myself into thinking that the babysitting appointment had not been firmly settled anyway. After calling my house for hours (my parents did not even own an answering machine in those days and they both worked late on Friday nights), my would-be employer finally got me on the phone and commenced to giving me one of the worst tongue-lashings of my life. It entailed a synopsis of what life was like for a forty-year-old divorced woman raising two children with no help and who looks forward to a night out now and then with a well-deserved glass or two of wine and flirting with a reasonably good-looking man.

I took my place by the Emperor's side.

III. Baby Jacob

Ok, this was before we were married and had the kids. We were visiting friends in Brooklyn, our only friends who already had a baby. We were all about 24 and their baby about nine months old. We left our shitty above-a-noisy-bar East Village apartment, stopped at a bakery for a box of rugalach, and took the F train to their place in Carroll Gardens.

Before dinner, I watched as David changed the baby's cloth diapers. He explained that they used a diaper service because disposable diapers last forever. His fingers danced over the retro-style safety pins as adeptly as he would later be sautéing pine nuts in fragrant olive oil.

David and Christi were good cooks and while they measured

and mixed, they handed me the baby. For a moment I thought, *uggh, can I offer to chop something instead*, but took the baby anyway. At nine months old, he was the perfect age for an inexperienced klutz like me to manage. His little body was sturdy and erect, and I soon realized I would not break him. I switched him from one hip to the other as I walked around the apartment showing him the dog, the Ficus, my dangly earrings. Suddenly it occurred to me, *babies aren't so bad*.

Nowadays I can honestly tell my children that they partly owe their existence to cute baby Jacob and a preparation-intense soft brie appetizer and baked salmon with dill sauce.

IV. Baby and Me, NYC

We brought our baby home from the NYU Medical Center in a yellow taxicab. Life in a small East Village apartment with a baby means: lots of outings. Within a few weeks, she became my intrepid companion all over Manhattan. Her life was sustained for the first four months by nothing but my breastmilk (always perfectly climate-controlled and ready to be served.) We bought the lightest sturdy stroller we could find, and I started stuffing diapers in my bookbag.

Since I was still a student, I would take my napping baby to cafes where I would work on my writing hunched over a cup of coffee. If she were to wake up from a nap and not find herself in her stroller next to a bistro table, her baby sign language would be like, "What the hell. Where are we? Are you ok?"

V. The Williamsburg Bridge

I started working at a community college on my daughter's first birthday. I couldn't find one (literally not one) Day Care Center in Manhattan that we could afford, so we got a part time babysitter and set up a dubious childcare schedule between the three of us. I don't know which was more acute: the anxiety of my morning drives across the Williamsburg Bridge or the return journey to relieve the babysitter. If I weren't going 75 mph, I wasn't going fast enough… hoping neither to hit the concrete median to my left nor the car to my right; I was always facing forward, gritting my teeth with the precarious passing of every T&LC.

VI. Mr. Baby, Esquire

After bagging a book deal and a promotion at work, I was feeling confident enough to go for number two. We had a little boy, and like his sister, my son also was a fun companion. Like a little Attorney General, he poured forth a steady stream of opinions and prognostications from his stroller. On my non-teaching Fridays, we would spend the whole day together. If the weather was too cold or wet to loiter in a park, we'd hit the shops. He could spend hours examining the Legos at Toys R Us, the fish at Petco, and especially the train set at Barnes and Noble. In every store, I followed the footsteps of a four-year old, grading a clutch of quizzes.

VII. So Good

By the time my daughter was ready for kindergarten, my son was only just starting day care. They went to Pumpkin Patch preschool, a place that I could both afford and which was full of wonderful people I trusted fully with my kids. Every day on my way to work I would think: "Dropping them off is so good. And picking them up is even better."

VIII. The Other Mother

The summer my son turned five we were visiting in Istanbul. My aunt had a Wii and a large collection of DVDs, so he was happy to be left at home with the big television while I would be out with my cousins. On one occasion I went for a haircut and returned with an impeccable blunt-cut bob. It was so perfectly styled that I couldn't help flipping my hair around like I was auditioning for an old Breck commercial.

My son took one look at me and shrieked "The Other Mother!" He went running into the next room and crawled under the dining room table laughing.

He had been watching the movie *Coraline*.

The "Other Mother" lives in an alternate dimension accessible from within Coraline's house. Her hair is a perfectly coiffed wall of shiny black. In the book, Neil Gaiman describes it as "wriggling like lazy snakes on a warm day." All she wants is to keep Coraline in her dimension and to love her forever. But as things go downhill, she reveals herself to be a spider lady who feeds on black beetles and death. No wonder my son went running.

Sometimes I am the Sweet Mother, very affectionate and supportive. I kiss my children regularly and cuddle with them everywhere. We are effusive with terms of endearment and regularly express them in multiple languages.

But then, I too am the Other Mother: the one who sets conditions that must be met. More activity, more accomplishments, more, more, more.

I lead by example. I am the one who is up early on Saturdays. I drink two cups of coffee, have toast and cheese, set up the Roomba and start a load of laundry. I go out and run for miles and when I return, I make a massive salad with many ingredients and bake multigrain muffins. Even though everyone else has just gotten up, I ask brightly, "Tennis, anyone?"

IX. Huge Stack of Laundry

I cannot lie; I still find myself doing most of the housework. I pay all the household bills. Not only do I have a full-time job which includes our health insurance, I also provide (most of) the child wrangling and serve the failure-to-perform consequences steaming hot from the oven. For Christmas, my daughter buys me socks that read: "You're fucking welcome."

X. Conference on Academic Moms

I was at the kitchen table working on a talk for a conference panel entitled: "Report on Academic Moms." I was in the process of writing a sentence about the unequal burden of work in most families. Statistics show that women partners continue to heft the majority of household chores, even when they are employed outside of the home. As I was typing away, my son came along, complaining that his radio car wasn't working. He held it out to me, with a plaintive, "Can you fix this?" I finished the sentence and leant back in my chair. "Why don't you ask Dad to help you?" He answered, "Because he's working."

Perfect.

My son was about nine at the time, old enough to know that my job often entails sitting around the house reading and writing. I didn't answer him. Instead, I typed a description of the scenario that had just unfolded, including his lines quoted above. Then I read it to him. He looked affronted and said, "Don't write that, it makes me sound sexist."

XI. Bad Moms

I was preparing for another academic conference. Even though the theme of the roundtable was "Mother Subjectivities," I ended up writing about Mother *Activities*. In the talk, I examined how authors explored the question: What must women do to be good mothers? (Is it because I, too, am always *doing* and trying to be so *good* at it?)

As I thought about literary moms, I began to notice how many of the Bad ones are the Best ones, that Bad Moms are entertaining: Bad Moms who strive to be Good Moms; Good Moms who bend the rules in Bad ways to be Good to their children; Moms who struggle to figure out how far they can pretend Bad is Good before admitting that Bad just sucks.

Euripides' Medea delivers one of the most intense speeches about the fears and hopes of mothers for their children, but she later murders her two young sons. Grendel's Mother is a "monstrous hell bride" (Heaney's translation,) but demonstrates deeply authentic grief at the murder of her son and a period-appropriate raid to avenge his death. Volumnia, the mother of Shakespeare's *Coriolanus*, "professes sincerely" that she would rather lose a dozen sons in battle than to have one who lives "voluptuously surfeit out of action." Maxine Hong Kingston's "No Name Woman" drowns herself and her newborn baby, for as Kingston writes, "Good mothers take their children with them," even if it's to a watery and ignominious death in order to escape social ostracism. And I think too of Sethe from Toni Morrison's *Beloved*, one of the most enigmatic mothers in American literature. Having killed her "already crawling" baby girl to prevent her from being sent back into the slave-state of Kentucky, Sethe must live with the memory of her action, ironically encapsulated in the single line, "Unless carefree, mother love was a killer."

XII. Did I Say that Out Loud?

My son and I were walking across the High School athletic fields. I was irate because he had made us late for the marching band show which his older sister was performing in. If his lateness weren't such a habit, I'd have been less of a raging bitch by then. I said to him, "If we miss the show, I'm going to beat your ass," and I must admit, the tone was not ironic. Then I noticed the mother of a kid we knew. I cringed at the echo of my own voice. Had she heard me? She seemed to have abruptly sped up her pace. I wanted to shout after her, "It was just a metaphor!"

XIII. Bad Kids are Fun Too

There's a scene in *The Sopranos* where Carmela and Tony are in bed talking about their daughter. Meadow is smart, ambitious, and spoiled. I think she scores a perfect ten (plus bonus points) on the Universal Scale of Unbelievably Obnoxious TV Teenagers. It seems to me that most of the time, Meadow deserves a smack, which you can't do, cuz that's uncool and that's why it's such a stroke of genius when the mob boss says to his wife, "Let's not overplay our hands, cuz if she finds out we're powerless we're *fucked*."

XIV. Happy Mama

I frequently practice yoga in the narrow column of space between my bed and the old baby changing table which I still use for my clothes. Just yesterday I was doing yoga after putting in a long day of work, shepherding my more than one hundred online Freshman Composition students through their virtual college experience. I was finishing up my practice with my favorite pose, Happy Baby. I often think that the world would be a much more humane place if all world leaders started the morning with a Happy Baby. Flat on your back, knees bent and splayed wide, holding on to your feet. Rocking left to right. Vulnerable and exposed, yet, balanced and natural.

Then I heard noises from below. While I was upstairs rolling around on my back, I realized that my husband and both kids were in the kitchen preparing dinner.

Ah, Happy Mama, at last (for now, anyway).

Four Walls

MICHAEL MARTONE

Bastion Cities or Trace Italienne

Gunpowder changed everything. Curtain walls of stone gave way, literally, with the shock of shot. Of course, it was Michelangelo who turned Florence into a star. Leonardo's Palmanova became the ideal city. The names for all the parts were like poems, little poems, like the parts of a poem. The Bastion and the Ditch. The Glacis, that grassy inflection. Horn works! Crown works! Dead zones now became deadly with intersecting fields of fire. Redoubts and Ravelins! Lunettes! Tenailles and Tenaillons! Counterguards and Cordons! Faussebrayes! Banquettes and Barbettes! Scarps and Counterscarps! They scan! They meter! Formal and beautiful! A Golden Mean! A raised ratio!

The Athenian Long Walls

Athens, Greece

Nothing is left of them now, of course. Finally, Sulla, in the Mithridatic Wars, leveled them for good. Four hundred years before, Lysander tore down the original walls that ran four miles from the city to the port. Xenophon reports there was much jubilation when the walls were dismantled to the song of the flute girls. Imagine you are standing on the Acropolis, the Lacedemonians laying waste, again, to all of Attica all around you, and this narrow strip, safe passage down to the sea, is your only lifeline. But it goes two ways. The Plague arrived by ship and had an easy time of it, funneled as it was along the corridor of ruin between the Long Walls, spreading from one citizen to the next, a safe passage through that long (what was thought to be) safe space.

Bam

Iran

There have been defensive walls at Bam for twenty-five centuries. Gigantic walls surround the city that are then surrounded by a moat. The walls are over twenty feet high. There are four gates and thirty-eight watch towers. There are sixty-seven "Stay Awake" turrets for which Bam is famed. On the Silk Road, the Crossroad of Spices, Bam is also still famous for its dates. The citadel of Bam was thought to be the largest adobe structure in the world, fending off invasion after invasion, siege, and mining until 2003. On 26 December an earthquake centered directly below the city center, leveled everything to the ground in a few seconds.

Vietnam Veterans Memorial

Washington, DC

There are 144 black granite panels that form the wall that grow in height as the visitor goes forward through time and deeper into the ditch. The stone on which the names of the dead are inscribed is from Bangalore, India, and selected because of its ability to take a reflective mirrored finish. You see yourself in the stone looking back at yourself reading the names. In 1912, a Captain McClintock of the British Army invented the Bangalore torpedo in Bangalore, India, an explosive device designed to breech hard defensive works like barbed wire, like walls. There are 58,320 names inscribed. Over 100 are misspelled. It is thought that five million people visit the wall each year.

Three Poems

RITA MARIA MARTINEZ

The Amazons Adopt Caylee Anthony

Wonder Woman pilots the invisible jet
to transport Caylee's remains to Themiscyra.
She and Queen Hippolyta enter Aphrodite's temple

and lay Caylee's small bones—skull once covered
in vines, eye sockets embedded with debris—on the altar.
Legions of Amazons perform holy rites, keep vigil

as Queen and Princess pray to the Goddess of Love
for regeneration. The Amazons long for another
child on their isle. One has not scampered across

its terrain since Diana. After Caylee awakens
without memories, Amazons argue over who gets
to babysit, to wash and braid her honey-brown hair,

teach her to play bullets and bracelets when she's older.
Caylee will show proficiency in ancient Greek,
shall run alongside deer, ride her beloved Kanga

across winding trails and forests. As an adult,
she'll operate the purple healing ray Diana invented
to restore battle-injured Amazons to optimum health.

Caylee shall enjoy immortality and daily sunrises
in this paradise abundant with mothers—haven where
children never worry about chloroform or duct tape.

* On July 15, 2008, Caylee Anthony, a two-year-old girl from Or-
lando, Florida, was reported missing by her grandmother. Casey
Anthony, Caylee's mother, was eventually charged with her murder. The prosecution argued that Casey had murdered Caylee by

administering chloroform and then duct-taping her mouth and nose, causing her to suffocate. The jury ultimately found her not guilty of first-degree murder, aggravated child abuse, and aggravated manslaughter of a child.

Every Girl's Got a Joker Hidden in Her Closet

I was irritated by Harley's ditzy Lina Lamont voice,
repulsed by the jingle jangle of her court jester hood,

by the red-and-black diamond-pattern jumpsuit hiding
Joker's signature brand: galaxy of cigarette burns

and bruises. I never understood why Harley Quinn clung
to the green-haired goon like one of Ivy's stubborn vines

until I recalled my entanglement with a slick trickster
who made me laugh. Like classic Mistah J, my joker's m.o.

included grinning from ear to ear—crooked teeth revealed
as he cracked jokes to elicit laughter from an audience

with pursed lips. When he blasted obnoxious Weird Al
song parodies or played mind games—like saying he didn't

love me, then taking it back—the grin resembled a slasher smile.
As Dr. Harleen Quinzel guzzled coffee and gin, listened

to Nine Inch Nails, and neglected a roster of psych patients
for extra sessions with Puddin', I concealed dark circles

under my eyes, woke early weekends to collect celebrity
autographs for my joker, attended his games to *RAH! RAH! RAH!*

from sidelines. While Harleen ditched her crisp lab coat
and specs and swiveled round and round on her office chair

fantasizing about J, I daydreamed and danced before a full-
length mirror. Fiona's *Criminal*—'90s bad girl anthem

undoing rational thought on repeat. When we ended just like
that I sulked to No Doubt's *Simple Kind of Life*. He'd snatched

my sunrises, evenings, and laugh. After learning he'd swapped
me for a groupie, I plunged into rage, into Alanis Morissette

and The Cranberries. How do we kill our attachments?
Dr. Quinzel dove into a vat of chemicals with aplomb

as if claiming her birthright. Swimming in toxic sludge
proved easier than getting over the Clown Prince of Crime.

* The line *He'd snatched/my sunrises, evenings, and laugh* is modified. The original appears in Stjepan Šejić's DC Comics graphic
novel *Harleen* and reads *He had stolen my nights . . . my days . . .
and my smile.*

The Savage She-Hulk

The girl recognizes sadness in her father's eyes so much like Doctor Banner's on *The Incredible Hulk* show, pities the scientist who wanders from city to city avoiding meaningful relationships because he never can stick around long enough to make them last. All Banner desires is a cozy lakeside cottage and a pair of golden retrievers flanked on each side as he curls up in his favorite reading chair with a cup of cocoa and a dog-eared copy of Darwin's *On the Origin of Species*. Despite attempts at a Zen lifestyle, inevitable triggers occur. Punks cross the line. Bullies brawl at bars. Caught in the crosshairs, cops are hot on his trail. Banner loses his cool, clenches his hands into two tight fists when the green rage overtakes every cell, incites him to administer destruction—like the girl's normally sedate father—who sometimes comes home from a loathsome job in a volatile mood she always fails to predict, always stunned when he smashes phones to smithereens, punches holes in doors, shatters her mom's favorite vase. The mother teaches the girl to swallow anger. The mother teaches the girl to pretend she has no mouth. The girl fears turning into her father, worries one day her own green rage will bubble to the surface until she rips doors from hinges, launches pick-up trucks across lanes of traffic like mere ping pong balls, destroys what she loves without remorse.

The Rifting

JULIE JONES

There are three primary theories entertained by the majority of the world's population for why, during the solar eclipse that occurred on August 17, 2017, the North American Tectonic Plate cracked in two.

The leading theory claims that Russian (or Chinese) special forces infiltrated the USA, sowed the path of totality from Oregon to South Carolina with underground mines that detonated in a cascade of explosions timed with the eclipse, which cracked the plate in two. Why the Russians (or Chinese) never invaded to seize control of the country while it was governed by chaos is still a matter of intense debate.

The second theory asserts that an extraterrestrial spaceship hid within the moon's shadow during the eclipse and shot a high intensity laser beam along the path of totality, which cracked the plate in two. Why the aliens never landed to seize control of the country, or whether they planted stealth agents in various governments, is still a matter of intense debate.

The final theory, popularly known as the Granger Hypothesis, was published in a peer-reviewed journal under the unimaginative title, *The Cause of the Rifting*. It posits that the path of totality loosely corresponded to a network of geologic rifts—the Snake River Rift, the Northern Reelfoot Rift, the Midwestern Platte Rift, among others, some known, some discovered only after the crack—which had been weakening sections of the plate for years.

Upon those weakened rifts, within that narrow path, for the duration of a few hours, millions of humans gathered, a weight calculated at over 5 billion pounds, which cracked the plate in two.

My name is Cherri Granger. I don't believe any of these theories, least of all my own. Tectonic plates are not dinner plates. They are not even thick slabs of bluestone for your backyard patio. Tectonic plates are 125 kilometers thick. They float on convection currents of magma which nudge these seven continental rafts at a rate of 1.5 centimeters per year. They have meandered for billions of years in a super-slow-mo choreography over the surface of our planet, crashing into each other, bouncing off one another, in an ecstasy of physics that is on a scale beyond most humans' ability to imagine. Magma plumes within the mantle are a whole other issue. Volcanoes also feature. There is much of the inner workings of the earth that we do not yet understand, just as there is much of the inner workings of the human body that remain a mystery. But I knew for a fact that a tectonic plate could not just snap in two like a broken candy heart.

My wife, Billy, if she had survived to read my article, would have critiqued it from an entirely different angle. She would have said it doesn't have a strong narrative arc. It features a non-sentient object, the Earth, as protagonist, and lacks an enemy beyond the vagaries of existence. It stars no stereotypical hero who should have saved everyone, including her, from the Rift. Quite the opposite, in fact. Worst of all, it has no emotional component, like me. She always joked that I had the emotional sensitivity of a rock. But she never understood how sensitive rocks can be.

Billy and I had flown from Chicago, where we lived, to Charleston, to witness the eclipse with our two miniature poodles, Marble and Granite. The eclipse coincided with our 25th anniversary. She'd already won the fight of where to vacation, a South Carolina beach instead of Carbondale, Illinois, the latter being where we would have enjoyed the longest duration of eclipse totality. I had been nervous to travel to a southern state, though not because of any concern about whether the hotel would welcome our dogs. For that we'd paid an extra fee.

I called Billy my wife, but we weren't married. I wore a ring.

She didn't. A fault line ran deep within the bedrock of our relationship. She said the laws of matrimony were based in patriarchy and asked why we should willingly clamber aboard a raft we had derided our entire adult lives just because it had recently, begrudgingly, allowed us to clamber aboard.

"Every other species on the planet manages their love relations without laws," she said. "Why can't we?"

Tax breaks are a thing. It's expensive to live in Chicago, and Andersonville, our neighborhood on the north side, became gentrified once it was deemed hip by the mainstream to be queer. Well-to-do hetero-liberals crossed the line that is Foster Avenue, invading our territory as proof of their acceptance of our "lifestyle." Starbucks replaced the local lesbian bookstore. Our rents, property values, and taxes rose until we couldn't afford our lives anymore, although money is a fiction. We agree that these slips of paper printed with white men's faces in green ink mean that they are worth exchanging for other things, which, in the case of taxes, include schools, roads, sewers, libraries, garbage collection, water purification, and a thousand other services that go unnoticed until something disrupts the machine. Marriage is one way to pay less taxes, though it has always been curious to me that people want to deprive the system that provides the services that maintain civilization.

Personally, I just loved Billy and had wanted to sign on the dotted line.

On August 21, 2017 at 2:37 pm, we were standing shoulder to shoulder with a thousand other people in a commuter parking lot off State Road S 20-52, just east of I-77, on the outskirts of Columbus, South Carolina, waiting for the moon to block out the sun. At present, the sun could be seen through our eclipse glasses as an orange crescent behind a flat black circle.

It was Marble and Granite, straining against their leashes, who sensed that something was wrong. They would not stop yapping. At first I thought they were being overly sensitive to their mommies who were angry after their fight that morning. Then I thought they were uneasy because the eclipse was eerie as it approached totality. The sunlight was a dull gray. Shadows were unnaturally sharp. The dimness had tricked nature into thinking twilight had arrived early. Birds rushed to their nests. Crickets started singing.

Humans were looking up and counting down.

"Ten! Nine! Eight!"

We were standing in this parking lot for me, because I cared more about the Earth than anyone else, according to Billy. But I couldn't enjoy it. All I could think about was how we got here. We had met during our junior year in college. She was my first and only lover. I majored in geology, she in business administration. She followed me to grad school in Colorado, saying that as an office manager, she could work anywhere, but when it was time for me to get my first real job, she suggested Chicago.

"But Chicago doesn't have any active faults," I said.

She reached out to hold my hand. "My parents are getting older." I saw in her eyes a spreadsheet entitled, "Sacrifices Made on Behalf of Your Significant Other."

"I read somewhere," she continued, "that every big city needs people like you to monitor the bedrock beneath their skyscrapers."

Bedrock, I told myself, was not uninteresting. It contains invisible lines that can grow over eons to gaping rifts. Rain water seeps into microscopic cracks, then in winter, freezes. The ice expands, widening the cracks ever so slightly, scraping loose fine particulates in the process. In the spring, the ice melts, washing away the debris. Alternating seasons act over hundreds of thousands of years to carve out space unseen from the surface. When an outside force exerts pressure upon the crack, a deep rift can appear in what seems a sudden occurrence, but nothing in geology happens suddenly. The groundwork for any major action is years in the making, millimeter by millimeter, unseen, creeping, building pressure, storing pent energy, until that moment of violent release.

That's how we ended up here.

"Three! Two! One!"

Totality dropped darkness upon us like a velvet stage curtain, leaving only a thin orange ribbon simmering around the horizon. Overhead, the brightest stars and planets glimmered in a bruised shadow sky, but everyone was craning their necks to stare at that singular black circle with its blazing white halo. It was a sight so inconceivable, so astonishing, that I understood why humans have believed it an omen of world destruction.

All around us people were chanting, "Oh my god! Oh my god! Oh my god!"

I wished Marble and Granite would stop yapping. I wished I could concentrate on this miracle of science, but I reached out to Billy, to cross the invisible line separating the sovereign nations that were our bodies, to explore with my fingertips the possibility of a cease fire. At that moment, it seemed safe enough to touch in public when all eyes were raised to the sky, but for the first time in my life, I didn't want to hold her hand. I didn't even know why I was trying.

That morning, we'd rehashed where to view the eclipse. She wanted to go to the beach, but I said that if we were looking at the sky, it didn't matter where we stood and we would get 59 additional seconds of totality by driving two hours northeast.

"We can go to the goddamned beach after we're done being awed," I said. "Alright?"

The people around us were still chanting, "Oh my god." A few cars sped by on State Road S 20-52, their drivers not caring about the flaming white ring in the sky except as it made traffic lighter for a short span of time. Billy, perhaps swept up in the moment, allowed me to hold her ring-less hand for a split second before letting go so she could swat away a mosquito that had activated in the artificial twilight, leaving me wishing she'd held on just a bit longer so that I could have been the one to let go first.

When I said that morning that I wanted to drive two hours one-way for 59 extra seconds of totality, she said that I was an emotionally stunted workaholic that was incapable of taking even one day to relax.

I asked what could be more relaxing than working with rocks? "They don't hurt your feelings. They don't require ten hours to get off."

To which she said, "Go fuck yourself," which I proceeded to do with her favorite twirling dildo with attached clit vibrator, which she had packed even when I'd complained that the TSA screening agents would see it, to which she'd said that she wouldn't need it if I was an adequate lover.

In the hotel room, she started counting how long I took. "58 … 59 … 60 …"

Time is a fiction. We say that that happened 25 years ago or this takes 2 minutes, but a second can span an eternity and years can crystalize in a single moment.

I came, but it was a lot of work, requiring a lot of lube, resulting in a weak orgasm that left me thinking that my childhood pet rock was the best friend I'd ever had.

In the commuter lot, Granite and Marble were yapping like crazy, twisting their leashes around my legs. Billy had the keys in her hand, ready to leave. She only came here because she wanted the dogs for company, although they were more mine than hers. I had a crick in my neck from staring up at the sky.

Everyone was counting down to when the nightmare would end.

"Ten! Nine! Eight!"

More time than it takes to destroy a 25-year relationship.

A single ray of sunlight shot out from behind the black disk and people began to jump up and downar screaming, "Diamond ring! Diamond ring!"

It seemed the entire population of the United States of America, plus half of Canada, an eighth of Mexico, and smaller portions from Japan, Germany, Australia, and Brazil, had travelled to witness the event. I imagined all the cars and buses and vans and trains and planes and people and dogs and luggage forming a thick line across the country, filling the moon's 70-mile-wide shadow from where it hit the rocky coast of Oregon, ran through Idaho, Wyoming, Montana, Nebraska, Iowa, Kansas, Missouri, Illinois, Kentucky, Tennessee, Georgia, North Carolina, ending in South Carolina at a sandy beach that kissed the Atlantic Ocean, which was where Billy wanted to be with her feet in the sand and a mystery novel in her hands. That entire distance, 2,482 miles, packed with awed adults and yapping dogs and crying kids, with all their food and water and gas and books and phones and laptops and shoes and clothes and thoughts and grief and love. Everyone unique, yet united, for the most part, in their desire to witness this celestial event which suddenly seemed to shake the earth beneath our feet.

"Oh my god!" someone screamed.

Society, at its most fundamental level, is a network of interconnected lines: electric wires, water and sewer pipes, fiber-optic cables, gas and oil pipelines, railroads, interstate highways. These lines are real, constructed of steel, plastic, and concrete, transporting all that is required for civilization from where it originates to where it is needed.

Nations, on the other hand, are imaginary lines traced upon the surface of the earth. Mexico, the United States of America, and Canada all occupied space on the North American Tectonic Plate, but look at the earth from the sun's perspective and you see no lines demanding that this language goes here and those laws go there. A nation is simply a fictional construct that humans agree upon.

The country formerly known as the United States of America didn't break immediately after the eclipse, even though our President had perished in the Rift. Every human, all around the world, held the construct of the country firmly in their minds. It was a strong fiction with a dramatic plot line that, Billy had once said, might someday be satisfying from a story-telling perspective, though not so satisfying for those of its residents who suffered the drama firsthand.

What broke first after the eclipse was not the fictional nation, but the physical lines that ran over and through the Rift. Gas lines exploded. Electric grids failed. Plumbing systems collapsed. Fires raged. Cell towers crashed. Flies buzzed in ragged swarms over dead bodies in the streets. No instant streaming of one's favorite TV series. Rioting quickly escalated into the Second Civil War. A feast for the vultures in the news industry, though no picture can convey the stench when the connective tissue of civilization breaks, and without internet, paperboys and girls were relegated to hawking headlines on street corners.

The main fault line between Billy and me was not obvious to those who knew us. It was not even obvious to us. Our friends lifted us as an exemplar of a relationship that could last. There were no secret lovers. There were not even crushes. We loved each other, and were well matched by nearly every metric. We earned in the same tax bracket and liked to snuggle on the couch with Marble and Granite. She took out the trash. I brewed the coffee.

We were different, but balanced, in a lopsided way. Where I dreamed of bedrock, she was down to earth. She enjoyed good wine, good food, and good company, whereas I enjoyed thinking. She liked to debate politics over drinks, watch movies on the weekends, read mystery novels at the beach. She grounded me in reality, and sometimes teased that I was like an ostrich with my head stuck underground, eating worms, unaware of my surroundings, leaving my ass up in the air, which was the best way she could reach me.

During the Second Civil War, trapped south of the Rift, I got conscripted into infirmary duty where I learned that a human body holds nearly 1.5 gallons of blood. That may not seem like much when you look at a milk jug in a refrigerator, but when 3,461 people bleed out, as they did in the Battle of Dentsville on September 25, 2017, that's over 5,000 gallons. That's a lot of spilled milk.

One of the wounded gave me a book on U.S. history before he died. It was a book Billy had given me for my 40th birthday. I'd never read it when she was alive. The author stated that 620,000 people died in the First Civil War. 40,000 in the U.S.-Mexican War. 22,000 in wars with Native American tribes, not counting those lost due to smallpox, nor those on the Trail of Tears.

Over 1 million gallons of blood. The earth drank it all, swallowed it down into the cracks of its bedrock with no regard to mother tongues or fictional boundary lines.

For 25 years I had mapped Billy's terrain, traced her topography, but she always kept a fissure hidden from me. I once went down on her just as her period was starting. I hadn't known it was starting, but didn't let that stop me from drawing down from her cleft the sweetness of desire mixed with the slow density of iron. But one mineral lay heavy on my tongue. A bruised shadow of sorrow. I tried to lap it up like milk, swallow it into my heart, bring her the pleasure that came so quickly to me.

"It's fine," she said after a while, touching my head. "No one can. It's not your fault."

From between her thighs, I propped myself up on my elbows and I asked if we should see a counselor, if there was trauma.

"It's not that," she said.

"Then if you don't trust me, if you can't let go, tell me why."

"No, it's fine," she said as she slid open the drawer of her bedside table.

It's fine that you have a volcano ready to erupt at the slightest touch while I allow you to toil for hours until you have carpal tunnel in your wrist, a crick in your neck, and your tongue is numb before I reach for my dildo and finish myself off in 30 seconds. It's fine.

All pleasure is simply the release of pressure. A bladder emptied. A trouble solved. A thoughtless word forgiven. A relationship you tried so hard, so long, to force, finally, let go.

The Second Civil War between north and south was short, lasting three months before the north let the south have what it has always wanted: a divorce. U.S. history had been an interest of Billy's, but our nation was only a few hundred years old, colonialism not even a thousand. Nothing compared to geologic time. She would try to entice me into discussions by pointing out how the earth's terrain influences the lines of nation-states, how mountains and plains inspire how humans fight or unite. She was right, of course, but my thoughts always drifted back down into the bedrock where the real drama happens.

The strange thing about the tectonic plate break, however, was not that it followed a network of geologic rifts—the Snake River Rift, the Northern Reelfoot Rift, the Midwestern Platte Rift, among others—but that it loosely traced the Mason-Dixon Line, the Missouri Compromise, and the former Mexican border that reached clear up to Oregon.

After the war, the states north of the Rift, except for Alaska which was repossessed by Russia, declined Canada's invitation to become a new province and join their health network. Instead, an alliance of Mohegan, Oneida, Ho-Chunk, Sioux, Cheyene River, Yakama, and other first nations, led a coup that resulted in the establishment of the Reclaimed Territories of North America. Conspiracy theories spread about how tribal leaders had received advanced warning of the Rifting from their spirit guides, but the new RETNA Chief managed to not roll her eyes while explaining that the warning signs of our country's collapse were not hard to read for anyone paying attention. By coordinating tribal police departments with casino security forces, who combined had tech and tactical training surpassing the FBI, they were prepared to act upon the opportunity that presented.

Like Canada, Mexico extended a similar, though less negotiable, offer to the southern states. After a few skirmishes, they took back all the land they'd lost in the 19th century wars, which included California, Nevada, Arizona, Utah, Colorado, New Mexico, and Texas, plus everything else south of the Rift in interest.

Cartographers were in high demand. Map lines were redrawn.

I never got Billy's body back. It fell into the Rift along with Marble and Granite, plus the bodies of 15 million other humans and untold numbers of rabbits, voles, chipmunks, racoons, cows, horses, fox, deer, prairie dogs, field mice, garter snakes, and other creatures that live on or in the earth. Birds were spared, and my job, of all things, was waiting for me when I finally made it over the border and back to Chicago after the war where I was a rock star of sorts. Author of *The Cause of the Rifting*. The Granger Hypothesis. I'd gotten it published in a peer-reviewed journal, though that's no guarantee of truth.

Every day I received new job offers in geologically active regions, but stayed in Chicago to take care of Billy's parents under the pressure of my guilt to be their substitute daughter. I occupied the cracks in Billy's and my condo, cluttered with the debris of our life. I ordered coffee at Starbucks, which survived after bankruptcy restructuring and the re-establishment of coffee bean shipping lines.

The eclipse, I learned while reading Billy's history books, had fallen on the 230th anniversary of our nation's 1787 Constitutional Convention, which wrote the fiction of the United States of America into existence; the 150th anniversary of the Reconstruction Act of 1867, which ended slavery and married the southern states against their will to the northern; and the 150th anniversary of the U.S. purchase of Alaska for $7.2 million from Russia. The timing seemed a strange coincidence, as if our tectonic plate held a temporal density.

It was also Billy's and my anniversary, which we counted from our first kiss. I had wanted to use the eclipse as an opportunity for us to open ourselves to the other again. Become cracked and open. Let the blood flow where our hearts had become frozen. Wash away the emotional debris in our veins. 25 years is a long time for humans. One day after another, making do with how we'd gotten in the habit of making love. Boring. But when we hit that anniversary, after we fought that morning, something between us broke like a slab of slate.

I worked all the time. I had no dogs. No friends. All our friends had been more hers than mine and I couldn't tolerate their sympathy, which would never survive if they saw a clip of Billy's and my last fight. If they saw how she'd died.

Like an ostrich, I held my head underground and ran the numbers over and again. My theory was wrong. There couldn't have been enough weight concentrated on that day to crack the North American Tectonic Plate, no matter what weakened rifts lurked beneath the surface. Which meant there was some weight in our world as yet unaccounted for, some force unknown to us, something here, on earth, that we had not discovered, or something so obvious that we could not see it.

When I shared my doubts with a colleague, he cocked his head and said, "Is your paper wrong?"

To admit an error of this magnitude would be the end of my career, but I was at fault. I knew it just as I knew that Billy had always lied to me. She had claimed she couldn't let go with another person. She had claimed that 14% of humans could only orgasm alone. But early in our relationship, when she'd paraded out the names of all her previous lovers, describing in detail what she liked best about each and why the relationship didn't work, vis-à-vis to compare to me and why we would, there was one that made her pause.

"Caroline was a total flake," Billy said, "but she taught me that I could come."

"Teach me how to do it for you," I said, and she promised she would, but either I was a bad student or she didn't really want to.

Not having the dogs, having no one to hold hands with, I turned to a psychologist for company. It was easier than finding a lover who faked their orgasms or lied and said it was fine. I paid. He listened. There was no reciprocity, just an exchange of his services for slips of freshly minted paper printed with new faces in blue ink.

At first, he was patient. He listened to my disdain for straight liberals who destroyed all that was wonderful about gay life with their unrelenting acceptance of us. He listened to my hatred of Starbucks and my guilt for enjoying the rewards I earned on its app now that cell phone towers were re-erected. He listened to my fatigue with the tedium required to administer the lives of Billy's parents. These topics I cycled through multiple times until I was relieved of many blue slips of paper and bored with the sound of my own voice. That's when he earned his pay.

"These are the things upon which you project your self-hate and survivor's guilt so that you can avoid feeling your sorrow and grief. What about the Rifting? Are you ready to talk about your wife?"

I'd dreaded this question even as I'd wanted him to ask. I saw Marble and Granite tumbling into the Rift, their leashes whipping past Billy who was begging me to hold on to her hand. If I mentioned the dogs, I would start to cry.

"What can I say? We were a stereotypical love story. You know in classic lesbian fiction, one of the women always had to die. The end."

He raised his eyebrows, but did not force the issue. "Then why don't you tell me about your work?"

That seemed a safe enough topic, so I told him how I monitored the sensors in the bedrock beneath Sears Tower and the rest of the skyscrapers in the Loop. Then I told him about my paper on the cause of the Rifting. Then I told him my doubts as to the accuracy of my calculations and my fear of being discovered as a fraud, which led to me saying things I didn't even know I thought, like how I felt like a fraud of a lesbian for having never given Billy an orgasm except by using a vibrator and how that didn't count. I'd never been with anyone other than her. Maybe I wasn't a lesbian at all, just a Billy-lover. Then I thought, this will be like the movies and he'll ask a tangential question about my sex life that will bring me an unexpected professional insight and boom! Mystery of the Rifting solved. But he didn't. He just nodded and listened as his eyebrows rose toward the light.

The strange thing about living in a country with blue money is that, while it is certainly preferable to not be killed for holding hands with your wife, it feels uncomfortably flat, like the prairies. Flat to a geologist is boring. It is pressure, rock grinding against rock, that creates majesty. It is release that creates beauty. Did not red and blue together make purple, the most fabulous color? But red alone, blue alone—there was no grinding, which was a relief at first, a tremendous pleasure, but peace quickly becomes boring. Blue soon divided into yellow and green and we were back to fighting amongst ourselves, though about different things.

Andersonville had one lesbian bar that the straight people tried to colonize, where they pretended they weren't uncomfort-able as they made a point of holding hands with their dates, obliv-ious to how lucky they were to hold hands whenever they wanted. I went out one Saturday night. My first night out. It was talking to the shrink that made me do it. I needed to prove to myself that I could. Also, in truth, I was horny. I was 46. My body was softer than bedrock with dimples in all my cheeks. Billy used to say that the two on my face were cute. Was I a good kisser? I thought I was with Billy, but we had kissed less and less over the years. She once joked that I tasted like dirt.

It was 9:30 at night. Early for being out, though past my bed-time. Music was playing. No one danced. I scanned the room. A few women at the bar were scanning me. I tried to act cool. Me. Hot mess of a rock nerd. I took a stool and ordered a mint julep, thinking it would be better for my breath than beer. The next three hours were agony. Then I was swaying back to my condo with someone who wasn't Billy, but Clair was friendly and had kissed me in the bar as the straight people pretended not to watch. I hated that we seemed to fit their stereotype, willing to hook up with any warm body, while they swiped right all the time. Could I help that I'd been born with an active plume feeding my volcano?

In my kitchen, Clair's lips were warm and wrong on my neck. My blood backtracked inside my veins, but I tugged her shirt out from her waistband and she lifted her arms overhead.

A vaginal wall is like bedrock. When stimulated and swollen, the barometric pressure in the flesh drops. This forces transudate, a semi-clear liquid, to weep through microscopic fissures and lubricate the cave. The pressure can be almost painful in its intensity until the muscles spasm like an earthquake, releasing pent up energy. People sometimes chant, "Oh my god. Oh my god. Oh my god."

Clair praised Jesus.

My lesbian membership card got stamped.

However, for the first time in my life, my bedrock was locked. The harder I tried, the more my body froze like ice.

"Sorry I couldn't do you," she said after 10 minutes before rolling over to Billy's side of the bed.

"Why are you giving up so quickly?"

She looked at me as if I had worms stuck in my teeth instead of pubic hair. "Why would you want me to push something your body doesn't want?"

One time, Billy said something I hadn't believed. She said that she could not force her vagina to play on demand, just as she could not force her heart to stop or start beating. She apologized, saying it was her fault, that it had nothing to do with me. She said we could allow the vibrator to do what human intention could not, like a pacemaker, but also, why couldn't we just focus on our pleasure until we were done being pleased?

"But I don't want to give up on you," I said. "I don't want you to think I'm a bad lover."

"This isn't about you. And honestly, it's too much pressure."

"But rock shifts after pressure. It's the most normal and natural release."

"I'm not your pet rock you can grind at-will against your pussy," she said. "And I'm not your wife. You don't own me."

It was low to bring up my pet rock when I hadn't mentioned her vibrator. "I don't want to own you," I said.

"And anyway," she went on, "I care more about emotional intimacy. Don't you?" Said the woman who once joked that I had the emotional sensitivity of a rock.

But I was filled with doubts. Was I wrong to care about sex? To enjoy it to the degree I did? Was my body coopted by hetero-normative patriarchy? Or was I just lucky to have a volcano tucked inside of me? I said, "Sex and intimacy are not mutually exclusive categories."

"Look," she said, rolling out of bed, "I can't force my body to behave the way you want. Can you please accept that and let it go?" She padded into the bathroom and started the shower.

Clair touched my arm where we lay in bed. "Earth to Cherri. Are you there?"

In a movie, this might be the moment when the camera zooms in on my face and the audience would see that I was having a sudden aha moment, a moment when the bedrock slips and the answer I had worked so hard for explodes into my mind. The close up would be followed by a montage highlighting my second groundbreaking article getting published in a prestigious journal, me taking a job in Denver, monitoring the Rockies, with the financial wherewithal to move Billy's parents into a nearby assisted living facility. We would live happily ever after, though their ever after would end quickly, and I would meet a new woman, possibly at a funeral. Our sex life would be amazing. We would click on every metric. Get married. Wear rings. Hold hands whenever we pleased.

But life isn't a movie and the city once known as Denver was now part of Mexico. Still, I was inspired. After Clair got dressed and left my condo, I banged out not an exacting, academic article for Nature Geoscience, but a whiskey-infused, grief-stricken op-ed to the Chicago Post, to wit:

The true fiction was that the United States of America had ever been united. It was an occupation of land that had always been forced. From its inception, the nation had been at war with its mythology and its reality, its ideals and its crimes. It resisted the suggestion that it should ever feel guilty, or apologize for where it had been at fault. The 2017 eclipse was the stimulus that brought the North American Tectonic Plate to its breaking point from all that pressure of trying to make something work that wouldn't. The mystery weight lacking from my calculations was the sorrow the earth had swallowed, the millions of gallons of blood, our grief frozen in the bedrock. The Rift exposed our collective wound in a sudden break that was centuries in the making. Time collapsed on itself. Our country's great stone heart finally snapped in two.

The day after my op-ed was published, I got fired. The job offers that had been a steady stream, ceased. I was not even considered for fracking surveys. But invitations to speak at New Age conferences began to trickle in. Sometimes I was featured on panels alongside men who explained their conspiracy theories about Russia or China or space aliens, but I needed blue slips of paper to pay my taxes, so went and presented my ideas. I discussed what science could tell us, and what my intuition told me. Sometimes, I even revealed that I lost my lover in the Rift beneath a diamond ring. People love a sad story, especially if someone dies.

But there is one memory I never share with any audience. I hate to share it even with myself. A roaring in my ears as I lay with rocks digging into my body, a thick cloud of dust choking my lungs, heart thrashing, one shoulder screaming, my arm stretched over the edge, holding Billy's hand, fingers crooked like cliffs aching with her weight as she hangs above the Rift while Marble and Granite soar into the void, their leashes waving goodbye.

I scream at her to hold on, which was the stupidest, most cliché thing I could have said.

I should have said I'm sorry, but that would have been worse.

I might have heaved her out like a superhero, but I'm simply not that strong.

All I could do was hold on, until I couldn't hold on anymore. I held on as I'd held on for 25 years. I held on because I thought love meant you hold on, even if what you're holding on to doesn't exist anymore. Maybe it never did. I held on until one by one, my cliffs crumbled and my hand became flat as a prairie.

I still wish she'd been the one to let go first. I wish I could let go of the memory. Every day I see her face falling away, her eyes registering at last the truth of who I am. A rock that can withstand only so much pressure. A human with a fragile, stony heart.

Four Poems

KIKA DORSEY

Trinity of a Life

1 Indiana

Grass wet with rain out my window.
Yellow station wagon, rhubarb
growing riotous beneath crabapple trees.
I bite an apple and watch the wind
on corn stalks, their nodding chins,
coffee and cream on my breath.
I write a river onto my name,
the dank smell of the St. Joe
like my father's breath when he calls out
my label like pounding a nail.
Here, Frances, close the window,
the wind is booming.
My body prying hips out of femur bones,
love out of blue-jay caws,
pillows out of bread.
Opening.

2 Colorado

Sounds of galloping horses
drowning out the yipping of coyotes
and bobcats screeching, fighting
on cottonwoods.
Smell of the ditch
like my wet dog.
Lovers the click
of closing gates, never final.
Some animal
in the milk of my breasts
managed to climb the fence.
Pour out bloody from me.
Raspberries, garnets, red jam.
Honey scooped from the willow's hollow.
Smell of leather boots

polished with monk oil.
Monk's Hood trumpeting purple.
My horse only took a hackamore,
mouth free of bit.
I bite into an apple.
Read a book.
Sand a desk gray with water stains.
Stain it the color of rust.
Even this desert has rivers.
They smell like iron, quartz, and stone.

3 Unknown

Mississippi, Danube, St. Vrain, Colorado, St. Joe.
What river will catapult me
into my future?
Zebra mussels sharp as shards of silver
from a ring's bed curling outward,
from a lover who left me.
In it turquoise.
Welded days to welded nights.
Roar of chain saws, lawn mowers.
Grass thirsty for rain.
Legs like fence slats or pine trunks.
Sky of satellites teasing stars.
My children diving into seas.
My name erased in the wind.
The cheatgrass bowing to snow.
Skeletal branches.
Chickadees counting two notes.
Three cups of bone broth
to make a soup thick as my marrow.
Fingers splayed, ringless.
We are always repairing
the broken latch of our gate.
The silver bed for lapis, garnets, pearls.
The bed for the riotous raspberries.
Sky like a mouth swallowing me.

The Angry Bitch in Me

She is the one that says, "Don't think your bad choices
don't affect me." The one with a bottle of truth laced
with arsenic when she says, "Get a life."
She lives in the deep well of an old marriage,
in the red pen grading papers written with AI,
in the chamber of my heart where a child
trips over the cane of an old, bitter man,
stupid as sin and erasing cradles in his poem
for a terrorist waterboarding our dreams.

The child couldn't know anger.
She just thought something was wrong with her
when born in a family with a father
who knew as little of love for his child
as a king knows of the pauper.
When born in a country where a beached whale
gave up in the crash of our sonar waves
pummeling his song, turning it to bones
he left for us on the shore.

She's the one who has given up.
The one resigned to aquariums instead of oceans.
In them a beluga whale swims in circles.
Round and round like a carousel.

I used to like those carousels.
I always chose the most majestic horse,
the one with a golden saddle.
I never did care
that I was going nowhere.

Self-Portrait as an Artichoke

Strip me naked, then
clothe me in butter and garlic.
Your fingers grasp my shoveling leaves
that curve like the arched back of a tortoise.
Olive-green suit with a pale heart,
spiky and thorned with a soft core.
I ask you for patience, for time,
to return to me again and again.
Where the leaves attach,
I release a smidgeon
of it for the sake of your hunger,
as you travel ever closer to a center,
my petals growing paler and softer,
journey to me a long road.
You have denuded me, a young flower,
before I had a chance to bloom.
Me with my invitation to ritual,
my tough stem, my birthing.
I watch how your lips love me,
how the journey has no return,
how you leave most of me behind.
I forgive you.

Eve

She tells me I'm a miracle, her gecko climbing the white walls,
pork rib in her mouth. God is nowhere to be seen. He flung

a jungle at her feet, shaped her out of what caged a man's heart.
He shut the sky-door. Now she climbs the ladder to the island

of me in future tense, the will-be, the seasonal ritual of spring
in her jouncing steps over hidden roots of grass. *Why do I speak?*
she asks,

when God is so silent? I do not answer at first, the fat and flesh of
a rib
in my mouth, a jungle of noise around me, God shut from me
like so much hope.

Fronds of city lights speckle my feet with shadow. A man flips a
burger on the barbeque.
I say, *So this world can be yours, will be mine. A gift.*

She buoys herself on my cloud, chooses again where choice was
made,
apple rinds at her feet, becoming past like a dusty desert ghost
town with bones falling.

And I am seven rungs away, my day of rest the last step into the
dust of a sidewalk,
my God as silent as a man who once said about my body in its
cracks,

This cannot be true, and I said, *But it is.*

Warsaw

LILLIAN ANN SLUGOCKI

My mom spent much of World War II in forced labor camps in Germany. She worked in a munitions factory alongside her family. They were not paid, fed very little, and if they tried to escape, they would be shot. When the U.S. Air Force flew over, they were bombed by them, too. History had them in a vise and always hungry. But my mom began escaping the camp at night. She dug a hole under the barbed wire fence and ran to a nearby village. I picture her breaking into houses, stores, and hen houses, smashing glass, and stealing bread, butter, eggs, and cheese. She's 10 or 11 years old. She's imprisoned, shot at, threatened to be shot at, and dragged out of her home, but she draws the line at hunger. I had to understand this as her daughter to tell this story.

They spent a short time in post-reconstruction Germany—remember that Dresden remained the gold standard for firebombing and annihilation until Gaza. My grandmother gave birth to her third child in a barn. But then they got lucky, booked passage on a ship, and landed at Ellis Island in 1948. My grandparents wept when they saw the Statue of Liberty. A commercial farmer in Northern Wisconsin sponsored them because they were farmers in a small village that no longer existed. Someone once told me it's now a parking garage for a high-rise in Russia. But, little do they know that my grandmother buried her amber jewelry somewhere deep in that dirt. Everybody buried their valuables because everybody thought they were coming home.

At the new and modern farm, they had a roof over their heads. My mother and her brother went to school after milking the cows. They weren't hungry, and nobody threatened to shoot them. The owner of the business and their sponsor said to Helen, my grandmother, I'm a single man and wondered if you could cook dinner for me. And make extra money. She said I have my own family to cook for. He said, ask your daughter. My mom is now 13 or 14. She went to his house at night, but she didn't cook. She told my grandmother what happened, and my grandmother said you had a dream about that.

At 17, she escaped to live with her aunt in New York City, in the East Village. She found a job in a typing pool off Madison on 44th. She and her best friend Francis took the D train to Coney Island on the weekends. They rode the Wonder Wheel, paid a dime to have their fortunes told by a mannequin in a glass-fronted booth, and ate hot dogs on the boardwalk alongside the Atlantic Ocean.

In Slavic literature, Baba Yaga is a sorceress, sometimes a monster who feasts on the small bodies of children. Folklorists who specialize in these things mostly agree that the word Baba means witch but also grandmother. In a strange twist, the linguistic roots of Yaga remain a mystery—Slavic, Russian, Polish, Ukrainian, Belarus, who knows. Is she a witch on a broomstick, a sorceress at the crossroads? Or an old lady with birds in her hair? Maybe she is an agent of change. The name can be pluralized—Baba Yagas—a collective of powerful women, like my mother, my aunt, and my grandmother.

In the 1970s, my mom had six kids from two husbands and wore cinnamon-colored pantyhose that came out of a white plastic egg, a black cocktail dress, and disco ball earrings. I watched her put on make-up. She favored a brown and taupe frosted combination on her eyes, coral blush, and a streak of vermillion on her lips. Her dark blonde hair was coiffed and sprayed.

I'm the oldest daughter, and I babysat on Saturday nights. One night, their car pulled up in the driveway; the headlights always lit up the kitchen. My stepfather came in the back door alone.

Where's mom? I said.

Your mother (his emphasis, not mine) is having a hard time standing up. Your mother is drunk.

I should check on her.

But she appeared at the screen door, swaying, her heels in her hands, hair askew, mouth bleeding.

Go to bed, he said to me.

I ran down the stairs to my room. A few seconds later, I heard banging, clattering, crying, glass shattering, and then a silence so profound it was like the air had been sucked out of the house. I waited a long time and climbed the stairs. The kitchen was dark. I didn't dare turn on the lights, so I opened the fridge as if I were getting something to drink. My mom's clothes lay strewn around the kitchen and the living room. Her black dress was ripped, inches from my feet, a disco ball earring glittered in the gold shag carpeting in the living room. Her shoes were scattered, one by the kitchen counter, the second under the kitchen table.

The next morning, she cooked scrambled eggs, buttered toast, sliced tomatoes with onions, fried a pound of bacon, and sat down to eat with us. She wore a pastel polyester housecoat buttoned to the top. Her hair was neat, her face washed, and her lip was swollen. Her neck was covered in red splotches, and she did not look up when he strode into the kitchen. He caught me looking at her neck and smiled.

He said, Get these kids ready for church.

And then he was out the back door.

All right, guys, she said, let's finish up. Everyone has something clean to wear. Brush your teeth and get a move on.

Mom, I said, are you coming with us?

No. Go on. I'm fine. Don't fight with your sister over pantyhose.

After we left, I imagined she poured a cup of coffee, grabbed her cigarettes, sat on the back porch, ran her feet through the emerald grass, and admired her bright pink pedicure. She sipped her coffee and smoked two cigarettes, changed out of the housecoat, and still barefoot, brought out a load of sheets in the laundry basket, the clothes pins in a canvas bag. She put two in her pocket, two in her mouth, and began hanging sheets. The wind picked up, and they billowed out like sails.

She was unshakeable.

SONGS 1-3
Part One

One

A tarot reader on YouTube with long turquoise nails said you have to admit you are sexually wounded. She tapped the deck and turned over a card, the Ten of Wands, in reverse. Expose it, she said, clicking her nails on the deck like castanets, and bring it out into the light of day. Maybe it will dissipate, lose some of its power, and you can fall in love again. The Gospel of St. Thomas (non-canonical) says essentially the same thing: if you keep your demons inside, they will destroy you, but if you let them out, they become angels who save you.

Two

There was this famous experiment with rats. They were alone in their cages and had two options: freshwater or water laced with cocaine. The rats drank the cocaine water until it killed them. Another famous experiment followed this one. Researchers took a group of rats and, this time, placed them in a rat hotel with all the amenities, everything you could ever want if you were a small white rodent. Rat heaven. In this experiment, they shunned the cocaine and drank fresh water. They had good food and company and a safe bed to sleep in at night. And the rats, btw, flourished, and some of their descendants are alive today.

Three

Dr. Gabor Maté says people who are addicted move the world like hungry ghosts. He uses the analogy of the mandala in Buddhism. Within it, there are six realms of being. According to this theory, they exist in a perpetual state of believing that their salvation lies outside themselves and wander through their own life like ghosts. There is never enough love, never enough food, and nothing can ever satisfy them. And that's what I mean when I say this is the weight we have to carry.

Part Two

The sun has been up for about ten minutes. It's too muddy on the aqueduct, so I'm walking through the commercial district of the village. Nothing is open; it's too early. I see a thicket of trees a half mile ahead. The sun is just beginning to hover over the branches. At the intersection of North Broadway, I walked north and, one block later, turned down Rochambeau Lane—also known as the Washington-Rochambeau Revolutionary Route (W3R). It's a steep hill, almost 45 degrees. The small houses with wide porches are almost flush with the narrow sidewalk and maybe the faintest echo of the soldiers who walked here. On the way back, I cut through a church parking lot. It's called Our Lady of Sorrows. It's Sunday morning. The bells ring.

Some people say that in a threshold space, like the dawn, everything has the potential to be transformative. I think the light this morning is a miracle, and so are the purple and pink buds on the cherry trees, the Gothic spire of another church on the crest of yet another hill, and the layers of pale blue and lilac in the western sky, and the faint sound of rushing water in the creeks that feed into the Hudson River. I hear it at the bottom of Rochambeau Lane, and I hear it on North Broadway. I hear it on Cedar Street heading west towards the Palisades. Maybe I'm a miracle, too.

My mom met my dad at a USO dance in the Village. He'd just joined the U.S. Army, but as a kid, he was exiled to a work camp in Siberia after his father was shot dead in the streets of Warsaw. They married in a Polish church on East Sixth Street and flew to Honolulu, where he was stationed. Things didn't last long in paradise because he was sent to Vietnam.

She joined the rest of her family in Southeastern Wisconsin, not far from Chicago. My father sends maps and postcards from Hanoi, Laos, Saigon, the Mekong Delta, and the DMZ.

Meanwhile, the basement of our rented home becomes infested with mice. We buy traps, fill empty boxes of potato chips with their tiny, stiff bodies, and put them outside in the snow. My mother cooks pea soup on the stovetop with a ham bone. We eat jelly sandwiches. She takes a job cleaning the house of a woman who lives in a mansion on Lake Michigan. She gives my mom her daughter's old clothes. I'll never forget a yellow cotton sweater with tiny pearl buttons.

I heard her crying to her mother. We don't have money for food. The army isn't sending the checks. How many bowls of soup can we eat? How many dead mice do I throw into the snow before someone helps me? She really needed to know the answer.

She met a shy young man at a house party with other emigres. He has a good job at the local factory. His family was part of a genocide—the massacres of Poles in Volhynia and Eastern Galicia, post-war. Apparently, it was a horrific time to be a little boy. She gets pregnant with her fourth child before divorcing my father. He's thrown in jail when he tries to beat the crap out of his rival. During this beatdown, my mom runs out of the house with us, barefoot in the snow, on a cold night in December.

SONGS 4-6

Four

I walked on the aqueduct all last summer. I left the house by 5:30 am to catch the sunrise. I saw brown rabbits in the ruts of the dirt path, robins, and dragonflies—fields of milkwood and wildflowers. Once, approaching a dense treeline of oak and sycamore, a deer appeared just a few feet ahead of me. It felt like I knew her, but it was transpersonal.

Five

At dawn, the birds sound like an orchestra tuning up, a cacophony of crows, cardinals, jays, doves, and chickadees. This morning, it was so foggy I could barely see the silhouettes of the trees, but I heard the sound of the waterfall at the bottom of the ravine. A mourning cloak butterfly flew by. When I say I walk on the aqueduct, I mean the trail that runs along it. It stretches 41 miles from Croton on Hudson to Van Cortland Park in the Bronx and brought fresh water to New York City.

Six

The tarot reader taps her long turquoise nails on a table with candles and crystals and turns over a card. She says this card works with the same consciousness/subconscious duality as the High Priestess. My guides tell me if you want to fall in love again, ask yourself this: who are you?

When I was seven, I took a train to New York City with my grandparents and my 17-year-old aunt, the third child, born in Germany. We stayed in the same apartment as my mom. My grandfather's sister had a rent-controlled apartment, bordering Tompkins Square Park, which was and remains the epicenter of anarchy. So god bless it. We rode the 7 train to the World's Fair in Flushing Meadows, Queens. Helen made garlicky meatloaf sandwiches wrapped in wax paper and stuffed them in her black patent bag. She said this is a big day.

The Unisphere dominated the entrance to the park—a stainless steel model of the earth, designed by Gilmore D. Clarke, and stands today—a silver globe 120 feet in diameter. I watched Abraham Lincoln, a robot, at a small theater. I looked at cars of the future, rode through the Small World Exhibition, and got in line for the mysterious event and the whole point of this journey. We stood in that line for hours. But we had food and took turns sitting in the shade to eat our meatloaf sandwiches.

As we approached a plain white pavilion, people lowered their voices. Then they whispered. We moved a few feet, and it grew even more quiet. And when we finally got out of the hot sun under an awning, Helen squeezed my hand. Don't let go, she said. We stepped onto a moving walkway. My aunt laughed nervously—who ever heard of a moving sidewalk? Helen shushed her and squeezed my hand again. The light of day disappeared as we slid into the darkened interior. It was pitch black except for a faint blue light, like a cloud, in the distance. We drew closer. I'd never seen a group of people become so quiet and still until we were enveloped in that blue light and saw, on a pedestal, Michelangelo's Pieta, sculpted in 1497, on loan from the Vatican.

It's carved from Italian marble but looks like it was created out of light. It represents one of the seven sorrows of Mary and maybe all women. Her son is dead, but the bodies are idealized, sensual, and perfect, almost alive five centuries later. My grandmother drew me closer as we moved away from the miracle, back into the chaos of sunlight, filled with a sense of wonder and deep love. I saw a much bigger world outside my own and chased it for the rest of my life. True agapé is a mark of salvation. Smart girls survive in many different ways. And god bless them, too.

Frittura

JUDITH GOODE

They were as light and fluffy as the small white clouds that floated across an otherwise spotless blue sky, of which Raffie and Kip had an unobstructed view from the balcony where they feasted on the fried scallops, clams, shrimp, calamari, and other seafood on the *frittura* platter. Raffie's father and his new wife were treating them to the first-class Pensione del mare's lunch while the parents went out on a tour of the islands. Raffie and Kip, who were living cheaply in a house without window glass in Positano, relaxed and enjoyed the hotel's luxury. Earlier, they'd spent some time on the parents' bed, having fabulous sex, as always. That was what kept them together, in Raffie's view, although Kip had asked her to marry him and was still waiting for an answer. He thought he'd heard "Yes!" but that was at the acme of Raffie's orgasm so she didn't count it. He did, however. He was one to hold her to promises of any kind. He also held grudges, small and large, but was himself free of guilt.

This could probably be attributed to his condition as a manic-depressive, which Raffie had learned about from the very knowledgeable French gynecologist they'd consulted together when they were still living in Paris. Dr. St. Claude thought Raffie might have an ectopic pregnancy because of her excessively bloody periods. Kip had asked to privately discuss with the doctor a bothersome irritation in the folds of his foreskin. Dr. St. Claude's manner was smooth and elegant, and he was not in the least ruffled at having two unmarried people with sex-related problems in his office. After all it was Paris, even though the year was nineteen-sixty, too early for the sexual revolution to have taken hold. Dr. St. Claude was outrageously handsome with a wide forehead and a widow's peak from which thick dark hair was combed in lustrous waves from his face. Later, when the pair was drinking un esprès at a café on the plaza near the doctor's fancy Right Bank office, Raffie blushed at the thought that he must have imagined correctly that they fucked day and night, and hence ended up in his office with their respective ailments.

Her pregnancy test was negative and months later, in Naples, an Italian doctor overdosed her on male hormones to stem the menstrual bleeding, and she ended up with a fine dark down on her upper lip and a few curly black hairs, like her pubic hairs, around her nipples. But these were minor annoyances compared to her worsening situation with Kip. He was declining into the depressive phase of his illness and she felt that he was dragging her down with him. Furthermore, she missed her husband Gianni and she wanted to go back to New York to repair their marriage. The repairs were really up to Gianni since he was the one who had initiated the separation one breezy June evening while they were standing side by side chopping raw vegetables for a pasta primavera in the large comfortable space that was both kitchen and dining room in their East Ninth Street railroad flat. A tall window opened onto the fire escape and the back yards below, the old maple dining table and chairs from Raffie's father's country attic stood by the window, and a handsome built-in cabinet with glass doors lined the back wall next to a large working fireplace. The floor was painted red, the trim Dutch blue. The bathroom was off the kitchen and held only a small bathtub, and the wood-covered wash tub adjoined the kitchen sink, as was typical in turn-of-the-century apartments. The front room, their living room, was large and sunny, and faced on the street. The room next to the bedroom was their shared study.

Gianni asked for the separation in the same tone of voice, with the same inflection he used when he asked her to pour olive oil into the heated skillet for the vegetables or to put the pasta into the boiling water in the stock pot. Gianni was Italian from

Tuscany and he had the profile of an Etruscan warrior, including the classical high-bridged nose. His hair was a sandy blond, and his skin fair and slightly freckled. He often began a sentence with "Dunque" or "Now then," at the same time energetically rubbing his hands together, which always smelled clean, just washed with the mild soap he preferred to the highly scented, fancy soaps Raffie would otherwise have bought.

"Dunque" was how he began the sentence in which he'd asked Raffie if she would consider a temporary separation. First, she undid her hair, which she'd pinned up in one of "her hundreds of," as Gianni said, referring to her collection of barrettes and combs. Why these annoyed him she didn't know but they did, possibly because she left her hair ornaments here and there when she did and undid her hair, depending on her state of mind. A change in mental state was always signaled by a change in the state of her hair, up or down. In this case it was down. She put her barrette on the counter next to the cutting board on which she'd been slicing mushrooms and went into their bedroom, the second from the kitchen of the two middle rooms in the flat, a small room, consisting entirely of their bed. The room was open on both sides and had a window on each of the two sides that faced on the adjoining rooms. For privacy while she cried, she put a red and white embroidered throw pillow from the bed over her head. Gianni came in and sat beside her on the bed. He liked to stroke her long kinky-curly hair. He stroked it away from her ear so he could whisper to her. She pulled away from him and tried to cover her ear with the pillow. He persisted. He said:

"Raphaella, amore, we've been together forever, I need to know what it's like to be on my own before we continue our life together. Just a few months, time for me to get to know myself as a separate person...."

Gianni spoke English with a British accent. He'd learned English in liceo in Italy from British-accented professors, then come to the United States for college, which was where he and Raffie had met, at the end of their sophomore year at Middlebury College in Vermont. Skiing, on cross-country skis, was where Gianni proposed. They were skiing in the woods after a night's snowstorm, when fresh snow was on the ground and light snow was still falling, and occasional and partial sun showing so that the temperature was not even eight degrees Fahrenheit. When they sat on a tilted log for lunch, careful not to put their sandwiches on the downward incline, they wore the khaki army half-gloves with the fingers cut off that Raffie carried in her pack. Gianni was delighted with these, as with Raffie's other mountaineering equipment, the ten essentials her father had taught her always to carry in her pack. Gianni was new to back country skiing. He'd skied the Alps, however, and was a good outdoorsman. Gorp was another pleasure Raffie introduced him to. Sticky mess that it was, Gianni loved the handfuls of raisins, peanuts, M&Ms, and too many other ingredients for the stuff to have a coherent taste which, Gianni said, was the beauty of it.

When they got to their destination, having traversed up a mountainside, skied down a bowl and up the other side, and reached one of many low peaks in the range, they stopped to rest and look out over the Green Mountains and valleys. It was chill and windy, but the view took their breath from them. They drank water from Gianni's water bottle. They stomped the snow off their skis. They took one more sweeping look at the view and prepared to go down. Gianni said to wait, he had something to say. He reached into the pocket of his wool knickers and took out a little box, which he popped open as he bent one knee in the snow. He took Raffie's left hand and put the ring on her third finger.

It was a signal moment in her life. She cried. He cried. They hugged each other. They chattered away in Italian until they realized they were freezing. Raffie covered her newly ringed hand with her mittens and they skied like demons down the mountain. The diamond and sapphire ring had been his grandmother's, and her mother's before that. It fit Raffie just as it was. They were married at the end of the school year at an old synagogue in Florence. Raffie's father, a widower, and her Aunt Rose and Cousin Jessica were there. The rest of the guests were Gianni's family. Afterward there was a dinner on the terrace of a restaurant unknown to tourists and populated only by Italians. Raffie translated for her family, and they all got slightly drunk and danced in mismatched couples—Raffie with her cousin Jessica, Gianni with

Raffie's father, and finally Raffie and her father, both of whom had forgotten that they were supposed to lead off with the first dance.

Because both families were secular Jews, no one said it but all the older relatives were pleased that Gianni and Raffie had chosen within the faith. Gianni's mother, who was frail and died soon after the wedding, put her hand lightly on that of Raffie's father and whispered to him, "It is good not to dilute—you know, they will have Jewish children." Raffie's father quickly took a swallow of his champagne, which went down the wrong way. He had to be thumped on the back by the guest standing next to him.

Kip was having a resurgence of his manic high that day on the Pensione del mare's balcony, feasting on the delectable seafood and making loud ahs and ums each time he picked an especially tasty piece.

"This is octapussy, Chèrie," he said.

"How do you know?"

"I know pussy when I taste it."

"Oh, shut up, Kip."

"At least I'm not telling you you've just eaten rocky mountain oysters," he said.

"You know what? You can be a real pain," Raffie said.

"Or that there were bugs in your watercress salad."

"That's enough, Kip!"

These were real dining events from Paris evenings that Raffie preferred not to remember. Kip liked to tease when he was happy. He liked jokes. In Paris he'd had a small entourage of admiring young American friends who accompanied him to bars, where he sang exotic French troubadour songs for tips in his beautiful reedy tenor. Kip was also beautiful to look at. He was a small delicate man with dark eyes and thin lips. He wore a closely trimmed Clark Gable mustache. Gay men looked at him twice on the street and tried to pick him up in cafés. At the height of his mania, his American friends would loyally stay out drinking with him when he'd finish singing and bring him home to Raffie at two, three, or four in the morning. She sat up in bed, rumpled and furious, to watch them standing in a line at the foot of the bed while Kip sang a song. Kip would present her with a milles feuilles, her favorite pastry, bought fresh from a baker he'd barged in on before the bakery was open. He'd say in his sweetest voice, which was indeed sweet, "Forgive me, Chèrie."

He made nicknames for her of sexual words, which he called her in a low voice when they were out in public and in a regular speaking voice in private. Kip's French was so expert he might almost have been taken for a native speaker. Raffie's French was good but her Italian was much better. Kip said you couldn't be taken seriously in any language unless you used the subjunctive with ease. Raffie had given this some thought and decided he was right. She'd heard him say, in French, "What do you want me to do?" using a forceful subjunctive. Literally, it was, "What do you want that I do?"

Kip was Greek-American. His last name was Kiprianos, his middle name, Christopher. He introduced himself as "Chris" to people whom he didn't want to meet again or people he wanted to confuse about his identity since everyone who knew him at all called him "Kip." His middle name was Alan and he used "Alan Chappelle" as an alias. Kip was in a line of work, when he did work, that required an alias. These were facts about Kip that Raffie didn't know until after she'd moved in with him in his Paris apartment on Plâce de la contrascarpe in the Fifth Arondissement in a building on which the letters Hôtel des grands sports were written in faded letters and from which the "s" at the beginning of "sports" was missing.

The apartment had no running water so Kip had constructed a hose in the kitchen sink to which he attached the pail he filled from the spigot in the hall. That way they were able to have a makeshift faucet for cooking over the one alcohol burner. Most nights Kip cooked chops, pork or lamb, on a grill over the fire in the fireplace. He seasoned the chops, Greek style, with olive oil and sprigs of fresh oregano from the open market down the street from the Plâce. They ate well. The toilet in the hall was Roman style—a hole in the floor over which you had to squat—which Raffie detested. But other than that, the apartment was pleasing. They sat on a sofa pulled up to the front window overlooking the Plâce, their faces in the sun on sunny days, and ate gooey Camembert on fresh bread with apples or pears for lunch. They washed in cold water at the sink, and once a week paid a dollar for a bath in gray lukewarm bathwater down the hall.

None of this really mattered because the arrangement was temporary as far as Raffie was concerned. She was on furlough, with a proscribed ending at which time she would return to Gianni in New York. She'd had a foretaste, however, of the difficulty of extricating herself from this relationship with Kip. It had been her plan to study in Italy, with only a brief stay in Paris to brush up on her French, when she ran into Kip and renewed their liaison. Kip had been a student at Middlebury too, until he was expelled for bad behavior, including cutting classes, insulting professors, drinking in the dorm, and having a girl in his room overnight. Raffie was that girl. For this, she felt somewhat beholden to him. And when he learned from a mutual friend that she was in Paris and turned up in the lobby of her hotel at midnight in December, wheedling her into going with him to have onion soup at Les Halles, she said she would.

Kip supported himself with the shady business of selling Bibles to American servicemen stationed in bases in France and Germany. It was shady because unapproved vendors were not allowed in the barracks to sell to directly to servicemen. Kip went at night and talked his way in or maybe he bribed the guard on duty, Raffie never knew the details.

She waited in the car, an old Citroen, in which Kip sat tilted back in the driver's seat and dwarfed by the dimensions of the car. But she hated those trips, except when they traveled through the countryside of the Loire valley or the Black Forest in Germany. Kip would return to the car with a greasy hamburger and fries from the canteen, crowing about a sale he'd made to a slow-witted lout of a soldier. But as he crumpled the paper the food had been wrapped in, he admitted that he felt sorry for the soldier he'd bilked out of money from his meager pay for a Bible he wouldn't read.

"But too bad, it's a job, and it's the only kind of work I can get as a foreigner," he said.

One time they took a night train to a base in the north of

Germany and slept in couchettes. Kip insisted that Raffie climb into his couchette with him and eat the sandwiches they'd brought, both turning this way and that to get comfortable in the narrow space, whispering loudly, laughing, and annoying the other passengers, even feeling each other up under the blanket. Finally a conductor came in with his flashlight and ordered one of them to get down to the lower couchette.

In a hotel in Germany, the desk clerk refused to give them a room together because their last names were different on their passports. In his excellent German, Kip persuaded the evening desk clerk, a stout, stern woman with deep vertical lines over her upper lip and small eyes with none or few visible lashes, to change her mind. Raffie had on her glasses so that she could sign her name in the register and when she looked up, the woman was examining her features. The woman, Fraulein Klegg, as the name tag on her lapel read, sighed, aggrieved.

"They didn't gas enough of you people," Fraulein Klegg said to Raffie.

Kip and Raffie left the hotel immediately and took a train back to Paris.

Raffie said she would never go back to Germany. In fact, she didn't even want to live in Europe anymore. She wanted to go home to the States. Back in their Paris apartment, she came down with the flu and ran a high fever. Kip gave her aspirin and peppermint tea, kept her in bed, and entertained her by reading Stendahl's The Charterhouse of Parma aloud to her in French. She said her head and body ached too much for serious fare so he switched to Inspector Maigret. When her fever came down, he went to one of their usual restaurants and brought home hot soups for her, and even a bowl of pot au feu. He gave her a sponge bath, which they both enjoyed, even in her weakened state. When she was fully recovered, Kip took her out for a celebratory meal on a barge in the Seine, where they ate bouillabaisse and drank several bottles of Côte de Rhone.

By March, Raffie was restless and wanted to pursue the research she'd intended for her European trip. She was translating the Italian poets that preceded Dante and needed to study some texts in Florence. Knowing that Kip wouldn't let her go alone, she conceived a plan with her best girlfriend, who happened to be on a Fulbright at the Sorbonne and needed to escape from her abusive husband. The two had the pensione reserved in Florence and their railway tickets bought. But the friend made the mistake of writing to Raffie at Kip's address, Kip intercepted the letter, a scene followed, and Raffie threatened to call the cops. Kip caved and offered to drive her and the girlfriend to Florence. The girlfriend patched it up with her husband, so Raffie and Kip drove across the Alps to Italy. Kip was beginning his downward spiral, which included his yearly bout with peptic ulcers. They stopped not in Florence but in a town on the Adriatic, where Kip went into a hospital run by nuns and Raffie slept in a bed next to him. She went to the bathroom at night to brush her teeth and smelled the sweet, putrid smell of the patients' feces samples placed on the windowsills to keep cool, a smell she never quite forgot.

A nun taught her how to give Kip the injections he would need after leaving the hospital. The sister took an orange and showed Raffie the correct way to jab the needle into the dimpled skin of the orange, instructing her to imagine that the orange was Kip's buttock. Raffie gave Kip her first trial injection in the hospital. Her hand trembled but she went through with it, making the quick jab as the sister had shown her. Kip sat up and said, "That was perfect, Chèrie, it didn't hurt at all." From that moment on, she became his nurse. They drove South, stopping only briefly for meals and petrol. Kip had to eat bland foods: "Tutto in bianco," he told the waiters, and was served spaghetti al burro and steamed vegetables. He said that driving calmed him. He unzipped his fly as he drove and asked Raffie to stroke his dick. This eased the pain. She would have been glad to drive but he wouldn't hear of it. In Naples Kip was laid up for two weeks and couldn't leave his bed. Raffie gave him the injections and went out to explore the unfamiliar city. She'd never been that far South and found it exotic, not minding that men grabbed for her in the streets, happy to be free of Kip and his pain. Kip had leased the house in Positano in advance and they moved in the day they arrived.

The house had an unobstructed view of the sea and the

terraced gardens below them. These were planted with bright-ly blooming flowers in dashing colors of red and purple, interspersed with rosemary and oregano that scented the air when the breeze blew in the direction of their patio. The path down to town was steep but Raffie managed to carry a few potted flower plants up, and a nasturtium, which she remembered her father telling her had edible flowers. She planned her day around Kip's injections, knowing, when she took the long trek to and from the beach, that she must not linger no matter how glorious the day because she had to be home at five for Kip's injection. Losing track of time would have been easy. It was June and the weather was fine, the beach and coves small idylls with no one around. One day, however, she made a shallow dive into the water and came up in a miniature oil slick. This ended her beach experience for the week.

The next eight days of steady rain were unbearable in a leaky house without window glass. The damp and cold were depressing even if you weren't in the depressive phase of manic-depressive disease. Kip was practically catatonic. Raffie tried to read contemporary Italian novels. Instead, she wrote letters to Gianni. She thought about the West Village bookstore where they lost each other browsing in the tall stacks, and were then reunited some-time later, as if after a long absence. "What did you find?" "What did you find?" they said, turning their heads to sideways to read the titles of the books each had chosen. Those were intimate times, even though they were in a public place. Both Raffie and Gianni were scholars and translators; Gianni was translating Dante; this was work they thrived on. Raffie missed her work and she missed Gianni. She missed her life. This interlude with Kip was drawing to its finish.

He called to her from the bedroom "I need you," he said.

"But I'm depressed and lonely myself—how can I possibly help you?"

"You have to!"

"I don't think so. I gave you your injection. You should be comfortable for a while."

"Raffie!"

She put on her rain jacket and stepped outside. The rain had stopped and she began walking down the path to the village. She could hear Kip calling her. He was a baby, she thought, he was reduced to infancy—eating, sleeping, complaining. Or maybe he was an old man. It was all the same to her. She smelled the clove-scented geraniums some people planted in their gardens and the wild rosemary that grew at the side of the path. With the rain stopped, the evening invigorated her and she walked faster, slipping occasionally on the slick stones of the path, laughing when she fell and getting up quickly so no one would see.

Raffie's parents were traveling to Florence from Positano the next day. Kip felt sick after his big frittura lunch and went to bed for the afternoon so Raffie had dinner with her father and stepmother and sat in their hotel suite with her stepmother while her father was out for his evening stroll. The parents were leaving by hired car in the morning. Raffie watched her stepmother brushing out her long thin hair, seated at the dressing table with a triptych mirror and a matching, amber-colored hand mirror on the dressing table. Raffie's stepmother wore a switch by day to make her chignon fuller. She didn't color her hair, however, leaving it the natural gray and near-black color. She'd told Raffie that the switch was made of human hair, her own mother's hair. Raffie had asked to finger it, which felt both creepy and sad, to think that it was a dead person's hair, but a loved dead person, her stepmother's mother.

Raffie asked if her stepmother, Alice, was enjoying her stay in Positano. It was her first time in Italy. She was from Vermont. Raffie's father had met her there at a farmer's market when they were both buying overripe organic tomatoes for sauce. Alice ate all organic food and used all-natural products in the house and on her body. Raffie's father had moved from Boston to Alice's home in Vermont. She had an organic vegetable garden and started seedlings in the house in leaky wooden flats. She also made cuttings of her house plants, which she put in jam jars on the windowsills to root. At night in winter she and Alice's father slept at about thirty-six degrees Fahrenheit in the bedroom, under a down comforter. Alice said that you got a better night's sleep in a cold room.

Alice said she loved Italy and everything about it. She was looking forward to seeing Florence. You'll enjoy it, Raffie said, if you don't mind that it's humid. She'd be too busy to notice, Alice said.

"Would it be all right with you if I tag along?" Raffie said.

"Not at all. But is Kip well enough?"

"Actually…I was planning on taking a little break from Kip."

"…But I—we—wouldn't want to come between you two…." Alice said.

"I'd appreciate it if you would, Alice. It would be a great favor to me. I need to get back home to Gianni."

"…Will you speak to your father about this?"

"Of course. I was planning to."

Her father was relieved. He said it was about time. He'd never thought much of the arrangement with Kip but he was waiting for Raffie to make a move. They could put her on a train for Genoa from Florence, he said. Raffie's father had a tall thin body. His frame was hollowed out, looking as though a persistent wind had blown in his direction for all the years of his life like some trees that happen to be exposed to unforgiving weather. He spoke in a whispery voice, the air seemingly expressed from his lungs. But he was lighthearted.

"And you, Dad? You're happy?"

"Never been more so."

"You don't mind all the—organics?"

"No, why should I?"

"No reason—forget that I mentioned it."

They talked about plans for sightseeing in Florence, what to show a first-time visitor like Alice.

"She's easy to please," Raffie's father said.

Raffie slept with Kip that night but left early in the morning before he was awake. She walked down to the grocery store and arranged with Antonio, who was driving them to Naples, for his wife Luisa to give Kip his injections. Of course Luisa knew how, Antonio said, she'd cared for her ailing mother for years and her grandmother before that. Raffie imagined Luisa's flat dirty hands on Kip's buttock, jabbing the needle into his flesh and Kip whining into the pillow, "But where is my Chèrie?"

Gianni listened to the news on WBAI assiduously for weeks and then he would stop for days, neglecting even to turn the radio on. When he was in his listening phase, if you spoke to him while the news was on, he would look at you through a watery expression and answer with something noncommittal like, "Really?" or "Is that so?" And if you tried to draw him out on whatever the subject was, you would guess correctly that he hadn't heard you at all. He was in his listening phase when Raffie climbed the four flights to their apartment and turned the key in the lock. He didn't hear the sound of the key turning or even the door opening. The radio was loud.

Raffie hadn't written or called to say she was coming home because she wasn't sure what to expect. She had a small suitcase, which she put down on the floor in the entryway and closed the door behind her. The rest of her baggage was downstairs in the foyer.

"Gianni! Are you going to say hello?"

He was slicing radishes at the kitchen counter and listening to WBAI. The radio was loud. His head whipped around and he took four quick steps toward her.

"You're home!" he said. "I missed you."

His arms held her tightly. Their hello kiss lasted a long time.

"I missed you, too."

"You cut your hair," he said.

"Do you like it?"

"It's okay. Shall I bring your bags up?"

"We can both go," she said.

"And you'll tell me all about Europe."

"Yes…how is your translation going?"

"Good, good."

They couldn't talk while they were carrying the suitcases up the four flights because they were out of breath. They put the suitcases in the bedroom. Raffie sat down on one of the hard leather suitcases that had been with her all over France and Italy, part of Germany, and even London over New Year's with Kip. Gianni sat down on another.

"Raphaella amore, I have something to tell you."

"What."

"In all this time apart, I have done some thinking. About myself."

"Yes?"

Raffi was getting impatient.

"And here is the answer to the question I asked myself about myself. I love you very much and want to spend the rest of my life with you!"

Raffi jumped up and sat beside him on the suitcase.

"Likewise!" she whispered.

Several weeks later, Raffie had a letter from a mutual friend of hers and Kip's in Rome to tell her that Kip had left Positano and come to Rome, very ill. He had gone into the hospital in Rome for the sleep cure, in which you're put into a comatose state and fed intravenously for eight days while the ulcer is supposed to heal. The friend wrote pointedly that Raffie should have been there with Kip during this ordeal.

Raffie thought of Kip with distant compassion then she wrote back to the friend and thanked her for her letter.

You're Not You Now

SUSAN HODARA

June 2023

I miss you, the you who has been my closest friend for nearly six decades—like a sister, like family. The one who knows me deeply, listens carefully and is always able to reassure me. For all these years, you have let me know that I am not alone in the world.

This other you—this not you—has splintered and flattened. You are joyless, defeated. Depressed in the clinical sense. You have become negative, distracted, inert. "No, I just can't do it." "No, it will never work." Tentative. We talk at least daily, long phone calls focused mostly on you. In the mornings, when it's especially bad, you speak slowly, with long pauses and lots of "um"s. "Is it okay if I go back to bed?" you ask me. "Yes," I tell you, "it's okay," and I promise to call you in 45 minutes to get you up.

You are cautious now. Afraid of ruining things. Afraid of doing things. Afraid of not doing them. Afraid of making mistakes.

You say your therapist keeps repeating that you haven't made mistakes, you've made choices. I imagine the choices he is referring to are about your renovation—the full gutting and redesign of your apartment in Cambridge, the one that your mother left you, the one that you moved to during the pandemic after you sold your apartment in Brooklyn. The renovation that you undertook to make the apartment your own but that, over months of miscommunications and disappointments and delays, has broken you.

Should I tell you that I also think there are other choices you have made throughout your life that you might now feel are mistakes. Like not having children. Not wanting a partner. I worry that you aren't able to embrace these choices the way you did when you made them. But this I know: Even though you don't have children, you do have family who love you so much. Even though you don't have a partner, you have me, who knows your life well. My mind understands that even those defining choices you made are adjustable. Your mind shatters with the possibility that they were "wrong."

With your other friends, you are meek and apologetic. You worry that they are getting sick of you, with all of your burdens. When it comes to yourself, you are harsh. "I'm an idiot," you say. "I am sick of myself."

I am alarmed by what is happening. "Don't say those things," I tell you. I want so much to fix this, to know what to do. Sometimes I get frustrated, and I want to say the thing you hate: Snap out of it. Just stop already. I don't know how to feel what you feel, the overpowering, undermining weight of it.

You call it anxiety. You call it "the thing that has gripped you." That has "taken you over." And finally, your "illness." You, who always chased joy, who wept tears over a towering beech tree or the power of a work of art in a museum—now you can't cry, and I fear you've given up.

And me? I observe myself, working, walking around, picking up tomatoes at the market, and I can't believe how lucky I am. I feel sharp and strong. I am filling my calendar, saying yes to everything. Your present state is making me savor my health and my aliveness.

Right next to that, your present state is a reminder of the fragility of everything I appreciate now.

Yesterday, on a walk, I played Meghan Trainor through my Airpods, and I couldn't help but bounce to her beat. I thought, Jenny should listen to this music, let this be her backdrop, and it will break through her defeat. But I didn't tell you this, because I remembered that you wouldn't do it, and if you did, you'd shake your head and say, "No, it doesn't work."

1965 to June 2023

Even before I met you, I heard kids talking about you: Jenni, so pretty, long dark hair. You spelled it "Jenni" then, with a heart over the i.

We were 11 years old, sixth grade. The following year, with all the elementary kids coming together, we'd be in the same school, junior high.

You were popular. Best friends with Linda. Sought after, I thought. It's what I wanted to be but knew I wasn't. I scurried behind Patty, Maureen and Lisa, certain that if I didn't keep up, they wouldn't wait for me.

So I couldn't believe it when, in seventh grade, you wanted me to be your friend. There we were, sipping vanilla Cokes at the counter at Brigham's. I sat silently as you told me about Linda. She was your best friend, you said, but I was your "fave" friend. It was our secret.

I spent hours at your house after school and on weekends. I remember the silliness, the wetting our pants with laughter. I remember the marshmallows that we stretched between our fingers to make sticky white taffy, and how, when the yellow wall phone rang in your kitchen, we crumpled into giggles as you tried to grasp the receiver with your elbows to answer it.

I smoked my first cigarette in your driveway, in the chilly October air, during your brother's 15th birthday party. Two years later, I smoked my first joint by the lake at your family's Cape Cod home. A year after that, you sat with me in front of my house in my parents' blue Chevy Bel Air while I confessed my darkest thoughts. You listened in a way I'd never been listened to as I spewed my inadequacies and self-hatred. You were quiet in the passenger seat. I looked down as I spoke, but I felt your eyes on me. I felt your attentiveness and your concern. I don't remember what you said, but you convinced me that my despair was baseless.

To me, you were the alpha: stronger, savvier, more glamorous, more desirable. Everything about you was better: Your mother was funny and sharp; the two of you were close the way I wasn't with my mother. Your father owned an airplane; one day he flew us to Provincetown, where we went to the beach and then came home. Your brother was so cute I could barely speak when he was around, playing rock-and-roll in his basement bedroom. When your neighbor Dave became your boyfriend, I tagged along with his friend Mike and hoped he might like me. You were always ahead of me, beyond me. A little out of reach. And yet, to my delight, there you always were, inviting me to stand beside you.

We absorbed into our own lives during college. After graduation, I moved to New York and worked in the film industry. You returned to Boston, where you fast-tracked in graphic design, a field I didn't understand. ("It's everywhere," you explained, holding up a menu in a diner where we were eating, showing me the many visual choices of font, layout and logo that I'd never thought about before.) When you traveled to New York on business, you warned me that you might be too busy to visit, although often you ended up finding time.

I decided to make a short documentary about you and your colleagues installing an exhibition of design work. When I arrived at the gallery, somewhere in Manhattan, you were giddy with excitement and full of questions about how to hang the show. In the first scene of the film, you are lying on the floor laughing. "I'm not me now!" you said, so beautiful, so young.

I married before you and became a mother, and you were godmother to my daughters, Sofie and Ariel. You were almost 40 when you married Geoff. He was also a designer, a quiet man; neither of you wanted children. You left your job to become a dancer and a visual artist; Geoff left his job in hopes of a better position, but no one hired him. Several years later, the two of you moved to San Diego. We talked more frequently then—long cross-country telephone conversations: You hated it there; too much nice weather, you said. Your parents were alone, aging on the East Coast. Geoff wanted to buy a house, while you wanted to leave. Your marriage was falling apart. You called to tell me when it was over. You said you fist-pumped in the bathroom, relieved to be done, but your voice sounded shaken.

Your next move was to a condo in Brooklyn, a commuter train ride to our house in Westchester County. It was then that you melded into our family. Melted, I could say. You had become softer, more vulnerable. Paul and I introduced you to our friends and included you in our travels. You were my sister, we said, or Paul's and my third daughter. And always, we were best friends.

You were spending the weekend with us when COVID shut down the city, and instead of going back to Brooklyn, you stayed. You stayed four months. Our guestroom became "your" room; you set up my sewing machine and transformed worn, yellowed fabric into frames for the drawings you made.

The more that was canceled, the happier you were. You had "your" coffee cup, "your" seat at the dining table. It was "your" job to stack the dishwasher and then empty it in the morning when the dishes were clean. You said you looked forward to it when you woke up.

I believe it was the pandemic that started to unroot you. It unrooted us all, of course, our lives misted in fear and caution. Nevertheless, the three of us had fun: We ate more dinners together in the dining room than Paul and I normally did (nothing too spicy for you). We lugged the big TV up from the basement and planted it in the living room, where we plowed through "Episodes" and "Schitt's Creek" and "Succession" (nothing too violent or scary for you). We walked for miles, around our neighborhood and in nearby preserves we'd never explored before, and often past the beech tree down the street that reminded you of your mother's love of the species.

We developed our separate Zoom routines—me teaching my classes and meeting with clients; Paul hosting virtual gatherings for the organization where he was volunteering; you joining regular calls with your extended family. I didn't mind you being there, and because you were there, I didn't mind the lockdown as much as I might have. And I believed—I still believe—that you felt the same.

Now, though, I can see that you were untethering in a way that Paul and I weren't. We were in our own home; you had abandoned yours and all your possessions. When you finally left us, you went to Maine, then to Cambridge, never back to Brooklyn. The bi-monthly magazine column you'd written since 1984 was suddenly eliminated for financial reasons. It seemed fortuitous at the time because you were about to begin your renovation. Instead of intriguing investigations of design and creativity, floorplans and functionality became your focus. Faucets and tiles became your obsession. Missteps and holdups and unforeseen impediments became your bane.

Months passed. It was late in the summer of 2022 when you first told your doctor about your anxiety and she prescribed an antidepressant. It was December, when we were all together for the holidays, when you upped the dosage. As winter progressed, I heard your speech slow; I heard the gaps between your words. I heard your desperation grow, and I worried. There was so much wrong with the apartment, you said. The mornings were particularly hard, you said. "Is it okay for me to tell you the worst?" you asked, and I said of course.

Paul called you, too. He kept telling you to come and stay with us. One day, after checking in on you, Sofie said you didn't sound good, and Paul insisted you buy a ticket to New York.

The next day, we pick you up at the train station and welcome you back to "your" room.

June 2023

Endpoints give me comfort. Put a finish time on a party invitation. Tell me how long a movie is before I begin watching. Give me an idea of the length of a traffic delay and I will wait it out more calmly.

When you arrive, there is no endpoint to your visit. A one-way ticket—no return date set.

The days creep on. When I make Paul's fruit smoothie in the mornings, I make you one, too. When I prepare my avocado toast with cottage cheese, I prepare a slice for you, too. I buy a larger container of milk. Instead of calling my mother or listening to music when I go for a walk, I invite you to join me, and we talk about you. Instead of grabbing lunch and sometimes dinner and eating in front of my computer, the three of us have sit-down meals. You set the table. You stack the dishwasher. But you are sick, and as well-intentioned as you are, there are often crumbs left behind.

I don't know what I thought. Maybe that if you lived with us, you'd be happy again. You'd forget the renovation. We'd be like we were during COVID, carefree and together in a safe bubble.

But there is no bubble. I have my clients and am teaching on Zoom; I don't cancel anything. And you? You aren't well.

"How are you?" I ask each morning. There we stand, in the hallway between your room and my office, in the gray light leaking in from the windows. You wear what you'd been wearing since you arrived: Sofie's oversized green hoodie from high school and gray athletic pants that I'd tossed aside years before. You are reed-like, frail; you have lost more weight. Your hair is white; you used to worry that your pink scalp was too visible, but now you don't care. Your fingers tremble uncontrollably. You wring your hands, one into the other. When you stand, I see you press your toes up and down against the floor, curling them under the soles of your feet, over and over again.

Besides the trembling and the compulsion of your toes, there are other symptoms. Med-caused constipation. Med-caused fog and fatigue. You aren't sleeping, but you don't want to nap: "It's always worse when I wake up," you explain. And your ears: They are plugged, you tell us. It's like you are underwater. You can hear us, but we sound far away. You pinch your nostrils, squeeze, shut your eyes and push, but it doesn't help. Paul drives you to Urgent Care, where they find nothing and refer you to an ENT. Paul drives you there, too, and again, they say nothing is physically wrong.

Days pass with no improvement. Each morning when I ask you how you are, you shake your head and say, "The same." After your remote therapy sessions, I ask you how they went, and your replies are unenthusiastic: "Okay, I guess," or, "I don't know about him." If we say something you don't want to hear, you press your fingers into your forehead and hang your face. Sometimes you look at me, your eyes flooded with bewilderment and anguish. "How is this my life?" you ask.

We aren't helping. "Yes, you are," you say. "You don't know how much you're helping." But I can't see it.

Another morning when I am on Zoom with a client, I see you and Paul from the window getting into Paul's car and driving off. When my meeting ends, I call Paul. You'd told him that the sensation in your ears was so painful that he decided to bring you to the emergency room at our local hospital. Again, no diagnosable malfunctions, but he describes your overwhelming anxiety and managed to have you see a social worker. I am able to join you there in time for the meeting.

The four of us sit on turquoise vinyl chairs in the overlit, chilly room, you between Paul and me, the three of us facing the young woman. I am hopeful; I want a professional witness. While Paul is more optimistic, I've been researching outpatient psychiatric programs and even inpatient treatment facilities. I know the latter are dire, but I feel dire. I am terrified.

I watch the social worker see your shaking, your hesitations, your sallow pallor. I watch her listen as you explain your anxiety, your depression, the discomfort in your ears. Her manner is kind, her eyes fixed on you. I want her to see what I have been seeing. I want her to admit you, give you medicine, make sure you eat. I want her to take the responsibility from us. I hear her ask you if you'd thought about hurting yourself, and I hear you say no. After an hour, she sends us home.

It is around this point that I notice my concern is being infiltrated by other emotions. Anger simmers. Resentment I can't risk articulating. And panic. Have I lost you? Where have you gone? What am I supposed to do when nothing I do makes you better? Sometimes I want to hug you and hold you and soothe you, and sometimes I do, but I'm afraid not enough. I'm afraid I let those other emotions get in the way.

And I want my home back. I want my time. No matter how non-disruptive, how invisible, how helpful you try to be, you are there. There are three of us, not two. You watch me way more than Paul does, and I feel your gaze. Your mannerisms, your indecision, the pauses between your words—it is all irritating me. I start steaming.

Everyone says what a good and giving friend I am. They say they wouldn't be able to do what I am doing. But I feel like a terrible friend. I feel guilty. Small. Selfish. By the beginning of the third week, I realize we are going to have to take you home. Still, I say nothing.

One day, on a walk, you interrupt our conversation. "What about you?" you say. "You are helping me so much. How can I help you?" You know as well as anyone about boundaries, and you are sensitive to mine. I mean, you're living in my house, inhabiting the second bathroom, eating the food I cook. "How can I help you?" you ask.

I know my answer, but how can I say it? We are walking, you by the curb, me to your left. Then I do; I tell you, the way I have always told you everything. "One thing I know," I say, "is that you cannot live with us forever."

You stop. You are silent. You don't look at me. You move to the grass along the side of the road, and you sit on the ground. I have done this to you. I am watching you, and your eyes meet mine. "I understand," you say. I know you do, but I also know you can't right now. You get up, and we continue on. Instead of remorse or sadness or self-loathing, I feel nothing.

Underneath that nothing, though, I am cracking. We are approaching week four of your stay, and bitterness has entered my heart. I don't like myself. "I can't do this anymore," I tell Paul. He seems less affected by your presence—more patient, more generous than I. "This won't go on forever," he replies. "We'll figure something out."

Then, after months on a waiting list, you are admitted to a ten-day outpatient program at a psychiatric hospital near your apartment. And your cousin Len's wife in Florida, Ellen, a retired psychiatrist, offers to come up to spend time with you. I am elated, relieved, grateful that these circumstances have materialized and aligned.

And so, on a Thursday, Paul and I drive you back to Cambridge. On Friday, we drop you off for the first day of your new program and in the afternoon pick you up and take you home. On Saturday, Ellen arrives, and we all have dinner.

Matthew joins us, too, the one other friend you had not yet pulled away from. You've known him for decades, lived together three times when you were both getting your master's degrees from NYU. Before COVID, he owned a gallery in Boston and represented your work. Since then, he'd risen in the ranks to manager at a nearby Amazon warehouse.

It is a simple dinner: pasta and salad. Ellen makes the pasta; I make the salad. We sit around the white round table that is standing in for the dining table you'd buy later. There are unpacked cardboard boxes against the wall. The conversation is cheery, the kind you make over a meal with people you don't know well. You are quiet, smiling feebly from time to time. I watch you, steeped in your discomfort, and I realize that by not hiding from us, by letting our talk surround you, you are trusting us with your darkness.

I carry an image from that evening: Ellen and Matthew standing side by side behind your sleek kitchen counter, Ellen with her straight, shoulder-length brown hair and black leggings, Matthew in crisp jeans and a tidy shirt, his reddish-blonde hair cropped short. Both are almost 60, a decade younger than us. Both are smiling. That night I am so grateful that they are there to support you. I have no idea, then, how much.

On Sunday, Paul and I head home.

Seven Months Later

Time has passed, and I can feel it. I can feel you coming back.

Seven months ago, when we left Cambridge, Paul and I boarded a flight to Denver for the July 4th weekend to visit Ariel and her family. I needed time with my one-year-old granddaughter, my only grandchild. I needed to be reminded of health and light. It was a last-minute decision, an urgent gulp of joy.

Ellen stayed in Cambridge for close to three weeks, and she took charge. She made doctors' appointments for you and accompanied you to them, speaking for you when you couldn't speak for yourself. She shopped and cooked for you, all organic and nutritious. She ordered supplements that she said would bolster your physical and mental health. She insisted on positivity. I could hear her in the room when I called you: If you told me how bad things were, she'd say you were improving. "She looks better," she'd say, taking your phone from you. "The mornings are hard, but there are good moments in the afternoons." Sometimes she would prompt you, like you were a child: "Tell her what we did today," and you'd report that the two of you had gone to Whole Foods or out for a walk.

Paul and I spoke with Ellen regularly. And I became the checkpoint for your friends. They phoned me for updates, troubled that you hadn't returned their calls or answered their texts. I want to remind you now of how much they care about you, even when you pulled away from them.

When it was time for Ellen to return to Florida, you were afraid. "What is my life?" you asked, not for the first time. Your outpatient program was finished. Your apartment was not. You didn't want to go anywhere or do anything, but you also didn't want to be in your home. Paul suggested that you come back to New York, but you said no. I think you knew that I still needed some distance. I did. I felt strongly about it, but I also felt bad.

Instead, you ended up in Florida at Ellen and Len's condominium. It was the peak of summer, so hot that you wouldn't go out during the daytime, even to swim. When the sun set, you walked around the development. That's when you called me, on those walks, the only time you didn't have to worry about being overheard. That's when I started to detect a tinge of spirit in your voice. You stayed in Florida for six weeks. It was there, I believe, that you began to return to yourself.

From Florida, you delegated all interactions with your contractor to Matthew. Appointing him as your go-between was a wise decision. He could address with ease the problems and questions that destroyed you to even think about.

At some point, Matthew began sleeping on the couch in your apartment—to oversee the workers, but also, you soon learned, because he was separating from his partner of 20 years. During one of your phone calls, you told Matthew that if he needed, he could stay with you after you returned from Florida.

Now, in an apartment built for solitary living, that notably does not have a guest room, Matthew has set up his bedroom in the office off the living room. An impassioned chef, he has taken over your kitchen, with its convection oven and shiny flat stovetop. Every morning he boils you a perfect egg and leaves it in a porcelain eggcup. He makes frittatas and soups. He has filled your fridge with aluminum storage containers stacked high, the contents of each identified in black marker on blue masking tape.

You have come to love your apartment: the openness, the custom shelving, the blond wooden cabinets, the specially designed lighting, the studio where you now spend much of your time. You roll up your new window shades to let in the view of Beacon Hill across the Charles River, where sculls press forward like dashes across the water.

I couldn't have told you any of this seven months ago. I couldn't have imagined the way you have found your way back. Your return to—and embrace of—the life you nearly lost is more than I had dared to hope for.

Recently, when we visited you for Sofie's birthday, she was talking about her dilemmas with her boyfriend and the strain of many unknowns. Sofie and I were seated on either end of your comfy gray couch, while you stood nearby. Across the room was the new dining table, circular and white, with round placemats made of plush felt in buoyant primary colors. To the right, a daybed, also gray, angled beside a cluster of leafy plants. Outside, it was dark, and the reflections of streetlights along Storrow Drive formed long twinkling cones that pierced the Charles. "I can guarantee," you said, your eyes on Sofie, "that something unexpected is going to happen that will determine the next step. We don't know what or how, but something will happen. This I know."

Now

Things happened to you. Unexpected things that led to other unexpected things. And now you are better.

I know you are shaken by the last year. You are still on medication, still in therapy, still hearing as if you're underwater. Still, you tell me, a little afraid.

I am shaken, too, and I watch myself for what is different.

Along the way, something in me stuck. Or stained. For a while I could not snap back to the way it was before. I came close. But something had changed. I no longer felt the deep pain of your illness—a mixture of my own dread and helplessness. Instead, I felt a transitory detachment, like a blip, like a momentary drop in cell service when the conversation becomes garbled and then re-establishes itself and you can forget about it and move on. Except for a while I wasn't able to forget about it. Maybe I could move on, but I couldn't forget about it.

I'd catch myself judging you; I couldn't stop. I hope I didn't show it, but my mind kept turning your actions into failings or fragility. When you didn't remember a word, your intellect was soft. When you second-guessed a decision, your will was tentative. When you told me you had fallen coming up the subway stairs, I conjured a grim projection of your decline.

Was it my silenced resentment towards you for collapsing onto me when you had to? Was it persistent fear? Was I more aware of vulnerabilities in you that had always been there, more able and willing to see? Or was I protecting myself from losing you again? Whatever the reason, could I still be the truest kind of friend that I wanted to be?

A few weeks ago, Sofie ended up in the ER with an infection in her eye. There was an hours-long wait. Should we drive to Boston, a trip I knew my body would rebel against? Instead I called you. No problem, you said. You would walk over to the hospital right away. It was a beautiful day, and you would bring snacks, sit with Sofie. I was flooded with gratitude, and it didn't escape me that it washed away the doubts that were plaguing me.

Last weekend I drove to visit you. We planned the trip because Matthew was away, so I could sleep on the couch in the living room. Sofie came over, and we ate up the food Matthew had left for you. We walked across the Longfellow Bridge and tried on clothes on Charles Street. You made us iced espressos with oat milk, and we talked. Well, you and Sofie talked. I think I listened more, happy.

Before I left on Sunday, you hugged me and lingered there. Then you told me to hug you back harder. And I did.

Left of Paradise

AVITAL GAD-CYKMAN

Look Backwards

Imagine the long dark hair of Lot's wife swirling around her sun-beaten face, her scarf loosened, her gown spotted with ashes and dust, thin like flour. Lot's family is on the run.

"But...Sodom and Gomorrah? Lot's wife says through fast breathing.

"Hurry! Don't look back. Look ahead," Lot says. His instructions rain like the sulfur.

But she must. The past is still present, outlining a future. She needs to see the burning ruins to reinforce her resolve. And her daughters. They walk behind her, her past and present.

Also, curiosity is stronger than obedience.

She twists her neck ever so slightly. Screens of hair, fire and smoke filter the abandoned city.

Her daughters are safe, well-covered from head to toes. They look straight ahead through slits in their headscarves.

She sees her city turn into history.

Her journey ends in a salt pillar.

Her name gone if it ever existed.

Curiosity and disobedience remain.

Have a Look

A woman named Alicia Albuquerque chooses fruit from a stall at the open-air market.

She declines to buy a watermelon without seeds, although the vendor promises that the watermelon is red as blood and sweet as sugar.

She's read about genetic experiments and found the idea revolting.

"This is the best watermelon in the market!"

"Do you have regular ones? With seeds?"

"You read too much, Lady," says the vendor.

She'll tell it again and again, for years. And keep reading.

Watch Out

Back in paradise, everything exudes a symphony of beauty. Eve is blessed with a perfect home. Well, it's all she knows.

She makes her way in a garden of forking paths. The possibilities are open. Open are flowers in bloom, and treetops open like palms. Open are other creatures who cross her path. Open is Adam. All opened up.

Her body plays a harmonious chord, smart and perfect.

She speaks, licks, smells, touches and experiments. Her curiosity nectar-thick.

Intoxicated, Eve learns the names, tastes, scents and textures. She touches the soft skin on her neck. Dogs communicate the traits of their breed. Snakes whisper secrets. Weeds weave carpets under her feet.

She's wide open. Commands are dispensable. Questions are heavenly, and the peeled unknown is sweet.

"What is this?" Eve asks once more.

She bites the apple.

Little Sister

JARRETT KAUFMAN

It's raining like all hell. Kay and her husband Ted loaf on the junk porch of their mobile home in Sunset Park. Kay is pecking her way straight to the bottom of a bag of Hostess donuts she bought this morning at a Conoco after she'd woken at dawn from a nightmare about her dead father. He was strangling her. But Kay doesn't tell Ted that. He sits there in his chair, leering at her. She knows the score. She knows what Ted's about. He's angling to swindle money out of her sister because he needs cash to get his new carpet cleaning gig off the ground and running.

"How long you gonna wait to talk to Pat? You found that money with him," he says.

Kay shrugs. She wolfs another donut then says, "She found it. It's her money."

"You fucking hoonyak. We can't live off your shit pay at Flowerama."

Lightning cracks the old, rusted water tower at the top of the mossy hollow. Beyond the blighted pines and past the rotted pavilion is Beacon Estates—the gated community Kay and Ted lived in eight months ago, before they lost their Tudor home, a BMW, the plumbing business—after Ted filed Chapter 11. He'd partnered with James P. Fudge, the smooth-talking contractor, to build a strip mall. But Fudge went on the lam when Ted was set to begin the pipe work.

Ted slaps a donut out of Kay's hand. "Pat'll waste it," he yells.

"That freak—"

She cracks a pot of sunflowers over his head and knocks him out cold. She mounts him and throws one wild blow after another. His front teeth go first. They roll over the patio. Next his nose. When the blood sprays her eyes, she staggers to her chair. She can hear him moaning. But she pays him no mind. She dead-gazes a patch of dandelions growing in the ditch thrash beaten in the rainstorm.

The wake was held in St. Louis ten months back in February. Kay and Pat stood at the casket to view the done-up corpse of their father Clem who'd died of a bad heart. Ted lingered in the parlor greeting a motley of grievers and Kay supposed some had come to witness Pat. She'd come out as trans after Clem passed and gossip stirred like valley winds. Even Uncle Walt, Clem's invalid brother, couldn't shake his awe. He gazed at Pat's open-toed heels as he asked if they knew of Clem's secret money. When Kay caught Maker's on his breath, she stared at Pat to see if she'd smelled it. Kay hated to fuss on Pat's recent sobriety. But Pat was an awful kind of drunk. She'd pop a bottle and drink with intent until her mind went lost in the fogs of a blackout.

"Money?" Kay said. "What money? He was a school janitor. He didn't have money."

Walt looked at her. "He told me he done hid thousands in the house after your momma left."

"What?" Pat said, but before Uncle Walt could answer, Pastor Ham took the pulpit.

Everyone scrambled to the pews. Kay and Pat sat next to Ted and Uncle Walt who toyed at tubes that snaked from his red nose to his oxygen tank. While Pastor Ham leafed at a Bible, Kay side-eyed the pale-faced Pepper twins who gawked at Pat. They snickered behind cupped hands and Kay felt their cold judgements like a fever chill. She wondered if they, like her, were shocked by Pat's clean-shaven face that'd been bearded a week ago. Maybe they were envious as she was by Pat's brawny figure and her long blonde wig that cascaded over her fine black dress.

Kay looked to mourn Clem but what grief she felt for the old man lifted like a dust cloud by relief when he died. She'd cared for him for months when he denied medical care after deciding he was saved. The idea came in a nap where a tunnel of light shined from a black sky and settled on his face and he'd known: this was God. So Kay took leave of work to look after him on the weekdays and Pat, returned from the city in the wares of a loyal son, helped on the weekends when she didn't work at Barnes Hospital as a receptionist. But doubt had clutched onto Clem in his final weeks. He'd dogged on Kay to make for a Christian funeral and she agreed. It'd be her last good deed for the bastard. Two days later, she found Clem naked and stewing in a pool of foamy diarrhea on the floor, clutching to his belly a Polaroid of their mother, Alma.

The sermon ended. Pat had wept fine but Kay had done nothing of the sort. She'd figured soon after their mother had left—a time Pat was too young to recall—that tears got in the way of living. They didn't help Kay, herself but a child, care for Pat. They didn't help her cook or keep house and they didn't help keep Clem's miserable face from shattering into a thousand pieces of hurt and outrage when he took notice of her likeness to Alma with her red hair and her fair skin.

After Pastor Ham closed the Bible and said, "Amen," he stepped off the pulpit.

"Amen," Pat said with the others. She stood from the pew, dabbing her eyes with a tissue.

"Amen," Kay echoed as she followed Pat to the altar to thank Pastor Ham.

It was Monday. The sisters sat at the kitchen in Clem's empty renthouse in Alton.

"Walt was right," Pat said as she divided the cash she'd found in a closet.

Kay yawned, spent from clearing out the house all weekend. "How much?"

"There's four hundred here," she gloated, then smirked.

Kay looked out the window at the streetlight. "It's late," she said.

Pat slid Kay's take across the cluttered counter between the cleaning supplies and a rusty crowbar and this blue dress they'd come upon in the attic. The dress had belonged to Alma, Kay knew, but it shouldn't have been there. Clem had forced Kay to torch Alma's clothes one night about a month after she'd gone when Kay kept nagging on him about if she'd come home. He'd yanked Kay off the sofa. He shook her. Then he barked, "the bitch left you," and dragged her to the fireplace in the basement. He said, "She's gone," and his eyes went empty like they'd do and Kay worried he'd quit his love of her so that was the last time they'd shared any words on Alma.

Kay swiped her pile of money off the counter and slipped it in her purse. She wiggled on her coat then she moved into the empty living room that'd been packed with Clem's grimy tables and chairs and a sofa that reeked of gasoline they'd donated the day before to the Goodwill. Kay opened the front door, the cold wind hurtling over her hair. She and Pat stood on the porch and the streetlamp sparked Pat's manicured fingernails as she shuffled her cut of the cash. "This is wild," she said. Kay nodded. She knew how Pat needed money for her reassignment surgeries.

Kay studied Pat in the still night and saw a despair in her eyes that betrayed her face. She'd witnessed with true pride Pat work hard to qualify for the male to female transition. She consulted a therapist, she was taking hormone treatments, and she joined AA. But her insurance had denied any coverage of the operations after they deemed them unnecessary and now she needed to find a way to pay for the surgeries herself. Kay hated to admit it but she couldn't deny she wasn't glad for it. There was a part in her that didn't want Pat to change.

Kay gazed over the empty street at the decrepit Village Motel as a heavy silence opened between her and Pat. She recalled when Pat was just a boy and how he'd come home after school with a torn shirt one day and then a busted face another day and she'd done nothing. She recalled when Clem would catch Pat prancing about the house in Kay's dress and he'd get blue and call Pat a "queer" or a "fag," and she'd done nothing. Kay knew the business of doing nothing well.

Kay saw Pat shivering out on the porch. "Where's your coat?"

she asked.

"I'm staying," she said. She stuffed the money in the pocket of her khakis.

"Come over. I'll fix dinner," she said, clomping down the porch steps.

"No," Pat said. "We've only got two days before the landlord takes the keys back."

Kay sat in her sedan. She said, "Fine," and shut the door. Then she left.

Kay parked the sedan next to Ted's Ford in the garage then bustled in the house. He was blaring the TV in the basement so she doffed her coat and went to the kitchen. She rushed to the sink then opened the cabinet. She removed the Clorox and opened it and stuffed the cash Pat had found on top of the cash already stored in there. Kay had plans herself. She'd been saving fifteen percent of her Flowerama pay for five years now by cashing her checks at a 7-Eleven before she deposited the rest at Regions to keep Ted in the dark. Once Kay saved thirty grand, she'd leave.

She closed the lid and hid the Clorox behind the Ajax and Dawn then glanced over her shoulder as she shut the cabinet. She stood and stared at the heap of overdue loan payments that piled on the table. She discovered Ted had forged her name on several loans he used to cover their expenses since all of their finances were tied up in the mall project. She found the paperwork in the trash and she pressed him on it good and Ted told Kay he had to lie because if he didn't, she'd sit at that damn flower shop all damn day and work herself into a bitter brood.

Kay was bitter. She'd been coaxed on a blind date with Ted when she was sixteen. She got pregnant not a month later and Clem went and forced a wedding on them. But before their marriage license arrived in the mail at the new apartment, Kay miscarried. They learned at her check-up Kay carried a disease that clotted her blood and because of it, she'd never bear a child. Kay hid in bed in the dark back at home until Ted opened the drapes. She felt naked and judged in the daylight and she hated how Ted lingered on her with a sad face. So she lied. She said, "I don't love you like a wife ought to love a husband," and when he slapped her, she was glad.

Kay heated a pot of water on the stove for tea. It'd become awful hard to ignore the cruel fact she and Ted had pretended to be happy together for more years now than she'd like to admit. They'd become so skilled at a shared muted hospitality that Kay, for a time, could forget how she'd grown to revile Ted. She poured steaming water in a mug and dropped a bag of black tea in it and as the leaves steeped, Kay went to the staircase. She looked at the TV glow splashed on the landing at the bottom. "Ted," she said. "Do you want tea?" She waited, but no reply came.

Kay returned to the house Wednesday morning to Windex the glass and shampoo the carpets before Mr. Stone, the landlord, came to collect the keys at four o'clock. She turned in the driveway and saw Pat was already there, her Bronco parked in the garage. Kay walked to the porch. When she opened the front door, she found Pat knelt down in the living room. She was holding the crowbar in her hands, clad in Alma's dress. Her pear-shaped face was dusted in grey lint and yellow wood pulp. Kay set the tote of cleaning liquids down and closed the front door.

Pat jammed the crowbar underneath a vent on the floor then used the claw to pry off the metal cover. She reached her hand in the duct and said, "We didn't check the vents," then she removed her hand and wiped the cobwebs off her fingers. "There's money. I can feel it." Kay sighed, opening the front door. She readied to leave, but Pat grabbed her wrist. Kay closed the door and flipped the wall switch, but there was no light. "Daddy didn't pay the bill," Pat said, then stood. She gave Kay the crowbar and Kay held the tool in her hands and she allowed herself to consider, at last, that there could be more cash stashed someplace in the house. When Kay slumped off her coat, Pat said, "Good," and they went to work prying open the vent covers.

Kay and Pat broke for lunch after coming up empty-handed. They walked down Horn Ave past the dirty-brick soup kitchen and a twist of oak trees by the Subway. They sat in a booth but Kay didn't eat, her stomach soured by doubt. She sipped her Diet

Coke while Pat gobbled her BLT and chatted about where they'd look next. Kay nodded as she gazed out of the window at the Mt. Grove Convent. When Kay was a child and Pat was an infant, Alma had taken them there the day she left. She'd waited until Clem went to work at Sumner High then she walked them to the convent. She prayed with the Pink Sisters—nuns donned in pink habits—as Kay moped in the nave. They weren't Catholic. They'd never prayed. Yet Kay watched in confusion her mother swaddle her crying baby as she and the nuns petitioned the lord in a sad harmony.

It was one o'clock when they got back to the house. Kay moved in the kitchen in a glum stupor so Pat pulled a red pill from her purse. She swallowed it then gave Kay one. Kay shrugged and downed hers. Within minutes, she felt a brain rush and in a giddy haze she and Pat tossed the garage and rifled through the closets again. But they found nothing. At two o'clock, Kay was beat and insisted they fix the mess and clean the windows and carpets before Mr. Stone arrived.

They waited on the porch at four o'clock. Pat said, "We can still look. We'll tell—"

"No," Kay said. She crossed her arms. "It's time. It's just time."

Kay elbowed Pat once she saw Mr. Stone's Buick motor past the defunct train yard and the rotten G&M lumber mill. He parked his boat of a car in the driveway next to the dead shrubs. It'd been twenty years since they'd last seen the old coot and Kay was tinged by jitters when she saw his fat snout-face crinkle nasty as he climbed the porch steps and ogled Pat. He collected the keys. Then he stuffed them in a soiled fanny pack and stared at Pat again as she was brushing her blonde hair aside. But when she smiled at him, Mr. Stone's face scrambled into a dark scowl. "God's love will never fail you," he said. He turned stiff-like. Then he moseyed off the porch.

After he left, Pat said, "Let's call Walt," and shucked a Camel out of a soft pack.

"Walt's fried. He drank himself into a nursing home. He doesn't—"

"We found money just like he said we would," she hissed.

Kay huffed, "It was just a few hundred dollars. I'm worried you're—"

"Don't," Pat said, then sparked the cigarette and took a mean pull.

"You'll be fine," Kay said. "Pat," she said. "You're brave."

"Brave?" Pat snorted. "Is it because everyone calls me a freak?"

"You're my sister. That's how I know," Kay said.

Pat exhaled smoke. "I'm fine. You know that. Don't you?"

"Maybe I don't know how to be fine," Kay said.

"It doesn't matter," Pat said. "I'm dirt. Your dirt. We're just all dirt."

"There's no money. You have to believe that," she said.

"Do I?" Pat said. She flicked her cigarette.

"I guess it doesn't matter," Kay sassed, then walked to the sedan.

"Wait," Pat said, jogging down the driveway. She hugged her.

That night, Kay lay next to Ted in bed. She couldn't find sleep, her mind all mixed up in worry over Pat and her fixation with the money. Ted slept on his side. They'd eaten chili at Applebee's for dinner and he'd been wrecked by brutal indigestion all evening. Kay listened in the dark to Ted snore and struggle for air. Some nights, she'd cup her hand over his mouth when she was certain he'd settled into a hard sleep. She'd squeeze her hand tight and hold it there until his face purpled like a bruise and after he'd wake in a coughing fit, she'd hold him in her arms.

It was midnight by the time Kay began to settle into a shallow doze but she was jolted awake in a spark of fright when her iPhone rang. Ted moaned then farted inside the twist of bedcovers. He tugged at his genitals while Kay turned on her bedside lamp and nabbed the iPhone. Ted rolled over. He cleared his throat with a thick wet hack and grunted in his stale breath. Kay answered the call, and Pat was rambling. "I know where the money's at," she slurred. "I snuck Walt some merlot at the Manor. And he told me. He said—" but the call ended.

Kay dialed Pat but the call was directed to her voicemail. She tossed the iPhone on to the bedside table and turned off the lamp. She lay back down then she turned on her side. She was angry. She wanted to forget Pat and that house and just sleep. But she couldn't. Her chest felt heavy with guilt. Kay eased out of the bed and shimmied into her jeans. She tiptoed across the dark bedroom and pulled on a shirt and her sneakers. When she was about to leave, Ted turned on his bedside lamp.

"Get in bed," he growled. He kicked at the bedcovers.

"That was Pat. She didn't sound right," Kay said.

"Goddamn it. I gotta meet Fudge in the morning to finalize bids," he said.

"I think Pat's at Dad's house," she said and slipped on her coat.

"It's not your Dad's house anymore," he said.

"I think Pat's drunk," she said after Ted groaned out a hot belch.

"I knew it. I knew HE couldn't stay sober."

"I'll be back," Kay sighed, grabbing the car keys off the dresser.

Ted yanked the lamp cord. The light went out. "Terrific."

Kay parked her sedan in the driveway then scooted out and peeked into Pat's Bronco.

She saw an empty wine bottle lying on its side on the floorboard. She said, "Bitch."

Kay plodded across the frosted lawn and climbed the rickety porch. The front door was locked so she trotted to the side of the house and crawled in through her old bedroom window with the broken latch. She scrabbled on to the dingy carpet and stood, slapping dust off her jeans. "Pat?" she said. She reached for the wall switch but stopped and pulled her iPhone out from her coat pocket. Kay turned on the flashlight mode and she shined the white light into the hallway.

She crept into the dark living room and her neck started to sweat when she smelled the stink of gasoline that lingered in the dank air. Then a sound came—a flurry of thuds that echoed from the basement—and she froze. She felt sick in the gut like she did as a child but she pushed on and took the stairs. "Pat?" she said. She surveyed the basement on the last step, the light catching the floor and fireplace. The thuds returned, and Kay played the light on the corner. She spotted Pat in that old tight blue dress and she looked stunningly tragic in the wash of the iPhone light.

Kay trodded over Pat's coat and purse and a half-full bottle of merlot standing on the floor.

"My cell died. I need that light," Pat said, holding the crow-bar like a baseball bat.

"You drunk," Kay yelled in dismay. "I trusted you. I thought this time was—"

Pat swung the crowbar into the drywall and jabbed her arm in the hole and pulled out the insulation. She said, "Walt thinks Daddy hid it here." Kay turned the light. She saw holes busted in all over the wall. Pat said, "Light," and Kay aimed the iPhone at her. She took Pat's arm. Kay knew Pat was lost in a bad way. So she refused to leave her here. "No," Pat barked and before she took another swing, Kay rushed her. She grabbed a clump of wig and threw the thing into the dark. They grappled some and the iPhone fell on the floor, a spray of light shining on the corner.

Kay pushed Pat against the wall and Pat dropped to her knees. She cried, "The money."

"We don't belong here," Kay said in the iPhone light as she helped Pat back on her feet.

They lugged their belongings up the stairs and shuffled out of the backdoor. Kay set Pat's purse and the bottle of wine on the patio then she helped Pat jiggle on her coat. They sat down, Pat's blonde wig cocked to the side. They hung their legs off the ledge. It was unusually balmy out and the sky, lighted by the winter stars, was clear as a prairie creek. On the knoll, a knot of apple trees towered. Kay had loved to climb those trees as a girl so she could look out past the sprawl of poor homes and marvel at the dazzling lights of St. Louis that paled the distant night.

Pat groped a Camel from her purse. When she bent over to light it, Kay pulled six rolls of cash from her coat. This was everything she'd saved—all twenty-six thousand of it. She tucked the money in Pat's purse, underneath a compact, some lipstick, and a bottle of estradiol. Kay sat there numb, staring at the night. But she'd be fine. There was no other way. She told herself that.

"Remember you said I was brave," Pat said, ripping on her Camel. "You're brave."

Kay swigged the wine. "I've always been scared," she said.

Pat took the bottle and gulped the merlot then handed it back. "No," she slurred.

"Here," Kay said. She guzzled the wine and passed it to Pat again.

"Hey," Pat hiccupped. "Do you remember how you said I was brave?"

Kay shut her eyes. She could hear the apple trees shake in the breeze. She said, "I do."

It happened at night. When the stink of gasoline seeped under the bedroom door, it woke Kay in grim alarm. She knew what this meant. She'd watched it happen many times before, spying from the dark hallway. She'd see this: Ted on the sofa in the living room colored by the TV. There was a can of gasoline cradled on his lap. He doused a rag in the fuel and cuffed it to his face then huffed the fumes. He sat in his sullied custodial uniform and gazed with hollow eyes at the floor as he inhaled the gas. But when Ted cursed God, Kay knew what came next.

She ran to Patrick's bedroom and woke him from sleep, grabbing him by the hand and dragging him to her bedroom. Kay closed the door. She cupped her hands over his ears so he wouldn't hear the furniture crash or the glass shatter. "It was her fault," she heard Ted scream from the living room. "She," he yelled. "She," Ted wailed until his voice began to shudder.

Kay opened the window and helped Patrick jump outside. She said, "Hide."

Ted came soon after and she didn't cry or beg when he hit her. She stared at him—at his mouth seeping in drool and his nose bubbling with snot—until he broke. Only then did she take his hard hand and lead him back to the living room where she slumped him on to the sofa. She sat, his head nestled in her lap and she fingered his hair until he nodded off into a fretful sleep.

Then she left. She rushed out of the backdoor and hurried on to the patio. Patrick wasn't hard to find. He liked to hide behind the row of apple trees. "I found you," she said, and she picked two apples off a low branch like she always did and the two of them returned to the house. They sat on the patio. She gave Patrick his apple then she hung her head low. Kay feared more than anything that if he looked into her eyes he'd find nothing good there. So she let the night fall over her and in the cover of dark she ate the apple that glowed in the moonlight like magic.

Morning Love Song, an Aubade

AMY SCANLAN O'HEARN

I heard a sound
come out of me

like a Mourning Dove,
in mourning

lying next to you
our breaths merge

then the heavy lifting
and the river

moving south
and your bones

older now and slower
and rocks laid bare

under a relentless
summer sun.

Couples

BOBBY NEEL ADAMS

Berndette and Bob

Todd and Tara

Wendy and Matt

Brett and Beth

Naut and Mitzi

Mike and Karen

Tim and Suzanne

Bruce and Deena

David and Del

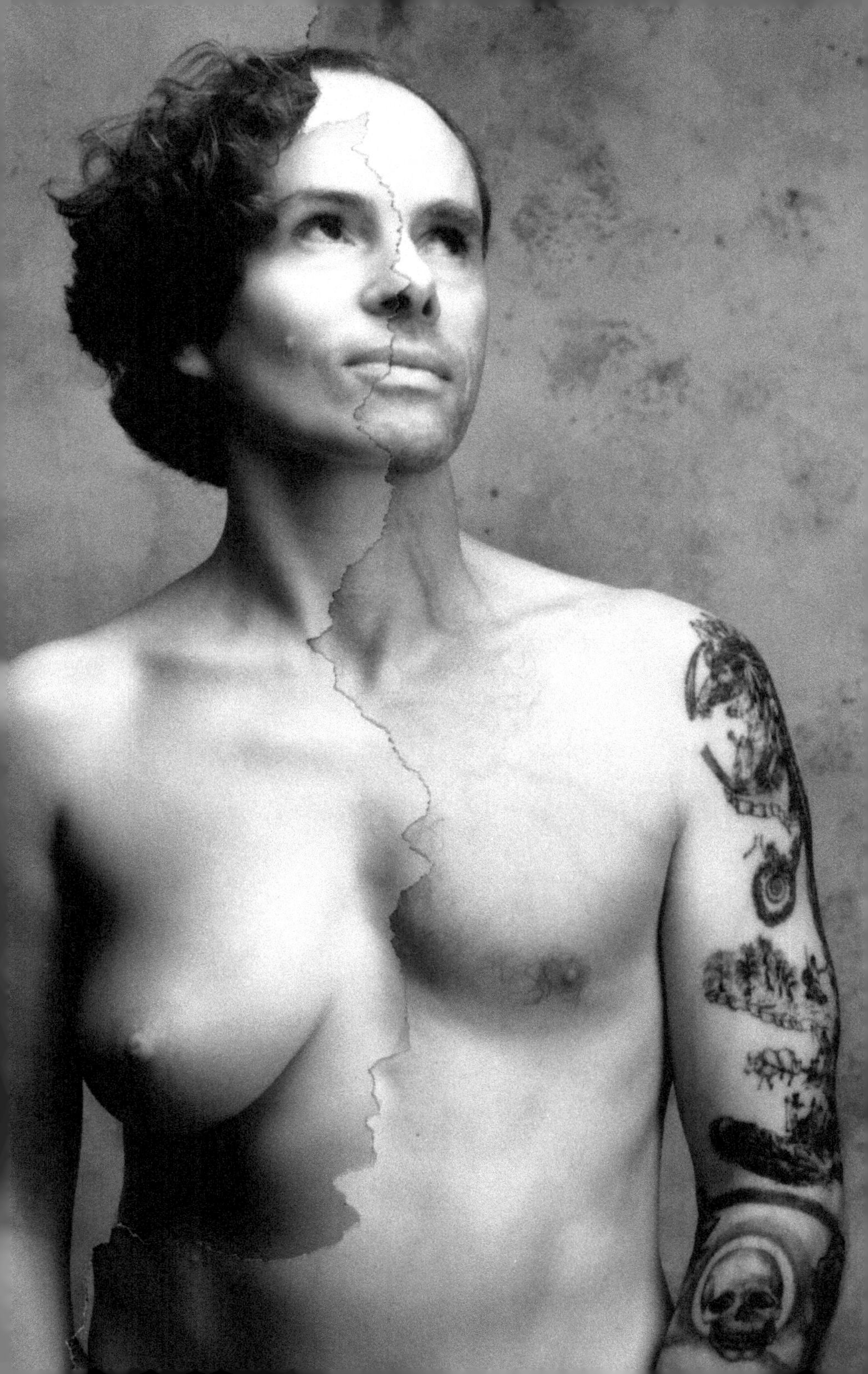

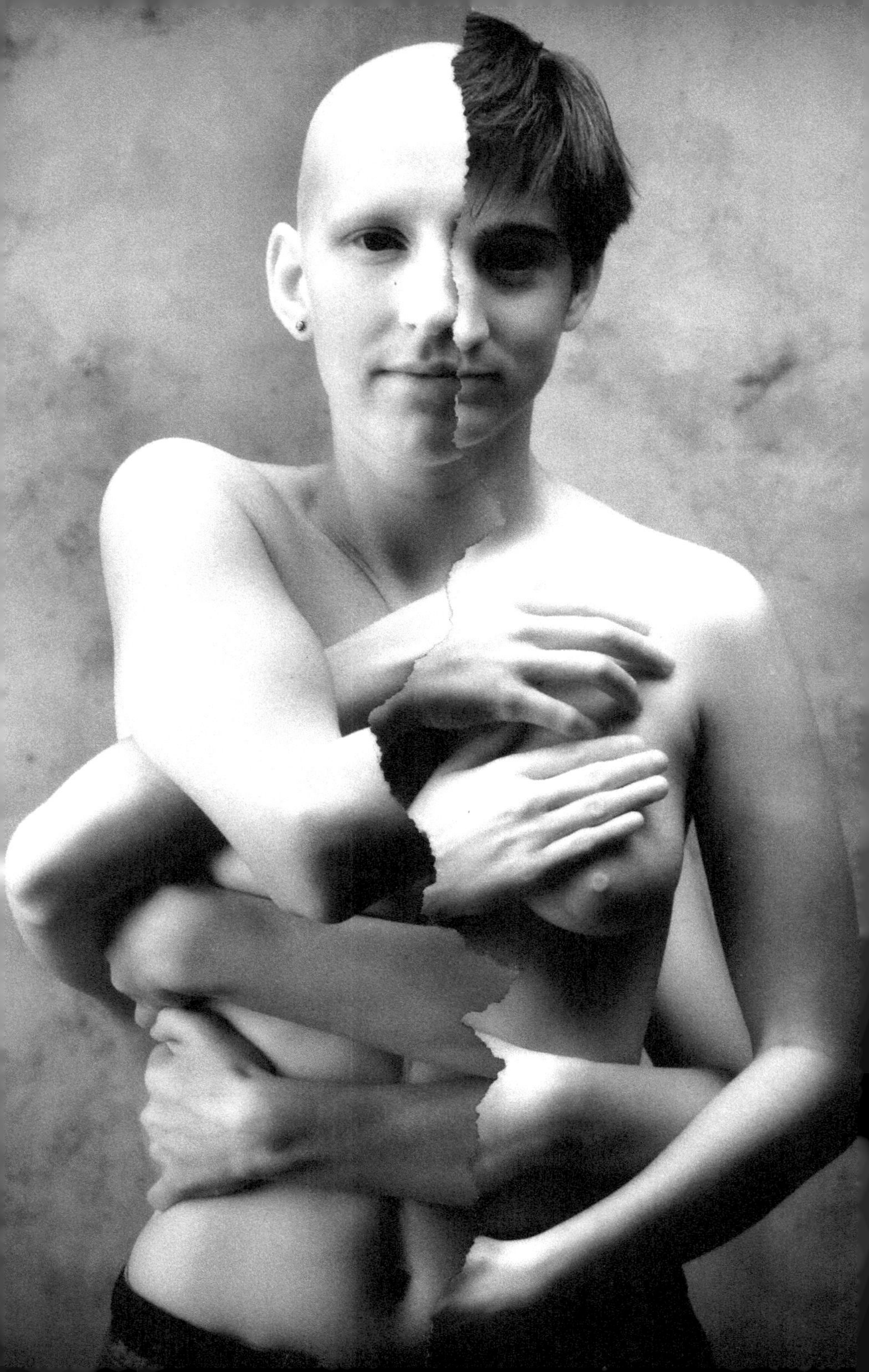

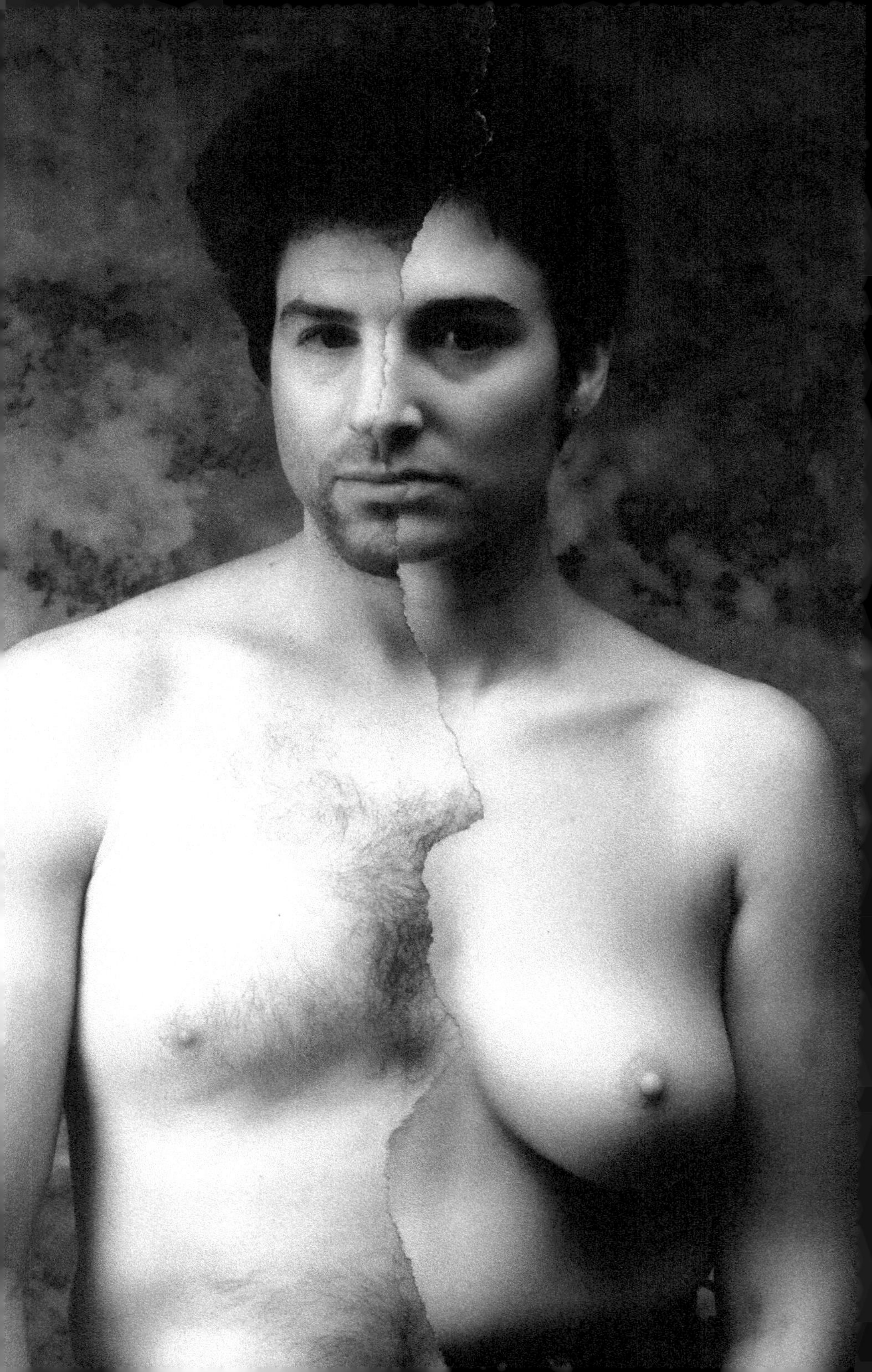

Artist Statement

Individual portraits are made of a married couple or two persons involved in an intimate relationship. These separate portraits are spliced together to make one image—a souvenir symbolizing the bonds of this couple's relationship.

I began making this series of photographs when it occurred to me that some couples visually resemble each other. My first composite photographs were a test to see if my theory was true. My thesis was that a person is often attracted to another when they recognize something of themselves in that person. In other words, one may be more comfortable around a person of the opposite sex if they share some of the same physical attributes.

These portraits have a secondary meaning: when the male is spliced together with the female—a representation bi-sexual being is created. The composite *Couples* image represents the male and female qualities in all of us.

—Bobby Neel Adams, Photographer

The Undefined Variable

ELIZABETH JAEGER

"He has to be math minded," Kati declared as she logged onto the sperm bank's website. We had been talking about having a child since we married three years earlier. And now, our dialogue was finally a reality. I was younger, healthier, and maintained a better diet than Kati, so we decided that I would carry the baby. Since he, or she, and I would be genetically linked, Kati wanted to find a donor whose interests aligned with hers, in the hope that someday she and the child might have something in common. Kati, a math teacher, loved numbers. I loved words. How cool would it be if our child loved and excelled in both equally? And so we had a starting point, a means to cut through the hundreds of profiles available, a way to narrow the pool of possibilities.

Shopping for sperm was surreal.

When you're shopping for a new camera on Amazon, there

is a thorough description of each model—company, pixels, zoom, picture. Customers have reviewed the product so you can compare—four and a half stars to four and three quarters. And you can read what others have said. The flash is finicky. After a week, the pictures started to blur. I bought this for my mother and she loved it. And best of all, there is a return policy. If the purchased item doesn't match the description, you can send it back. Or if it's damaged, you can count on a full refund.

Finding and settling upon the perfect sperm is far more abstract. There is absolutely nothing tangible about the product. One may plug too many variables into the equation, ensuring no possible guarantee that you will end up with a pleasing result. There are no customer reviews. My son has the sweetest disposition. He didn't get it from me. Love the donor's DNA. My daughter is brilliant writer. I can't string a serious of words together to form a cohesive sentence. So glad we went with the journalist. I wanted blue eyes. I specifically chose this donor for that reason, but my child's eyes are gray. Wish I had made a different decision. And most frightening of all—no refunds. If you are displeased with the product, you can't send it back. If the sperm doesn't result in a child, Oh well. Or if the child is born with seven fingers on one hand or an inability to calculate fractions, too bad. Like with any child, DNA is a crap shoot. But when an attempt to have a baby comes with a price tag—$500 a pop—there seems to be more at stake.

How does one settle on the perfect product? We started with math, weeding through donors, and looking for ones who had degrees in either science or math. Each donor had an extensive profile—education, hobbies, family medical history, photos, ethnicity, religion, etc. The catch, however—and there is always a catch when there is an opportunity to make money, this is America after all—only a limited profile is available for free. The more details, the more money the search will cost. Since the outcome relied upon chance, and since, as teachers, we didn't have excess money lying around, we decided to make our decision based on what we could review for free.

To maintain the anonymity of the men, the website offered no names. Instead, the sperm bank assigned each of them a number. Since I, unlike Kati, did not orientate my life around numbers and since referring to people by a number seemed so sterile, I decided to name them. I based their monikers on ethnicities. For a while, "Mario Sowinski" topped our list but after further perusal, we chose "Hans Armstrong." Hans was part Danish (hence Hans, as in Hans Christian Andersen, whose fairy tales I loved). and an avid cyclist, (hence Armstrong, although, had we known then that Lance had been doping, we probably would opted for a different name).

"But what will you tell your child?" my dad asked one weekend while visiting. "What will you tell him when he asks why he doesn't have a father?"

I shrugged. I hadn't thought that far into the future. "Let me have the kid first, and we can figure everything out later."

Dad shook his head, "He's going to want to know. He'll look around at all his friends and want to know why he's different."

I knew Dad was right. And there was also the element of other kids being mean. Kids were often cruel. But my kid wasn't even conceived yet, so why stress out about something that may never happen. And it wasn't like we were the first lesbian couple intent on raising a child. Queer families may not have been common, but they certainly existed.

Kati and I agreed on Hans and started our search for a fertility doctor. Usually when searching for a new doctor, we turned to friends for recommendations, but in this case, we had no one. None of our friends had need of one, so we turned to our insurance company for a list of doctors in our network. We chose one whose office was a five-minute drive from our condo. At the time, it seemed like a good idea, considering all the driving back and forth we expected to do. In reality, the doctor proved to be a nightmare.

During the first four inseminations, I had no less than two ovarian follicles, and Hans's samples—arriving at the doctor's office—always had a high sperm count. Following each insemination, I did everything possible to ensure that I'd get pregnant. I reduced my level of exercise. I didn't drink. I rested more than I wanted to. I prayed and meditated and hoped. But nothing took. After four cycles, I started to lose hope. I desperately wanted a child, but it seemed as though my body had other plans.

After four failures the doctor finally decided to run a fertility test. Kati and I took a day off from work and early in the morning drove to some obscure hospital near the New Jersey/Pennsylvania border. The test was supposed to be fairly simple. The doctor would shoot dye through my fallopian tubes, a process he would monitor on a screen to determine if they were blocked. "If nothing else," he spoke in his usual monotone, "It will clear out the cobwebs."

It was at that moment, in that hospital room as I lay sprawled on the bed, that I realized the doctor was a quack. He fumbled with the equipment as if he were an intern auto mechanic. Realizing he hadn't selected the proper instruments, he left the room without an explanation. For a quarter of an hour, we waited, wondering if he had abandoned us. When he finally returned and commenced the procedure, pain ripped through my abdomen. Kati asked if pain was normal but the doctor only shrugged, leaving me to speculate how he obtained a license to practice medicine. At the test's conclusion—there was no blockage—I felt nauseous and I doubled over, invisible claws ripping at my insides. Briefly, I wondered how it measured up against labor pains, but as long as I knew a child was definitely on the way, pain, no matter how sharp, would be more bearable than it was at that moment.

On the way home we stopped for breakfast. I stepped out of the car and onto the sidewalk and doubled over. The walking intensified the pain, and in the parking lot of Dunkin Donuts I threw up, my regurgitated breakfast splattering the hubcap of our car.

In April, arriving back at the doctor's office for our fifth attempt, I refused to allow the doctor to touch me, insisting instead that the nurse do the insemination. On the morning of Good Friday, I had just one ovarian follicle—no possibility for twins—and the sperm count was exceptionally low compared to other vials. To add to the odds stacked against us, due to our work schedules—teachers were not permitted to take a personal day before a long vacation—we were unable to make an appointment for the previous day, the day on which my body was allegedly most fertile.

I had a terrible sense of foreboding. This time, like the previous four, I would not get pregnant. And five strikes was two more than we should have tolerated. It was time to find another fertility clinic. Immediately following the fifth insemination, Kati requested my records and we made an appointment elsewhere to start all over again.

Since I knew pregnancy was out of the question, I drank wine with my Easter dinner. I went out with friends and ordered gin and tonics. And I didn't bother to rest or cut back on my exercise. In fact, about three weeks after the insemination I went hiking. I planned on a six-mile loop, but halfway through I felt incredibly exhausted and painfully parched. During the last two miles, I had to stop frequently to catch my breath and drink water. But no matter how much I ingested, it wasn't enough. My body absorbed it all and then begged for more. Six miles should have been nothing. I should have been able to complete the trail without having to tap into my energy reserves. By the time I got home, an hour after I intended, all I wanted to do was sleep and hydrate. I drank another liter of water, and then when I had to pee, I figured what the hell, I'd rip open one of the home pregnancy tests left over from the previous month. I followed the instructions, waiting for the negative sign to appear. Instead, the plus sign slowly grew visible, my eyes staring at it incredulously, certain there had to be a mistake. It couldn't be. I opened the door, the testing stick still clutched in my fingers, and called to Kati, "Come here, you're not going to believe this."

"What?" She asked, pausing the television, and reluctantly heading over to the bathroom.

Unable to speak, I showed her the test. For a long moment she stared at it, her mind grappling with the impossibility of the evidence before her. Then finally, looking up at me, she said, "You've got to be fucking kidding me!"

The stick didn't lie. The following Monday I went in for a pregnancy test and an ultrasound. Kati and I were overjoyed when the nurse handed us the first photo of our child, a small dot that looked as though someone had dripped a drop of ink on the paper. It was nothing more than a speck, a collection of cells, but it was our child, our baby, and suddenly the next eight months seemed eternal. I couldn't wait to hug and cuddle him or her.

As soon as the tests confirmed my pregnancy, Kati returned to the sperm bank's online database and purchased every component of the donor's profile. We learned that while Hans had a degree in engineering, his GPA didn't reflect the habits of a dedicated student. In his free time, he enjoyed hunting and his French-Canadian grandfather had been a fisherman. He credited his mother with cultivating in him a love of reading. And he was married with two children of his own. The pictures spanning his life—toddler to adulthood—we found most exciting. Having a face made Hans seem less abstract.

I didn't want to know if we were having a boy or a girl. The anticipation, the guessing, the drawn-out surprise appealed to me. However, within two months, Kati felt certain that I was carrying a girl. Her conviction became infectious and in a few weeks my doubts had dwindled to nothing more than a shadowy whisper. At five months, when I went in for an ultrasound, the technician asked if we wanted to know the sex of our child. With a flick of the wrist, I indicated Kati, "No, she's confident it's a girl." The technician rolled her eyes and laughed, "Okay, just don't go out and buy anything pink." And so we learned that Kati's instinct was wrong.

January 3 was my due date, but it was dangerously close to December and I did not want my child to have a December birthday. I feared it would get lost in Christmas and I always considered the week after Christmas to be the most depressing one of the year. Sure I had off from school, but after all the holiday hype, the following days felt like a dead zone. Friends tried to persuade me that a baby born in the latter days of the year would brighten them for me, but I didn't want them brightened. I wanted my child to hold off and wait until the final page in the calendar had been turned to make his appearance. But his day of birth, like the genetics he'd inherit were not up to me, and fate or the gods or mother nature would do as they pleased, whether or not it satisfied me. I was just excited to know that in a short amount of time, I would be a mother. And really, that's all that mattered - holding my child, kissing him, and loving him.

On the night of December 30th, at around 10:30, my water sprung a leak. It didn't break. It didn't gush, drenching everything in its wake. It literally leaked, like a faucet you meant to turn off but just didn't twist tightly enough. Drip, drip, drip into the toilet bowl. Drip, drip, drip slowly but steadily. There was no stopping it, no plugging it up. Damn! More than twenty-four hours until the new year and my baby was on his way.

I did not sleep. I expected the contractions to commence at any moment, but the night passed in a blur of expectation. When I got up in the morning, I felt no different. The drip persisted so Kati called the mid-wife who told us to go to the hospital. I phoned my parents to let them know their grandchild was on his way. My dad was anxious and elated. Thinking practically, he favored a December 31st birth. If my son arrived before midnight it would mean a tax deduction. Kati and her dad had the same mentality. But I held out. Leaning forward as far as I could, I spoke to my son, "Hang in there. Sixteen more hours. That's all, sixteen and you can make your way out."

For breakfast, we stopped at the diner. Who knew when I'd be able to eat again, so I filled up on home fries, a veggie omelet, and toast. Once I checked in at the hospital, the odyssey began. My expectations were simple: water breaks, contractions begin, contractions continue, baby is born. But I should have realized that my life very seldom followed the prescribed script. My water still hadn't ruptured, and I hadn't even had a slight twinge, much less a contraction. And so, the nurses hooked me up to a heart monitor for the baby and stuck an IV in my arm.

I had been adamant with Kati. I didn't want drugs. Nothing unnatural. But Pitocin, the midwife promised would kickstart my contractions. It was necessary if I didn't want to put my child in danger. But still, even with the Pitocin, my body rebelled until they had me on a higher dosage than usual. I felt the pain. I meditated through it, determined not to scream for painkillers. But I didn't dilate. So after a long day, as we inched toward midnight, it appeared as if my wish would be granted. We watched the ball drop, and as 2010 lit up on the TV screen, a massive contraction ripped through me. I looked at my bulging, gigantic stomach and once again spoke to my son, "Any time now. December is over." But as obedient as he had been all day, he now grew defiant.

So that I could sleep, the nurses stopped giving me Pitocin. But even then sleep eluded me. It was obviously time, so why weren't things progressing as they should? The morning brought with it more Pitocin. It was slow to work, and so I lay in bed, writhing in pain, and watching the clock. At three o'clock in the afternoon, the midwife insisted on an epidural. I needed to relax. As soon as I did, my body would open up, and my son would come. Angry and frustrated—I hadn't wanted drugs of any sort—I relented, accepting the needle.

Sometime after 10 o'clock at night my son's heartbeat suddenly plummeted. Without warning, without an explanation, the hospital staff whisked me into the OR. One second I was lying there waiting for something to happen, and the next, the orderly was pushing my bed through the hall. He speedily and skillfully navigated into a brightly lit room. Someone placed an oxygen mask over my nose and mouth, a curtain was pulled across my waist, and while I didn't feel the incision, I felt the tugging, pulling, ripping apart of my flesh. And then the cry. The doctor held our baby aloft, announced that it was boy, and in that moment Kati snapped a picture—my abdomen splayed open, the umbilical cord dangling down, and our wrinkled little man scrunched up in the doctor's hands.

I wanted to hold him, kiss him. But the doctor had to staple me back together. As the staples bit into my flesh, a nurse held my son next to me. I rolled my head to kiss him, but I couldn't. It was as if I were bumping my head into glass. My lips couldn't reach his cheeks. I couldn't understand why until the same nurse removed the oxygen mask and I kissed my little boy for the first time. But then I started to gasp. I couldn't breathe. And I started to shake, my body rumbling. The oxygen mask snapped back into place, and as Kati went off with our son, the orderly pushed me into recovery. It took nearly an hour before the shaking subsided and I found that I could breathe on my own.

After tending to our son, cutting the umbilical cord and seeing him washed and weighed, Kati walked into the recovery room and sat down beside me, more elated than I had ever seen her. "He looks just like your father," she told me. "Especially his chin. He has your father's chin."

Later, shortly after being wheeled into my room, our son joined us and all I wanted to do was hug him, hold him tight, and kiss his tiny forehead. We named him Gary Alan III—a traditional way of naming, bestowed in a non-traditional way. My father is Gary Alan and my brother (who has no children) is Gary Alan Jr. As a child, it always upset me that the honor of being a Jr. had been granted to my brother. As the oldest, I felt it should have been given to me. When I complained, my father impatiently explained that girls can't be juniors because: 1) Girls have different names than boys, and 2) When a girl gets married she changes her last name and therefore, can't pass on the full name to her child. Well, I wouldn't have minded a "boy's" name and since I refused to change my last name, there was no reason for me not to give it to my child. So, I hijacked it for my son, breaking the rules, and re-channeling it through the maternal line.

Our son loves being the third. He signs everything, even his homework, Gary III. A few people, including teachers and classmates, when they learn that he has two moms question how he can possibly be the third. Even my dad once commented, that strictly speaking, he should probably be the second. But Kati and I just tell people, "We're lesbians, we make up our own rules." A few people roll their eyes, some chuckle, but ultimately they all accept it.

A name isn't all our son shares with my brother. Genetics are quirky that way. The only thing G3 and I seem to have in common is our love of reading. I had been an athlete through college. I continue to love hiking and have an aversion to sedentary activities. When my son turned four I signed him up to play tee ball. I even volunteered to coach, but he had no interest, preferring to dig in the dirt to catching the ball. Soccer and basketball also bored him. And to this day, he hates to walk. Hiking is a chore. Though I suppose I didn't strike out completely in sports since he does enjoy taekwondo.

In many ways G3 is a mini version of my brother. He can sit for hours constructing Legos, and he enjoys movies more than anyone I've ever known, except perhaps my father. His sense of style belongs to an experienced fashion designer and, even though he attends public school, he wears a button-down shirt and tie nearly every day. I once asked him why he likes dressing up for school, and he answered, "I get more compliments than anyone else. Besides, I like to dress like my uncle."

He collects knowledge the way most kids collect Pokemon cards, and his memory for random facts amazes me. Impressing others, including his peers, motivates him more than the desire to get good grades. Even though he is only eight years old, he can hold his own in a conversation with adults on topics as varied as politics, history, and nature.

My parents never seem to miss an opportunity to comment on the similarities between Middle and Little Gary. Perhaps it's because G3 doesn't have a father that he has chosen to emulate his uncle. Last year, he enthusiastically joined Cub Scouts, telling everyone who would listen that he wanted to be an Eagle Scout, "Just like Uncle Gary."

There are many moments that I can point to my son's behavior and think, "Yep, he's just like Middle Gary." Occasionally, I can even identify a trace of me in something he does. But there are times, when he acts on his intriguing imagination or when his sense of humor, so different from anyone else' in the family, carries him off into a fit of laughter, that I wonder about Hans, about how his DNA has manifested itself in my son's personality. At age two G3 looked very much like Hans. The similarities were striking. But as he got older, he looked less and less like him.

So far we have been fortunate. Other kids seem to accept, without question or criticism, the fact that G3 has two moms. It's never seemed to bother him that he doesn't have a father, except for one fleeting moment when he was three. He and a friend, Sabrina, a girl two months older than him, were painting outside. She was an outgoing and bubbly child, and as she enthusiastically worked on her picture, she rattled on about how she was going to give it to her daddy for his birthday. Then suddenly, in the midst of her chatter about her father, G3 started to cry, "I don't have a daddy." Immediately aware of how her words had inadvertently hurt G3, she put her arm around him and said, "But you're lucky. You have two moms." The tears promptly stopped and my son smiled.

A few years later, after school a classmate once asked him if he had a father, and my son, without a moment of hesitation, responded, "No, but I have a grandfather." And that was that.

Sometime around G3's fifth birthday, Kati started to ponder, "When do you think we should tell Gary about Hans?" The best answers I could come up with were, "When he's ready." Or, "When he starts asking." For a while that appeased her, but then two more birthdays passed, and she grew impatient. She wanted to pull out the binder with all of Hans's information, sit G3 down, and tell him where he came from. But I wanted to wait until G3 initiated the conversation, until he was ready to hear the truth. I figured that when his curiosity piqued enough to ask, he'd be more enthusiastic about listening. We both expected it to be a momentous occasion—the day our son learned about Hans.

But he never asked. He never questioned why he had two moms when almost everyone else he knew had a mom and a dad. We were his family. He accepted it without question.

Then last summer, we were driving home from a day at the Point Pleasant boardwalk when I remembered that a local church was having a blood drive. I suggested to Kati that if we got home early enough we should stop. It had been a couple of years since I last gave blood, and I liked setting an example for our son. Kati, despite her abhorrence of needles, agreed. This ushered in a conversation about blood types. Kati and I are both A+. Out of curiosity, I asked her if she matched her mother or her father.

"Why does she have to match one of them?" G3 asked. Without pausing to think about the words tumbling out of my mouth, I explained to G3 that a child gets his blood type from one of his parents.

A few minutes later, again without fully thinking through the repercussion of my words, I told G3 that he was O+.

"Oh no," he quickly countered. "You're wrong. I can't be O+."

"Why not?" I asked, fairly certain that I wasn't mistaken. When the doctors typed him in the hospital after he was born, I very clearly remember thinking, What if he ever needs blood, or an organ? I won't be able to give it to him. And only then did it realize that perhaps blood type should have been part of our initial search for a donor.

"Because you and Mommy are both A+ and you said that children get their blood type from their parents. So I have to be A+ too."

Our heads—Kati's and mine—turned simultaneously toward each other, and she mouthed the words, "Now?" I shrugged, not knowing how else to explain my way out of this conundrum.

Kati peered at our son in the rearview mirror, "I'm your mother, and you know I love you, right?" she asked. When G3 nodded, she continued, "Even though I'm your mother, we do not share any DNA. Two women can't make a baby. A mother needs a man's help, which is why most children have a mother and a father."

"But I don't have a father."

I turned around, and even in the fading light I could plainly see his confusion, the wrinkled brow sifting through this new information, searching for something solid to grasp hold of; the bright eyes glowing from the strain of processing exactly what Kati was saying; the effort of trying to figure out precisely how this sudden revelation might affect who he was—his concept of himself. But curious, excited, and intrigued he listened intently as Kati and I told him about Hans—the fact that he was French-Canadian and Danish, that he enjoyed cycling, that he once served in the military, that he liked to hunt, and that he had two kids of his own, which meant that G3 had half siblings running around somewhere in the world. When we finished, pausing to answer questions or respond to comments, silence seeped into the car.

Then G3's eyes grew wide, his smile infectious, as the words exploded out of him. "I'm French-Canadian!" His mouth hung open, his eyes dancing with the light of discovery. "That is so awesome."

Again, Kati and I exchanged a look, totally flabbergasted—this, of everything we had just told him, this French-Canadianness is what elicited a reaction.

"Do you have any questions?" Kati and I asked simultaneously, wanting to make sure he understood, wanting to ensure that he knew we'd talk about anything he wanted to discuss.

"Yeah, when can we go to Canada?"

Two Poems

KAY COSGROVE

Feeding

Closed all the windows to the heat   How still Frances
at this time of day   How still I   Feeding you means
          sitting means
my body does my work   I'm so hot with you against me the way
it used to feel in New York in July   when loving was new
          and my body
a poor translation of a language   I can't speak   can't decipher
          one insect's song
from another   windows open now to the summer
a small person in my arms   I read an article today
"motherhood is a privilege"   I want to spend time
          thinking
about the past or reading about a girl in Chinatown eating
her way through   heartache I want to swim laps in a pool
and have my brother follow   to drive on back roads
          singing
songs by heart   When did I get so
When did my heart open like the door across the street   the
          old woman's been sitting
at her window waiting   Who is a hero?
I'll fade into the background soon I haven't already   have
          I? All I wondered about
as a child has already been   resolved and now just
          a matter of waiting
Outside all the mother animals feed the babies   to sleep John
          left my toothbrush
on the sink already tooth-pasted   Does he still reach my hips in
          the dark I forget
if I dreamed   it or if I was there next to him or was it outside
          in the grass
a squirrel running home to eat   the squirrel does

Don't Move

I'm fascinated with my face
how the eyes don't match.

And with yours,
the long gray streak suddenly

an accessory like glasses
or a big leather tote.

I made a joke about my legs
to my OB/GYN.

I was pregnant and had
varicosities cropping up

all over the legs
I let everyone compliment

since high school. "Not to be vain,"
I said, "but I love my legs."

He laughed so long
I felt the blood pumping

back up to my heart
bypassing those bulges

set to ruin my idea
of me. Sometimes

I lie still to imagine myself
from the outside in,

a jigsaw puzzle
whose contradictions fit

perfectly. In what
cold jar do you place

your own sick and hungry heart?

The Last Days of the Survivor Dance

SARA LIPPMANN

On the second Tuesday of January the survivors gather for the annual survivor dance. They gather in the ballroom of the historic synagogue on Ocean Avenue. Like many things, the place is a shadow of its former self. Spanning half a city block, it now sits cavernous and crumbling, like a mausoleum at Greenwood. Like an abandoned sandcastle desiccating in the sun, its future doomed. When congregants die, there are no new members to replace them. As a result, there is little money for maintenance, for heat. Who wants to fund institutionalized religion these days anyway? Religion is the start of all wars.

Amidst the neglect and decrepitude simmer rumors of grandeur: an indoor swimming pool (or perhaps, mikveh), a basement bowling alley, a former high-spirited life. But at 2 o'clock on Tuesday the building is as good as dead. Organizers have their pick of parlors: auditorium, stained glass chapel, main sanctuary with leaf-strewn, cut-out skylight. They opt for the ballroom with its mirrored walls and six-foot windows for maximum light. Round tables draped in polyester cloth flank the fold-out dance floor like a wedding, a bar mitzvah, like any other simcha. Crystal teardrops wink from the chandelier. Helium balloons glide like lovers along the ceiling in silver and blue.

Slowly, survivors are ushered in. They shuffle one by one, two by two. They have walkers on tennis balls, wheelchairs, functional canes. They wear thick-soled orthopedic shoes. Their arthritic fingers clutch the hardy arms of their home health aides. Transportation has been provided by the organizers. That is, the survivors have been rounded up.

The survivors at the survivor dance self-segregate. They sit according to nationality and native tongue. One entire side of the room is boisterously Russian—Are they even Jewish? one says too loudly, about the FSU (former Soviet Union) attendees. What? Her companion shouts. No one can hear much of anything.

"It's awful growing old," they say in unison.

Yet this is precisely what they've done, of course: grown old, by surviving. They survived—in attics, in forests, in cellars, in oak casks and steel barrels, in secret rooms, they survived by baptism, survived parents and siblings, uncles and cousins—they survived by passing, they survived in hiding, on the benevolence of strangers, of gentiles, on false papers, via Kindertransport, they survived because they were—all of the surviving survivors at the survivor dance—merely children in the war. They survived the ghettos, the roundups, they survived those putrid, sloshing trains, they survived the camps, selection after selection because they vanished like specks of dusts in the barracks, or because they were tall enough to slip into the sturdier adult population, to prove capability beyond their years. Ultimately, they survived as children by ceasing to be children.

They are Polish, Czech, Belgian, Dutch; they are Slovakian, Hungarian, Romanian. They are Margot and Fanny, Elsie, Anya, Ruth. They were born in 1932, 1935, 1937. Every year there are fewer. For example, there are no more German survivors. It is 2025. Do the math.

The unspoken code of the survivor dance: Do not ask about survival. Do not say: what happened to you? Ravensbrück was not a sorority. Survivors are suspicious. They get competitive. Better to say nothing. Better to take a seat, tuck in, be raring to eat.

First, the survivors are served a proper luncheon of chicken dry as bone, string beans wrinkling in their blanched skins. Slick, bloated bowties peek out of a bottomless pit of kasha.

"In the orphanage, Kasha is all we had," one woman—Bella—says, forking a noodle, her eyes a watery blue.

The meal is meant to be a buffet, but because of the survivors' limited mobility, volunteers circulate with platters of thighs and breasts, ladle vinegary cucumber salad, cutting up meat with plastic knives to assist in the feeding hour as if survivors were exotic animals trapped at the zoo.

Immediately, there is an anxious demand for take-away tubs. Survivors at the survivor dance never leave empty handed. They squirrel away enough to last them the week. This is what survivors do. They eat their share but do not gorge themselves, rationing out portions for later. Logs of marble cake hold up well in the icebox and make a presentable, last-minute funeral platter—or shiva gift.

It used to be that the survivor dance was a monthly occurrence. Survivor dances were held across the nation, in multiple cities, in all five boroughs, and even then, they would sell out. Survivors flashed IDs, wove through velvet ropes. Today there is but one survivor dance a year. In one borough. Such is the cruel march of time.

Still, the ballroom half-fills. One osteoporotic survivor dressed in camel clucks her tongue in the direction of another jovial, Russian-speaking table. They will say anything for a free meal and dental insurance.

The aides try to placate their cantankerous charges. Hush now, Miss Dora, they say. Be nice. Aides are from Belarus, Ukraine, from Haiti, Trinidad and Guyana. They compile their own doggie bags: Sanka, Sweet n Low, they stuff creamers into coat pockets and load up their own clamshells with little red potatoes. Leftovers won't eat themselves. Over tea with lemon they tilt their chairs toward each other; grateful for a reprieve. They blow into their Styrofoam cups, lower voices. Survivors are no walk in the park, don't you know.

Survivors go to the beauty parlor. Survivors go to the bank. They are moody, stubborn. Survivors startle at the slightest sound: phones ringing, car horns, ambulance sirens. They are always complaining. Survivors lament their loss of independence—after what we've been through. Children give them agita, grandchildren don't call. They don't come. It's like we're invisible. Or else, family members are too dependent. They don't stop calling. They won't leave the survivors alone.

Sure, their survivor status has its perks. Health care. A rotation of cheerful volunteers. High school students adorably adapt their stories for "witness theater." Authors turn them into beach reads, Holocaust blockbusters. If they're lucky, Spielberg might immortalize them as a hologram. Otherwise, it's a lonely life. It's not like they all know each other. And when they do, half the time they don't get along anyway. Differences abound. They grew up communist. They grew up Catholic. In displaced persons camps. They migrated to Italy, were shipped off to Cuba, Australia, Shanghai. They took a one-way boat ride to Palestine. Some of them ended up back in their birth countries, only to cast their eyes on Ellis Island long after the survivor dance had seen its prime.

The microphone sputters to life. It's time for music! Dancing! The emcee is a supple Puerto Rican in a checkered sportscoat and a jaunty summer cap. Sal Rodrigues has been performing the survivor dance songbook for the past thirty years. He pushes play on his karaoke machine and takes a deep breath. He sings from memory: Hava Nagila, Am Yisrael Chai. He belts out Sweet Caroline and Mac the Knife. He knows he must capitalize on the narrow window between lunch and naptime. A few survivors stiffly rise to their feet. They shed their puffy coats, hobble to the dance floor.

If there are 50 survivors, 4 of them are men. Women live longer, but men have it made. They can cut a rug with anyone, but most of them cling to the sidelines, collecting cake crumbs in their hollow laps. One man in an argyle sweater vest nuzzles the bosom of his bottle blonde health aide, slyly placing his parkinsonian hand along the hump of her rear.

"Russian," Dora scoffs.

Survivors watch as a lone couple makes a respectable go at the tango, strutting across the foldout floor like they own it, like they've been together 50 years. It's really been more like ten, having met at a survivor dance after becoming widowed. These days, they are lost without each other, but their feet remember even when they don't know who they are.

Miriam lifts her plastic cup of seltzer at the first chord of "Kalinka," her hand trembling. "When we were sent to Russia, we thought it was the worst thing in the world."

"Deportation was supposed to kill us. But it saved our lives," Edna agrees. Their mothers were sent to the gulag. To Siberia, to Kazakhstan. To penal colonies, to mines, to potato farms. They were forced into hard labor. Over a million Poles were exiled. If they survived the cold, the brutality, if they survived the relentless rape, if they did not break their backs or catch their death, if they did not bleed out in childbirth or get murdered by the Soviets, they survived.

Not everyone was so lucky.

"The Germans killed my mommy," Halina says as if she were a doll with a back string.

Bella wipes her eyes. "Kasha thin as water on a good day."

Margot says, "When she returned from hell, I refused to go with her. I said, 'You are not my mother.' Can you imagine? But I did not know her anymore. Hell had made her very sick. Soon she would die. My father was dead. A neighbor took me. All three of his children were gassed."

Miriam says, "In Tomsk we dipped our clothes in water because ice sealed in body heat."

Fanny gazes wistfully at the dance floor. "Once I was a professional dancer."

"Nobody cares about old people," Dora again.

"We were children," Bella drifts off.

"This is what we lived for?" Anya says.

"I danced for the New York ballet," Fanny whispers.

"So shut up and dance already," Ruth says.

A few more survivors have drifted onto the dance floor. They snap their fingers, wing elbows, purse lips like they're blowing out candles, slam imaginary tambourines against their thighs. They step to the right, to the left. They spin slowly around, clap, spin back again. They rotate in a circle, wave to those seated across the parquet hunched into their chins.

"Come on!" Their recruitment is more like a commandment.

The home aides oblige. They bounce right up, slip into rhythm, raise the roof, bump their hips. Sal strikes up La Bamba, coos into the mike, "Go on, ladies, shake what your mama gave you." The microphone buzzes in back feed.

Others won't budge. They are arguing. Today's cake, is it chocolate or poppy? Who can tell, with a loaf so stale one could crack a tooth. Poppy is richer in flavor, but the seeds are a nuisance, causing a spike in blood pressure no one needs.

Sal pivots to holiday tunes. He sings Hanukkah, O Hanukkah, even though the festival of lights is over. Survivors observe the stack of empty chairs in the corner. What happened to Edna? Adele? To Milena? She died. She had a stroke. She broke her hip. In winter it is harder to leave the house. Survivors stay in. Survivors watch the local news. Weather broadcasts every seven minutes. They watch the funeral procession of a former president. Fires ravage the California coast. Air strikes flatten entire cities. Strangers stab strangers on subway platforms. Survivors don't look away. They watch horror upon horror. In their overheated apartments. With their silk carnations and needlepoint pillows. There is no end to it. Once they slept on warehouse floors, working double shifts to scrape together enough for a measly balcony in the sky where pigeons come to roost, and where, on clear days, they might catch a glimpse of the ocean. Lately, the surf is deserted. All there is is rain. Of course, a person can die of a broken heart even after surviving, eleven stories high, fall through the glass as new year hopefuls go rushing, handheld, into the raw, foggy sea.

But today's not that day. Today the survivors sitting like cement are surrounded by other survivors. Up, up, up. In another five years there will be no more dances. In fifteen people will claim they never existed. AI will take over, erase the word Jew from the story.

"Dance with us."

"My dancing days are over."

"Make an exception."

"Who am I dancing for?"

"Why must you dance for anyone but yourself?"

"The world is such ugly."

"Exactly. What else is there to lose?"

Like that, they are yanked off their sad, flat asses and pushed into the hora, buoyed by Sal's New York, New York.

It is there, holding bulbous hands on the dance floor, that memories of an orphaned life come tumbling back. How they carried and cared for each other: changed diapers, soiled sheets, became mommies without mommies. Forged family from no family. Ate raw onion and kasha broth from spider-cracked saucers. Rubbed their cold toes against each other like insect wings where they lay four to a cot at night. Where children arrived half frozen to death. Babies, toddlers, salvaged from crawl spaces. Nuns took them in. Nuns gave out prayers and purpose. They took communion. Took up hope. Who would come for them? Who? Who? Relatives in America. Every survivor will tell you: One day they were here, gone the next.

Nadine

VIMI BAJAJ

"Why don't you bring Ashok over for lunch?" Nadine was an anthropologist and had to get to the bottom of things. All these days and months she'd gotten a second hand account and now she wanted to see the mystery man in person. I somehow knew she'd be disappointed, but I also knew in a subtle sort of way, that not meeting her's or anyone else's expectations was to be a part of my journey.

"Wonderful! I'll tell Roger. How does noon on Saturday sound?"

The next day, Nadine and Roger shook our hands warmly and invited us in. They were expats and had lived quietly alongside my family in Delhi for the past twenty years.

"Hello hello!" Nadine led the way. She held onto Ashok's hand and asked him something inaudible. The two of them laughed and then we all settled into the living room.

Roger and Nadine were charming hosts. She asked questions and looked at us with interest, while Roger served the drinks. She was dressed in a simple blue tunic with white leggings. Her hair, which was normally tied back, was bouncy and open and had a silvery shine. Nadine's made-in-India clothing made her look active and young, though she was in her sixties. During the course of the afternoon, she flitted about from the kitchen to the dining room. She left a sweet smelling fragrance behind.

Nadine asked that I come in to the kitchen to help. She was placing warm spanakopita on a platter. "It's a traditional Greek dish." She wiped her hands on her apron. "I like him," she said, "your Ashok." She grabbed two pot holders.

"In so far as my wife's temperament is concerned," Roger was saying, "I'm at her mercy."

Muffled laughter.

Nadine picked up a heavy platter of paella while I held the spanakopita and walked toward the dining room. We sat down to lunch.

Roger was careful to offer everyone their plates of food first, before taking his. Nadine began before anyone else. I saw that Ashok was observing her from the corner of my eye.

"It's really good." I broke the small silence.

"Yes," she said. "I finally found a shop that sells gourmet cheeses. It's in a mall in Gurgaon. Run by a European of all people. Imagine that, another expat. I buy all my meats and my cheeses from him. He lets me taste everything. Wonderful man. Roger and I go there all the time, isn't that right dear?"

Roger nodded in agreement. He was her second husband. She'd left what was then Rhodesia and ran away with Roger twenty years ago, leaving two small children behind.

After we were finished, Nadine rose to clear the table. I rose as well.

"No, my dear. You two sit in the drawing room a bit while Roger and I clean up. We won't be long. Come, Roger." They had a tacit understanding, their movements a dance as they began clearing the table, swiftly picking up the dishes and the glasses and the silverware in one go.

They served dessert in the drawing room, chocolate mousse.

When we were leaving, Nadine told me to come by tomorrow. I said I would call instead, as I was very busy with work and wouldn't be available. She kissed Ashok's cheek and told him how happy she was to finally meet him.

"I really like her," he said later in the car.

The next evening, Nadine admonished. We were speaking on the telephone. She was munching on cumin crackers which she'd baked herself, she said.

"Remember, this is a battle. We can't let them win, not all the time."

She was a staunch feminist, as they say and though I was stepping into an arranged marriage, I was leaning on her heavily during that time, perhaps because of her history and how she had led her life.

She was stern, but she had the ability to soften at whim and become more engaging and womanly. It was her caprice, as they say.

These are the peculiar wonderments of life, she'd say in that impervious way, when she was more lucid and willing. Her voice was crisp and distinct and seductive. She had a strong emotional intelligence and spoke authoritatively on many subjects having to do with relationships and decision making and living in general. Sometimes she could sound self-righteous.

It was easy to imagine her with her landline phone on its long cord, which she many times put on silent during her off hours, only answering at her convenience. I could picture her wandering around the small kitchen or around the counter to the drawing room during our conversations. She liked to wear loose clothing: white sleeveless tunics over light cotton pants or leggings, which she'd brought from Fab India or Cottons or some such place or off in the lower markets from shopkeepers that she could out-bargain like a native. Her Hindi was pristine.

The only jewelry she wore was a sterling silver ring on her forefinger the size of a large bug, and a thick black string around her neck with turquoise pendant.

She was going on about rings in general and how even middle aged men wore them these days. Rings on every finger. "Garnet, crystal and tanzanite, all semi precious. I don't know why."

Some things are better left alone. I plead ignorance on these matters. But I can't help noticing these things. India is full of strange delightful matters.

"But there are also many horrors, goodness knows." How old she was in her way of speaking. And yet how progressive, in everything else. "I often tell myself, 'you know too much.' But the truth is, I don't know enough." She'd put another cumin square into her mouth and offered another apology for eating on the telephone. Her plan for living intrigued. "First you bake and then you eat. No need to serve anybody. It's only for ourselves that we live and move. I don't mean to rush, dear. But it's getting quite late."

It was almost eight at night and we'd only been on the phone for a few minutes. She guarded her time with a religious zeal.

"Winding down," she said yawning.

In fact, it was useless to talk to her at these times. Mornings were off limits as well.

This is my sacred writing time, she'd say if you happened to call her between eight and ten in the morning. *Please don't call me then*. In fact, it was better if she called you, preferably when it was time to make dinner.

We met at her house the following week. I was free from my teaching duties now that school was out for the summer. She was going on again about Alan, her first husband. "Thank heavens I came to my senses and left."

But what about him? Was he the right person to take care of the children? Shouldn't she have taken them with her?

"I realize, my dear, that after what I've just said, and all that I've told you in the past, that I might have given a one-sided impression of my first husband. He loved his children, you see, much more than he loved me. And that also, is a dangerous pickle to find yourself in, mind you. While it is true that Roger's support and encouragement are what have enabled me to write sans encumbrances all these years, that kind of attention can also be suffocating and wearisome.

There are many days when I just want to walk out. And I did once. Did I tell you? We separated for a time. He was getting too clingy. He moped. He was sullen. He could never say anything good about himself. It's very hard to live with a person like that. It makes me come across as the selfish one to others. You know, with my dietary restrictions, my adherence to my body's diurnal rhythms, all my issues. I come across as a real bitch and I know it. *Poor Roger*, everyone says. *He's such a saint*, they say, implying by their silence, the worst about me, by default."

They had separate bedrooms, her requirement, not his.

"Sleep is precious. I'm useless after eight or so. We cuddle in my room for an hour, listening to the BBC, and we're each in our beds by nine. I'm a very light sleeper. We have our own bathrooms, in fact. Mine is en suite, his is the one in the hall."

The house was an anomaly, a quaint adobe style cottage with thick walls that blocked cellular signals, a real annoyance when visiting Nadine, since you would have to stand next to a window to make a phone call. But it had its own peculiar charm and was unlike the grand mansions and havelis that towered behind private walls and had, for the most part, crowded out the smaller homes almost to extinction. The gated area was home to politicians and high ranking government officials, and was soon becoming the hub for multinational companies to take up residence by leasing space within three and four storied buildings built just for that purpose by enterprising residents.

"Very cold in the winters, almost unbearable," Nadine was saying. "I sleep with an electric blanket. The previous owners must not have had those worries; he travelled a lot for work and they lived here only half the year. It's really not built for Delhi winters. A heated floor is out of the question. I've gotten estimates. But most older homes are like that. We've wanted to trade up many times, but the house just doesn't want to let us go. It has a pull on us or something."

Why would they want to trade up? They were older, in their sixties, just the two of them.

"Actually, the prices here have really gone through the roof, as they say. I'm afraid our realtor doesn't take us seriously anymore. But no matter. The place is small, but it's just the two of us. I've gotten used to throwing things away to make room for the new. I told you about my plates?" She'd found a set of cobalt blue dinner plates to replace the bright yellow ones. "I was forced to part with them. And the same with my glassware. I had to buy matching stemware and bowls and I just threw out the other things to make way for the new. I have to be very selective with what I buy because of limited space."

She was beginning to sound immoderate.

"Not to mention the summers. Roger and I leave for the hill stations. Ooty is a favorite. Have you been? No? You must go there then, with your new husband. It's lovely. Lots of honeymoon couples."

It was from Nadine that I learned to pay heed to myself. Nadine usually called while prepping in the kitchen.

"Are you free, dear? Is this a good time?"

There was the incessant clang of pots and pans during the conversation, or the sizzle of something in a fry pan, or the rush of water when she was rinsing, presumably one of her large copper pots.

In me, Nadine had found an enduring listener, after sifting though a few others she had met over the years, fellow emigres, a collection of ever changing women from her book group, and a few of her student lackeys from her weekly drawing room talks, all of whom eluded her, after a time.

"They never like it when I multitask like this. One of them told me as much. She said she'd only talk to me if I gave her my undivided attention. Can you believe the nerve?" Another loud clanging of pots. "Sorry. I'm looking for the big shallow pan to sear my fish in. Hold on." She sneezed loudly, more like a short scream. "I just opened my spice drawer. Are you still there?"

"We had grilled pomfret on a bed of seasoned cauliflower. I made a nice tomatoey sauce to go with it. What's that you say, dear? Oh yes, the cauliflower. It's a great substitute for starch. Roger and I try to stay off carbs. We never eat rice and I can't say how long it's been since I've had any bread."

But she ate ice cream on a daily basis, sometimes even substituting it for her midday meal.

"I feel I must allow myself a few guilty pleasures. Excuse me, while I eat in your ear, Mm." Sounds of her eating and breathing and swallowing. "I've gained about three pounds."

"I weighed myself today. I lost a pound. I stopped eating so much ice cream. I was getting awful headaches again. I'm very chemically sensitive, as you know, and if it's not the right brand, well. So I just gave it up." She was munching on something. "Now I'm onto homemade chocolate chip oatmeal cookies. Have you tried them? No? Oh my goodness, you have got to try some. I'll make some for you. So delicious, my God."

Whenever I talked with Nadine, I felt self-indulgent, as if every other sentence that Nadine spoke was either a coded message to my own brain that it was all right to be so, because Nadine was, or a blatant call for conversion.

"You wouldn't like this novel I'm reading right now. It's got too much sex in it."

I remained silent and annoyed at her predictable assumptions.

"Oh? I thought you'd be offended. Well. I'll let you borrow it for a few days then."

With Nadine, I was given a license to be rakish in my thoughts, to manage a bravura without shame. A descent into an immorality of the mind, an opening of a door with a key that Nadine had provided because she had lived it. She had left a husband and two small children without so much as an afterthought, and in fact could be said to be boasting about it years later. But it had amounted, in some eyes, to abandonment, had it not?

"He's quite hot."

"Pardon?"

"Sexy, dear. Sexy. You never told me he was so sexy."

"You find him sexy?"

"Yes, don't you?"

"Of course, but, not in that way."

"In what way, then? Is there another qualifier for sexy?"

"I just think he's nice and all."

"He'll do, you mean. I see." Nadine nodded her head appeasingly.

"Well, I have to say. I've noticed a change in you." She was clamoring away with her post and pans and her wooden spoons or the spice bottles in the jammed up spice drawer. "Excuse me while I eat in your ear." She chomped on something which sounded like crunchy tuna salad, a favorite Nadine breakfast item which synched with her diet. "Hm? Why do I think that? Because you've become a little distant." More pots clanging. "Sorry, I can't find my favorite saucepan. The one with the red handle. Here it is. I'm making Roger's favorite dish, seared tilapia on a bed of swiss chard and tomatoes. Absolutely delicious. You have to try it. Oh dear, excuse me." She sneezed a short scream into the telephone. "Must be the spices." It always seemed to happen while she was cooking. "Not that I don't like it for you to have your own friends or anything. I mean I have my book group. We're meeting tomorrow at my house. But you wouldn't like it. We're always reading edgier stuff. It's not up your alley. Besides, they're women of a certain age."

"These things happen, it's nothing new. What I don't understand is why you can't see it when it's all around you. I sense your confusion, dear," she said.

We were having tea with pistachio biscuits. We sat at the little dinette. Nadine's kitchen was spacious and modern and well lit. It had a ventilation hood and the best appliances.

Redbirds frolicked in the birdbath outside.

"Didn't you see it in your parents? It's in every household, I imagine. I defy you to tell me it's not."

They were trilling and chirping and the sun shone upon them like drips of gold.

"What? Have I said something false?"

I watched as the birds fought for a spot in the birdbath.

"The male of the species is like a bull," Nadine said. "His gaze is stuck; at a certain point he is immovable. You can see his face and he is strong and he knows he is strong, as if that were the only quality worth having in this world. He smells the scent of the female and he must have her. You see, he is ready. His bull faced gaze won't leave her. And it's the same everywhere. You must have seen it. Look closely, it's everywhere. The female is receptive to all types of ill. It's like she becomes a magnet, unless she collects herself, comes on her own, so to speak, breaks away from that type of thinking, a brutish way of thinking."

Was she saying they were all that way?

"Take Roger, for instance. If left to his own devices, he would have succumbed to the general consensus. He was awakened to right thought and right action by yours truly."

How could she say that? She'd had an affair with him while they were both still married.

Nadine touched her hand and gave it a squeeze. "Don't think too hard, my dear. Plunge in. You've done enough of it. It's time to make a move." She pointed to the birdbath. "Look at the birds. They have a hierarchy. I've studied them, informally of course, here in the garden. It's not a gender based hierarchy, like ours. It has more to do with practicality and survival. It has to do with warding off danger and warnings and signals. A sound for a snake outside their nest and so forth. I've watched them. I've seen how they behave." She pouted her lips and did a birdcall, ending with a perfunctory comma at the end of the trill. "They have a separate sound for humans, one for weather, for rain and so forth. It's fascinating. I can't prove it, but I know there are research scientists that have studied it. But it's a mystery. A higher order than mere subjugation."

"The fact remains that a man can do what I did and no one bats an eye. But I never did it out of spite. It just so happened that I felt he, Alan, my first husband, could do a better job in the parenting arena. Joint custody was out of the question, it would have been the end for me. I was slipping, you see, losing who I was at my core. I had small children. We did. He owned up to the responsibility. I did not. And that is the honest truth. Now they're grown and bygones are bygones and I've attended a wedding and I absolutely have no regrets. None."

"You are denied power and then you are denied pleasure. Don't you see it, my dear? Open your eyes. It's all around."

The redbird splashed and turned in the bath, expanding first one wing and then the other, a thorough washing."

"I was becoming like that. I was becoming like her, like your sister. I was giving him the power. He began to notice a shift . It was about the time I began to get published. Small things. You know, local paper and magazines. Nothing big, but it was a start. It set me on the road. I don't know what possessed me to lift my pen. I suppose it was always there, but I never paid much attention to it; pooh-poohed it away like a bad child, until it began to eat away at me." She started sniffing, as if she had a bad allergy to something. "In those days, we'd been raised to be good wives and that was all. Well. I was not good. I was bad. I was snooping around, checking his papers, his wallet, his pockets, tracing his calls, following him after work sometimes. But it occurred to me finally, to ask myself what I was doing. What was I really doing? Why was I disrupting my peace of mind? Over whom? This man who had a chokehold over me? Why?" She spoke calmly, and without emotion. Her voice was flat. "But you know what the funny thing is?" Now she was wistful and sounded far away. "The funny thing is that he sensed what was coming, like animals can instinctively sense a natural disaster. He returned from a trip abroad, where who knows what activities he was engaged in, and I with my midlevel trust, sometimes yes, sometimes no, but I could never uncover anything. And he became the nicest he'd ever been. If I were any weaker, I might have succumbed, but I summoned all my strength and remained cynical. I did relax a bit and relished all the niceties for awhile. We did what married people do. As if that would make any difference. I was immune to him. We did all the usual things with the children, they were now five and seven. And so it went on. I waited for the pendulum to swing the other way, to the ugly side of life, the side where he was angry with me and my poor mothering skills. But he never did. Maybe that was his fatal flaw. He seemed somehow convinced of my value now. He paid me one compliment after another. It felt odd. He held my hand and put his head on my lap in the evenings. But it was too late. I had made up my mind to leave him one day. And then I remembered Roger and we had our affair, and then we left."

"I finally trusted someone with my whole heart and soul. Roger led me to see that. It was only later that I found out about his internet addiction." She said something that was not helpful. "Yes I know it's a big problem. But when it happens to you, to someone you love, I can only say, you have to be in my shoes. You begin to doubt yourself. I felt it happening all over again. I got mad. I threw his laptop into the dust bin. I slammed that heavy door in his face. I made him leave and stay at a hotel for a few days. But then poor Roger. He finally broke down and told me that his pharmacologist, oh." She broke down for a moment. "His pharmacologist, thank you." She blew her nose on the tissue. "His pharmacologist had halved his medication, and added another one."

"I knew he had done something, dear, but I couldn't prove it. I knew but I really didn't know, you know? I suspected but I had no evidence, not even a shred. Only a lack. A lack of connection, a bond with my husband. That and my own overworked imaginings were a lethal combination. I hated him. And for the longest time, I couldn't confront him. Why? Because if I was wrong? How would that look?" She began fanning herself. "On those days that he was abroad, I was in a panic. Such a state. I became delusional. Such a state. But then I found Elaine. Elaine was Roger's wife. They were a couple we had gotten to know. We had dinners together. Alan and Roger got along well enough. They had children in college. Elaine was older. I still had the traces of youth upon me."

"I felt I betrayed by these things, these events, these exclusions, these familial loyalties (though I later found out that he had never in the strict sense betrayed me with another woman or a fly by night or anything). I felt excluded from all his most meaningful relationships, like his mother, his brothers, the gang of four I called their secretive, speaking in whispers, club. Oh it was worse than anything I'd seen in any backward culture. The gang of four. Worse than any group of cackling women. Finding the worst in other people, then puffing themselves up from it. Pah. Left a bad taste in one's mouth and all that."

"So you see, it's everywhere, like a polluting cloud that darkens the skies above and makes you choke, suffocating, oppressive. We must break face, each in our own way, within the context of our lives and then one hopes, out of a revolutionary context.

But you are much more sensible. You've waited. You've discerned. I can tell. And since you've asked my opinion on the matter, I'll tell it to you. He's made a very good first impression on me. But I don't wish to sway you one way or the other. I can only tell you what I like or dislike. I don't want this to be a major factor in you decision. I can only ask that it be one of the factors. You have to go with that gut feeling. Do not deny it or you will pay for it later."

"The gang of four were blind, don't you see? They were blind the whole lot of them.

Alan remarried. He has a child with this woman and my boys have grown up. That's about all I know and all I care to know. I started a bit when I referred to them as my boys just now. I don't in fact think of them that way. I haven't had a hand in raising them. I never called, even on their birthdays. I made a clean break. I only know that it is what I have done. I do not mourn or grieve or do any such thing. I only move forward. Some revolutions are quiet revolutions. It is hard, you see, when one is born into that sort of thing? The vast majority of lives are like that.

When we were together it was never like that. I prayed daily for courage, for grace, for patience, for love, fortitude, peace, all the Christian virtues. But the one day I decided to leave. I sought out a way. Roger presented himself before me. His face. His face became the face of friendship and the way out. I was friends with both of them, you know. Elaine, his wife, knew everything, all my personal troubles with Alan, my anxieties and my weaknesses. She even knew of the gang of four. I shared all that with Elaine and she with Roger. Elaine was quite a few years older than I was, like how I'm older than you are, what is it, fifteen years? Something like that. But she was an ideal friend. Roger was also younger than Elaine, closer to my age. It was a May-December thing, only the other way round. Quite advanced for that place and time, I tell you. Roger says he respected her intellect. But nature can be very cruel. And nature was on my side back then. Roger and I became lovers. Elaine dealt with it bravely, as if she half expected it some day.

This went on for about six months. Alan was away for months at a time. I tell you it was liberating. I was no longer searching my husband's pockets. I was living my life. And do you know, my leaving became a local news story? A reporter came and interviewed me. The article was about 'the surprising trend of women leaving husbands and children behind to pursue their goals and new love.' And there was a picture of my head shot and a separate photograph of my husband and children eating dinner in our kitchen sans yours truly. I was vilified. No one could digest it. But I don't think myself a maverick. I am not a trendsetter. They were wrong about that. It was not my intention to set a new standard. Where would the world be if everyone did what I did? My case was completely different. I should have never married or had children.

One day someone recognized me on the street. Aren't you that woman, he said. That woman who left her children? In the paper? He shook his head in disgust and spit at my feet, calling me a whore and what not. I knew that day I had to leave. Roger asked his company for a transfer and we decided to come here.

I hardened myself. I'm no saint that they could bend and break, who says nothing and lets the man grow big and solid while she gets wiry with stones in her eyes. I'm not one of those."

"I remember sitting by myself, this was before Roger. The children were in school. No. There was only the one. He was in the nursery with the nanny and I was all alone in the sitting room, looking out at the golden light above the river. We had such a nice view from our house. I could see a mix of light and shadows. The trees on either side of the riverbank were dark. And there was the last of a golden light that fell on the water. Nothing stirred. It was like some dream. But I was raging inside. I wanted to scream at it. At the stillness and the light, at the river and the shadows of the trees. It was as if I was being attacked by some invisible hand, and I might be going insane. My husband was not there. He was at work overseeing things. I put myself in his shoes just then, a sort of mental telepathy, and I saw that he was breathing, doing something, and also not doing something. He was not doing something with regards to me, his wife of some few odd years. When he came home it was dinner, then a drink, and then a phone call to his mother and one of his brothers."

"There were all these little disturbances that did not let me progress down my path, that kept holding me back. So finally I said to Roger, we were married by that time, I said to him we have to leave, to go somewhere else. Isn't there somewhere we could go? Somewhere where your company might send you? I was just beginning to write, you see, and I really had no prospects before me."

Nadine pulled up her pant legs for her massage. The woman had let herself in through the back door, heated some mustard oil in the kitchen and sat down at her feet. The woman wore a prominent silver nose ring, in the shape of a flower, and when she smiled, her teeth were red orange from chewing betel nut. Her skin was brown and uniform and when she rubbed her hands with the first dab of hot oil, the palmer surfaces were pale and anemic, next to the rest of her. She began the massage in earnest, grabbing Nadine's ankle and working to the calf. At first Nadine grimaced with pain but then she relaxed with the rhythm of it. The woman's glass bracelets clinked as she worked.

"May I say one thing, dear? You must marry the right man. You must do your due diligence. Marriage is not a must, you know. In my day it was. But yet and still, it is a very viable thing, I think, for both parties."

The woman was still at her feet, now on the other leg, both of them shiny from the mustard oil. It had a rancid odor that stung your nose and made your eyes water, especially when it was worked into the flesh.

"What's that? My children? Yes, very much so, I left them with him. And I have never regretted it." She rubbed her eyes from irritation and blew her nose. "Of course, this can only be possible if the other party, you know, is willing to carry on, and usually it is the woman, but in my case it was him. And so when one is of a mind to live one's life the way she wants to live it, when one finally comes to that crucial point, well then, a decision has to be made, one way or the other. It was that way with me, you see. (I simply cannot say…)

What's that? Do I keep in touch? With my son, you mean? I've been to his wedding a few years back. Both Roger and I."

Nadine's legs had become red.

"Bas. Do hers now. Would you like a massage, dear? She's excellent. Yes, yes. Raise your pant legs, dear."

The woman left to get more hot oil from the kitchen.

"It gets the blood circulating." She became pensive. "Roger and I fell in love while we were both still married to other people."

The woman came back with the hot mustard oil.

"I had a sterilization procedure. It would have been easier for him to get fixed, and he did offer, but I insisted. I wanted no more and that meant no more. Not by him, not by anybody."

Again she was quiet.

"They will try to push things on you. They will do their best. But you must resist. First and foremost, take a kind of action within yourself.

Her face glowed in the lamplight. Her left eyelid drooped a bit, giving her an artificial look of humility, the sort of imperfection that could easily be mistaken for kindliness.

"It hasn't been quite that big of an adjustment for us. Life in Rhodesia was much the same as it is here. Servants and cooks and launderers and ladies' maids. And all of the same red tape."

We met again at the Gymkhana club at Nadine's request. She liked to have a light breakfast after her morning swim.

A group of middle aged women sat at the neighboring table. They were well dressed and raucous. It seemed they were celebrating someone's birthday with lewd gifts. Nadine rolled her eyes.

"What these females don't see is the harm they're doing. They accede to the comforts, they laugh and talk and joke in the manner of men and then they go home to the husbands that in some way, subtle or overt, run their lives. They stand in the way of progress. They show other women, women like yourself my dear, an aspect of themselves that takes away from the spirit of our efforts. It makes all of us seem small. 'There is no struggle, there is no injustice,' they say with their body language. Themselves blind, they raise daughters that men would love to pillage. More subjugation. More of that which we have seen since the beginning. This will continue on for ages and ages."

Four Poems

MELISA CAHNMANN-TAYLOR

They Kept Putting a "D" in Front of Her Name

So it spelled *Dumbell* instead of *Umbell*.
Infuriating, after she'd twice corrected
the error by email. Everyone
wants to mess with what's yours,
make an ass out of a cluster.
An umbel is an inflorescence,
but just because some flowers radiate
from a single point, doesn't give license
to butt a consonant where it doesn't belong.
Like *umbrella* she'd said, like *umbilical*.
For the umpteenth time she explained,
her name was all she really had.

How to Do Things with Words

Wedded by a husband's childhood priest
through language, "I do"

check every Sunday evening:
who on volleyball, who on AP;

who on therapy, who
on teeth cleanings, who- words

that move to hurry and wait.
"I resign," each proclaims in jest

betting by morning pronouns
have put the food away, cleaned countertops,

one calling all the shots for others.
According to morning radio mine

is the 16th state to withdraw
"divisive concepts"—*critical,*

equity, systemic, racism, disallow
even *Roe* and *Wade* from government

exams. In linguistics Austin wrote
about "infelicity," when language

barges, uncontrollable, without the least
intention of making good. *Protesters,*

legislators think, are the terms themselves,
and they, infelicitous captains, justify

chokeholds as a "last resort."
You know, holding a weeping teenager

that words *do* things. Just listen
to *narcan* and *overdose*, new

declarations of independence & pain
foretold in only two to three syllables.

America, You've Assumed Things

You still think
everything's counted
by degrees,

your language stuffed
with stolen phonemes.
What else explains mean

indifference at your
immigrants' collapse?
Some strokes or heat

others electrocuted,
flung 3000 feet
down incomplete

stadiums. Never enough
words for excess,
in your green

arenas. America,
your adages—
ass, you, me—

assume things, and you
know what they say.
—*Give Way, No Entry*—

your signs tell
only what's "yours."
Block buster state-

ments singing
contagious choruses:
out of pocket to treat

the disease. Everyone knows
your fool's measurements
are inches and feet.

Ars Poetica: it's not enough to write looking over a cliff

Devastation looms as big as high rises on the horizon,
then sits on chaise lounges watching episode
after episode, wanting to fill   old sorrows with new
     ones.

A reviewer, an acquaintance, bemoaned everyone's   "trauma
     admissions"
submissions she claimed inadmissible in Art's court.   She wor-
     ried
Pain was trying to replace   *True Talent* rather than ignite it.

Those of us comfortable, keyless,   frazzled
by car lines and the steep cost of airline tickets, want to
     read,   don't we?
Comfort wants its own poems, too.

Write pretty troubles, jazzed by caesuras, fancy   spaces
on White pages. Where one least expects   color:
demands to appear and reappear.   Taken seriously.   As Art.

It's not enough to look over the cliff if we're   not already falling.
Look at   Loneliness in the bathroom mirror.
When the series ends   almost go to sleep.

Numbed again on hard seltzer, she tired of being useless.
Until her career as a writer started to take off.
Because of cancer.

The Accompaniment

LORI TOPPEL

The boy is smaller and thinner than Sol, with heavy lashes under black eyebrows. His light eyes are noticed; his hair is a buzz cut. He stands by his father's side, holding a cell phone in a red case. He's the only child in the donut shop, where there are ten plastic tables, but most are empty. Caroline watches the father drink his coffee at the counter.

No school today? she asks the boy, and he holds out his hand to shake hers.

No school today! he says. Look at that big sculpture. He points outside the window.

She glances at the monument. Here she is, at the tip of Manhattan. On her way here from the train, she passed sculptures and stone buildings, and she thought: the end of the world has a beautiful facade.

The father says to Caroline, Hello, you are a volunteer? Thank you for coming. My name is Renzo, and I've never missed a check-in. Today my son—this is my son—wanted to come with me, and I think why not? He should see how we try to live here.

The father is clean cut, wearing a white shirt with a tan button on one cuff and a white button on the other. The boy runs across the room to a woman who must be his mother. She's talking to the group leader, a heavy woman who looks short of breath. The group leader brings the mother over to Caroline.

Mirabel doesn't speak much English, she tells Caroline. I understand you're bilingual so you can help her if she has any questions. Last month, we had dozens of volunteers, but, with so many hearings, we're spread thin, and…pfft. She spits air.

The boy turns to his mother to show her a video on his phone—Caroline hears a frenzy of guitar music—and he grins. The missing teeth, the dimples.

His mother whispers, ¡Apágalo, Gabriel!

It's September, six months after a judge ordered that the separations stop, but the situation is messier than ever. When Caroline woke up at 6:30 that morning, Raul and Sol were still asleep. She parted the curtain to check on the house across the street as if something might have been snatched away in the night. The same green shutters and the same mailbox with the American flag. Every morning, she peeks out.

Today, she didn't linger. In the bathroom, she closed the door and washed her face. She dabbed cream on her forehead and cheeks. She'd read too much and couldn't forget the numbers. How a child could be detained for 200 days, how the government had lost track of almost 1500 boys and girls, how over 400 parents were deported in one month without their kids, how parents had been told their kids were going to take a shower, yes, they'd be right back, but they were taken to a different facility, how the shelters were five times as crowded as they'd been the previous summer, how they were kept too cold to prevent the spreading of germs.

She glanced at her phone, tapped it to check the time. She bared her teeth in the mirror, brushed quickly, made a white mess in the sink. She dressed in lightweight pants and a cotton blouse. It was going to be hot. Indian summer.

On her way out, she grabbed her breakfast, a banana, thinking she'd call her grandma once she was in the city.

I'm late, I'm late, for a very important date…

These days, she's rattled. She thinks in song. A defense mechanism of some sort?

Mirabel is twenty-six, four years younger than Caroline. The two women sit by the window and make small talk in Spanish as the group waits for the last volunteer to arrive. Caroline says she's from White Plains, this is her first accompaniment, and she has a six-year-old son, not much younger than Gabriel.

Gabriel's eight, Mirabel says.

I forget how tall my son is for his age. Then again, my husband and I are big, too big.

Mirabel laughs. She can't be an inch over five feet. She wears small rose-shaped metal earrings, a drop of red against the shine of dark hair that's parted in the middle.

Where do you come from? Mirabel asks.

I grew up in Queens.

Where did you learn Spanish? Mirabel asks.

I've been taking it since third grade, and my husband's Puerto Rican. That helps.

Good to practice, Mirabel says. It's good.

But you speak well.

No, not very.

The door swings open and a slight man walks in. He's flustered. He apologizes for being late. His silver hair looks wet but isn't, his tie is loosely knotted, his shoes have been polished.

Mirabel zips up her handbag and throws out her coffee cup.

What brings each of these volunteers here? Caroline wonders as the group walks to Federal Plaza. The country's Zero Tolerance policy or something else, something personal? There's Carla Somers, a tall woman in her sixties, a florist, from the Upper West Side. This is her fourth accompaniment. There's Cindy, who didn't give her last name, a fifth-grade public school teacher. She's on crutches from having stumbled on a tennis ball in a playground. There's the latecomer, Tim Jackson, a wiry, middle-aged insurance executive. Caroline is sure he attended the same training session that she did. She feels embarrassed for him: he's struggling to communicate in Spanish to Mirabel and Renzo, telling them it's supposed to cry tomorrow.

Llorar is to cry, Renzo says, tilting his head to the side. You say llover—that's to rain. Like English, Spanish is hard.

Caroline's phone lights up. Her grandma's texting her: Did you get to city?

She texts back yes. Another text is from a work friend who can't believe she took the day off, but Caroline doesn't reply. Her boss, a well-known graphic designer, at least in southern Westchester, isn't so easy-going. She told him she had a gynecological procedure with anesthesia that morning.

Every night, she reads Sol a book, stories about doctors, firefighters, architects, and engineers. He wants to build bridges. London Bridge is his favorite. In his mind, where nursery rhymes loosely take root, London Bridge will never fall.

For days now, he has asked her to read from Alice in Wonderland. They watched the movie twice, the classic version from 1951, the bold and clean animation. Alice is blond and innocent, and Sol can't get enough of the White Rabbit, the Cheshire Cat, or the March Hare, animals who come off as impulsive or crazy. For Halloween, he wants to be the White Rabbit.

Every night, after he falls asleep, she lies beside him. On the ceiling, there are glow-in-the-dark stickers, a T-Rex, a pterodactyl, a brontosaurus. Thinking of the girls and boys in Sol's class, she imagines their faces next to the dinosaurs. Is it true the guards might taunt the children? Your father broke the law. You can't go with him. But maybe you're not even his kid. Are you?

Oh say can you see by the dawn's early light. No singing that anymore. State it.

Sometimes, after leaving Sol's room, she wanders through the house and hunts for an out-of-place thing that she can return to its proper place. Maybe the container of butter on the counter, out of the fridge.

Every night, around midnight, Sol rushes to her side of the bed, and she shifts over to give him room. He's scared to be alone, and she and Raul are right down the hall, a jump, skip, and a hop away.

There's no separation of heart and mind. None what-the-fuck ever.

The training session for volunteers took place in July at the Episcopalian Church in White Plains. The coordinator described herself as an "illegal" from El Salvador, a sloe-eyed woman with a forceful voice.

All of you will serve as witnesses for the undocumented men and women who must plead their cases in court, she said. International Refugee Law states that a government can't criminally prosecute anyone for seeking asylum, but that's what's happening. The government is prosecuting everyone now, even those families who have been here for years and haven't been able to get papers through legal channels. They're also being rounded up. Imagine this: your hearing is coming up, and you've been told to pack a small suitcase in case you're detained or deported. What would you bring if you had to leave everyone behind? It's a frightening prospect, isn't it?

The coordinator reviewed the rules of an accompaniment—Be respectful, don't pry, don't antagonize—while Caroline wondered what she might pack in a small suitcase. A hand towel, a bar of soap, hand lotion, two outfits, and the photo of Raul holding Sol like an airplane. A few granola bars, a bag of Swedish fish, red ones only, two bottles of water, a small sketch pad, pencils. Then she reconsidered, weighing towel against shawl, fish against peanuts, water against whiskey.

People were raising their hands, and the coordinator called on a woman with short white hair.

You said some people go to court because they've been charged with a crime, she asked. What sort of crimes are we talking about?

We're not free to provide that information, the coordinator said. We're not here to judge. What is your concern?

I'd have a tough time helping someone who's been accused of a violent crime, like rape, for example, the woman said.

That's the crime everyone picks. I can tell you that we've never had a rapist as a client. Most of our friends go to court for traffic violations. If you want to know all about a client, this might not be the right volunteer work for you, and we respect that.

The white-haired woman nodded, sat back down, and whispered to the man beside her, whose name, Caroline now knows, is Tim.

The coordinator took the next question. A young woman stood up and scanned the room as if she were a fan in a football stadium. She turned to the white-haired woman and said, I'm just curious. Do you feel more American than all the undocumented immigrants who have lived here for decades, all those men and women who have raised kids here, worshipped here, and paid taxes here?

The white-haired woman responded in a loud voice, louder than that of the young woman, If you've been charged with a violent crime, I don't care who you are. You can be American, Russian, or a Martian, but I'm not going to help you until you're acquitted.

She wore a black sweater, the sleeves long enough to cover her hands. With her arms crossed over her breasts, she looked as if she were in a straitjacket.

Raul is sensible. Caroline often heeds his advice, but she rarely sees him these days. He gets home late, they talk, he sometimes dozes off in the middle of a sentence, his or hers. He's a trusts and estates attorney, graduated law school a few years ago. After his first month at work, he told her that Americans take advantage of many loopholes, and a loophole, by definition, is an inadequacy.

He's from a town on the northern coast of Puerto Rico, close to a sprawling resort built by Rockefeller. For two decades, Raul's father has managed the resort's outdoor dining room. After Hurricane Maria, the resort shut down for a year, but management provided employees with generators, meals, and jobs to rebuild the resort and replant the soil. It's a pretty island, swept by trade winds, given to the United States in 1898.

She and Raul are amazed that so many people still don't know Puerto Ricans are American citizens, who, if they live on the island, can't vote for the president yet can travel freely to and from the territory. When they move to the States, they can vote. Another loophole.

After Raul had cast his first ballot in New York, he asked a stranger to take a picture of him in front of the machine. Cameras weren't allowed, but the stranger got away with it. The small photograph still hangs in Raul's office. Her grandma got it framed for him. Whenever Caroline visits Raul, and someone with heavy footsteps passes by, the photograph tilts to the left, and Raul stops whatever he's doing to straighten it.

26 Federal Plaza. Like a steel monolith held up by blocks of ice. As the group approaches the entrance, Caroline hears Tim tell Carla that over twenty activists showed up for his first accompaniment, and after the hearing, they all marched around the building seven times. It's called a Jericho Walk, he says, and it's like a prayer in action.

What's he talking about? Caroline asks Carla.

In the Bible, Tim answers, God offered Joshua, the Israelite leader, the city of Jericho and instructed him to march around it for seven days. On the last day, the walls collapsed.

Then the Israelites invaded the city and slaughtered everyone in it, Carla says, except for the prostitute who'd helped their spies. I'm pretty sure I've got that right.

Tim says without any modulation in his voice, That's a gross misinterpretation but not an uncommon one.

A Jericho Walk is a march of solidarity, the group leader tells everyone.

Tim tells Caroline, There are ways to help others heal.

Are you always this serious? Cindy asks him. I could use a little levity right now. She glides ahead, unimpeded by her crutches, to get in line for a security screening.

The group leader's air of detachment makes sense to Caroline. So many personalities and opinions. The possibility for discord is high. As sweat trickles down the back of Caroline's thighs, she watches Tim fish a white handkerchief out of his pants pocket and dab his upper lip. He isn't even perspiring.

Her legs don't match. The left one is smooth, and the right bears a long scar from her hip to her knee. Caroline thinks of the scar as alive, like a school of salmon swimming upstream to spawn in calmer waters.

Always look both ways before crossing the street, she tells Sol whenever they're in the city.

Caroline told him about the vacation she went on with her mother. They were in Bermuda, at a resort where guests rode around on mopeds. Caroline was fifteen, on her way to the beach with a girl she'd met at the pool. They found a moped with the key in the ignition. The girl dared her to ride it, and Caroline hoisted herself up on the seat, turned the key, and jolted forward. Within seconds, she fell. The bike landed like a boulder on her right leg.

Never show off, she tells Sol, and always pay attention.

At age eight, Caroline had focused on one thing: dance. She'd been accepted at a prestigious ballet school in Manhattan, a feeder school for Juilliard. Her family lived in Woodside, in a 1930s townhouse, with a small attic where mousetraps were laid out, traps Caroline used to throw out before the mice were caught. Her mother used to pick her up after school and drive her to ballet. One time, she had a shopping bag on the front seat with two dead mice inside. Sorry, she told Caroline, I forgot to dump them in the trash outside. I was rushing. I know you've thrown out my traps, which is a waste of money, but we can't have rodents living with us.

Caroline sat in the back, her head out the window, trying to fend off waves of nausea. What's wrong with a few mice?

You just focus on what you love and want in life.

Her mother was all about discipline. She made sure Caroline was always on time. Without traffic, they could get to midtown in under thirty minutes, her mother singing along to all the top hits on the radio.

By age twelve, Caroline was enrolled in Latin, ballroom, and modern dance classes. Weeks before the trip to Bermuda, she tangoed in an off-Broadway musical.

She hadn't wanted to stop dancing.

Her leg stopped her. Polly wanted a painkiller. Polly lacked confidence. She named her leg in the hospital. She pitied Polly, always lagging behind. Despite two plastic surgeries, Caroline's scar hardened like a taut rope.

When she first danced with Raul, they were at Salsa Nation in Brooklyn. She was twenty-one. The autumn trees outside the club, their leaves shining under the streetlights, matched the fiery strobe lights inside. In love with Raul, in love with his music, she felt her body becoming lighter, as it used to when she was a child practicing to Tchaikovsky and Stravinsky, Madonna and Prince, even to old movies. She'd curtsy to Fred Astaire, sing with Gene Kelly, marvel at Ginger Rogers. Gigi—watch that with me, Caroline told Raul. I was like Leslie Caron, just giddy whenever I performed. Even her grandma would put on Chubby Checkers to twist with her.

For her sixteenth birthday, her mother took her to see The Royal Ballet of Canada, and Caroline held back her tears, knowing she'd never again belong to the otherworldly species on the stage.

Months later, after her mother died of a pulmonary embolism, Caroline held back nothing. She moved in with her grandparents and cried with her grandma for days.

In a long line, removing shoes, passing through the metal detector. In a cold lobby, the thirty-foot ceiling, a white sky. A large portrait of the president in the center of one wall. Carla stops in front of the painting and wrinkles her nose.

On the ninth floor, the group meets Renzo's lawyer, a pro bono attorney. He's a middle-aged white guy, with an avuncular beard dyed black. He gives Gabriel a fist bump. The intimacy reassures Caroline. A trust touch, she thinks. The lawyer winks at Gabriel before disappearing with Renzo into the offices of ICE.

While the volunteers pause in the hall, the group leader pokes her head into the waiting room, and says, I'm told we can't sit in there. It's too crowded but go see for yourself. In any case, let's wait in the cafeteria.

Has this ever happened before? Carla asks.

Not to me, but I've heard it's been happening. They don't want the families nearby; they don't want us nearby.

I thought the whole point was to stay close to Renzo. Carla shakes her head. I'll sit in on a hearing up here, wherever I can get in. I'll find you later.

Caroline peeks into the waiting room. Five people are sitting in one corner. Over a dozen seats remain. On a television mounted high on the wall, the debate on healthcare policy drags on.

Gabriel pulls on her elbow. He wants to know what she's doing. When Mirabel glances into the room, she takes a few photos with her phone, ruffles her son's hair, and asks if he's hungry. Then she and Gabriel take the stairs to the cafeteria.

Caroline is about to pay for her coffee and jelly donut with a ten. There's an ink smear across Hamilton's eyes that looks like a mask peeling away. She gives the cashier another ten and tucks the stained bill in the back of her wallet.

She doesn't need the donut. She's too young to be pre-diabetic, but she is. Raul never eats donuts, calls them devilish delights. At home, after sitting at the computer for hours, he'll drop to the floor, do fifty push-ups, twenty burpees, and a hundred jumping jacks. She hadn't ever heard of a burpee until she met him.

The volunteers find a table, and Tim takes the seat across from Caroline. On his tray, there's an egg salad sandwich and a pint of chocolate milk. His cup, plate, napkin, and plastic utensils are arranged as if he's about to be tested on the rules of etiquette. He picks up the sandwich and says, Last time I was here, the client was very popular. Two congresswomen came to support him.

Why so popular? Cindy asks.

Tim finishes chewing before he answers. In this world, it's often about who you know.

Avoiding the question—happens when you feel uncomfortable, Caroline thinks. She glances at a nearby table where three women are talking. No, they're barely women. They're in their late teens, should be at school. She asks the group leader, How long do you think Renzo will be?

There have been days I've waited for eight hours, she says. Let me see what I can find out.

Gabriel slips off his seat to approach Caroline. Do you want to play a game?

Sure, what game?

Prove Me Wrong, he says and scrambles up to share her chair. Mirabel tells him to get his own, but Caroline says it's fine and scoots over.

On his phone, he shows her a photograph of Renzo holding a fishing pole. My dad, he says. Then he finds a photo of another man, older than his father, standing alongside a young girl in pigtails, an open market behind them. That's my uncle and cousin. I don't know them.

You've never been to Guatemala?

I'm made in America, he says and flashes a smile that would land him a role in a Disney film. He moves closer to her. I promised I'd be quiet. Let's whisper.

He loads the game and explains that, on his turn, he must answer five questions. If she challenges him, and he can't prove he's right, he loses. He answers every question correctly, and a feisty female British voice congratulates him for acquiring twenty extra points. He jumps up and dances for a few seconds, and Caroline and Cindy laugh.

I win, he says.

Mirabel tells Gabriel they should walk around, Cindy announces she needs more tea, and Caroline tries the donut, hoping it will be as stale as the coffee so she won't eat it. The glaze is sticky, the donut not soft. She pushes away the plate.

Tim says, I think I might have seen you at the training session in White Plains.

Yes, I remember you.

Then you must also remember Freida, my wife. She raised some eyebrows with her questions.

She had some reservations about volunteering, Caroline says. Under the bright light, Tim's lightly freckled forehead reminds her of a robin's egg.

My wife is tough, but I empathize with her point of view although I don't necessarily agree with her. I believe in what St. Augustine thinks: although we might succumb to corruption, we are, nevertheless, good. If there's not a shred of good in someone in the first place, he or she can't be corrupted.

I'm not sure about that, Caroline says. She has never heard of St. Augustine.

You believe some men are inherently evil, as Frieda, my wife, does? You don't think a strong will or rehabilitation can save a damaged soul? Yet here you are. You don't know if Renzo has ever been accused of harming someone in the past. Your ignorance permits you to have faith in him.

Caroline gets up and says, You have no idea what I know or why I'm here. Excuse me, I have to make a call.

As Caroline steps into the hall, Gabriel skips past her into the cafeteria.

My baby just cares… Nina Simone sneaking into her head. This song, that song, anytime, anywhere. Like the hiccups.

In the hall, the air seems too thick. The world outside, the one Caroline left that morning—Raul scrambling eggs for Sol's breakfast—feels irretrievable. That time Sol asked for green eggs and ham, and she didn't have green food dye, only blue, so she made him blue eggs, and he was delighted. She wants to return to the kitchen, to her husband and son.

What if Raul or Sol were to get hurt while she's here? She thinks of a close friend of Raul's, also Puerto Rican, who was recently stopped by ICE. He had left his wallet, with his driver's license, at home and was taken to the station to verify his immigration status. I'm American! he shouted. Why are you putting me through this? And Raul later told Caroline, He should know better than to yell at anyone in a uniform.

Do you think you're more American…?

Young American, young American.

She thinks of the ten-year-old Venezuelan girl who died recently in federal custody at the border. She had the flu, wasn't treated. Wasn't the first child to die.

Down the narrow hall, Caroline sees Mirabel on the phone, crying quietly. Has she heard something, or could it be nerves? Caroline drinks from the fountain, thinking she'd like to comfort Mirabel but also wants to respect her privacy. The stream of water shoots up, splashes Caroline in the eye, and she wipes it dry with the heel of her hand. She returns to the cafeteria where Gabriel is standing next to Tim's chair.

The kid's a champ. I can't beat him, Tim says. His smile is tight.

Caroline's hands are clammy. She pretends to want something at the counter but returns to the hallway. Carla has reappeared. She's with the group leader who's talking to Mirabel, and Caroline's legs feel like switchgrass in a storm.

She's in a chair, in the cafeteria. Cindy's at her side, offering her a cup of water. Are you better now? You turned as white as a ghost.

Caroline puts her head between her knees, stares at her worn black sandals.

Everything's okay, the group leader says. You'll be okay.

Cindy says, Everything's great. Renzo is going home. He'll come back next year, but isn't that great news?

Thank God, Caroline whispers, something she never says. She feels as if she's being poured back into her body.

Tim, who's sitting close by, asks if she needs anything. No, she doesn't. She apologizes for any trouble she might have caused and looks around for Mirabel. The cafeteria is crowded and noisy. In the corner, Carla is talking to Gabriel, who is on Mirabel's lap, resting his head on her shoulder, the phone in his hand. Caroline manages to walk over to Mirabel and tells her she's happy for her. Gabriel glances up at Caroline, his heavy lashes closing over his eyes, and says, Thank you. God bless you.

Yes, it's good news, Mirabel says. But are you okay? Sit down, no?

I got so lightheaded. I don't know why.

You probably didn't eat enough, Carla says. When you're dealing with a stressful situation, it's important to feed yourself.

Maybe so. Where's Renzo? Caroline asks her.

The men's room, I think. I'll be back in a sec, Carla says.

I'll go with you, Caroline says. I need the restroom.

Wait! Gabriel is on his feet. Picture time! He instructs his mother to stand and Caroline to sit. Now you're the same size, he says. Then I'll take pictures of everyone.

Enough photos, his mother tells him and strokes his head.

Near the restroom, a small group has gathered. Caroline counts those crying: two young women and an older man who looks to be in his fifties. A security guard orders everyone to head downstairs. The hallway can't be blocked, he says. A fire hazard.

Do you know what's going on? Caroline asks a woman beside her.

I heard that gentleman's wife was just deported, she says, her chin pointing to the older man. I swear…I feel like I'm in the goddamn Twilight Zone.

The group leader pushes past Caroline and talks to someone in uniform who's shepherding a few women and children toward the elevators. A young girl starts bawling. A rash of heat spreads through Caroline's body. She looks for the older man, he's by the elevator, he's staring at the floor. He has brown hair, flat curls that appear to be drawn on his forehead, and a light mustache. He wears a cornflower blue shirt. Vermeer's blue—lush and indelible. Almost the blue of twilight, of hanging in between.

So late in the afternoon and not a touch of humidity. It feels like another day altogether. Caroline passes Foley Square and stops in front of a sculpture that is shaped like a ship. The Triumph of the Human Spirit. The placard says the sculpture was built on top of African burial grounds, where slaves were interred from 1625 to 1827. Up close, the sculpture reminds her of a tall dancer in arabesque.

She gets on the subway, longing to get home. There's one empty seat near the bathroom. She considers moving up the train to find a seat near a door, to get off the train if she suddenly feels dizzy again, but she's tired and sits by the bathroom. I'm late, I'm late…She closes her eyes, picturing the older man in the cornflower blue shirt, and dozes off. At Grand Central, she takes the train to White Plains and makes her way down the crowded platform. Going down the stairs to the garage, someone walks up to her. It's Tim, Tim saying hello.

Oh, hey, she says, surprised to see him, I thought you lived in Mount Kisco.

I do, but I'm meeting Freida, my wife, for dinner at the Turkish place in town. His briefcase hangs from his shoulder, his hand covering the lock. He's flushed.

Caroline says, You have a good night.

Her right leg feels stiff from sitting around all day, and she wants to get home to stretch. Thankfully, she's parked on the first floor. As she approaches her car, she glances at a heap of food scraps by the wall—the mild stench of decay. That's when she sees Tim again, coming in from the street.

Caroline, he says, I'm glad I caught you. I can't find a taxi. Is this your car? Would you mind giving me a lift to the restaurant?

She doesn't want his company. I'm sorry, she says, but I've got to get home. I'm late as it is.

Two young men pass her. She's tempted to stop them, engage them, so Tim will go away.

I see, Tim says. I'm glad you're feeling well enough to drive.

I'm fine.

May I ask you something?

What's up? She steps back.

Why don't you trust me? I imagine you'd give Renzo and Mirabel a ride. You'd trust them over me. That's the trouble with people like you. You love the underdog. I volunteer because I have faith in people, that's all. I believe in second chances even though I know nothing about the clients we support, like Renzo.

I'm not sure why you're talking about him, but I've got to go now.

Pressing the briefcase to his chest, Tim says, You must realize that although Renzo lives a quiet life, he also lives in the shadows. Even if we tried to find out more about him, it would be hard, but anyone can look you up, or me, for that matter. Maybe you read about me last year. The story was all over the local papers. Maybe that's why you have an attitude about me.

I don't know what you're talking about, Caroline says and unlocks the car door with her remote key.

That's why you won't give me a lift, isn't it? You must have read about me, but you realize the charges were dropped. You read about that, too, I hope. That's why Freida, my wife, is on my side.

Caroline gets in the car, turns on the ignition, and the locks snap down. The wetness at the back of her knees. She looks in the rearview mirror, about to put the gear in reverse, but Tim is standing too close to the car. She swings open the door, plants her smooth leg on the ground, and says, Get the fuck out of my way. I told you I'm late.

Back in the car, about to dial 911, she checks the rearview mirror again. He's gone. She shifts into reverse.

Raul brings home Peruvian-Thai takeout. She burns her tongue, the chicken still hot, and stares at her plate. Raul is picking out the white meat for Sol. With her chopsticks, Caroline stabs at the string beans, thinking about Tim, red-faced and rambling on about charges—what charges?

What's wrong with the string beans? Raul asks her.

Nothing, they're so green, greener than usual.

Your Mom's being a little weird, he says to Sol.

Sol smiles. He's in his Batman pajamas, the only pjs he wears these days. From the other room, he fetches something to show her, a robot he made from pieces of macaroni, stuck on cardboard. A typical kid's robot, she thinks, boxy, antennae ears. But the eyes—they're human-like. Little blue donuts on two globs of translucent glue.

He's just like me, so clever, Raul says and asks Caroline about her day. She reaches out and touches him under one of his eyes where his fatigue swells. The man we were accompanying went home with his family, she says. So that's good.

Sol folds his hands in prayer and whispers, Gracias a Dios.

That's Raul's doing. Before bed, before dinner, after a flight to Puerto Rico, after Sol's fever has broken, Raul thanks God. Sometimes he'll even say it in good fun while buttering a slice of toast or stamping an envelope.

She has taught Sol other things. Drills disguised as games—drills she never had to learn as a child—in case a madman starts shooting. Whenever she and Raul are on a bus or subway, they pretend to play hide-and-seek.

Time for bed, Raul announces.

She ruffles her son's hair, something she rarely does, and he says, Stop, that tickles.

Once again, she reads to him. Alice is chasing the White Rabbit down the hole. He falls asleep within minutes, but she doesn't stay with him and doesn't wander through the house. She gets into bed. Why was she so lightheaded in the city? Next time, she'll have a big breakfast and bring her own water bottle.

She hears Raul in the shower. He likes to take his time. Tonight, she hopes he doesn't. She picks up her phone from the night table. There's a text from Mirabel thanking her with two emojis, a heart and an American flag, that includes the photo Gabriel took of them.

Caroline begins her search on Google. The results appear quickly: two articles in local papers. She reads the first one, puts down her phone, shakes out her hands and is shaking them hard when Raul soft-shoes toward her.

Hey, what's wrong? He sits beside her on the bed. Your client wasn't detained. His hands hold hers, quiet them. What are you doing? Tranquila, Carolina.

Drops of water, a patina on his stomach, his eyes pushing into her, the way they do when he's about to seduce her.

But there was another family, she says, and the mother, the wife—I don't know—she was deported a few hours ago. Also, there was this man, another volunteer, but I can't talk about him right now. Everything feels wrong. I've been hearing songs in my head for days now. I can't tell you how unsettling it is.

But that's a good thing. You're dancing in your head. Tell me, what are you listening to now? He lies down beside her.

You, she says, just you.

Almost midnight, and Nina Simone is back in Caroline's head. That sweet and sassy My Baby Just Cares for Me.... Her mother knew all the lyrics by heart. Caroline can only hear the chorus for the umpteenth time. She rests her hand on Raul's shoulder. He's been asleep for a while. When his body feels this hot, she knows he's in a deep place, possibly dreaming. Soon she hears Sol running down the hall. He slows down as he gets closer to her side of the bed, waits for her to shift over, to give him enough room. There—where the sheets are already warm.

Ms. Beaver

ANNA MARIA JOHNSON

For much of the summer, my husband has been spending the evenings with another woman. After supper, or sometimes even instead of eating, he makes his escape. Steven shoulders a blue plastic kayak, crosses the road, and puts in on the upstream side of the low-water bridge on the North Fork of the Shenandoah River. There's very little planning and prep work; he just disappears for a few hours.

For weeks he's been stalking beavers who live in a bankside lodge: a simple mound of branches piled in a heap a little way upstream from our house. He thinks they live with a houseful of noisy kits because of the squeaks and yelps he hears when he paddles past their simple bank lodge and because at least one of the beavers has visible nipples—evidence that she is a nursing mother. Under normal circumstances, according to Ben Goldfarb's book *Eager: The Surprising, Secret Life of Beavers and Why They Matter*, male and female beavers are notoriously difficult to tell apart cept by scent; only when nipples are visible can the novice beaver-observer be sure about her sex.

Each night around 7:40, Ms. Beaver paddles from her home to forage. When she returns after an hour or two, another beaver ventures out to eat. Based on his observations, Steven thinks the two beavers may be a mother and older child who are raising this year's kits together. When he passes by their lodge, he hears yelps like the sound of kits, and he has seen at least one baby. Our own children, ages eighteen and twenty, are transitioning away from home, so I imagine Steven takes comfort in seeing the young beaver family.

Steven, a conservation photographer, recalls another beaver six years ago whom he witnessed grooming herself in the sunlight. She had reached her claws into her glands somewhere near her lower abdomen to collect oily secretions, then applied them carefully all over her fur. He described her as resembling a woman performing her skin care routine or like a Degas painting of a woman toweling off beside a tub. He said that when he watched her, he felt as if the veil between himself and nature had been lifted.

One night, feeling a little jealous, I decide to go out with him to watch the beaver ladies. The night is warm after a summer's day, but not too hot on the water. Steven helps me carry my kayak across Route 259, an awkward, vision-obstructed endeavor. Every time, I expect I will be hit by a semi-truck hurtling at 70 mph. Steven sets my kayak down upon the shoulder then dashes back for his own kayak.

We put in on the shallow river. Since it hasn't rained much this summer, the river is so low that it's only knee-deep most places, so we have to paddle shallow. As soon as I am floating on water, I wonder why I don't do this every night, too. It's quite peaceful and beautiful, so long as you ignore the sound of the traffic. If you are reading this, know that if you are driving along a river and see a couple of folks kayaking in the river, you don't need to honk your greetings at them.

Almost immediately, the first thing I notice are the *Odonata*—damselflies and dragonflies flicking the surface and having orgies on nearly every floating leaf. A mated pair of damselflies, each the size of a darning needle, lands on my arm. The male is bright blue with large, indigo eyes set close together, while the female is light sage with greenish eyes. I could see why people used to call them "blue darners" and imagine why folks feared they could stitch an unsuspecting summer napper's eyes shut. These two, however, pose no harm as they are busily focused on making the next batch of damselflies. Soon they flit off, only to be replaced by another pair with nearly identical color patterns—the lovely, muted sage green female clasped firmly by her bright metallic indigo companion. The evening light twinkles over the waters, rendering the river's blues, greens, and browns a golden-edged Vermeer.

Steven catches my attention as we near the beaver lodge. Nearby swim a water snake, a musk turtle, and a wood turtle. The beaver lodge isn't what I had pictured based on my knowledge of children's book illustrations; it is more like a tangle of branches in the roots of a large eastern sycamore. But I hear the yips and cries of what we hope are baby beavers from within, and we glimpse a swimming mother paddling away from the din like she is escaping domesticity for a little me-time.

Based on our observations and our reading of beaver books, we believe Ms. Beaver lives in a household with her weaned juvenile child of 1-2 years and newborn kits, with the juvenile helping to care for the newest litter. The mama and juvenile take turns swimming out to forage, leaving all the kits in the care of the other for an hour or two of peaceful grazing. Forgive my anthropomorphism, but it sure appears to me that Ms. Beaver enjoys her autonomy away from the children while she observes life along the river.

The beaver family home, Steven surmises, includes a family of muskrats as well. Sometimes he must closely examine his photographs to determine whether the smaller creatures near the lodge are beaver kits or muskrats. I am not sure how their cohabitation works; do they have separate apartments for beavers and muskrats? Do the beavers view the muskrats as vermin, or as neighbors? Is there commensalism involved?

I imagine that if I could hold my breath long enough, I could swim under the lodge and peep through the branches to see how the table is laid for tea.

Steven recalls seeing a different mother beaver six years ago paddling along the river with two of her kits riding along behind, perched on her broad, flat tail as if it were a raft. What a way to first experience the broad, bright world! Not too different, perhaps, than human children whose parents bring them along on errands to the grocery store and credit union—little hands clinging to coattails and apron strings. I picture our own children as if they are little beaver children dressed in pinafores and bonnets like Beatrix Potter characters.

Steven recalls how the beaver kits of six years ago were wide-eyed and curious, unafraid, while the parents seemed skeptical, cautious, wary. When the kits played in the river, the parents swam in circles around them, patrolling for danger.

We remember doing the same when our daughters were young. In any new place, Eliza, our eldest, would eagerly explore, testing boundaries and reaching for electrical outlets, climbing bookshelves and couches, naive of the horrors that could befall her at any moment. We constantly ran circles around her, blocking off stairs and other dangers, keeping her safe from harm. Then we had a second child, and we dared not relax for years.

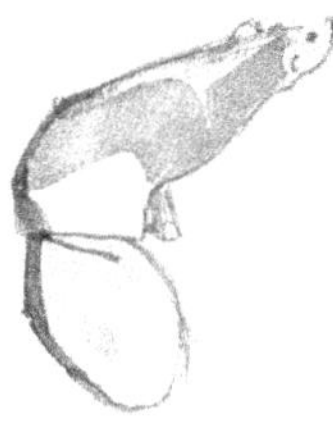

Tonight, on the river, both of us away from the responsibility of kits, Ms. Beaver eyes me directly, sizing me up. I feign less interest than I feel, blinking my eyes slowly, and turning my head away. This is a strategy that has worked well in the past with house cats, so I assume it might also work with beavers. I cease paddling and let the kayak float harmlessly while Ms. Beaver assesses the situation.

I must have passed muster because, for the next quarter-hour or so, she paddles a little distance ahead of our kayaks, sometimes swimming back toward our direction when she outpaces us. I feel that her curiosity toward us is as great as ours towards her, and at the same time, that she has plenty of confidence in her ability to protect herself from danger.

Steven remarks that the beavers he has watched and photographed over the years have taught him about boundaries and respect. "The adult beavers," he says, "teach me the limits of their comfortability. I slowly, cautiously approach, and if I get too close, I am rewarded by a big slap of the tail! When I was finally able to get through a photo session without a tail slap, I knew I had learned to recognize their boundaries and what they have tolerance for." His words sink into my mind like a stone in the river.

Over the course of our twenty-plus years of marriage, Steven and I have had ample time to negotiate boundaries and practice respect. It has not been easy as we both came from family systems where boundaries had—in some cases—not been well-maintained. This man and I both value autonomy yet crave deep and meaningful connection. We married young and had our first child barely a year later, meaning that, for many years, neither of us had quite as much space nor as many resources as we might have preferred. We've had to develop our own personal cues and signals—the slapping of words or silences.

Now, in just a few weeks, for the first time since our beloved offspring came into the world, more autonomy than I dared to dream of will be opening up, and I am not sure how to feel about it. Our youngest will be heading off to college. What will my life mean if each day doesn't focus around my children? What other identities might I find within me besides that of mother, and might I like them? Will Steven and I still find enough to connect us without the shared project of raising our children? Can I remember the long ago dreams we shared before our children became our universe? How will I cope with the pain of missing my daughters when, so soon, both will no longer be living with me on a daily basis? The silver lining of the COVID-19 pandemic has been having my young adult children home more than I had expected during these past eighteen months, but now as life blessedly returns to semi-normal, my daughters will go off into the world to seek their fortunes.

Pressing pause on my mental vortex, I glance at the man with whom I have shared my entire adulthood from age twenty-one—exactly half my life. At age forty-eight, he still has a similar physique as when we first met, thanks to the hours mucking around in rivers and ponds and wandering forests and fields. The evening sun hits his graying beard and lights up his brown eyes still holding the wonder of a child. I am reminded of the times together before marriage and children, when we canoed on a Maine lake, and I steered while he photographed dragonflies and damselflies; when we watched amazed and horrified by a pair of turtles mating violently in Moss Lake in western New York; when I got eaten alive by mosquitoes in a Georgia swamp while he was filming me for a grad school art project, and we both laughed when my gynecologist reprimanded us for hanging around mosquitoes while I was pregnant.

I know now—just as I knew then—that no matter what stage of life, we'll always have this together: this lifelong project of observing the natural world, discerning how to make our home within it, and documenting it in texts and images.

Ms. Beaver's furry body is smooth and svelte in the river like an Olympic swimmer or a dolphin. Her wet brown fur reveals her sculpted body structure, reminding me of the soft rounded curves of river rocks or of the eddies that flow around them. She glances at me now and then, eyes alert but not afraid.

Something—I don't know what—spooks her, and she dives, tail slapping the water like a bellyflop. I think we've lost her, but soon she appears alongside us, her body submerged but completely visible beneath the golden-lit river water. Brown, supple, sensuous. I am mesmerized by her movements and time seems to cease flowing. There is just Steven, me, and this mysterious other creature investigating our presence.

When we come to a deep place, she dives contentedly and swims smack-dab between our two kayaks, turning her head to keep watch on us both. This surprises me more than anything so far; I would not think she'd want to be surrounded. She must trust us, or trust herself, enough to follow her curiosity to the place where she can observe us both, her view unobstructed. There are maybe ten feet between Steven's kayak and mine, with Ms. Beaver between us, so close I could probably touch her with my paddle. I hold my breath a little, noticing the dragonflies and damselflies which alight on my vessel and my arms every few minutes, then dance airborne in a pas de deux as they fulfill life's purpose.

Soon Ms. Beaver swims to the other side of Steven's kayak and finds her way to a muddy bank covered with a large willow tree and young willow shoots. She hauls herself out of the water like a mermaid, revealing hips much wider than I had imagined. The wide hips shimmy not ungracefully as she waddles up the bank, selects a desirable willow shoot, then carries it back to the water to eat. Out of the water, she is startlingly large—the size of a largish dog. She probably weighs north of forty pounds.

Her upper body out of the water, she dunks the willow a few times as if to wash it, then begins munching, making little beaver-chewing sounds as she efficiently devours the leaves. When she finishes the shoot, she tosses the remaining twig into the river, then hauls herself onto the bank again to fetch a new shoot. Again, she takes the shoot back into the water to eat it, keeping the leaves wet as she munches. She leaves some untouched, seeming to select the tastiest ones only. It is apparently very important that the leaves be very wet while she is eating. Her teeth and chubby cheeks are as adorable as a stuffed animal's, but her expression is serious, and I would never dare to talk to her in a cute voice as I would to baby animals. This woman is all business.

After eating three shoots in her accustomed manner, she comes back for a swim. Just when I think she may have finished eating, she simply chooses another site along the riverbank for fresh willow. After a few minutes of journeying upstream, she spots another healthy willow tree and hauls herself out to select fresh shoots. This time, she eats only two. Then back to the water.

I wonder if our presence disturbs her in any way, but Steven says he has never seen her so relaxed and comfortable. I wonder what she thinks about the human man in the blue kayak who shares her river most evenings, and what she thinks about the companion he has brought this time. What do beavers think? I can't guess. What I can tell you for sure is that beavers like to eat willow. And they appear to enjoy the quest for willow as much as the process of eating it. I can also tell you that beavers are noisy eaters, like you may have seen in cartoons. With each nibble, she smacks her lips loudly enough that I hear every tasty morsel from a couple of kayak-lengths away.

When we get to the place with small rapids, Steven turns to me and says, "From here, she does one of two things. She either goes up on the bank to forage, or she climbs up the rapids. If she picks the rapids, we can get out and portage to follow her."

Tonight, to our joy, she picks the rapids. When I say the word "rapids," you may be picturing something from Yellowstone with whitewater and danger. This is not what it is like here. The Shenandoah is narrow like a creek and the rocks form something like a small flat waterfall. It's more like creek walking than navigating rapids upstream.

Ms. Beaver resembles a bear cub as she carefully picks her way along the rocks upstream. It is hard not to think of her as a small person in a costume. We watch her, speechless, until she is comfortably past the rocks and again swimming. Steven has the presence of mind finally to portage his canoe up the rocky water, and I follow.

I feel sure we have lost her by now. My portage is far less graceful and efficient than our lady's dexterous movements. Steven moves smoothly in his water-appropriate Chaco sandals. My muck boots, however, quickly fill with water so that small puddles are attached to my feet. I galumph like the awkward land mammal I am and tumble (wetly) back into the kayak.

It isn't long before we glimpse her swimming past us again. If she had wanted to lose us, she could have easily done so. But she seems to be purposeful in allowing our company. I could describe my new acquaintance in three words: svelte, confident, and thicc (as the young women say in 2025).

After perhaps an hour-long communion with our lady beaver, we decide it is time to return home. We steer the kayaks so that they point downstream and float, barely needing to paddle except to steer. On our return, we see a musk turtle, its back coated with a thick blanket of moss as if it is trying to grow a new world on its back. The damselflies flick about the air in tandem as the stream of life flows ceaselessly on. Back at the bank lodge, we pause briefly to listen to the yipping kits. But they are quiet now.

Artwork: Photography, *Beaver* by Steven David Johnson; Illustrations, *Beaver I*, *Beaver II*, *Beaver III* by Anna Maria Johnson

The Spell

MARIJA STAJIC

We drove over a cobblestone alley, passing front and back yards with chickens and pigs roaming around, and leashed dogs barking after us as if begging to be freed from a lifetime of slavery. There were trucks parked there, and tractors and haystacks, and strawberry gardens, plum orchards and more fields, some of them infant with nothing but tilled earth that smelled of a thousand potted plants. We reached the end of the alley, "the blind end," in Serbia, not "the dead end," and Mirjana parked in front of a green gate with barbed wire and steel spikes. It was quiet there, no dogs, no chickens.

"We're here. Bring Travis' things," Mirjana said.

I grabbed up a Ziplock bag from the back seat.

The click and the beep of Mirjana locking her car made me wince.

"Yeah, somebody's going to steal your car here. The deer and the wolves," I said.

Mirjana ignored my sarcasm and focused on opening the gate.

"Ring", I said.

"There's no bell."

She searched up and down the gate, felt her way around the lock like a professional thief and found a hook. She pulled it up and voila, the door opened as if we had said Sesame. She pushed it in and showed me through. I now stood on the other side, holding my Ziplock bag, with my purse nabbed into my ribs as if I were in the middle of Tangiers.

"I don't like this... something about it."

"Give me a break," she said. "Nobody's going to bite you. It's just an old lady, with some spells."

She strolled into the yard and I waited behind, like a child in front of a dentist's office. She walked up the concrete stairs and knocked three times. It was a two-level house with a basement and no second floor, but with steel poles sticking up, tearing the sky and impaling the naïve birds, as if somebody planned on building up then ran out of money or out of life. The door opened with a long screech, and I saw Mirjana talking and waving me over. She leaped inside and the dark space beyond the door swallowed her, and all I saw after Mirjana's dark head of hair were white, spider web-like strands and a black headscarf.

I followed gingerly, I had to, Mirjana was there for my bene-fit, or so I believed. The door was left open for me and I walked in, wide-eyed, shoving my purse deeper into my ribs. Behind a white curtain on the left, hung from the doorframe's wooden rod, Mirjana sat at a dining table with a woman who looked about eighty years old.

"Baba Dusanka, this is my best friend Ana," Mirjana said, pointing her whole upward-facing palm at me. I drew my cheek muscles into a smile.

"Come in my poor child, come in, don't be afraid, Baba Du-sanka is here to help." She got up and I heard her bones popping. I sat in the chair next to Mirjana's, and placed my purse on the host's hand-woven doily-style tablecloth. Dusanka pet my head three times.

"Coffee?" she asked. "Sugar?"

Mirjana handed Dusanka her own sturdy plastic bag, trans-parent, with half a kilo of ground Turkish coffee, a white paper bag of sugar, a bag of flour, a bottle of rakija, and one red thou-sand-dinar bill at the bottom of it all.

"Rakija," I requested. Mirjana beamed at me and said "same here," and in ten seconds Baba Dusanka placed a shot glass in front of each of us, and a bottle of green liquor swimming around one single herb.

"Ziveli," she said, and poured the contents of the third glass right into her own mouth like medicine.

Mirjana and I looked at each other and giggled. We both sipped rakija, which tasted bitter and smelled as strong as a ninety-proof bottle of rubbing alcohol, as something they used in hospitals in the States to disinfect wounds. My mouth shrank as if I had eaten a bowl of starch, and my throat burned. I had another lick out or respect and fear and that was it. Dusanka of course downed her second glass without a frown or a squint. She got up and walked into her kitchen behind a wooden bar, and came back with a large metal bowl. She took the flour out of Mirjana's giftbag, and poured some into the bowl, about two spoonfuls. She then swirled the flour around, holding the bowl with both of her hands, in practiced movements and purposeful joint swerves while staring at me. She then began her analysis.

"What's your husband's name?"

"Travis," I said, as obediently and without hesitation as I was indeed seeing a doctor for a serious condition.

"Tre?"

"Travis."

"Tra…I can't say that. It sounds like grass. Foreign?"

I nodded. "American."

She hummed and nodded as if it all now made sense. As if only Americans left their wives for younger women.

"And his mistress?"

"What about her?"

"What is her name?"

I looked at Mirjana. "I honestly don't know and I don't want to know," I said.

"You poor child," Dusanka said, still twirling and shaking the flour bowl. Then she began to hum. She stopped abruptly, as if she remembered something important.

"Children?"

And there it was. The inevitable question for any married woman.

"No children."

She stared at me with her pink webby eyes. She began to shake the flour again.

"How long were you married?"

"Ten years."

"Why no children? You couldn't? He couldn't? You could have adopted, you know. Plenty of unwanted little souls out here, God help them."

"I didn't want any."

Dusanka stopped her bowl magic and looked deep into me. She squinted and blinked as if I were the Lock Ness Monster at the very least, a mythical creature she didn't know existed. Not only mythical but evil, because, by Serbian unwritten law, two children were the meaning of life. Three were socially acceptable. But zero or four? There was something wrong with you. Especially if your number was zero. Not physically wrong. The worst kind. Head-wrong.

"Why?" she asked, searing my retinas with hers. I began to shiver, cold all of a sudden. I zipped up my jacket.

"I was…I am…afraid."

She kept staring down my eyes, piercing them with pity.

"Of what my child?"

I looked at Mirjana, who was dead serious. I looked down at Dusanka's dirty carpet, with animal hair and breadcrumbs and dry mud. I wondered if she had any children why were her floors dirty, why was her headscarf old and washed out and torn at places, why were her nails long and black, her palms blistered and dry like firewood, why her stockings had holes in them, why her whole house smelled of mold and decomposing meat, why could one barely see through her gray-yellow curtains and her coal soot-covered windows. Why were there no pictures of grandchildren framed and hung on the walls.

"Of what? What are you scared of?" she repeated.

"Of never being whole again," I whispered.

Dusanka brought us into her "study," and by study, I meant an unheated, unpaved and unpainted room where she threw the flour against the wall, then analyzed it. Most of it, by the laws of gravity that existed even in Serbia, fell on her cracked bricked floor. But some of it stuck, but I was pretty sure it was because the walls were damp. Everything smelled of mold, an ancient mold, a mold whose great grandchildren lived in that room. Mold and years of unwashed bleached white flour.

She placed a pair of heavy reading glasses on her nose, glasses that made her eyes look like a cartoon character, and began reading the flour, studying it as if under a microscope. She ran her fingers over the white cracks in the concrete and studied the shapes the flour made on the floor. I stood there looking at Dusanka, then glancing at Mirjana who shrugged her shoulders and silenced me with her finger at the same time, as if we were in church and I was about to shout, in the middle of a service, that God is a hoax.

Ten minutes of flour reading ritual and I got antsy. I shifted my weight from foot to foot, scratched my scalp, pulled at my cuticles. Mirjana grabbed my shoulder, steadying me. I stopped fidgeting and placed my palms on my thighs, trying to stop my legs from having a life of their own. Then Dusanka turned toward us, removed her "ashtray" glasses, placed them in top right pocket of her wool cardigan, and showed us back into her dining room.

We sat down again, in the same chairs, waiting for the verdict and the cure that should follow.

Dusanka clasped her hands on her crummy tablecloth and twirled her thumbs. Then she spoke in a deep and solemn voice.

"As I thought, my child, he loved you, he did, I saw it as clearly as I see you right now, and he still does but…"

"Is that with or without glasses?" I blurted out.

She blinked.

"What?"

Mirjana grabbed my hand.

"Apologies, baba Dusanka, it's Tourette's." Mirjana said sternly, rolling her eyes at me.

Dusanka cleared her throat and ran her tongue over a few front teeth she had left.

"As I was saying, he needed children. That's why he was vulnerable to this young woman. She promised him the whole pack if he left you. And he couldn't fight that. The urge for a family, for descendants, for someone to bury you is stronger for men than any love for a woman."

All I did was keep sitting on that wooden chair that grew more and more uncomfortable on my bones and flesh, and listened and stared at her twirling thumbs. She traced my gaze and stopped the twirling.

"And I didn't see you two getting back together even if you wanted to have children now. So, you should move on, while you still can. How old are you?"

I wondered if my mother paid her off.

"Forty."

"Forty what?"

"Forty years old."

"Oh. Well, you look so young. I thought you were 20 something. Maybe your ovaries still work. Don't tell men how old you are. Burn your birth certificate."

I looked at Mirjana with my premeditated razor gaze.

"Baba Dusanka, thank you, that's great advice, but what about the other part we talked about on the phone?" Mirjana took over.

"What other part?"

"You know? Having him pay for what he's done to her?"

"Oh. That. A spell. I don't do those. You need a vrachara for that."

Mirjana now looked at me.

"Aren't you one?"

"Not that kind. I'm a fortune-teller. You need a VRA-CHA-RA."

We looked at each other, in silence.

"A witch, you need a witch. They do the cure. I only diagnose."

"Well. Fine. Do you know one?" Mirjana asked.

"There's one in the first house you passed. The big, yellow one. But she won't see you without a note."

I could see Dusanka thinking about it for a few moments, sizing us up, then she tore a strip from an old newspaper, wrote something and handed it to Mirjana. Not me, but Mirjana. As if she were my mother, not my high school friend of the same age.

"I'm not sure he did anything wrong, this Trav…Tre…grass fellow of yours, but suit yourselves," she said. "It's going to be the same with all men until Ana stops being spoiled and selfish and realizes what life's all about."

I opened my mouth but Mirjana grabbed me by the armpits and pulled me up.

"Time to go," she said, pushing me toward the door.

When we were back in the car, she read the note.

I glanced over.

"She knows how to write?"

Mirjana placed the note in her pocket.

"What does it say?"

Silence.

"Mirjana?"

"Who cares? It's our ticket in."

"Just spill it."

She hesitated, then pulled it out her pocket, dropping it in the beverage compartment. I picked it up. It was smudged but I could still make the words out.

"Childless by choice?"

Mirjana shrugged and stepped on gas.

She drove the whole alley backward, looking over her right shoulder through the back window. We passed the same cows, and pigs and chickens on our way back, and the same old women in headscarves and farmers in overalls stared at us from their yards and fields and orchards, as if they have never seen a car. When we got to the beginning of the alley, there was indeed a yellow house on the left and Mirjana leaned over my body and sized it through the passenger window. She nodded and parked, pulling the parking brake on.

"Really?" I said. "Haven't you had enough?"

"Get out. You wanted revenge, remember?"

Did I? I almost forgot. But then I recalled the last three months of Travis slipping away like an eel without the balls to tell me face to face that he met somebody else, that he fell in love with her, and that she was 25 and wanted to have seventeen of his children. And I recalled the Marine smelling of sour milk at my doorstep even before I had a chance to drink my morning latte, and I once again felt bile bubbling in my stomach and crawling up my esophagus. The bleaching effects of Baba Dusanka's rakija also could have caused it. But either way, my desire for revenge awoke.

"Let's skin that sonofabitch!" I stepped out of the car and slammed the door.

This time there was a bell at the gate, and I rang it.

A few minutes later, a girl of about ten got out of the house.

"What do you want?" she yelled out toward us.

"We're here to see your grandma Masha. Is she home?"

The girl was quiet, her chin tucked in. She pulled on her blonde braids.

"It's Sunday. She doesn't work Sundays."

Mirjana and I looked at each other. "We could come back tomorrow," Mirjana whispered.

"Baba Dusanka sent us. Please ask your grandma. We came a long way." I yelled out toward the girl. "All the way from the United States of America. On a big airplane." Then I stretched my arms out wide and imitated the airplane sound. As if I were talking to a toddler, not a tween.

She stood there for a few moments, blinking and staring at my act, then ran back into the house, her braids disappearing last.

Five minutes later, as Mirjana and I turned our backs to the house and approached the car, a woman in her early 60s came out.

She walked briskly and unlocked the gate. She showed us upstairs and we found ourselves taking our shoes off in a foyer that smelled of hyacinths.

"I'll make coffee," she said as she showed us into her living room that was as clean and tidy as my mother's. We sat on a brown sofa next to each other, and looked at framed photos of children and adults, alone and in packs. A glass cabinet with antiques, gold-trimmed coffee cups and teakettles, flowery porcelain china and silver dishes for special occasions stood in front of us. Every item sparkled and shone on starched, bleached doilies.

Masha came back with a large silver tray that held two Turkish coffees and a saucer with Turkish delights, walnut and rose-flavored, as well as syruped pieces of quince called slatko.

We thanked her and stuffed our burned mouths with delights and yellow cubes of slatko, our lips covered in powdered sugar.

We licked ourselves like cats while Masha sat across from us in an armchair and began talking in her modulated voice.

"May I see the note Dusanka gave you?"

Mirjana dipped into her pocket with her white sugary hand, and pulled the dirty yellow piece of paper, handing it to Masha.

Masha didn't look like a peasant to me, she didn't look like she belonged in this God-forsaken Southern Serbian village. As I waited for her verdict, I wondered how she ended up here. Her hands were clean and manicured, her nails painted white. Her hair was colored dark-brown and curled, her clothes ironed, and she smelled of perfume and hairspray and French soap. She wore embroidered slippers, black slacks and a pink cardigan with a white shirt underneath. White pearls peeked from her slick neck. She was more put together at home than I was at work. I thought about the pink bathrobe and slippers waiting for me in America.

Masha read Dusanka's paper for quite a while, or maybe it just seemed that way to me. I knew there were only three words on it but I guessed she was either concerned about God striking her dead for working on a Sunday, or she was trying to read between the lines of "childless by choice." As Masha read the paper, or contemplated what she just read, I began to feel nauseated about the word childless. After all, it wasn't the plague, it was a choice. And I was American now, damn it, there were plenty of American women choosing not to have children. There was nothing wrong with me. There was something wrong with all of the people believing that a woman must want children, otherwise there was something wrong with her head, there was everything wrong with her head. And what about all those spoiled children, all those children who took off and never saw their parents when they grew up. What about murderers and rapists. They were someone's children too. As a Serb, I felt that I couldn't make that choice, that I should maybe lie and tell people that I was barren, or that Travis was. As an American, I bloody wanted to stick to my choice, to write "I don't want little brats" on my forehead and shove it in everyone's face. But I knew that in Serbia people would either pity me or think that I was insane, and that I couldn't reason with them. They couldn't understand children as a choice, just as they couldn't choose not to breathe.

Masha lifted her head from the paper and sized both me and Mirjana, who has been unusually quiet.

"How can I help you?" she said.

Was it possible that this woman who had a house full of children and grandchildren, was willing to help me? Me?

Mirjana spoke first.

"Her husband left her for another woman. A younger one. Just, you know, poof, left! Arrivederci. And sent a nasty mover to pick up his things. On a weekend. Early morning. Before she had her coffee. He should be castrated if you ask me…"

Masha listened to Mirjana but read my face.

"Keep going," she said in her unburdened voice.

"Well, we want revenge. We thought, maybe, a powerful spell, you know, to destroy him without hurting Ana?"

"What kind of spell?"

Mirjana and I looked at each other.

"It was Mirjana's idea," I said, pointing my finger at Mirjana.

"Is there a catalogue?" Mirjana asked.

At that moment, I thought Masha would throw us out, but she remained as calm as ever. I began to wonder what kind of clients she saw on a daily basis. What kind of lunatics and damaged people when she remained as unmoving as a pole to whatever bullshit we served?

"Did you bring his possessions? I would need something of his."

"We have his various hairs, a piece of his sweater, and his toothbrush, for DNA, I presume?" I said.

Not even an edge of lips little smile. She proceeded as if she heard this kind of thing every day.

"Let me see the items."

I gave her the whole Ziploc bag and she looked through it.

"You realize that you will have to face him, or get into his new home to activate the spell?"

"No, I didn't know that. I sort of figured, it could work remotely?"

"It has to be placed on him or under his pillow or under his bed. Or under hers."

Her. Her. I never thought about that possibility before. But I didn't even know who she could be. That's how cut out of Travis's life I had been.

"That would be impossible."

"In that case, you're wasting your time."

"Since we're here, why don't we buy one, and then we can figure out later how to use it?" Mirjana whispered.

I nodded. Sounded harmless enough.

"What would you like to have happen to him?" Masha asked. I wanted to kill him, but only metaphorically, so what was equivalent to killing someone in Serbian Voodoo?

"What are my options?"

"Well, when my husband left me, I made sure he could never have children again," Masha said.

Mirjana and I looked at each other.

"And, did it work?" Mirjana asked.

"Oh yes," Masha responded.

"Please tell us more." Mirjana propped her chin on her knuckles, and her elbow on the edge of the sofa.

"What is there to say. He was a cheating pig. I forgave him once, twice, a dozen times, before I found out that he actually had another wife in Nis. So, I had to act, before he impregnated her. I got some of his hair from his comb, I cut a tiny piece of his sock, and wrapped all those in some fibers from his shirt, and solidified it with chicken fat. "

"And?"

"I chanted to it, I cut the vrachbina into small pieces and hid them in several of his pockets, but I also rubbed it against the crotch of his pants and placed tiny bits into his shoes, and his underpants."

"So, what happened?"

She was quiet for a few seconds, as if she considered whether to tell us the end of her story or leave it unfinished.

"His other wife was already pregnant."

All three of us became silent. I could hear Masha's grandchildren playing in the yard, the yelling and joyful screaming and running and jumping. I could even hear the cuckoo clock ticking in the foyer. I could hear somebody's cow moo. Then somebody started a tractor.

I waited for Masha to speak again, and I knew Mirjana did too. The room was now stuffy, and my chest filled with stale breath bursting to be released. I didn't know if I should remain still or if I could get up and leave. Was I allowed to leave? I just met Masha and she ruled this moment of my life. I watched her breathe, blink, twitch.

"I'll be right back," Masha said, taking my bag with Travis's things with her.

Mirjana and I remained alone, sitting next to each other on Masha's sofa, melting into her feather cushions that smelled of lavender for quite a while in silence, until we heard murmurs and soft chanting in the next room.

"So, she made the other woman miscarry?" I whispered to Mirjana.

"I guess so."

"What else could have happened?"

"I don't know. Maybe her ex and his wife live happily ever after and have a dozen children."

"And Masha still works as a witch because her spells don't work."

"Ask her," Mirjana said.

"You ask her."

At that moment, we could hear Masha's footsteps.

She walked up to us and offered a box as small as a ring one.

"As I said, if you want this to work, you need to place it either on your husband's person or under his bed, his mattress, his pillow. If you manage to place it under the mattress, it will be virtually undetectable. The same goes for his girlfriend. There are several pieces here. If one misses its mark, the rest should work. Bring them all, use them wisely. And be specific before deploying the spell. Consider well what you want it to do. Say it. Seal it…"

"Seal it?"

"Blow on it. Kiss it. Or rub your tear on it. Even a drop of urine would work. Or spit."

I opened my palm and she placed the box on it. I swear, it radiated. My hand tingled. Vibrated.

"If you change your mind, don't throw it in the garbage yourself. Have someone else dispose of it. Not you personally."

"Why?" I asked.

"Just don't do it. Don't anger it. You don't want it to turn against you."

I looked at the box, then back at Masha's face.

"How long do I have to decide?"

"As long as you need to. But it's powerful, so make sure you are sure."

She stood by us, silent and still, her arms by her side, and Mirjana got up first.

"How much do we owe you?" Mirjana asked.

Masha waved her arm in front of me, as if shooing a fly.

"Nothing."

Mirjana glanced at me.

"We would prefer to pay you for your time. And your expertise," I said.

"You can pay me if you are happy with the spell's effect."

"But, it could be a while. Ana is not going back home for the next few weeks," Mirjana added.

"I'm not going anywhere," Masha said.

I got up as well and Mirjana and I walked toward the door together. Masha followed. We put our shoes back on quickly, and when we crossed the threshold, I held onto the door frame with one of my hands, and placed the box into my purse, zipping it shut.

"Did your ex deserve what happened to him?" I turned and asked Masha.

She looked into my eyes, then looked away. Her face darkened, staled in front of me.

"He did. His baby didn't."

Now I looked downwards. Shivers appeared at the bottom of my spine and traveled upwards. I examined my Chucks, Masha's pointy Turkish slippers, her pristine white shaggy rug in the foyer as my hands began to shake.

Who was I? Could I do such a thing?

"Ana?" Masha spoke softly, jolting me out of my rumination. She reached for one of my hands and placed it in hers.

"I know how you feel. I know what you're thinking. I have been where you are now. And it's a hard place to be."

I nodded. Felt burning in my eyes, pressure in my temples.

Mirjana stood silently behind me. I couldn't see her, but I could feel her.

"Why don't I take the spell back, and give you a few days to think about it? I will store it safely and if you don't come back, I'll dispose of it myself. No harm done."

Masha extended her other hand. Palm facing upwards.

All I had to do was unzip my purse, fish the box out and place it on Masha's hand. And walk away.

I closed my eyes, one of my hands still warm and moist in Masha's. I tried to run the movie of me and Travis in my mind. The moment we met, the moment we got married, moved away, bought the townhouse. The good stuff. The laughter, the trips, the kisses, the safety and smell of our bed. But instead, other pictures, sounds, smells popped up like clouds: the smelly, sweaty mover swearing at my front door, Travis' girlfriend breathing in the background of our phone call, how I had so start from scratch at 30 with other American-born 22-year-olds just to be with him, my Serbian mother's shame for having a divorced daughter, false promise of "till death do you part," all the lies and sneaking around, making me feel blind and stupid. I pulled my hand out of Masha's. I cracked my neck, rolled my shoulders back as if getting ready for a fight, and opened my eyes.

"He doesn't deserve to begin a new life as if I never existed, does he? Nobody does."

Both women nodded. Mirjana pushed the front door open and I stepped out, the smell of freshly cut grass washing over me, my spine straight and my hands steady.

Rocks, Fox and Wendell Berry

RUTH ANN DANDREA

The only real, practical, hope-giving way to remedy the fragmentation that is the disease of the modern spirit is a small and humble way—a way that a government or agency or organization or institution will never think of, though a person may think of it: one must begin in one's own life the private solutions that can only in turn become public solutions.

—Wendell Berry

If we are to be properly humble in our use of the world, we need places we do not use at all. We need the experience of leaving something alone. We need places that we forbear to change, or influence by our presence, or impose on even by our understanding; places that we accept as influences upon us, not the other way around, that we enter with the sense, the pleasure, of having nothing to do there; places that we must enter in a kind of cultural nakedness, without comfort or tools, to submit rather than to conquer. We need what other ages would've called sacred groves. We need groves, anyhow, that we would treat as if they were sacred—in order, perhaps, to perceive their sanctity.

—Wendell Berry

You will see how we bear / children in ruins.

—Wislawa Szymborska

The fox stops, half turns, half stays. The way a fox will, being two things at once and daring both. Mottled coat, those delicate fairy tale feet, one poised as if to point the way, a way for me to follow. As if to say I know another shape-shifter when I see one. Those dark deep eyes which never leave the forest which carry trees with them, in them. I let the curtain fall closed. Walk my bare feet back to the kitchen. The kettle whistles. A train passes. Oh, the welcoming call of the train whistle waking a world, setting the air a-hum. Iron wheels chugging east, urging, reminding, breathe, keep moving on and on and on. Oh, the sound of that train whistle fading in the west, warning, times a-wasting, work, play, love, echoing its call all the way back to a simpler symphony, soft rain whispering, it's okay, it's okay, it's all okay. Ease. Reprieve. All of it reminding me I am alive and still of this world. This world that slaughters children in the streets. All the Palestinian children, Ukrainian children, Vietnamese, Sudanese, children, children, children, dead in the streets. While I, old woman that I am, lived on. And now this latest child. Countable blocks, walkable, from my own backyard. A thirteen-year-old with a pellet gun, made, by some unscrupulous manufacturer, to look like a Glock. What does a Glock look like? And why should a thirteen-year-old know? And the big policeman who chased, tackled, punched, and then, they say, fearing for his life from the gun he did not know was not the real thing, shot the boy dead with a bullet into his small chest. While I slept. With birds nesting in the trees. And the bunny tucked under the front stoop steps.

This world. That we've lost.

If we ever held it.

Split apart, it seems, at its seams.

Those old ties, family, home, community, land, church, sundered.

The binding of mattering.

When my husband left, just when the kids were grown, and we had before us all that time to be together, just us, to see some places, to come home, I felt as if my skin had failed. That my veins and organs, the flesh of me, was floating, without anything to hold it together. Just the way the world feels now.

Everything drifting off.

Away.

Change, I know, is part of life. If it weren't there would be no life. Stasis surely equals death, sooner or later. I don't want to be one of those old women yearning for youth, the way things were, whining about today, I decide, and pour the rest of my coffee down the drain. Rinse out the breakfast dishes and stack them in the rack.

I stretch and shower and dress. Deliberately.

Somewhere in its wanderings my mind has made a decision.

It has decided to do.

Through the back yard, past the herbs, the pussy willow, the sweet grass and the comfrey, strange and burdensome plant that it is, straight to the tomatoes, I go. Basket in hand. A-tisket, a-tasket. A green and yellow basket, I sing. But my brown basket will have to do. To lade. To fill with ripe and ripening tomatoes. Clumps of San Marzanos, those giant bloody teardrops. Beefsteaks as big as my hand, heavy to hold, like a human heart, weight the basket. To gather leaf by leaf, curls of kale. To pluck an Italian frying pepper. I cut a whole head of lettuce, about to go to seed. And pick small tender ovals of basil, stems of flat-leafed parsley. My bare feet mud-smeared from the garden, tingling in the dewy grass.

It is already warm.

It is Independence Day.

I want to go into the woods and create a small monument to the woman who said, "If terrorists kidnap me, please don't kill four thousand children to get me back." Instead, I put a big pot of water to boiling. Plop in tomatoes until their skins burst. Fish them out with a slotted spoon and plunge them in an ice bath. Cool enough, I pare away their loosening skin. Like stripping a sunburn to tender flesh. Use my knife to quarter the big ones, halve the small ones in the palm of my hand, then stir them into the already sautéing slices of onion, nubbins of garlic. Bubble it all to simmer. Add water and wait. While I wait, I toss thawed chopped meat into a bowl with egg, breadcrumbs, cheese, dried herbs and garlic. Into the mix, my fingers go, squeezing and blending, then fingering bits, smaller than my palm, and rolling and rolling, forming balls that I lay in concentric circles in the frying pan. When I was a child, making meatballs with my grandmother, I was taught to roll the meat between my palms at least fifty times before putting it in the pan to fry. And hers were the best meatballs ever. I don't do that anymore. I don't know why. So, I try, with the last batch of meat, counting the revolutions of it in my hands. I put it in the pan, scrutinize it against the others. Will it taste any different? I give up the quest. I will never know the answer, these meatballs are not for me. Tomato sauce simmering on the stove on Sunday morning. Is there anything more comforting?

A couple hours in, I add handfuls of basil and parsley. A couple more hours and the sauce is smooth and thick and ready.

I have cleaned the greens for salad, massaged the kale to make it tender. Kept one small tomato from the pot for slicing over the bed of lettuce.

From the cupboard I gather boxes of macaroni. I find a pound of rigatoni, another of ziti, one of regular spaghetti. I take them all.

Packing is not going to be easy.

But I like to pack. To find places for necessary things. To tuck shoes into leftover spaces and flatten books atop clothing.

This is a different kind of packing.

I am ready.

I have retrieved the map of my small city from the glove compartment of the car. It is spread on the kitchen counter beside the sauce cooling in a large glass bowl, the only one I have that has a cover. I find the street. Count the blocks from mine. Too many to walk.

I rummage the attic to find a box the right size. Cover the sauce which is still steaming. It's too early to cover it, but I cover it anyway. Gingerly lift it into the box. Surround it with boxes of macaroni to steady it. Tuck the salad in beside it.

Dinner for six.

The newscast never told how many in the family. They are one fewer now.

I carry the box to the car, secure it with blankets on the floor of the backseat and drive it across town. From Genesee Street, I count the blocks to Shaw. Shaw. Funny name for a street. The first boy who ever took me to a dance was named Shaw. I shake my head. Put the disaster of that dance, that boy, aside. Focus on the Shaw that is the street.

It seems like any ordinary street.

Not one where a police officer could've chased, tackled, punched, then shot and killed a child.

But there it is. A ribbon of yellow tape waving like a white flag from some shrubbery.

I slow, pause until I can make out a street number, then creep the car along, counting out the houses until I get to the one.

It looks like any ordinary house.

Not one where parents grieve the loss of a child, one they brought from a faraway land that was dangerous, to this one, that was supposed to be safe, who is dead, anyway.

I don't know what I expected.

But I did not expect this ordinary day, ordinary street, ordinary house.

Something should show the killing of a child. Some permanent lightning flash above the spot where it happened. A brighter light haloing the place the body lay. Even blood stains. Which, if there were any, there must have been some, have been scrubbed clean.

I carry the box from where the boy was killed, processing down the sidewalk to where the boy lived. Where his parents, his brothers and sisters, for all I know, his aunts and uncles and grandparents and cousins might live.

It is heavier than I thought, this box of atonement. And heat from the sauce steams my face. Sauce, sweat and tears. I trudge. Climb the wooden steps feeling dizzy. Fold myself over and place the box, as gently as a communion wafer, on the tongue of the doormat. Recite its prayer in English, I am sorry. And in Latin. "Mea culpa, mea culpa, mea culpa." The rhythm of my leaving feet beats in my breast. However, did I let my home become a place where cops kill children, it asks, over and over again.

And how do I heal the wound?

Knit together the torn pieces?

Make a world, any world, livable again?

I think I hear a door open, close behind me.

But it was maybe only the one I opened and closed to get into my car and drive away.

Away from the house, the street, the small city where it happened, into a countryside, all the way back to the last place where I knew, absolutely knew, for certain and for sure, that the world was good.

And I am there.

Wherever there is now.

It is not my grandmother's garden, my grandfather's farm. Even the old house has been torn down. Just straight fields of corn, straighter fields of corn, and more, and more fields straight with straight corn rows. Fences and irrigation ditches. Looking more like a factory than a farm. If a worker—are there any workers here whose hearts aren't engines? If a worker slices a hand here, do the neighbors—are there any neighbors here? Do the neighbors stop their own work and rush to tend the injured one? Bandage and carry? Pay his hospital bills if there are any? Feed his family while he is laid up? Offer their prayers for his swift recovery in the small white church that isn't there anymore? Is there any connection here, to anything but money?

There is one.

And I may be the only person on the planet who knows about it. Who remembers.

Again, I park the car. Again, I walk the distance to an opening, squeeze between the No Trespassing sign and the electrified fence. I know there are no animals here. No farm dogs waiting to greet or eat me. No random bull in a pasture waiting for a cow. Not even a flock of chickens clattering up a commotion if I come too near the coop.

It's just me.

And acres and acres of corn.

I think the ears hear me. They rustle their thanks for human footfall.

I disappear between, among them.

There is no straight line to where I am going. I cross between rows, zigzag among single plants, tall as, taller than, I am and tasseled under a golden sun that no one's figured out how to chain in or fence out.

I am looking for a rock.

A needle in a haystack, you say?

No. A rock in a field. A boulder of a rock. Gargantuan and great. A rock, the story goes, my great-grandfather found when clearing the land a hundred years ago. Some stray erratic left behind by the last retreating glacier. Taller than a man. Taller than two men. My great-grandfather and his brother couldn't see over it standing on each other's shoulders, couldn't reach around it, holding hands. They said what must be said. "Let it stand." Let stand, too, a stand of trees. Birches and maples, even an old oak. A shady spot for the animals in summer. A place for women to spread the picnic blanket when they carried out the men's lunches. A sacred grove to go to retrieve lost faith when mortgage payments were missed, old folks died, children left the farm. Old Jack, the first dog I ever knew, is buried there. No one ever spoke these words, but in my heart of heart I know my grandparents are buried there, too. In spirit if not in body.

It is hard to figure direction in this maze of anonymous corn.

It is hot and the ground is harder than I remember. Lumpier and difficult to walk.

But I walk anyway.

Walk and walk and look and find.

There, in the clearing. The rock. The rock all the machines in the world couldn't break and crumble or carry away. A gleaming monolith to another time.

I come to it slowly. Reverently. A trio of immature birches has sprouted near its base. Those paper white beauties. A pioneer species, my grandfather taught me. Just like us. But round back of the rock, the old oak is still there. Rough-barked and ornery as ever. Alongside it stands the towering white pine. I can walk beneath its lowest branches. I turn and align my spine with its trunk, press against it. The Haudenosaunee believed that if you stood with a white pine long enough, it would absorb your worries. I wait and wait. Then see the familiar fingernooks, footholds, and my old body forces me forward into the face of the rock.

Which, carefully, gingerly, with none of the agility of my youth, but with muscles that remember the climb, rise to its rise, find their way to finding me atop. Sitting, as my grandfather used to sing, on top of the world. Looking out on creation. Like any god or goddess. And loving it all. I find I am still loving the beauty and the horror of it all. The sun beats hard on my old gray head. Soft breezes push through sweetly scented pine needles to ease my soul, slippery with sweat, and thinking, feeling, it might settle into stone forever.

A rustle in the corn stalks.

A flicker of red in the green and yellow landscape.

The fox stops, half turns, half stays. The way a fox will, being two things at once and daring both. Mottled coat, those delicate fairy tale feet, one poised as if to point the way, a way for me to follow. As if to say I know another shapeshifter when I see one. Those dark deep eyes which never leave the forest which carry trees with them, in them. Carrying everything.

Five Poems

TOTI O'BRIEN

Cinderella, 2

The slippers that, you said, "made me
look Latina" have expired almost.
Two years. They did a good job.

I had purchased them at the dollar store.
Silver rubber
with a large bloom in the front.

I wore them all day, even in the garden
where they got caked with mud,
encrusted with dry leaves.

I duly took them off
at the door, then
tiptoed through the kitchen.

I washed them (and my feet, in turns)
in the sink. I dried them with a rag
and put them back on.

My Latina flip-flops...
and what did you mean?
I know, but will not say.

You, half-Mexican and half-Puerto Rican
don't tell me that it's fine to self-ridicule.
That's a trope I've never believed.

Don't pretend your remark was a joke.
I can tell humor
from sarcasm.

When you looked down

and frowned
I don't quite recall what I felt.

We were meeting in person for the first time.
We were pondering the opportunity of an affair.
You had made up your mind. I still dallied.

I recall a slight pang of... disappointment?
We were still at the stage where truth is a china
we prefer to keep locked in the curios cabinet.

Born in Rome
raised by the Mediterranean
I felt Latin as Latin can be.

Must be why I grabbed those mules
without a second thought.
They fit me, flowers and all.

But, no, I didn't come to the States
from South America, and Latinas
would never say I'm one of them.

Where did your words put me? Were you
assessing what I was, wasn't, should, or else
shouldn't be? Did you even know?

I wore the slippers in your presence, and much longer
without you. Now the left sole has crumbled
and a flower is gone.

I will wait for the other to wilt and wither at leisure.
Some things can only die a natural death.
Some things are meant to stay.

Farewell

In the bright, full-packed amphitheater,
the man who has made himself into
a myth but is still a man, though—
and then so, then more so—

can't get off the microphone, and we
guess he's bidding farewell. He's been
ill and now is gripping with mortality.
Losing foot, he breathes in

the crowd like a last cigarette. Then
he exhales words, and each falls
like a drop of sweat from a cross
hoisted up on Mount Calvary.

Each word floats in a bubble of sound.
Each is wrapped with echoes. The full
house punctuates his pauses
with moans

in a giant, ceremonial orgasm. And
the woman who supposedly shares
the mike and the honor with
this man, is silent.

Sitting a bit askew, she looks up
at the standing figure that now and then
gestures her way and asks
for a sip of water.

She hands a plastic bottle, then quickly
resumes her pose that, as the hour
grows late, becomes quasi-fetal—
her spine imperceptibly

spiraling on itself, her neck tilting forward.
On our way home, the super blue
moon is shining. It is huge
but yellow.

Maybe it isn't quite full. It looks
bruised on a side, as if someone
had knocked it hard, indenting
the beautiful curvature.

Invisible

No one mentioned prodigal daughter.
Not once. No such thing existed,
as the girl who'd take off would be
simply called a whore.

Well, she wouldn't be called. Should
someone imprudently inquire, Dad
would say, "Mate, I've only one gal
—right here, pouring wine."

Absence didn't breed opportunities
for reflection, didn't mature pardons.
It cemented oblivion. All relatives
went by the code of silence, in unison.

Should she ever return, she'd choose
siesta time, pace the desert sidewalk,
skirt the wall opposite to the family
home.

Sunshades on her face, she'd cast an
askew glance at the window, shutters
close, shielding the masters' afternoon
rest.

From the street, she would inhale dust,
twilight, old ink, lukewarm coffee,
soap and a tang of bleach. No smells
of roasted meat.

No perfumes. She'd move on, as
empty as she came. Only later, at the
end of her life, Mother sometimes
recalled.

They were flashes, so brief that they
left no trace. Mother recalled small
hands, chubby fingers hungering for
her cheek.

Maybe a polka-dotted dress, morphed
into kitchen rags. Wait. Who used to
wear it? And the clickety-click of
varnished Mary Janes.

Dark Matter

"Layla will come at noon." "Who is she,"
you distractedly ask. The sky is porous.
This is far North, past the border. The air
gleams a strange halo, as it did when we lived
on the river barge. In our shower, we saw
small waves through the transom window.
Water made the light eerily phosphoresce.

She storms into the bar and nods at the
waiter. Looking straight in your eyes, she
cockily says, "Did you know that your wife
and I go way back? She was hot!" For a
second her bragging thrills me, sort of.
Then I feel tension rising—a kind of
melancholy, as well.

She still sports the sloppy buzz cut she
favored by then. No one else in the joint,
except for the waiter. A brief pause, then,
"Truly," I stutter, "we never were lovers.
Now and then, we cuddled in bed with
a German shepherd, because it was
damn cold."

"She still was my entire world," I think
and don't say. She stands up, nervously
sways right and left. I go grab her thin
wrists, wrap her long arms around me.
Sex has nothing to do with this. Never
had. This is just ancient love, revived—
and the embers irk my scars.
We go way back, a long history—a
legend—of velocity, drugs, excess and
trespass. Those were years of lead. That
was war. We have escaped, and since we

lost track. It seemed that time went by,
smoothed all edges. But now it seems
that it stopped instead.

It is noon and it is midnight. The air
vibrates as when the stuff we had washed
down was too poorly cut, and darkness
kept glaring—no rest—and the dog, wiser
than we were, watched our listless
wake, our scattered, and then shattered
dreams.

Excused

A thick cloud of dampness, as if
the whole world had wept.
You hug me as you would the mat
of a sailboat in the eye of the storm.
All is dark green, interspersed by
windows of pale—peaceful oases
where still you can't find rest.
Underneath, your tremor never remits.

I am an ultra-mundane epiphany,
a figment of dream.
You are a ghost of your former self,
pretend flesh and blood.
You bend over to unplug the bathtub.
Stooped shoulders, frail back,
hardly shield from my sight
your flabby, overhanging gut.

Memories elude you. They brood
on collateral items. Rubber slippers
that made me look "too Latina." Or
"Wops have no sense of privacy."
Childishness doesn't make you
innocent, darling. Your profiling,
your cheap stereotypes
dig a groove.

Hell is always a room away.
Through the door, I can hear
its labored breathing. A snake
tries to bite me, then bites its tail.
Please, leave nothing behind. I will
burn all traces, then burn sage
to embalm the surrounding air,
dissolve nasty fumes.

I don't hate you more than I would
a mirage, a nightmare. I have
walked right into the noose
you had laid on the floor.
You have pulled the rope tight,
as a lad of yore
would have caught a butterfly
in his net.

Thelma and Louise

ADELE GARDNER

Night swimming in Keuka Lake,
my sister and I
talk Thelma and Louise, and how the strong woman
always has to die—
or, seen from another angle, the only sure escape
from an oppressive patriarchy
is death.
              I have to justify
Why I disliked this movie, with its unrelenting violence
against two adult females who simply want to live their own lives,
who dare to dream, to speak up, to act out.
In the popular mind, they might be Bonnie and Clyde—
another duo mythologized and maligned,
whose violent end—betrayed by the system
intended to protect all citizens
(but enforcing the rule of the rich)
remains a tragedy no matter what triumphant spin some take.

I don't condone suicide as solution
(even with friendly hands clasped and a triumphant yell)
any more than I believe "self-defense" justified the murder
of Bonnie Parker, who never fired a shot,
nor even Clyde in that moment, who'd stopped to help a friend,
caught in a trap of lies lined with love and trust,

his hands nowhere near his backseat guns.
No trial.
       Thelma and Louise
could have fled to Mexico;
toured Macchu Picchu under assumed names;
taken up pens and transformed their life experiences into the gold
of transgressive women writers;
found sanctuary as torch singers of Brazilian jazz;
campaigned for women's rights;
become the women warriors of a new Amazon.
Where were their mentors, all those females who dared—to live?
Not Joan of Arc martyrs—radiant but still dead,
believing the lie that a woman's lofty goals can only be fulfilled
by the ultimate sacrifice—
the ultimate silencing of women who dared to dream.

My sister and I
swim now in this lake, alone in a family
that reveres its males,
all of them good and wise and worthy.
But so are we.
The strong matriarchs of our family
have praised us but vested their power in their men
despite the brains and talents of the female line.
We've sought these women out for love and wisdom,
heeded their tales, recorded their words with love,
and imbibed their ultimate message,
that to be a good woman
one must put everyone's welfare above her own.

But now, alone in the secret, dark lake,
by the light of the smiling moon,
we think of Thelma and Louise
and swim up the moon path
away from our family cottage,
determined to choose life
and stand firm against society's training
that teaches women to belittle themselves
and warns us we'd be throwing ourselves off a cliff
if we dared to make
our own way.

Three Poems

DEBORAH A. LOTT

Dress Up

At your house on a weekday afternoon
we are playing that two grown up men want us.
Movie stars.
We take turns choosing:
there is only one Tony Curtis with his long eyelashes
Dean Martin with his wavy hair.

We put on our mothers' discarded dresses.
Ball gowns.
Admire ourselves, one another, in the mirror,
smiles aligned.
The Arrival of the Boyfriends:
we close your bedroom door and pretend a knock.
When they come upon us in our beautiful gowns,
Tony stands back and flutters those lashes,
Dean lets out a low wolf whistle.
They take us in their arms,
bestow the close-mouthed movie kiss.

Good girls: we resist, then go limp,
raise one heel in the air behind us,
the semaphore of female surrender.
Bad girls: we squeeze their necks and kiss harder.

When your father is due to arrive home,
your mother rushes to put on lipstick with a pop-up brush.
We have clicked it up and down, up and down,
letting its soft bristles tickle the tenderest spot in our palms.
We never touch the douche bag that hangs every day in her
      shower.

After your brother is born,
we add a birth scene to follow the kiss.
Staggering down the hall,
we collapse onto your bed,

where we spread our legs wide
and painlessly deliver a baby doll from between them.

When our breasts start to protrude,
nipples burning and stinging
under the training bras that constrain them,
when the boys at school—no movie stars
leer and snap our straps,
we see that the dresses are worn,
never ball gowns at all.
When some angry fist inside us
spasms out blood,
we can feel how a baby's big head and sharp shoulders
could tear at our insides.

When womanhood looms before us, within us,
the fun goes out of the game.

Breakfast Room at the Wayward Inn

This motel off the highway,

identical to every other in its chain.
It could be anywhere and
no one here knows where I came from or where I'm going.
 I don't remember much
this morning.
Free breakfast
not just continental
Real Cooked Breakfast, the sign says.
Behind a door
like the door to any guest room
a utility table holds
coffee urns

and giant plastic dispensers
disgorge cheerios.

A blonde with crude black roots
sleepwalks.
Lip resting on her mug's rim,
last night's nightmares leak from her
like nuclear fallout.

A toddler
wearing a tee shirt from the last tourist stop on the road
drools down his dinosaur.
So giddy with dumb
morning energy
I want to knock him unconscious again.

A buff man cooks my breakfast
behind a plastic shield.
No stove, just portable burners and a waffle iron.
Slick black hair pulled back in a ponytail,
he pours fluorescent yellow solution
into one-serving-sized pans
four or five going at once,
just the way he learned in prison.
Behind him, a faux needlework sign:
"I'm the boss in my kitchen.

A blue-inked tattoo peeks out the rolled up sleeve of his chef's
        coat.
I point at onions, tomatoes, olives,
his eyes refuse to meet my eyes.
I watch the eggs bubble,
and wonder if I could just ease into his life,
erase all memory of mine.
Set up housekeeping here,
and every morning, take my finger,
 trace the path of that blue-inked line
up his bicep,

where it slithers into a reptile's tail
or undulates into some part of a woman's body,
or maybe it's all just words.

Missing

In dreams I search for you
through rooms teeming with unfamiliar dogs.
I will know you when I see you
but can no longer conjure your face.
Imposters,
their markings off,
the space between their eyes altered.

One day when I was a child,
a stranger inhabited my mother's body.
I could tell by the stiffness of her wrists
when she held them up out of the dishwater
by the singsong in her voice when she cooked the eggs.
Could my touch will her back into the flesh she had abandoned?

When you finally appear in my dreams
your eyes are vacant
your outline dimmed
like a too-many-generations removed copy.
I try with a touch to revive you
but this is not the return
when you arrived down the airport luggage ramp
barking and howling,
declaring yourself alive inside your wooden carrier.

My touch could not revive my mother either,
her absence in presence insurmountable.
Now the losses keep adding up.
Each morning I wake and name my missing.
 In the mirror, I am bleached pale,
made strange with mourning.

Tragicomedy for the Fallen: Part I

KURT BAUMEISTER

Odin's spear struck Valhalla's golden floor with a mighty thud, silvered veins of sorcerous power erupting from the point of contact, energy flying electric and jagged to the four corners of his vast throne room. This was One-Eye's signal for quiet, and I went along. We all went along.

"Mr. Hitler has a proposition," spake the All-Father, clearly pleased with himself.

1924, and it had been a long time—ages, literally—since his failed Great Integration, nearly a millennium since the Norns had deserted us. Finally, though, Odin could see himself back on top. He was practically giddy.

"Ahem," Hitler cleared his throat.

The would-be Master-of-the-Thousand-Year-Reich smiled fully—disturbingly so given his uneven, copper-tinged teeth. But behind that smile, I could see the rage in Hitler's gaze, the malice not so much masked as controlled. The ruddy-sweaty speed-freak complexion, the dark stains under the arms of that baby-shit-brown shirt, that weird shiny hair, and ridiculous half-stache. As the cops say, the guy was wrong, so wrong.

"Ah, right," Odin explained, sounding flirty, submissive. "He prefers 'Führer'."

"Führer of what?" I asked, wriggling free from a couple Valkyries, Helvetica and Nonchalance if memory serves. Yeah, I know, strange names. Strange Valkyries, by the way. One-Eye never let me play with the ones I really had something in common with, Peace, who plays a mean game of chess, and Silence, who can really sing.

I swayed to my feet, grabbed a fresh tankard, and drained it as I composed my thoughts. I hadn't seen any of this coming, though I should have known there was a reason for Odin bringing me back after so many years on the outs. There always was. At the moment, though, I was just so happy to be home. It had been centuries.

"The Fatherland," Hitler replied.

"Father-…what? Was this your idea?" I asked, turning to Odin.

"Germany," Hitler said, as if he meant reality.

"You mean the Weimar Republic? There are no Führers, no Kaisers. Anarchists, Marxists, socialists, democrats, that's what you've got…it's a fucking fractious mess."

"That's all going to change. That's what Mr.—"

Hitler cleared his throat again.

"The Führer wants to talk to us about."

Odin was being so deferential, so polite. It was surreal, and I couldn't take it. I started breaking up, laughing. Practically, yeah…OK, fine, I was cackling by that point. Cackling like a mad scientist alone in his lab. Odin Asgard, Lord One-Eye, Mr. Hotshot-Topshit King of the Gods Himself, was groveling to this sweaty, little, Viennese weenie.

"Well, by all means, let's hear what…the Führer has to say."

"Ah," Hitler said, exhaling heavily, a grand mystery solved. "You must be Loki; this Jew the All-Father has told me of."

Yes, he said it just like that, said it right there in golden Valhalla, said 'this' and 'Jew' with a derision he'd hidden well until that moment.

Man, did that little weenie have some guts, let me tell you. But then in my considered estimation, crazy will do that. I mean, look at this Vekk guy over in Germany. He's talking about Jews again, talking about how great they are at math, how great they are with money, how much he loves them. No one's standing up to him either, not even in Germany. I guess one of his daughters is married to a Jew—a Jew who incidentally has had enough plastic surgery to make him look a perfect Nazi. Apparently, that's Vekk's out. As long as you have a Jewish son-in-law who looks like a Nazi you can say whatever you want.

"Jew?" I asked, turning to Odin, who feigned surprise. "I'm a pagan deity, you nitwit."

Hitler sneered; the hate no longer masked. If only I'd done more that day, if only I'd been able to stop them. I tell myself I tried, and I did, but I could have done so much more. We all could have, including you. And not just then, but now. Today.

I turned to Odin, "You're not actually thinking of helping this schmo, are you?"

Odin raised his tankard, the sign for a refill. "We'll talk later."

Hitler finally disappeared, dematerialized really, dissolving in a waterfall of dying light, like Princess Leia telling Obi-Wan he's our only hope. Which is when Odin buttonholed me. He hauled me into one of the throne room's antechambers and closed the door behind us, leaving the others to plot and scheme.

"Son," he began.

"Oh, here we go."

"The reason I called you back is this Hitler guy."

"Yeah, I get that from the meeting we just had."

"I need your help. If we're going to make this work, we need everyone on board. And..."

"What?"

"I don't know. I was hoping you'd tell me. Aren't you supposed to help me with image consulting?”

“I already told you,” I said. “I’m not helping with this.”

“Will you at least give it some time, see how things develop, watch what he’s doing down there, the way he’s unifying them all. It could really work to our advantage. He could get them to worship us again. Wouldn’t you like that?”

“Not really. I’ve never had many worshippers, remember?”

“Oh, sure you have.”

“A few. But nothing like you. And I don’t really care whether I have them or not. I never have.”

“But I care. Can’t you see how much it matters to me?”

There was Odin’s “real” emotion. He was playing me for the thousandth time and even then, even when I knew it was happening, I couldn’t stop it. What is it with family, that makes you want to try again and again?

“But he’s evil.”

“So are you!”

“Says you.”

“Fine, maybe you’re not. But, son, I need you. Will you at least give it a little time? Watch him, see how things go. Help me make it work. I know we can do it.”

“Yeah?”

“Yes. And if we do well enough maybe that will even get the Norns to come back. Wouldn’t you like to see Sunshine again?”

“Of course, I would. But it’s been eight centuries. I hardly think us helping some tin-pot dictator preach ‘law and order’ will bring them back.”

“Couldn’t hurt,” he said, gaze going wide, looking down. Was that a little mist in his eye?

“Well, that doesn’t really make sense. But I’ll do what you ask. I’ll watch and wait, at least for a little while.”

And there I was, a victim of Odin’s real emotion, yet again.

The Perilous Beauty of Golden Angles

JASON MARC HARRIS

Geometry has two great treasures: one is the theorem of Pythagoras, the other the division of a line into extreme and mean ratio. The first we may compare to a mass of gold, the second we may call a precious jewel.

—Johannes Kepler

Stacey pulled the bowstring back to her right ear and let go. The green arrow stuck half an inch from dead center in the yellow circle.

David stood amazed. "Nice!"

"Want to give it a try?" She patted his left shoulder and the touch jolted electric through his body. He spotted a glisten of sunlit sweat in the crook of her elbow, that golden hollow of smooth tanned flesh opposite her tilted joint.

He notched the arrow, lined it up with the guide. It thunked into the red circle.

"I bet we'll have you getting bullseyes in no time." Her right bicep flexed as she pulled off her armguard, and he witnessed the benevolent genius in the geometry of her golden joints, the shape of a triangle. Not just any triangle—an equilateral triangle which he pictured haloed within a perfect circle bifurcated by two Kepler triangles! The key to the golden ratio of a pristine 1.618.

His geometry was limited to art and anatomy, but he knew that Stacey's bend was perfect. The twin epicondyles of her humerus joined the prominent cap of the olecranon to form that legendary 60-degree angle from which George Odom proved the golden ratio might be derived, inscribed in a circle. Kepler's jewel nestled within.

As the sun set in the horizon and Stacey's elbows bent in elegant harmony, he hungered to reach out and feel for himself her golden ratio. He could no more resist that angle of desire than he could stop breathing.

He touched the back of her right elbow. The olecranon pressed into the tip of his middle finger while the medial and lateral epicondyles rested beneath his pointer and ring fingers.

She flinched. "Yeah, you don't need to do that."

"S-sorry. I just noticed your elbow is building up tension. It can give you tendon issues."

She cocked her head. "Really?"

"I've been reading about it in my sports medicine book. I'll bring stuff to help Saturday."

The next Saturday, he set his supplies down on a picnic table beneath the sloping shelter. Stacy was stringing her bow. She folded her arms into a fortress of skepticism. "What is all this?"

"Massage relieves toxic tendon tension in the elbow."

"Toxic?"

"Lactic acid from holding the bow string taut can erode microfibers. It could tear—"

She rubbed her elbows as if they itched. "I don't want toxic tendon tension."

"I won't charge for the jojoba oil. Not cheap, you know." David squirted oil on his right hand and stroked the slick goo on the front of Stacy's right forearm.

She giggled and drew back. "It's cold!"

He caressed her radial and ulnar bones and up the back of her humerus, pressing in a staccato burst of finger-drumming massage.

"Wow, that feels really good." She closed her eyes.

He closed his eyes for a moment too. He'd found the notch, that hinge of perfection.

"What the hell?" The low male voice preceded the swat to his head.

David opened his eyes to see Stacy's boyfriend, Mike, sticking knuckles in his face.

"I should kick your ass, Maples."

Stacy pushed Mike away. "Stop it. David helps me train."

"He had his hands all over you."

David backed farther away. "I was helping her loosen up."

Mike turned to David and raised his fist again. "Shut up, Maples."

Stacy grabbed Mike's wrist. "He was helping. Jojoba oil is what pros use to reduce toxic tendon tension in the elbows."

"If Maples wants elbow-action, how about this!" Mike thwacked David's right arm with his chunky knuckles just below the olecranon, striking the ulnar nerve complex. David's arm twanged with pain down to his pinky, his elbow shrieking with pins-and-needles.

Worse than physical pain was the stab of exposure. Mike saw his crush. David couldn't risk confirming it. He'd never be able to hang out with Stacey again. The teasing would be torture.

"Fun times with the funny bone!" Mike laughed and walked away.

David left the scene of infamy. He turned into his retreat.

Stacey called after him. "Sorry…."

He couldn't look back as he staggered into the redwoods, tromped over a creaking wood bridge, and crossed the dry stream. He circled the trails deeper into the forest and found a tree: hiding behind its thick trunk, he masturbated once.

When he walked into the parking lot, it was dark. Mike and

Stacey were long gone.

For years, he researched the geometric, fleshy affliction—what had made him an elbow epicurean? He read evolutionary biology and aesthetics articles, scoured the internet, dug into fetish magazines. Symmetrical features demonstrated healthy genes. This made sense but "why the elbow?" remained the question. And where were any women at all who shared his predilection?

In Seattle, he studied sports medicine and read through the "Takes All Kinds" website personals. Transexuals offering watersports to sugar daddies, erotic mannequin aficionados, clown costume roleplay, celebrity lookalike naked theater, orgiastic painting frenzies paired with edible clothing and expensive wine. Perhaps among the more artistic set of erotic adventurers, he might come upon a woman who would pose for him while he drew her pivotal voluptuousness upon the easel.

And then he saw the ad:

Madelyn the Muse

28 SWF Leggy fetish model, former-gymnast, roller-derby cheerleader, and contortionist offers her beauty to the adoring male world. I will allow you to put me on a pedestal where I belong. I am art in motion. I am the whisper of exquisite stillness. Marvel at my perfect breasts, toned arms, and legs, and feel the joy of worshipping this Goddess of desire. No strings attached except for the ones I tie you up with. Poet and college dropout. I am irresistible. All fetishes entertained. I am strict, but I am not strictly a "professional." Curious? You should be. Contact me. Now.

Her peremptory gaze was hard to deny. Blue eyes. Pink and blond streaks through ebony hair. Samurai sword. Her olecranon looked stellar. He dialed the number. "Uh, is this Madelyn?"

"That's right. Who are you?"

"D-David."

"What's your fetish, boy?"

"Elbows. I guess."

"Elbows? That is fantastic." A pause. "Tell you what, Daniel, I'm not much for phone-gabbing. Meet me at the Romadrome."

When he arrived, a man was getting ready to play his guitar. The feedback from the amplifier whined. He sat down with his organic strawberry lemonade at a table in the corner and surveyed the crowd, a human tapestry of ink-splotched skin—snakes, lions, cheetahs, an assortment of Biblical quotes, proverbs from Sanskrit and Buddhist texts.

And then Madelyn walked in. The orange heels clacked and clipped on the wood floor as she strutted long legs to the register. She wore a cherry red shirt. Her hair was the same pink and white in her photograph, silky and clean against the backdrop of rough characters less groomed.

She spotted him and nodded. He remained seated and waved, a small gesture.

After retrieving her cappuccino, she marched up to him and sat down and smiled. Pretty face. But he could not see the elbows tucked beneath that damn shirt.

"I'm Madelyn." Her voice was less husky than on the phone. She extended her hand. Her grip was firm. Erotic. She glided fingers across his palm at the end of their handshake.

"I'm David."

"Elbow-boy." Her smile was brief but not contemptuous.

He took a swallow of lemonade. She sipped her cappuccino and leaned back, shaking her hair, and crossing her legs beneath the short leather skirt. Then she rolled up her sleeves and raised her arms in a stretch. In the yellow light of the coffee shop, the knobs of her elbows flattened into smooth skin as her arms straightened. The tautness of her bicep and brachioradial muscles flexed underneath the butterscotch opacity of her soft skin. Then the notch of her forearms became inverted cupolas, shallow-sloped without abruptness, the bulbs of her elbows ripe with the fertile promise of healthy arms. He could not see every inch of elbow, particularly on the left side, but he could take his time later.

"You're checking me out big time. You gonna whip it out and

dick-beat right here?"

He held both his palms up. "I'm not—I wasn't…." He let his words dribble away, knowing what he said was as absurd as the gesture of his hands on top of the table.

"Forget it. I enjoy toying with the deviant sexuality of fellow humans. Especially pathetic men. Congratulations, you qualify. Nothing personal, Diego."

"David."

"Whatever. Let's go." She stood.

"Where do you want to go?"

"I live five blocks away." She slurped down what was left of her Cappuccino.

The last rays of sunset glimmered on the pinkish shreds of cellophane cirrus clouds in the grey-blue sky. Following Madelyn, he noticed a large purplish beetle crossing between them, a crane fly shaking its spindly legs, a Daddy-Long Legs on its web going in for the kill. He swallowed hard. "It's a nice night," he said.

"Every night is nice." Madelyn stretched her right leg over a puddle swollen from the gutter and creeped into her driveway. "Here we are."

The heavy wooden door to the brick apartment building clunked shut and she beckoned him to follow up the stairs.

Her apartment smelled fruity and spicy like incense. A purple dildo perched on the granite countertop. On the walls where fetish photography of women in gas masks, huge boots, and latex pelts. There were shots of burlesque shows and bondage clubs from downtown. A print of Waterhouse's Hylas and the Nymphs hung among the fetishes, Hercules's homoerotic pal, Hylas, being lured to his watery demise by sultry, pouting, milk-white faces. And a Hello Kitty poster, a little pink ribbon in the cat's puffed fur, a halo of sparrows above its head. It wore a quizzical expression, to swat a sparrow or not to swat a sparrow?

"Seems like every woman likes Hello Kitty these days," he said.

She ballerina spun in her orange heels. "She kicks ass. Soft and cute. An archetype of female power."

"Archetype? Have you studied mythology?" He noted the perfect spread of her elbows as she placed her hands on her hips.

"I'm a student of life. I dropped out of U Dub after I realized there wasn't a single major that did what I wanted. I even considered being a sexy librarian, but I don't like being quiet. Now, I make my money any way I want to. I say what the hell I want. I do what the fuck I want. Glassblowing, modeling, contortioning, dancing, photographing. I'm a courtroom sketch-artist sometimes. You name it. I can do it. From the carnival to the courtroom. I'm also a professional and lifestyle seductress, muse, and goddess. So, sit down already and get ready to worship me."

She pointed to the nearby sofa and winked. Beside the sofa stood a lamp with multi-colored appendages like an octopus, each tentacle a different color.

He sat tentatively on the couch beneath a black-and-white photograph of a naked woman with crown of deer antlers. She sat beside him and stretched out her legs, using his lap to rest her attractive yet somewhat threatening heels.

Madelyn grinned. "Comfortable?"

"Yes?"

"I never want men to be too comfortable near me." She pushed her heel down into his inner thigh, close to the groin. He winced.

"So," She breathed through her teeth, "how about I get you on your knees while you beg at my feet. Or maybe I should whip you and stomp while you cry for mercy, tie you up while you squeal like a pig, fuck you with that ten-inch purple dildo over there, or perhaps you'd like to wear one of the glittery girly wigs from my collection…." This wasn't a question. She had plans.

"None of the above." He blushed and folded his hands over his groin.

"Oh, that's right, you're not the run-of-the-mill. Pardon me." She slid her legs off his lap, stood up, and glanced back at him. Then she removed her red shirt, revealing a black brassiere, and started to sway from side-to-side.

He swallowed the dryness in his throat and watched as she wrapped her arms across her abdomen and cupped each elbow with the opposite hand, rhythmically showing the bulb beneath in a peek-a-boo maneuver.

"You're elbow-boy, right?"

"Yes." He watched her wobble her arms around.

"Tell me when it looks good to you." She bent and unbent her arms.

"It's all nice."

She advanced, pressing her fists together against her chin and thrusting her elbows in front of her like a great proboscis stabbing forth from her chin or a strange sideshow performance, a human hybrid with stag beetle pincers. She moved closer, the knobs of her flesh-draped bone touching together and cleaving apart in repetition. She pushed her elbow in front of his mouth.

"Suck it."

"It's not something I really want to do." His face reddened.

"Then lick it. Do it." She put her right hand behind her head in a fetching pose and pushed her left elbow against his lips, parting them. He intended to protest but his tongue darted over her elbow, and she sunk it deeper.

"See?" She whispered and removed the elbow from his mouth. "Wasn't so hard, was it?"

"No." He chewed at his lip. It wasn't that great either.

"How about you pay me two-hundred-dollars for the privilege of kissing and licking my elbow for a half-hour. Sound fair?"

"I didn't think money was going to be part of this." He crossed his arms and leaned away.

"Some things I do just for fun. Like I wrote in my ad, I'm not 'strictly professional.' You're just a poor college student though, aren't you?"

She pulled back her shoulders and tossed her head to the side, glanced out the window at the puffs of fog. She scratched at the black lacey strap of her brassiere.

"Yeah, big student loans."

"Been there. One of the reasons I dropped out." She pulled up a stool from the kitchen bar and spread her legs before him.

"Sorry to hear."

"Don't be. I found other things. The carnival and contortioning. Could do some amazing shit till I had an accident with a glass door and a dumb slut. Cut up my ulnar nerve, which fucked up my drumming. Before that happened, a guy from the Blue Man Group told me I was almost good enough to be the first Blue

Woman. Somebody else is now."

Her face paled in the waning light, crinkling eyes, tightening lips, hollowing cheeks. She almost looked poignant, self-righteous, otherworldly, as though she were the ghost of some dead mother summoned to a trial, testifying about her dead son. She stroked her left elbow and extended it as she looked out the window over the declining angle of the eaves below, the last drips of sunlight speckling a few freckles on her forearms.

He winced as he saw now the milky-white scar, whose wriggling shape suggested a caterpillar burrowed into that fold of flesh around the elbow bone.

"You have a problem with my scar?"

"It's just unexpected. I'm surprised I didn't notice it earlier."

"Uh huh." She was frowning, growing fierce in the dim light. He squirmed in the silence. The shadows over her face hollowed her eyes now. It reminded him of a skull.

"So," she said, crossing her legs and arms and leaning forward, "got any idea why you like elbows so much that you want to slurp all over them?"

"That's not really what I wanted to do. It's just how they look with some women. It's about the perfect beauty of the angle."

"Oh really? How about this angle?" She bent her elbows forward and raised her shoulders. He thought he glimpsed the triangle of her elbow joints balanced in symmetry—two sides of Kepler's golden isosceles triangle perfectly outlined. Leonardo had merely to reach out from the heavens with his silver stylus and protractor to trace with glittering ink across the air to complete the triangle. That elusive golden mean actualized in the flesh at last coming to embrace him. But before he could contemplate this vision of perfection, with a quick thrust, she bent her elbows in the other direction, backwards. Each elbow joint appeared to separate, and a secondary lower bulge appeared while her arms bent into dislocation. The caterpillar scar squished into a crescent, a winking eye.

He felt dizzy. Sweat started from his forehead, and he swam with a disorder of thoughts. He thought of a twisted pretzel on a spit, or a butterfly unnaturally stretched on an anatomist's table, the proportions jerked out of symmetry. The pulpy, stucco ceiling billowed down on him.

He stood and turned toward the door.

Madelyn laughed and switched on the tentacled lamp. It illuminated the walls in a carnival of madness, the appendages, splotching the room with swirling shapes and primary colors.

It had been one thing for David to learn in his anatomy classes of the deformities and injuries that plagued elbows—psoriasis, arthritis, bursitis, and dislocation—but to see the naked horror of this inverted elbow while a madcap parade of color mottled the room, that was a very different thing. The world was undone. The very spectrum had turned against him.

"Is there a problem?"

"That is just sick." He couldn't speak another word. He gasped and stiffened and panted and choked. He backed away from her, wobbling the octopus lamp.

She grinned and in the shaking yellow, green, and red lights, her face shifted through the shades in a surreal flutter, nightmare of Cubist Dadaism. He forced himself to take slower breaths. In. Out. Make it to the door. One step at a time.

"It's one of the reasons I'm such a good contortionist. It's all about slipping the ulnar bone out of its little groove. I'm one of the lucky rubber people."

She twirled her arms and resumed her normal proportions.

"Did I destroy your dream?" She leaned close to him, her blue eyes bulging.

"What do you mean?" He raised his right hand protectively to his waist while feeling the other behind him to avoid tripping over any other chaotic furniture.

"Your dream of perfect women with perfect elbows." She sneered. "I hope I did. I enjoy being a dream-destroyer. Especially for boys who don't pay. Now, get out."

He stumbled away from the couch and to the door, which he swung open as she watched him, smiling prettily. He half-expected her to crab-walk along the wall, pursuing him with those deformed and accusing elbows, intent on perforating his ribcage and drawing out his heart and soul, tossing his innards to the devils that surely must be watching as they laughed to see the firmament collapse upon him now. The harmony of the universe no longer stood intact upon the perilous beauty of golden angles.

"Don't fall down the stairs," she called after him. Her laughter lingered in his ears as he closed the door and hurried to the waiting street beyond.

He walked quickly away along the slick streets wet with drizzle. The dark grey sky sagged as he breathed heavily, sucking up the damp air. Mildewy fog wound its way among the brick buildings along the Avenue. A few houses down, a pizza delivery vehicle stopped, and a young woman got out. Her red hair tied in a braid hung out the back flap of her cap, and she balanced the pizza box in one hand and whistled as she approached the door.

The air felt cottony in his ears as David watched her. He felt no thrill at the marvel of skill and beauty in her perfectly pivoted elbow. He walked on.

The raindrops quickened and the night grew chill.

He came upon the crest of the hill overlooking Puget Sound and could see the bare hill next to Gasworks Park and the twisted edifices of abandoned rusty pipes beside the cold saltwater shore.

The Space Needle sat amongst the taller skyscrapers, black, grey, and greenish in the dense cluster of downtown. Further yet, Mt. Rainier's creased glaciers glowed dimly in the distance, its dormant volcanic dome frozen and still. Unlike Hawaii, the myth of creation had long gone quiet in the Pacific Northwest.

Orion the Hunter later emerged from the rags of cloud, and he paused in his walk and studied the dark sky and golden stars. He did not see Artemis, Aphrodite, Stacey, or Madelyn in them. How many archers, he wondered, practiced their crafts, and looked skyward, knowing their perfect marksmanship, their purity of joy and art and love and beauty had their dwelling place in the stars alone?

The Child
Who Opens
Windows

MARJORIE MADDOX

—for Karen Elias

What is a locked room to a child
who has just learned to read?
She knows the meaning of "open,"
"close," deciphers "together" and "left
behind." Her teacher didn't mean
to lock her in the room all alone.

But there she is by herself. All alone,
she peers outside, watches the other children
skip to the playground. They didn't mean
to leave her behind. At six, she's already read
about resourcefulness: the Box Car Children left
on their own. She knows that only she can open

the window, call out. With this thought, she opens
her life to action and determination. Alone,
she finds the hooked pole, stands on a chair. Her left
hand steadying her, she cracks open the transom. A child
learning to save herself, she calls out the window. She's read
what should happen next: Everyone returns. It wasn't mean-

ness that made them leave. She was in the cloakroom, meaning to snap her snowsuit, latch her boots, then step into the open
classroom. But by the time she announced "Ready!"
teacher and classmates were gone. Now she is alone;
no one hears her calling. She is just a forgotten child
in an adult world. She bangs on the walls, refuses to be left

behind. In the lonely classroom, it's all that's left
to do. An adult comes. The child doesn't mean
to scream, to hug the woman who saves her, to be the child
she is, but she is relieved and vows to open
windows for others, show them they aren't alone.
She will unlock doors, write what they need to read,

and fight to save those left behind. Reading
and a locked classroom teach her to leave
no one out. She understands being alone
with no one noticing. She understands the meaning of both hopelessness and courage. She will open
her life to saving others. Even as a child,

no longer alone, she vows to help. Look closely. Read
her child's face. Decipher her eyes. She will not leave
anyone. She means it. At every window and door, she chooses
    "open."

Artwork: *The Child Who Opens Windows*, design by Karen Elias,
    graphics by Freepik

Mil and Me

MICHELE HANSON

Hardly anyone is named Mildred anymore. According to the U.S. Census, Mildred was in the Top 10 of girls' names in the first quarter of the 20th century. My mother, Mildred, was born in 1928, so that checks out. In 1920, it ranked sixth in popularity, and 18,000 Mildreds were born that year. Compare this to 2020, when only 96 girls in the country were graced with the name.

She may have been born Mildred, but since 1952, when she married my dad, she has been more commonly known in public as Mrs. Edward F. Hanson. Her bank accounts are in the name of Mrs. Edward F. Hanson, even though Edward himself passed away in 2016, after nearly 92 years on earth, 64 of those married. "Mrs. E. F. Hanson" is how Mom signs her checks and for her credit cards.

She called him EdDear; Dad called her Mil. If you call yourself a friend, you will call her Mildred. Just one thing: Do not call her Millie. She won't correct you, but she will make a mental note and (this is my perspective) think somewhat less of you. I get it. I'm Shelly to my cousins and no one else, except my dogs when they're in a talkative mood. Never has it occurred to me to introduce myself as Shelly. Only my siblings, a friend I've known since high school, and my ex call me Shell. (Once my mother called me Shell in a text, and it felt very, very wrong.)

When I got married, I had been a Hanson for thirty years—

in other words, my whole life. Reading Gyn/Ecology by Mary Daley in grad school had been my political awakening, which meant that changing my last name to that of my husband's was a non-issue. (I am aware how inadequate a statement of independence this is. As a descendant of Ole Hansson, who immigrated from Norway in the 1880s, I trail in the wake of all those "sons of Hans," so the feminist bucket doesn't really hold water.) Hanson is stamped on various records that verify I exist: birth certificate, social security, bank accounts, passport, school transcripts. Going through the bureaucratic nonsense for a name change would not only have been recklessly time-consuming, but it would also have meant an existential reckoning at every turn. Who was I, as a married woman? Should I be henceforth née Hanson and morte someone else? If I became famous under this assumed name, how would my former elementary school comrades recognize me as the same girl who wrote a couplet about hummingbirds in second grade?

Rarely does a man choose to change his name upon marrying, and even then, he would still own his birth name as part of a hyphenated cocktail. (I have friends who simply merged their two names, so both were changed. This strikes me as a win-win or, if you like, a winwin.) A man's last name is a constant throughout his life, whereas a married woman's choice unavoidably reveals something about her social status or self-image. Who does she think she is? Keeping her name suggests she may be a professional with a recognized history or that she has a nontraditional view of marriage. If she does change her name, it's likely she has more conventional values. Or the choice might simply be practical: it's so much easier as a couple, and certainly as a family, to be a legal entity as well as a unit of meaning. Then people can say, for example, "The Carrutherses put their house up for sale," or, "Do you think the plural of their name should be Seligmans or Seligmen?"

The sociolinguist Deborah Tannen has claimed that "there is no unmarked woman," meaning that the decisions women make, consciously or not, from momentous to minute, telegraph something about her identity. Whether we apply artful makeup or just a little or none at all; wear heels that impede our stride and endanger the alignment of our spines or "sensible" shoes that fly in the face of fashion; dye our hair or yield to gray; go commando in yoga pants or reveal a prudish panty-line; are called a female CEO or a woman mechanic, or even a congressperson or fisherperson, bearing the weight of all those excess syllables—we have no neutral default.

We are questioning these distinctions more and more, but women still have a smorgasbord of titles to choose from—Miss and Mrs. and Ms.—each one open to interpretation. I imagine a rainbow-filled day when we've gotten over this hostile backlash about gender identity and we adopt "Mx" as a title. Mix! Everybody can be a Mx. She can be a Mx, he can be a Mx, they can be a Mx. If you're an adult, you're a Mx. Children will call me Mx Michele, for example. We'll call children "Mixxy," as in, Hey, Mixxy. Watch your language.

My choice not to repurpose myself had repercussions. It rankled. How do I know? Not because my mother complained, challenged me outright, or even asked out of curiosity why I would flout centuries of tradition. No, her opinion was conveyed through a package sent through the mail, on which she had written my first name and address in her careful cursive, and Hanson was in my dad's distinctive, squat print.

As was typical in our family, my oldest sister, Nancy, the responsible one, stepped up to restore equilibrium to the universe by getting engaged two years after I was married. Whereas the ceremony for my then husband and me took place in a mayor's office with only the three of us in attendance, Nancy and Mom planned a beautiful wedding on a mountainside in Lake Tahoe with all the things: the double-enveloped invitations; the white dress and veil; friends, family, and flowers; a photographer; and a band that played "Macarena." My other sister and I wore matching bridesmaid dresses and sandals with modest heels. At some point, Nancy was probably introduced as Mrs. Not-Hanson. When dinner was served, the guests found their place by the name cards propped in tiny silver goblets made for that purpose. Mine was designated with a hyphenated last name, a compromise that I assumed had been engineered by Mrs. Hanson.

At 96 years old, Mrs. Hanson—Mom, that is—still lives by herself in the same house she's lived in since 1957, where she and

Ed raised a son and three daughters. Her legs can be unsteady, but her mind is strong. She still balances her checkbook to the penny. It's her sharpened pencil and register versus the bank statement, and you'd better believe she gives no quarter. She folds her dirty clothes before laying them in the laundry; she irons her t-shirts. Since Dad died, her responsibilities have expanded, and she has seen to a number of home-improvement projects: new lighting in the living room, an automatic garage door, a fence across the driveway. She fills up fat books of word-find puzzles and carefully counts off the stitches for her latest needlepoint project.

I remember her saying that her father, whom she referred to as "Daddy," decreed that his four daughters could either become teachers, nurses, or secretaries, and three of them each pursued one of these paths. The eldest got married young, making the necessity of a job moot. Mom worked as a clerk in the office of a junior high school so she could have the same vacation time as her children. But I have long thought that if she had been born into a different world, she could have directed a sizeable company. She would have delegated this, followed up with that, gotten through the meeting agenda early, and still had time to sew everyone matching outfits, as she did for my two sisters and me. She would have devised ways to reach out to shareholders, restructure the company hierarchy for maximum efficiency, and still make sure the next event was properly catered.

She isn't much for reminiscing, but she has told us the story of how she first came to know my dad. As a young woman of twenty-four or so, she worked at a branch library in Santa Monica and checked out books to this handsome, soft-spoken man who had served in the Coast Guard and was now at UCLA on the GI Bill. I imagine Mom's heart wildly, quietly aflutter when she looked out the window and saw him arrive on his Indian motorcycle, wearing his leather jacket. She said the other young women who worked there would exclaim excitedly, "It's Eddie Hanson!" But it was Mildred he was there to see, under the pretense of having to study.

My son is named Cosmo. You don't hear of too many people named Cosmo. It's a fine name for a dog: maybe you've met one or two of those. In the year he was born, according to the Social Security Administration, only 20 boys were named Cosmo. (That's three more than "Quentavious," but still not wildly popular.) We had several reasons for choosing it, not least because it's distinctive yet simple. The etymology is from the Greek, meaning an orderly or harmonious universe. We didn't expect him to be orderly (he is not), but, as it turns out, he is musically inclined. The possibilities intrigued us: A cosmopolitan is a citizen of the world; a cosmonaut is a person who sails through boundless space. Cosimo de' Medici was a generous patron of arts and culture in 15th-century Florence. We debated. We realized it was unusual. Would we be comfortable yelling it to call him away from the playground? Hearing it announced from a commencement stage? Would he? Who could know? We considered other names but kept coming back to this one.

When we introduced him as a child, people used to comment on the Seinfeld character or, for a much younger crowd, the name of a cartoon fairy, but these allusions have faded with time. Now most people just think it's cool. My mother had a different response. When I called her from the hospital just after he was born—we were living on opposite ends of the country—and told her his name, she said flatly, "You're kidding."

If I could have chosen a name for myself as a kid, it would have been Kristi. I didn't know anyone named Kristi, but to me Kristi must be that girl everyone liked, confident, fun, with a happy disposition. She never felt at a loss for words, never questioned her place in the group or the decisions she made. Kristi had blond braids. My parents kept my hair short; Dad was handier as a carpenter than as a barber.

In terms of poetic meter, the name Kristi is a trochee, with stress on the first syllable. Michele, on the other hand, is an iamb, soft, the stuff of sonnets. Since I have a soft voice, saying ImMichele can sound like mm-shhh, perhaps leading people to assume that I have little to say. Nevertheless, it was my name (or rather, my name sung by the Beatles) that led me to study French, starting in ninth grade. In that language, people pronounce the Mishh as Meesh, and it's music. Introducing myself with je m'appelle Michele is inarguably la poésie. I once asked Mom why she and

Dad chose to spell it with only one L, and she said she just liked the way it looked. Maybe she just thought it looked neater, like a woman whose wild hair could be easily tamed with a barrette or a haircut—one of her favorite complaints. She has a point, though. In writing a lower-case H, two Ls, and two Es, one might very well lose track and add superfluous loops, sending the name into a spiraling doodle, making both writer and reader dizzy. Also, in French, Michèle-with-one-L is written with an accent, like an insouciant tilt of the beret or a small, graphical act of résistance.

In other words, I'm fine not being Kristi. (As I write this, though, I notice the similarity between Kristi and Cosmo, the five letters, two repeating vowels of differing pronunciation, and the s. Both are trochees: Was that my unconscious preference all along?) Cosmo's middle name is Hanson (trochee) and his last name is one syllable, an arrangement we thought would preserve his shared heritage without the hyphenated saddlebags. My middle name is Gudrun, which I used to dislike for its strangeness but am now proud of for the same reason. Gudrun is also my mother's middle name and was her mother's first name. Growing up, Grandma had the nickname Goody, leading perhaps inevitably to the association with shoes—two of them, that is, with a nod to Goody Two-Shoes. (I've read that the origin of that expression may go back to the seventeenth century but was first popularized in a book published in 1765. It tells of a poor girl who grew up with only one shoe but whose virtue is rewarded when she eventually marries into wealth. With a new pair of shoes and a husband, all is well.) People used to give Grandma ceramic shoes to put on the curio shelf, and my mom has at least two pairs of these. As the inheritor of the name, I am also the de facto inheritor of said shoes. I have one pair already, white porcelain pumps an inch long, with squared toes, a little bow at the instep, and a low, sturdy heel. I marvel at their simplicity and wonder at their purpose.

A few years ago, my sisters and I took on the project of straightening up Mom's garage. We filled a recycling barrel and a garbage barrel and made a trip to the Goodwill with all the stuff she no longer wanted. At one point, we dragged out a steamer trunk that had belonged to one of her relatives and opened it to find a trove of old photographs. Some of the faces we recognized, and some had names scribbled on the back: Clarence and Florence, Joseph and Myrtle. Mom could only hazard a guess at the ones who weren't identified. The photos were mostly dispatches from the twenties and thirties: women in loose-fitting dresses that reached to their knees, men with baggy pants, easy smiles that suggested they knew each other and were caught in a moment. Relatives, friends—who could say? They were lost to time.

One professionally done photo was of Grandma with three little girls, dated 1932. Mom and her twin, Margaret, were four years old, and their older sister was six or seven. The youngest, Joanne, had yet to arrive; Gudrun may well have been pregnant at the time, not yet showing but still knowing. One print was in black and white; a copy of it was hand colored. In this one, Gudrun is wearing a pistachio-green, V-neck blouse with a loosely tied bow, and the girls are in pink dresses that match the rosy glow on their cheeks. Although none of them is smiling, it is Mildred, with her mouth turned down at the corners and her direct gaze, who seems the least compliant, highly skeptical of the entire charade, recognizing pointless display when she sees it. Would she rather be doing something productive, like running around outside, playing with her dog, Trixie? Or would she prefer to be the one behind the camera, organizing the scene for posterity?

I was reminded of a photo of my sisters and me, taken when I was about eight. They would have been eleven and thirteen. The photo is in black and white, but I remember well those matching dresses that Mom had sewn for us: short sleeves; a simple A-line shape with a mock turtleneck collar; and the print a kaleidoscope of small diamond shapes in groovy colors of bright green, yellow, and pink. Like four-year-old Mom, I am not smiling. I've jammed my hands in the big patch pockets because that's what pockets are for, damn it. In these seconds, I will stand still because it is required of me. But then, you'd better believe, I'm off in search of something else to do.

Birdnesting

ANGELA YOUNGBLOOD

I never learned embroidery in the classical sense. It was a wisp of a memory like a loose thread. Something I kept pulling at. Something that kept pulling me. Ignorant and unsteady, my hands shook as I tried to pass the tulip red thread through the eye of the needle. I had resolved to learn by feel. Intuitive movements. The burlap was heavier than most fabrics meant to pass through the narrow rings of a standard wooden embroidery hoop. Because of this it sagged in the middle, the edges that should have been taut and flat around the ring folded in on each other. My first piece of stitching was off to an unbalanced start. I held a thin square of cardboard—the kind you might find wedged behind a stock image of a smiling family in a cheap photo frame—to the back of the burlap to help temporarily support my work. Let my needle pass through the fabric and then the paper. A glide into a crisp snap. Repeat.

Rummaging through a shoebox of photos I came across a polaroid of my Uncle Danny and Grandma in a desert. Thinking about the last time I saw them both [in a box] and stumbling upon this photo [in a box], I find the closeness of the space overwhelming, claustrophobic. I pull Danny and Grandma out of the box. Dust them both off, as if to say, "No, you! You don't belong here." I also pull out an old photo of ripples on water—nothing more. Nothing to distinguish it from any other photo of water. Nothing to determine space. No marker of when or where, just something general like, "It was probably morning or evening," because the black and blue is punctuated by sherbet hues, light dancing on water.

I bought oil pastels and glue. Wine for good measure. I drew the parts outside of the frame. The parts I couldn't see. More dusty rolling hills. More squat sage plants. I drew a cactus, cartoonish in color and size, and stitched it into the scenery. Something that looked alive and vital. Something that held the piece together before more landscape faded into the rippled water that, tilted on its side, looked so much like a mirage. Squiggles on the horizon, before fading into black.

This will be their new resting place, the both of them. Younger. Stronger. A place that I created for them: Danny with his gap-toothed grin, and Grandma. Squinting at the sun. Squinting through the frame, at anyone, like me, who cared to look at them.

In loss, we learn to assign meaning to things that did not hold meaning before. I think about this as I look at bowls and baskets and think about all they hold even when empty. Contemplate the weight of the brass elephant on the table. Handmade Christmas stockings and the thought put into their creation. Photos kept in boxes that I periodically pull out and blow the dust off. Memories that play on repeat.

We are all creators, even if we aren't parents. We bring so many things to life in ideas and thoughts. In our homes we create mini-universes. We create families outside of the nuclear.

Grandma collected tiny spoons. Grandpa made her a bunch of wooden shelves with small U-shapes to hold them. So many spoons. From all over the United States, places she had been and places she would never go. I often wondered as a child if her spoon collection had anything to do with all of the mouths she had to feed. Eight children and a sister young enough Grandma raised her as her own. So many mouths to feed before her own. And with a family that size, things tend to multiply rapidly. I have cousins cast to the winds, blood, that mean nothing to me. Phantom memories from a family reunion or two when Grandma was still alive. More life means this too; more death.

Grandma was the thread that binds. Her eyes flashed like needles. Sharp. The point at which every family member met, connected. There was a fierce closeness to her love which spread over everyone like a blanket. Her cancer grew from inattention. From holding the lives of every other family member to the eye of her needle before her own. How quickly that thread of family unraveled after her passing.

A common trap is birdnesting. A pulling of the thread without mindfulness and a nest can form a small knot that grows. Tangled. Hung up. A collection of inattention. If dealt with right away a small knot is no big deal. But if grown unnoticed, requires snipping. Pulling out the threads and starting again. Snip, snip. How long have you been sitting on that particular nest? How long have you been building it? Snap! The thread breaks.

I never considered myself a creator. Despite building worlds outside of myself on page. Because writing felt as essential to me as breathing, I never considered pen as needle.

The needle is the essential device. It is the driving force. The catalyst for creation. For mending and repairing. There is a balance—too much tension and the thread breaks. Too little tension and the fabric is a peek-a-boo of backing. A glimmer of past peeking through, a shifting of design.

My muse for my first stitching came in the form of a bargain hunt. I was in a Goodwill, under a cascading bombardment of fluorescents mirrored in flashes of chrome fixtures. The shelved section. The section that houses home-goods and knick-knacks—things people have discarded for other people to sort through and find. My dad taught me this; to look behind what was placed at the front. Beyond the exterior. The true treasures are hidden where most people don't want to reach. Behind bundles of posters with curling edges, their rubber band bindings stiffened with age, my hand brushed against coarse fabric. I pulled the fabric up and out of the bin, a nesting of brown burlap swaddled into itself. Its heft felt earnest in my hands. Its weave, loose and open. It looked to be an old seed sack, black outlines of flowers and pots stamped onto the fabric. A textile coloring book. All twenty-six years of me yearned to create something with this cloth. Something was there that I couldn't quite visualize yet, but I could feel it in the stiff contours of the material, wanting to come out. It took two more months of sitting at the back of my closet before I bought a hoop, a set of needles, an abundance of thread.

When looking at a blank canvas you must decide how much negative space to leave. To fill or not to fill? That is the question. Fill stitching is the most common stitch in embroidery. Used to cover a large area, it takes on the flat look of foil without the sheen, of a sky without turbulence, a blanket with no texture. Does it mean more to show the emptiness or to fill in the space?

Portrait of Mother

Your domain was the domestic and I realize now that these hands, my hands, are not so very different from your own. How many times did I almost trip you? A silent observer at your feet as you shuffled about the kitchen in your soft pink slippers, your head further than Mars and just as uninhabitable. A hum vibrating on your lips. Pajamas. Always pajamas when at home. And cooking that involved a lot of steps. A lot of dishes. Like you had to leave evidence of your labor in the sink. Dishes spilling out the sides. And me, always wanting to handwash despite the dishwasher. I wanted to physically show you I was helping. That I could reside in the warm glow of your enclosed space and lighten the load. I got soap and suds everywhere. Perched like a bird on the stepstool, my sleeves rolled up to my elbows, sopping. I realize now that you indulged me. That I made your work more difficult. Take longer.

Here, I moused around your ankles as you busily hummed. Avoided getting in your way—by the sound of your hum I could tell when your head was above the clouds; if I made you come down too far it would be Nimbostratus for perhaps the rest of the day. Perpetual rain. A blotting out of the sun.

This was your space. And I was just in orbit. The space you created nourishing meals for us. Floured hand to wooden pin. Ladled spoon to soup. The timer chirping like a happy bird. I think about the linoleum. Faux tile, the pattern indelible: the place I loved you most.

Portrait of Father

You always apologized for the mess as you leaned over the cab bench to unlock the passenger door. I would mumble no-worries as my feet crinkled over empty cigarette packs and hostess snack cake wrappers and scooched my way in. There was a fine layer of ash on the dashboard, the ashtray always at the same level of overflowing. We would hand crank the windows down—did you ever have a truck with AC that worked?—and pop a tape in the tape deck.

We'd sing old country songs or Steve Miller Band's greatest hits. You'd say, "Well, lookie here, Ang…" as we came across a neon sign and bent our course for a deal. We'd climb out of the truck and you'd say something like, "Looks like they've got some books, Ang." You'd walk up in a lackadaisical way, casual, as if you had all the time in world. Your hands would reside in the front pockets of your jeans, as if you didn't want to touch anything unless seriously interested in purchasing. "Howdy-do," you'd nod at the sellers. We'd go our separate ways, gander at the trinkets and possessions people wanted to give up for nickels and dimes. I would always make my way to the stacks of books, rummage through, find a classic. You would always get a cookbook for mom. Or a random do-dad for your shop. A piece of wood to repurpose with your hands. Maybe a book or two for yourself. "Welp, Ang, did you find anything?"

We'd do this for a couple hours, maybe stop at a thrift store or two. Mom would say we didn't need any more junk. It wasn't about the stuff. It was about the windows rolled down on a fine day. The familiarity of a song. The seeking and finding. It was you saying, "I'll gladly pay you Tuesday for a hamburger today," before we grabbed a bite to eat or singing, "I love little baby ducks, and old pick-up trucks, and I love you too." It was our little slice of amity, sandwiched between blue collar and television.

I've noticed when I show someone my embroidery, they always want to see the back. They look at the front, what I want them to see, then they flip it. See where the thread trails. The litany of birdnesting. The bulbous and varying knots. Their fingers trace where the pattern isn't consistent. From the front, the work looks precise, made by educated hands with a purpose. But the backing? The backing is messy. Stop and go. I watch them looking, exposed. I watch them looking for the demarcations of creation.

If the initial fabric is supportive, the design can be visualized. Completed with little upset. Tear-away backing is different. Initially it is there to provide stability, but once the pattern is done, it is ripped away. If the backing is not cleverly conceived, is not pulled away cleanly, stitches rip. Edges are left ragged. Raw.

Block # 05116. This patch of quilt is of my grandma's design. A combined collection of her stitching and the stitchings of other women in the family. Backdrop of cerulean. "DANIEL L. YOUNGBLOOD" in a dark blue, the lines straight and concise. A photo of a young Danny printed on a patch of fabric. A section of bible verse, but I can't make out the words, just the images: Eagles and Jesus, a church with child-like trees; triangles atop miniature rectangles.

The AIDs quilt now weighs 54 tons. I can search for block # 05116 on an online database. The image is pixilated. Blurry. The only gap I see is the one between my uncle's teeth. This gap contains multitudes.

When embroidering now, I use no tear-away backing. No scraps of cardboard. No supporting infrastructure other than the hoop and fabric with a close weave. I know to not trim the edges of the fabric too close to the hoop so it doesn't give with the repetitive motion of the needle piercing and tugging. Piercing and tugging. Everything is freeform. No outline. A woman, her needle, a blank canvas.

Are you wondering where I am? I am the mouse at my mother's feet. The umbrella holder to her Nimbostratus. I am the consummate yard-saler, growing around the edges of my father's anger. Assertiveness is difficult to graft into learned passivity. I am the shame and guilt of feeling. Of holding in. I am the little girl who loved the gentlemen of her family. An admirer of spoons. A filler of stockings and bowls. I am the stitcher, the bird-nested tear-away backing, you'll see me in the gaps.

Mommy's Monsters

PEGGY HENDRY

"And this is Mandy," Mommy says. The man picks me up over his head, laughing with his mouth. When he puts me down, he pinches my cheek so hard it hurts. He has eyes like Daddy had. I don't like him.

Mommy and I follow him to his pickup. She bends over to me and says, "Isn't he handsome? He reminds me of your father."

We get into his pickup. I sit in the middle. "You're gonna love this," he says, and drives off, making dirt fly. "We're gonna to see the monster trucks."

I'm confused. "Are they Transformers?"

He laughs and pats my knee. "You'll see."

He drives us to a place he calls the rena. We climb a lot of stairs before we sit down. There isn't any shade. In the middle of the rena, trucks are hitting each other on purpose. They make loud crashes and big clouds of dust. It's stupid.

I want to get away from the sun and noise, so I say I have to go to the bathroom. Mommy nods. I scootch my way past the people between me and the stairs. Most of them are nice about it.

The inside part of the rena is cool and gray. I can still hear the trucks, but not so loud. I sit down and lean against the wall.

I look down at the purple flowers on my skirt. It's the most prettiest thing I wear. When I have it on I look beautiful like my friend Mindy, the purple princess. Mindy lives in a castle in a purple flower, and she wears purple dresses all the time. I let her wear the light-purple hat Mommy bought me for Easter. Everyone in the castle says she looks pretty in it.

When I know Mommy would want me to come back, I walk up the stairs. It's too loud and too bright. I squinch my eyes.

The man and Mommy are drinking beer. "I got you a soda," Mommy says. The soda is sweet and cold. I use the big paper cup to shade my eyes. My head hurts.

The truck crashes go on and on. "When can we go home?" I ask.

"Shhhh," Mommy says. "Don't be rude."

"Can I go downstairs again?"

"Yes, go on, but come back soon."

"Okay."

As soon as I turn the corner, I run down the stairs as fast as I can. I know Mommy wouldn't want me to, but I don't think anything bad will happen. When I get to the shady part at the bottom, I hop up the stairs on one leg and hop down the stairs on the other leg. That makes my head hurt more, so I stop.

I go into the bathroom. The sinks turn on when you stick your hand under them. I run up and down the row, trying to get them all to turn on at once. Some ladies frown at me, so I stop. I take water in my hands and splash it on my hurting head.

I go back and sit against the wall some more. I think about the bathrooms in the purple palace. They have sinks that turn on like that, too.

After a while, I go back to the seats. "Let's get hotdogs," Mommy says.

"Yeah, good idea. We need more beer, anyway," the man says.

We get hotdogs and bags of chips, and Mommy gets me a chocolate bar with nuts in it for after. It all tastes good, but then my tummy feels icky. "Mommy," I say, and then I throw up.

The man says a bad word and jumps up. "You got vomit on

my shoes, you little —" he says.

Mommy wipes my face with tissues and hands him some, too. "She didn't do it on purpose."

People are looking at us, especially the ones sitting in front of us. I think some throw-up got on them, too.

"We can't stay here now, the smell is disgusting," the man says. "Come on, let's go."

As we start down the row, someone shouts, "Hey! Aren't you going to clean that up?"

He says, "I'll find somebody who works here." He doesn't. He heads right back to his truck, and we follow him. "You better not throw up in here," he says.

"Tell me if you might throw up again, okay, baby?" Mommy says. I nod.

When we get home, Mommy asks the man if he wants to stay for dinner, but he doesn't. I'm glad. I go to bed and Mommy puts a cool washcloth over my eyes. I think about Princess Mindy's cabbage-leaf bed. It rocks in the cool breeze from the castle lake. I go to sleep.

The man is back. Mommy's making company dinner for him, while he and I watch TV in the living room. He puts his can of beer on the coffee table. I pick it up, wipe the table off with the bottom of my tee shirt, and put a coaster under it. "If you don't use a coaster, it leaves a ring."

"Think you're pretty smart, don't you?"

I don't say anything. Daddy taught me not to talk back.

He comes over more and more. He brings Mommy flowers a lot. He brings me some gummy bears, but I won't take them. The next time he comes, he brings me a chocolate bar with nuts in it. I know I'm not supposed to take it, but it's my favorite, so I do. He says, "Don't tell your mother." I don't tell Mommy, because I know we'll get in trouble. After that, he brings a chocolate nut bar every time. I eat the candy, but I still don't like him.

Kitty Cat doesn't like him, either. When she hears him coming, she runs to my room and hides under the bed. I know he did something bad to her, but I don't know what.

Before we got Kitty Cat, we had a kitten. I called her Baby. She was so sweet with her big eyes and her teeny feet. One day, Daddy's car hit Baby in the driveway. I ran to her but she wouldn't look at me and she wouldn't move. I got Mommy, and she said Baby was dead. I asked her when Baby would stop being dead. "Oh, Mandy," she said, and hugged me. "Baby's not ever going to stop being dead." I cried, and Mommy did, too.

Daddy said, "We're not going to let you have cats if you're gonna cry when they die."

Mommy and I dug a hole in the yard and put Baby in it, wrapped in a towel. I was sure Mommy was wrong. Baby followed me everywhere and slept on my pillow. I knew she'd come back to me. After a few days, I went and dug in the dirt, because maybe Baby needed help getting out of where we put her. What I saw in the hole didn't look anything like my Baby. That's when I knew what dead is.

Mommy tells me to entertain the man while she's fixing dinner. "I'm making lasagna. I'll be out as soon as I put it in the oven…. Oh, Mandy, I hope this works out. You like Clint, don't you?"

I don't want to hurt Mommy's feelings, so I say, "Uh-huh."

He and I are sitting on the back porch, the one that faces the pasture, when he picks me up and puts me on his lap. I try to get down, but he holds me there. Something bad is coming. I try to say no, but it won't come out.

"You like that, don't you?"

I shake my head no no no.

"Sure, you do."

I shriek.

"Mandy?" Mommy comes fast from the kitchen. He pushes me off his lap and I fall face-down on the floor. "What happened?" she asks.

"She fell." He pulls me up by one arm. "This is our secret," he says in my ear, "like the candy."

I run and hide behind Mommy's legs. She goes down on one knee to look me over in her Nurse Mommy way. "You're okay, baby. You just fell down. Come to the kitchen and I'll give you a chocolate-chip cookie."

In the kitchen, Mommy sits me in a chair and looks me in the eyes. "How did you fall, Baby? Did Clint do something to hurt you?"

I want to tell her, but I can't. If I do, he'll tell about the candy. So I say, "He didn't do anything."

"You sure?"

I nod, and she gets me a cookie.

That night, after I go to bed, I hear the man yelling. Something goes crash.

There's a monster in the purple kingdom. Princess Mindy and her friends don't know what to do. They hide inside the castle and be very quiet.

Mommy's telling him to keep his voice down, "For God's sake, Mandy's right down the hall." He yells even louder and she yells, too. Then there are ugly sounds. I hear Mommy crying. The next day, Mommy looks like she fell down and skinned her face.

Mommy comes into my room. "Mandy, is Clint hurting you? At all? Even a little?"

I shake my head.

"You'd tell me if he did, wouldn't you?"

I don't like lying to her, but I have to.

"Okay." She hugs me tight. "Okay."

My Mommy's a hopsis nurse. She helps people who are trying to die. I don't know why people want to die, but I know my Mommy's a hero. She brings home flowers and candy all the time that people give her because she's so wonderful.

Mommy works at the hopsis on Sundays. Karen used to come stay with me, but he says he'll do it from now on. "No point paying for a babysitter. It'll give us a chance to get friendly. I'll teach her all about football."

Mommy's about to go out the door in her blue nurse pants. She gives me a hug and a kiss. "You call me if anything doesn't feel right," she says real quiet. "If you don't feel safe, you run next door to Miss Millie and call me."

I nod.

"What do you do if things don't feel right, Mandy? Say it."

"I run to Miss Millie and call you."

"Okay," She hugs me again. "I love you, baby."

"I love you, too, Mommy."

"I love you more."

"No, I love you more."

She smiles and leaves. I don't think she wants to go.

As soon as she's gone, the man gives me a chocolate bar. I eat it and we watch football. It's ugly and boring. He likes to watch the men knock each other down, and he explains to me every time how they did it. Sometimes the men who get knocked down are carried away and don't come back. "Are those men dead?" I ask.

"Dead?" He looks at me and frowns. People on the TV cheer, and he looks back at it. "Dammit! I missed a touchdown! Don't ask questions, just listen to what I tell you."

I don't listen. Instead, I go in my head and visit Princess Mindy and her friends, Rose and Daisy. Daisy can be so silly sometimes.

At half-time, he says, "Now we get friendly."

I don't like the way he says it. I remember what Mommy said so I try to run to Miss Millie. He grabs me from behind and shoves a sock in my mouth. The sock makes it hard to breathe. I kick and thrash. After a long time, he stops moving. We sit like that for a while.

"This is our secret," he says. "If you ever tell, I'll kill you. I'll kill your mother. Understand?"

I nod. He takes his hand away and lets go and I pull the wet sock out of my mouth and grab my underpants off the floor. I want to run away, but it's too late for that now.

"We better get cleaned up," he says. "Come on."

I follow him upstairs. I'm scared for him to be behind me.

He washes in the bathroom sink. I hide in my room and peek under my locked door. I'm scared he might come after me again, but he doesn't. He just goes downstairs.

I go to the bathroom and fill the bathtub and wash and wash. The blood comes off, but I'm not clean.

I stay in my room until Mommy comes home. The Peter Pan and Wendy dolls watch me from over my bed. They can't help.

My body hurts. A lot. Where he did it.

When I hear Mommy come in the door, I run so fast to see her that I trip at the top of the stairs and fall on my hands and knees and slide down. I stop when my head hits the wall. Now my head hurts, too, and I start to cry.

Mommy runs up the stairs. "Mandy!" She looks at me all over. "Are you all right?"

I have a bump growing out of my head. I poke it with my fingers.

"What's going on?" He yells from the living room.

"Mandy fell down the stairs." She's hugging me.

"She okay?" He doesn't come out of the living room.

"She's skinned up, but she's okay." She talks loud to him but she talks to me in her soft, I-love-you voice. "You scared me, Mandy. You could have died falling down those stairs."

I put my arms around her and cry harder. She hugs me some more and we rock back and forth.

"What did you trip on? How many times have I told you not to leave your toys around the stairs?"

"I dunno."

She lets me go and walks up the stairs. I wipe my nose on my sleeve when she's not looking.

"For Heaven's sake. The carpet has come loose up here. No wonder you tripped. I'm sorry, baby. I'm sorry I blamed you and your toys."

We walk down the stairs into the kitchen.

"Here, baby, let me clean you up." She washes my face and elbows, and gives me an ice cube in a dish towel to put on my head.

She brings me a pill and some orange juice. "Take this." I make a face. She tilts her head and smiles at me. "Ta-a-a-a-ke it."

So I do. The orange juice tastes good, and I hold out my glass for more. She kisses my cheek and brings me some. "There was an old woman who swallowed a fly," she sings.

I love that song.

"I don't know why she swallowed a fly." She opens her eyes

real wide. "Perhaps she'll die."

I giggle. We sing the whole song. The ice is dripping down my face, and Mommy takes it away. We keep singing silly songs while she makes dinner.

I promise to be quiet now. He doesn't put the sock in my mouth when he holds me. When the hurt comes, I put my teeth together real hard and go to the purple kingdom, where Princess Mindy and her friends whisper about how to make the monster go away.

Mommy worries because I have so many headaches. We don't talk about her bruises under her clothes.

I hate him. I hate him so much.

Princess Mindy wears purple armor and rides a unicorn that spits fire. She has a big sword with purple ribbons tied on it. Rose and Daisy have big sticks with knifes on the ends of them. They ride dragons as big as the houses in the village below the castle.

They make a big paper monster and prop it up in a field, like a scarecrow. Mindy rides her unicorn and Rose and Daisy fly over on their dragons. The Animals shoot fire at the paper monster and the girls stab it. The paper monster tears apart and burns. Daisy falls off her dragon and breaks her leg. She says it was worth it. They write castle hero all over her cast.

Sunday. Mommy kisses me and goes out the door in her blue hopsis clothes. He and I watch football. He talks about how the men knock each other down. This time, I pay attention.

Half-time. I follow him upstairs.

I wait in my room, peeking under the door. I wonder if my plan will work, and I wonder how much trouble I'm going to be in. I watch his feet leave the bathroom and walk down the hall. When he's almost at the top of the stairs, I run as fast as I can and throw my whole body at the back of his knees. We both fall down the stairs.

I wake up on the floor. My head hurts but my arm hurts worse. Everything I see is blurry. I look at him. His head is on his body wrong. He looks like Baby after Daddy hit her with the car.

Good.

I try to stand and throw up.

The room is woozy and I walk to the kitchen, leaning on the wall, and call the number Mommy put on the fridge.

A lady I know answers the phone. "Mercy Hospice. How can I help?"

"This is Mandy. I need my mommy."

"She's pronouncing a death right now, honey. Can I have her call you back when she's done?"

"It's a mergency."

"What kind of emergency is it, Mandy?"

"I'm bleeding a lot."

"Okay, I'm going to get her right now." The phone starts making music in my ear. I'm dizzy.

The music stops and Mommy says, "Mandy, what happened? Nancy says you're bleeding."

"My head's bleeding and it hurts real bad. Come home."

"Let me talk to Clint."

"I can't. He won't wake up."

Mommy says a bad word. "I'm coming home. I'll be there as soon as I can."

I rinse my mouth and sit at the table, holding my hurt arm in front of me. I hope Mommy won't be mad.

She runs in the door and sees him on the floor and drops her purse. "Clint!" She squats down and touches him on the neck, strokes his hair. She starts to cry and shakes his shoulder. "Not you."

Mommy wipes her eyes and looks at me. She makes a scared noise when she sees my bloody head. She rushes over and pushes all around on it. "Don't!" I say and pull away.

She starts to hug me, then sees my arm. She touches it gently, but she still hurts me. I cry harder.

"I think your arm's broken, baby, and your head needs help,

too. We have to go to the emergency room."

"Okay." I try to stop crying. Mommy gives me a tissue.

"Blow."

I do. She picks me up and carries me to the car.

"What about him?" I ask as Mommy walks around the dead man.

"No one can help him now. I'll…think about him later."

The people at the hospital all know my Mommy. They let us cut in line. The doctor is real nice, but he hurts my arm when he moves it around. Mommy says he has to move it, if it's going to get better.

Loud blue men come. I know they're policemen because of Sesame Street. They ask Mommy questions. She keeps shaking her head and saying, "I don't know, I don't know." The big men want to ask me questions, too. The doctor won't let them.

I sleep in the hospital that night, in a white bed that goes up and down. Mommy stays with me and sleeps in a chair.

The next day the policemen ask me what happened. I say I don't remember. I do remember, but I don't want to get in trouble. The doctor tells them it's normal for someone who hit their head not to remember what happened. They don't bother me again. But they keep asking Mommy questions.

I thought we'd go home after the hospital, but we go to Grammy's house. When Grammy sees us, she hugs us and hugs us. "I'm so sorry that happened," she says to Mommy. "We'll talk later?"

Mommy nods.

Grammy smiles at me, and says, "I made those cookies you like, Mandy-pants."

"Will you draw something pretty on my cast?"

"You bet I will. Now, let's get those cookies while they're still warm."

In the kitchen, Mommy says, "Are you sure you don't mind us staying here?"

"As far as I'm concerned, you could both move right in."

Mommy gets her mad face. "You know I can't live in this

house, Mom, and you know why."

"But your father's been dead for years."

"To me, he's everywhere in this house." She puts her arms across her chest like she's cold. "Clint may have been a bastard, but at least he didn't—do that—to my little girl."

"Well, I've made up the bed in your old room for you." Her voice sounds funny, not like my happy Grammy.

"I won't sleep in that room. I'd rather sleep on the pull-out couch."

And we do. It's fun, but my head still hurts. So does my arm.

A man in a suit comes and asks us more questions. Mommy says she doesn't know. I say I don't remember.

The suit man says Mommy has to go to a n-quest. I thought a quest was what knights went on. Mommy says they call it a n-quest because of the number of questions she'll have to answer. "I hope they'll stop asking after this. I'm tired of telling them I don't know what happened."

When we go home, there's yellow ribbon all over the hall and white tape on the floor. Mommy puts me to bed with a bowl of soup. I hear her down by the bottom of the stairs, crying and talking to herself.

After the N-quest, Mommy goes back to work. Karen comes, and we play Old Maid and Go Fish. Karen makes the best brownies, but my Mommy's are better.

Princess Mindy makes a big party in the purple kingdom. All the chocolate you want, and the unicorn and the dragons get medals with purple ribbons on them. Princess Mindy tells Rose and Daisy they can be princesses now, too, because they were so brave when the battle came.

In the fall, I start first grade. The other kids are loud and run around all the time like they're crazy. I like learning stuff and I like my teacher. She's pretty and she smiles a lot.

The girls in the purple kingdom go to school, too. They wear purple bows in their hair and take bunches of grapes to their teacher.

In school, we make red and yellow and orange leaves and tape them all over the room. Later, we make pumpkins with big yellow smiles. Pretty soon, we take the pumpkins down and put up turkeys.

"We're going to Wanda's for Thanksgiving this year," Mommy says.

"What about Grammy? We always go to Grammy's house."

"Wanda says Grammy can come, too."

"But why? Why can't we go to Grammy's house?

"Don't whine, Mandy. It's not nice. There's someone Wanda wants me to meet. Someone I want to meet."

I stamp my foot. "But it's Thanksgiving! We go to Grammy's house!"

"I'm sure we'll have a good time—we'll all have a good time. And Grammy won't have to cook."

I stick out my bottom lip. "But Grammy loves to cook for us!"

She gives me her don't-talk-back look. "We're going and that's final."

I bet Mindy gets to go to her Grammy's house for Thanksgiving.

We go to Wanda's for Thanksgiving. I wear my new light-purple skirt. The old one got too little. This one has dark purple kitties on it. They have red hats on.

I'm mad because I don't get to sit at the grown-up table like a real person. Grammy comes and sits next to me, and we have more fun than anybody.

After dinner, I go outside and play with the other kids. When it's getting dark, we go back inside and ask for more pie.

"Mandy," Mommy says. "Come over here. There's someone I want you to meet." The big man sitting beside her stares at me. "Mandy, this is Vern."

The man looks down at me and says, "Well, howdy, little lady." He smiles with his mouth, but his eyes are like Daddy's. I don't like him.

Red Feather Boa

ALICE LOWE

I **turned six in an empty house,** four days before my family's departure from our Long Island, New York suburb, destination California to start anew in the land of sunshine and opportunity, our furniture and bric-a-brac in a moving van already headed west. A few neighbor kids joined me on the bare living room floor, where we donned paper party hats and balanced cake and ice cream in paper bowls on our laps.

At ten I had a slumber party, my first. I invited Len, who lived on the next block and with whom I'd been hanging out at the beach that summer. She had a white mother and a Black father, the first biracial family in our provincial Southern California town. I was surprised and disappointed when a couple of the other girls, or their parents, cancelled with polite excuses; my mother explained that they didn't want their daughters consorting with Len. I didn't get it. I still don't.

Twenty-one at last, though I'd been drinking since my mid-teens. Like Dorothy's scarecrow when awarded a diploma as proof of his intellect, I now had the long-coveted certification of my adulthood. At lunch with co-workers, my boss announced the occasion as he ordered my first legal martini. I flashed my ID at the bartender, who sputtered: "But I've been serving you for years."

I invited forty friends to celebrate my fortieth birthday, mixing and matching people from my multiple lives as graduate student, single mother, program assistant at Planned Parenthood. A friend brought a tray of California rolls, sliced and arranged in large numbers 4 and 0, a candle in the middle.

I flew to Seattle to spend my fiftieth with my boyfriend, now husband. I told him I wanted a low-key birthday, not to fuss over me. He took me literally and then some—no card, no gift, no flowers, no song. No breakfast in bed, no celebratory dinner a deux. Nothing. Back home, a close friend hosted a brunch with several friends and my first Dom Perignon champagne, first Osetra caviar. She understood "low key."

My workmates gave me a red feather boa when I turned sixty. Photos from our in-office celebration show us in hats—mine a red beret—with platters of food on the table, banners on the wall. Or so I recalled until reminded that the boa was for my fiftieth, leaving sixty a mystery, a black hole, just another day.

At seventy I got my first tattoo, ran my first half marathon, welcomed my first great-grandchild. To paraphrase Gloria Steinem, this is what seventy looks like.

And now eighty. I celebrated in Maine with a close friend also turning eighty, and again at home at a festive brunch hosted by my daughter. Maybe because my mother died at sixty, I never visualized myself on this lofty peak. Anne Sexton said, "In a dream you are never eighty," but in life—if, unlike Anne, you're lucky—you are.

Four Poems

JESSICA MELILLI-HAND

Jane's Tongue Flops Out

Jane swallows so many sharp words her tongue severs
and fish-flops to the kitchen floor.
Jane's eyes say *Oh, oh*! as the cat bats it about.
It goes *schlop, schlop*, the cat shakes its paw at the insult
of dampness, and Jane tastes faint cleaner and crumbs.

Jane tries to call for help:
Mah mah she cries *Ba ba ha ha pah*!
She tries signing but only knows the words
Hello, beautiful, and more.

Hello beautiful, she signs when she means help.
The people wave. Hello more beautiful
hello beautiful, more. More hello more hello.
The people wave. She can say *puh*.
Hello she signs. *Puh* she says.
Hello*puh* hello*puh* hello*puh*.

A fly lands on her tongue and it thrashes about, spooks the cat.
Thwack thwack her tongue says.
Hello*puh* MahMah. Hello*puh* Pah. Hello*puh* beautiful.

Her mother waves. Her father waves.
Someone beautiful keeps walking.

Duet for Flute and Voice

Sometimes I am willing to believe you
must be a god; grass falls prostrate

with each step. What would Whitman say?
Dear Walt, you taught us with your mouth full

of grass, and we are trying to listen, trying to live
like life is enough. When you breathe, Love,

across the flute's empty spaces, sound is born
where before there was nothing. I am listening.

Don't worry, Love. No other woman's sounds
can ever fill my ears. My mouth is full

of you. When I lie in the grass and listen,
your flute's sine wave is a bowl rolling

rolling over,
never empty.

Wedding Poem
for the ghosts of my living parents

Because your ghosts hollow
the space beside me, a bride
with a bride, guests ask me when
you both broke back to soil and sky.
When I tell them, no, you are alive,
it still feels like grieving,
like sinking beneath gravity.

Call me daughter again.
You vanish.
Call me daughter.
Your mouths: sewn shut.
So many preachers
with needles for tongues.

In my left pocket, the blackbird I carry.
I wish you could see.
Inside the body of another woman, my heart
is a bird building its nest.
You scissor toward wings.

I want you to remember *Feelin' Groovy*

into our spatulas while you taught me to fry okra.
Wish I could waltz with my dad
when the first song plays. I can't find my mother
as the rice rains down.

We do not have time.
Like Jeremiah lamenting Jerusalem,
you pour your livers upon the earth,
but you do not have Jeremiah's eyes,
and I am not the virgin
daughter of Zion. Look at me
and call me daughter. While we cry
get thee behind me at each other,
we do not have time. A hand holds
a C-shaped stone, grinds your livers
to feed that final dark. Its mouth seeks.

Consider the Orange

The weight in your palm,
the way your palm takes its shape.
Consider the sound of the peel spiraling—
our DNA—and the orange still present after
the peel falls away. The release of juice anoints
your weary tongue, drips down your arms. When you
hold the orange to your mouth, it looks like prayer.
Consider the seed inside the orange, the orange inside
the seed inside the orange. When I hold you to my mouth,
your dress spirals to the floor. Sunlight slants through
the window, the window a seed of the world outside
inside. Outside, water has gathered together after
a rain. The roots of the orange tree pull until
each orange swells with alchemy. Your shape
weights my palms. Let me taste.
Bless me, Love, as we pull
together, as we stay.

Contributors

Bobby Neel Adams was born in Black Mountain, North Carolina and presently resides in Arizona on the Mexico Border. Adams has exhibited worldwide and his photographs are in the permanent collections of: International Center for Photography, Houston Museum of Fine Arts, Station Museum, diRosa Foundation, and the Norton Family Foundation to name a few. Adams has received grants and awards from the Aaron Siskind Foundation, LEF Foundation, MacDowell Art Colony and the Hermitage. His book Broken Wings was published by the Greenville Museum in 1997. Adams is currently working on a series of Memento Mori photographs of insects, birds, and mammals. He is the *Eckleburg No. 22* featured artist.

Vimi Bajaj is both a physician and a fiction writer and graduated from the Bennington Writing Seminars. While she is currently working on a novel based in her native India, her other works have been published in journals such as *Eckleburg*, *The Asian American Literary Review*, *The Bristol Short Story Prize Anthology*, and others.

Kurt Baumeister is the author of the novels *Pax Americana* and the forthcoming *Twilight of the Gods*. His writing has appeared in *Salon*, *Guernica*, *Electric Literature*, *Rain Taxi*, *The Brooklyn Rail*, *The Rumpus*, *Vol. 1 Brooklyn*, *The Nervous Breakdown*, *The Weeklings*, and other outlets. An acquisitions editor with 7.13 Books, Baumeister holds an MFA in creative writing from Emerson College, and is a member of The National Book Critics Circle and The Authors Guild. Find him at kurtbaumeister.com.

Melisa Cahnmann-Taylor, Meigs Professor of Language and Literacy Education at the University of Georgia, is the author of *The Creative Ethnographer's Notebook* (2024), the poetry-book, *Imperfect Tense* (2016) and five other books on the arts of language and education. Recipient of six NEA Big Read Grants, a 2023 NEA Distinguished Fellowship, Hambidge Residency Award, and the Beckman award, her poems have appeared in *Georgia Review, Bitter Southerner, Lilith, Poet Lore, Rattle, American Poetry Review, Barrow Street*, and elsewhere.

Kim Chinquee grew up on a dairy farm in Wisconsin, was a medical laboratory technician in the Air Force and elsewhere (most recently, during COVID). She's the author of seven collections: *Oh Baby, Pretty, Pistol, Veer, Shot Girls, Wetsuit, Snowdog*, and the novel *Pipette*. She's Chief Editor of *Elm Leaves Journal* (ELJ), Senior Editor of *New World Writing*, and Contributing Editor of *Midwest Review*. Her work has been published widely and received three Pushcart Prizes and a Henfield Prize. She's a competitive triathlete and lives with her three dogs in Tonawanda, New York.

Kay Cosgrove is the author of *Anybody Home?* (Blue Edge Books 2023). She received a BA from Fairfield University, an MFA from Sarah Lawrence College, and a PhD in American Literature and Creative Writing from the University of Houston. She is the recipient of awards from The Academy of American Poets, Inprint Houston, and *The Westchester Review*. Her poetry has appeared in *The Southern Review, The Missouri Review, American Poetry Review, Prairie Schooner*, and *EPOCH Magazine*, among other journals. She lives in Philadelphia.

Ruth Ann Dandrea spent more than thirty years teaching high school kids to believe this truth: "Sometimes you need a story more than food to stay alive" (Badger in Barry Lopez's *Crow and Weasel*). Her stories, poems and essays have appeared in literary magazines, newspapers and education publications. She is co-author of a book on women's kayaking, called *WOW: Women on Water*, which was named the Adirondack Center for Writing's nonfiction book of 2012. A book of her poetry, *Castings*, is forthcoming from Doubly Mad Press. She serves as fiction editor for the literary magazine *Doubly Mad*. Summer Thursdays you can find her paddling a yellow boat on quiet Adirondack waters.

Kika Dorsey is an author in Boulder, Colorado. She has a PhD in Comparative Literature and her books include the poetry collections *Beside Herself, Rust, Coming Up for Air, Occupied: Vienna is a Broken Man and Daughter of Hunger*, which won the Colorado Authors' League Award for best poetry collection, the novel As *Joan Approaches Infinity* and her recent collection of poetry, *Good Ash*. She has been nominated numerous times for the Pushcart Prize and for Best of Net. Currently, she is a lecturer at the University of Colorado in literature and creative writing. In her free time she swims miles in pools and runs and hikes in the open space of Colorado's mountains and plains.

Karen Elias taught college English for 40 years, Dr. Karen Elias is now an artist/activist, using photography to record the beauty and fragility of the natural world and to raise awareness about climate change. Her work is in private collections, has been exhibited in several galleries, and has won numerous awards. She is a board member of the Clinton County PA Arts Council where she serves as curator of the annual juried photography exhibit.

Avital Gad-Cykman is the author of *Light Reflection Over Blues* (Ravenna Press) and *Life In, Life Out* (Matter Press). She is the winner of Margaret Atwood Studies Magazine Prize and The Hawthorne Citation Short Story Contest, twice a finalist for the Iowa Fiction Award and a six-time nominee for the Pushcart. Her stories appear in *Spectrum, Eckleburg, Iron Horse, Prairie Schooner, Ambit, McSweeney's Quarterly* and *Michigan Quarterly, Best Short Fictions*, W.W. Norton's *Flash Fiction International* anthology and elsewhere. She holds a PhD in English Literature, focused on minorities, gender and trauma and lives in Brazil.

Adele Gardner (they/them, Mx., MLIS, MA) has over 500 stories, poems, art, and articles in *American Arts Quarterly, The*

Cape Rock, Pedestal Magazine, Flash Fiction Online, Analog Science Fiction and Fact, Legends of the Pendragon, and more. Adele's poetry collection, *Halloween Hearts* (Jackanapes Press) celebrates in part the creative spirit of Edgar Allan Poe. Twelve of Adele's poems won or placed in the Poetry Society of Virginia Awards, Rhysling Award, and Balticon Poetry Contest.

Judith Goode was awarded a full fellowship to the Iowa Writers Workshop. Her short stories have been published in numerous literary magazines, such as *Calliope* and *The Forge.* She was born and raised in New York City, and lives in Saugerties NY. Her short story "Frittura," originally published in *Menacing Hedge* is the *Eckleburg No. 22* Gertrude Stein Award First Place winner.

Michele Hanson teaches English and French at Colorado Mesa University. She hikes often with her dogs and tries to devote some time to oil painting and finishing a novel. Her work has been published in *Eckleburg* and in the anthology *Mothers Tales: Journeys of the Heart.*

Jason Marc Harris teaches creative writing, folklore, and literature, and is the Creative Writing Coordinator at Texas A&M University in College Station, TX. He graduated with a Ph.D. in English Literature from the University of Washington, and an MFA in fiction from Bowling Green State University. Creative work includes his novella *Master of Rods and Strings* (Crystal Lake Publishing 2024), and stories in journals such as *Arroyo Literary Review, Marvels and Tales, Midwestern Gothic, Psychopomp Magazine, The Saturday Evening Post,* and *Writing Texas.*

Kathleen Hellen is the recipient of the James Still Award, the Thomas Merton Prize for Poetry of the Sacred, and prizes from the *H.O.W. Journal* and *Washington Square Review.* Her debut collection *Umberto's Night* won the poetry prize from Washington Writers' Publishing House. She is the author of *The Only Country Was the Color of My Skin, Meet Me at the Bottom,* and two chapbooks. Hellen's poems have appeared in the *Colorado Review,*

Evergreen Review, Gargoyle, jubilat, Massachusetts Review, North American Review, Poetry Northwest, Prairie Schooner, The Rumpus, Salamander, Sixth Finch, West Branch, and elsewhere.

Peggy Hendry's work has appeared in *The Storyteller, Journal of the Society of Southwest Authors; DASH Literary Journal; Months to Years Magazine*; and, *Eckleburg*. She is in the process of publishing her novels, *Witch Interrupted* and *Emily's Asexual Romance*. She lives in the beautiful Sonoran Desert with her husband and the cat who owns them.

Susan Hodara is a memoirist, journalist and teacher. Her articles have appeared in *The New York Times, Communication Arts* and other publications. Her short memoirs are published in a variety of anthologies and literary journals. For over a decade, she has taught memoir writing workshops at the Hudson Valley Writers Center in New York's Hudson Valley. Hodara is one of four co-authors of *Still Here Thinking of You: A Second Chance With Our Mothers* (Big Table Publishing, 2013). Read more at susanhodara.com.

Elizabeth Jaeger's memoir *Stolen: Love and Loss in the Time of COVID* is forthcoming from Unsolicited Press. Her essays, short stories, book reviews and poetry have been published in various print and online journals, including *Margate Bookie, Caustic Frolic, The Blue Nib, Capsule Stories, Watchung Review, The Doctor T. J. Eckleburg Review* and *Italian Americana*. She is a history teacher and she lives in New Jersey with her wife, son, and three cats.

Anna Maria Johnson earned her MFA from Vermont College of Fine Arts and now teaches in the School of Writing, Rhetoric and Technical Communication at James Madison University. She spends her free time studying the natural world and figuring out how best to respond to and live well within it. She makes her home with conservation photographer Steven David Johnson along the north fork of the Shenandoah River in Rockingham

County, Virginia. She volunteers as a Virginia Master Naturalist and serves as president of the Shenandoah Chapter of the Virginia Native Plant Society. Her proudest publication thus far has been the collaborative project, *Plant Ridge & Valley Natives: A Guide for Gardeners*, which encourages people to convert their yards to ecological gardens that support the natural world.

Steven David Johnson is a conservation photographer and Professor of Visual and Communication Arts at EMU in the Shenandoah Valley of Virginia. His photography of the natural world has appeared in *Wildlife Photographer of the Year*, *Nature Conservancy Magazine*, *Ranger Rick*, *Virginia Wildlife*, *Biographic*, and *Orion*. When he's not in the office, you'll probably find him crouched next to a vernal pool or kayaking the North Fork of the Shenandoah River.

Julie Jones has been nominated for Best Microfiction and Best of the Net, and honored as a contest finalist by *River Styx* and *f(r)iction*. Her short stories have appeared in *Eckleburg*, *Cincinnati Review*, *Chicago Quarterly Review*, and *Atticus Review*, among others. She earned her MFA in Writing from the Vermont College of Fine Arts and lives in Connecticut. You can find her at juliemjones.com.

Jarrett Kaufman has been awarded scholarships from the Lighthouse Writers Workshop, the Cambridge Writers Workshop, and the Minnesota Northwoods Writers Conference. His fiction has been nominated for a Pushcart Prize and has won numerous literary awards, including the Mary Mackey Fiction Award, the Gertrude Stein Fiction Award, the Missouri Writers Guild President's Award for Fiction, and the Ernest Hemingway Flash Fiction Prize. His stories have been published in over a dozen literary journals. Most recently, his work has been published in *Fiction Southeast*, *Arkansas Review*, *Another Chicago Magazine*, and *The South Dakota Review*.

Jessica Lanay (She/They) is a Black feminist interdisciplinary writer, poet, and art journalist raised in Key West, Florida. Their/Her debut hybrid poetry collection, am•phib•ian won the 2020

Naomi Long Madgett Poetry Prize judged by Toi Derricotte from Broadside Lotus Press. They/She is a Cave Canem and Callaloo Fellow. Their/Her poetry can be found in *Indiana Review, Prairie Schooner, Poet Lore,* and others. They/She has performed her poetry at the Brooklyn Museum, The Cave Canem and Bowery Presents First Book series, and with Brooklyn Poets. Their/Her personal and craft essays can be found in *Salt Hill Journal* and *Black Warrior Review.* Lanay's art writing can currently be found in BOMB Magazine where she has interviewed artists such as El Anatsui, Howardena Pindell, Vanessa German, and Shikeith, among others. Their/Her art criticism can also be found in catalog contributions for The Andy Warhol Museum's exhibition Fantasy America, Nona Faustine's monograph White Shoes, and the Washington Project for the Arts exhibition curated by Tsedaye Makonnen Black Women As/And The Living Archive.

Sara Lippmann is the author of the novel *Lech* (Tortoise Books) and the story collections *Doll Palace* (re-released by 7.13 Books) and *Jerks* (Mason Jar Press.) Her fiction has won the Lilith Prize, been honored by the New York Foundation for the Arts, and her essays have appeared in *The Millions, The Washington Post, Catapult, The Lit Hub* and elsewhere. With Seth Rogoff, she is co-editing the anthology *Smashing the Tablets: Radical Retellings of the Hebrew Bible* for SUNY Press. She received a BA from Brown and an MFA from The New School, and has been teaching creative writing for over 20 years to students of all ages, most recently with the teaching cooperative Writing Co-lab, of which she is a founding member. Raised outside of Philadelphia, she lives with her family in Brooklyn. Read more at saralippmann.com.

Deborah A. Lott is the author of the tragicomic memoir *Don't Go Crazy Without Me.* Her work has been published in *Alaska Quarterly Review, Bellingham Review, Black Warrior Review, Rumpus, Salon, Los Angeles Times, Cimarron Review, Crazyhorse, StoryQuarterly,* and many other places. Her essays have been thrice named as notables in Best American Essay. She teaches creative writing and literature at Antioch University Los Angeles and oversees its literary journal *Two Hawks Quarterly*.

Alice Lowe writes about life, literature, food and family in San Diego CA. Recent work has been published in *Bluebird Word*, *Burningword*, *New World Writing*, *Skipjack Review*, *Big City Lit*, *Bridge VIII*, and *Bookends Review*. She's been cited twice in Best American Essays. Read and reach her at aliceloweblogs.wordpress.com.

Marjorie Maddox is a professor Emerita of English at Commonwealth University, *Presence* assistant editor, and *WPSU-FM Poetry Moment* host. Maddox has published 17 collections of poetry—including *Transplant, Transport, Transubstantiation*; *Begin with a Question*; *How Can I Look It Up When I Don't Know How It's Spelled?*; *Seeing Things*; *In the Museum of My Daughter's Mind*; *Heart Speaks, Is Spoken For*; *Small Earthly Space, Seeing Things* and *Hover Here* (forthcoming)—plus a story collection, 4 children's books, and the anthologies *Common Wealth: Contemporary Poets on Pennsylvania* and *Keystone Poetry*. Read more at marjoriemaddox.com.

Rita Maria Martinez is the daughter of Cuban immigrants. Her current poetry raises awareness about triumphs and challenges navigating life with chronic daily headache (CDH) and migraine. Her Jane Eyre-inspired poetry collection—*The Jane and Bertha in Me* (Kelsay Books)—was a finalist for the Andrés Montoya Poetry Prize. Martinez's poetry appears in *The Best American Poetry Blog*, *Ploughshares*, *Pleidades*, and *TupeloQuarterly*. Her work is also featured in CLMP's 2023 Disability Pride Month reading list. Follow Rita on Instagram @rita.maria.martinez.poet or visit comeonhome.org/ritamartinez.

Monica Marioni was born near Treviso and moved to an area of Vicenza when she was still very young, and here she still lives several months a year. She obtained a degree in statistical sciences because of her passion for **mathematics**, a science in which she has found ample space for creativity. In 2005 she began to devote herself to a full-time art career and started to translate her matherical attitude in the dense material nature of her first abstract works, created on the most disparate supports, with a wealth of strong juxtapositions between metals, plastics, earth and resins, which she commanded through an intense manual action of selection and transformation. Her work has been shown in Venice, Washington DC, Miami, Lima, Rome, and Capri, and she was the recipient of the First Prize of the Fiorino d'Oro for Painting in Florence, Italy. Read more at monicamarioni.com.

Michael Martone's newest book is *Table Talk & Second Thoughts*, a memoir in flash. Recently retired after teaching at four universities over forty years, he lives in Tuscaloosa, below the Bug Line, where he putters in his gardens and works on his new book, *Fort Fort Wayne*, which includes the pieces printed here.

Jessica Melilli-Hand, an associate professor of English at the College of Coastal Georgia, is published in *Eckleburg, CALYX, Hunger Mountain, Painted Bride Quarterly, The Minnesota Review*, and elsewhere. She won first place in the Agnes Scott Poetry Competition three times: when judged by Terrance Hayes, Arda Collins, and Martín Espada.

Toti O'Brien is the Italian Accordionist with the Irish Last Name. Born in Rome, living in Los Angeles, she is an artist, musician and dancer. She is the author of four collections of poetry and three of prose. Her short story collection *Alter Alter* was released by Elyssar Press in 2024.

Amy Scanlan O'Hearn is a writer and teacher in southern New Jersey. She is a 2013 graduate of Rutgers University MFA in Creative Writing, recipient of the Oregon Poets Association New Poets prize for 2015 and has worked as Poetry Editor for *Typehouse Magazine*. Fiction and poetry appears in *Helen, Bacopa Review, Mom Egg Review, Per Contra*, and *Panolplyzine*. Her essay "Hopkins Pond" appears in *The Doctor T.J. Eckleberg Review* of

August, 2019.

Lillian Ann Slugocki has created a body of work on women and sexuality for print and for the stage including; The Public Theater, HERE, Circle Rep, Naked Angels, Labyrinth Theater, National Public Radio, and WBAI. Her creative nonfiction has been published in *Longreads, Tupelo Quarterly, The Taoist (Medium) Salon, Hypertext, The Atticus Review, Entropy, Bloom/The Millions, Beatrice, HerKind/Vida, Eckleburg, The Nervous Breakdown*. Books include *The Erotica Project* with Erin Cressida Williams (Cleis Press), *How to Travel with Your Demons* (Spuyten Duyvil Press) and *CREDO: An Anthology of Manifestos and Sourcebook for Creative Writing* (C & R Press).

Marija Stajic's short stories have been published in dozens for literary journals, including *Prairie Schooner, Best Small Fictions, Hudson Review, Eckleburg* and more. Her work has been awarded, anthologized and nominated for Pushcart. She is a writer/editor for the U.S. Federal Government. She has an MA in International Journalism and a BA in Literature and Linguistics. She is represented by Tobias Literary Agency representing her second novel *America Sorceress*, currently on submission.

Lori Toppel is the author of *Three Children*, a novel, *Still Here Thinking of You*, a collaborative memoir, and *The Word Next to the One I Want*, a novella. Her stories and essays have appeared in *Antioch Review, Atticus Review, Del Sol Review, Dorothy Parker's Ashes, Eckleburg*, and *Inkwell*.

Filiz Turhan's work has appeared in the *Threepenny Review, The North American Review*, previously in *Eckleburg* and elsewhere. She has been a Professor of English at a Community College for a really long time; like many of her students, she is a first-gen American and was a first-gen college student. Her academic publications explore the topics of Romantic-era Orientalism and Contemporary World Literature.

Julie Marie Wade writes and publishes poetry, prose, and hybrid forms. Her most recent and forthcoming collections include *The Mary Years* (Texas Review Press, 2024), selected by Michael Martone for the 2023 Clay Reynolds Novella Prize, *Quick Change Artist: Poems* (Anhinga Press, 2025), selected by Octavio Quintanilla for the 2023 Anhinga Prize in Poetry, and The Latest: *20 Ghazals for 2020* (Harbor Editions, 2025), co-authored with Denise Duhamel. A recipient of the Lambda Literary Award for Lesbian Memoir, Wade teaches in the creative writing program at Florida International University in Miami and makes her home with Angie Griffin and their two cats in Dania Beach.

Angela Youngblood lives and writes in a small northern California town. She holds a B.A. in English Literature from CSU Chico. Her non-fiction essays have been published in *The Watershed Review, Pithead Chapel, The Boiler Journal*, and *Eckleburg*. Amateur plant enthusiast, but not-as-vigilant-a-plant-caretaker-as-she-would-like-to-be, she tries to nourish things to grow. She sporadically posts on her nebulous blog youngofblood.wordpress.com.

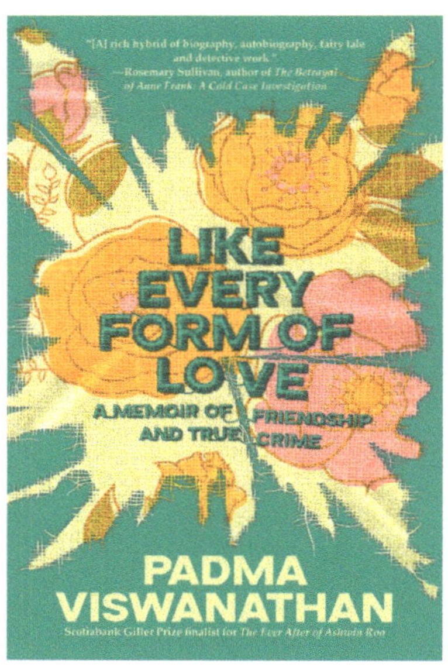

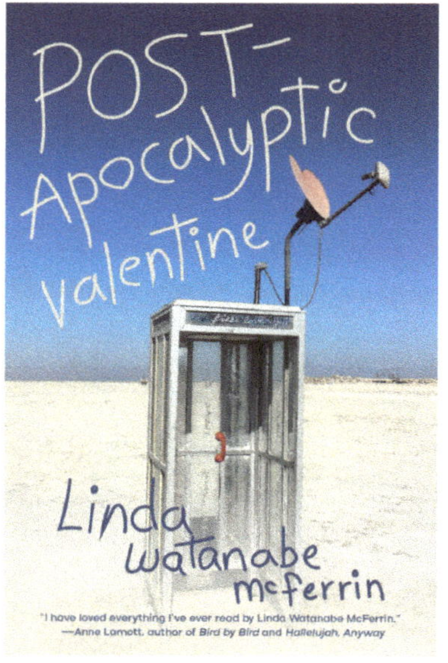

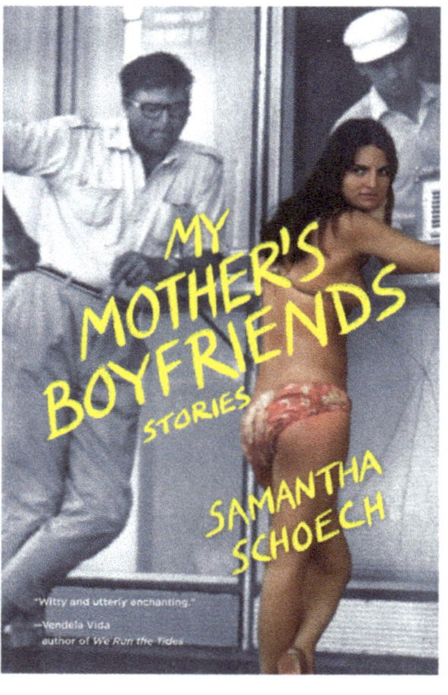

AN AUTHOR-RUN INDIE PRESS
Order from Amazon or Bookshop
Submit your best work at
713Books.com

KURT BAUMEISTER
TWILIGHT OF THE GODS
A NOVEL
PUBLISHING MARCH 11, 2025
STALKING HORSE PRESS
"A LOKI LIKE NO OTHER"
PREORDER IT NOW!
"Timely, hilarious, and wildly original, Twilight of the Gods is unlike any book you've ever read and finds Baumeister at the top of his game."
— Jonathan Evison, author of Again and Again
STLK KNG HRS PRS

"Love, pain, and nearly magical meatballs
make the story of Bella Donato a
delightful read."
—*Kirkus* starred review

FOREST AVENUE PRESS

Paycock Press

Gargoyle Magazine

gargoylemagazine.com

LITQUAKE
SAN FRANCISCO

LONGLEAF
Read. Write. Beach.

EMERALD COAST
STORYTELLERS

NEW YORK
BOOK FESTIVAL

LIBRARY OF CONGRESS
NATIONAL
BOOK
FESTIVAL

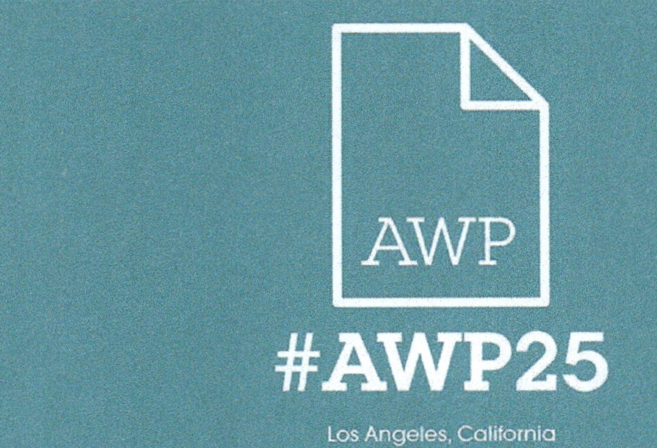

AWP
#AWP25
Los Angeles, California